GEEK MAFIA:
Black Hat Blues

Eli
This book is weird.
Happy holidays!

love
M

PM

GEEK MAFIA:
Black Hat Blues

Rick Dakan

PM

Geek Mafia: Black Hat Blues
By Rick Dakan

ISBN: 978-1-60486-088-7
LCN: 2009901383

PM Press
PO Box 23912
Oakland, CA 94623
www.pmpress.org

Layout: Karl Kersplebedeb
Cover: John Yates

Printed in the USA, on recycled paper.

This is a work of fiction. All characters in this book are fictional and events portrayed in this book are either products of the author's imagination or used fictitiously.

Foreword
Thanks to All The Hackers

This is a work of fiction, so let's keep that in mind, but it wouldn't have been possible to write this book without the welcoming, friendly, helpful, and sometimes intimidating assistance of numerous real live non-fictional hackers from all over the United States and Germany. I spent the better part of a year traveling to hacker cons, interviewing participants, attending talks, and taking copious notes. Almost without exception the organizers, speakers, and attendees I talked to welcomed me into the fold and helped me to, I think, really understand the world of hacking. It's a community I've come to love and now consider myself a part of. So some of you out there might recognize yourselves in this book, some of you are even mentioned by real name. In the latter case, real names are used entirely fictitiously and shouldn't be taken as real-world reportage. Many other incidents herein might seem familiar to those knowing few who were there for the real world events that inspired them, and I hope you'll get a smile or a thrill from my fictitious versions.

For everyone else, welcome to the world of hacker conventions. If you've never heard of such a thing before (I certainly hadn't until a couple months before I attended my first), I encourage you to get online and find out more. Watch some videos of some talks, check out some websites, and if it looks interesting to you, try it out. What's the worst that could happen? Well, I guess this book is one version of the worst that can happen, but really, you wouldn't be this crazy, would you?

Chapter 1

Paul

"I was going to, but even at this one I never log on using the wireless at a hacker con, it's like suicide, except your porn collection gets stolen too." Paul Reynolds smiled at the overheard bit of conversation as he balanced three pizza boxes and two six-packs of Coke in front of him and wove his way through the cluster of shivering smokers huddled outside the hotel entrance. It was a relief to take the awkward twirl through the revolving door and come in from the cold. No one seemed to pay him or his pizzas any attention. This crowd had seen a lot of pizza delivered in its collective lifetime. He picked up more snatches of overheard data as he moved through the mostly male conversation clusters that milled about the spacious and surprisingly elegant hotel lobby with no purpose other than to meet, greet, and discuss the topics of the day. "They have Jason Scott speaking opposite Dan Kaminsky again... How many Shmoo balls are you going to buy?... I actually kind of hate room parties... You have to try the Ethiopian place this year... I'm thinking of not sleeping at all and seeing if I actually start hallucinating in code."

It was certainly the nicest hotel Paul had ever attended a hacker convention in—usually they inhabited rundown economy chains out by the local interstate—but the newly remodeled Wardman Park Marriott in Washington D.C. catered to businessmen, politicians, and lobbyists more often than hackers, and Paul imagined the con's organizers probably sold it to the hotel staff as a "computer security conference" instead of a "hacker con." But looking around the crowd, he recognized the quintessential types well enough after a year of moving among them.

They were hackers: mostly male, casually dressed, lots of black t-shirts, interesting hairstyle choices. Fewer had laptops than he'd first anticipated, but there were still more of them per capita than even a hotel lobby catering to traveling business execs was used to. And a lot more of those machines had stickers advocating various flavors of Linux or BSD or proclaiming the owner's allegiance in the great pirates vs. ninjas debate. Paul came down firmly on the side of the pirates of course.

The con hadn't even started yet, and Paul knew that there would be hundreds more hackers arriving over the course of the evening, and tomorrow morning the large ballrooms up the escalators would fill with over a thousand people interested in hacking, hackers, or hacker culture. There would be parties, and arguments, and debates, and games, and wildly entertaining rants mixed with droning, mind-sappingly dull presentations. And unlike the previous cons he'd been to, this time he would miss almost all of it. He wasn't even registered to attend. In his polo shirt, cardigan sweater and khakis he looked more like a vacationing yuppie father of two toddlers than your typical con attendee, but that was just his cover. Just like the con itself was providing cover for why he was really in DC and what he and the Crew were planning.

Paul bypassed the throng waiting in front of the bank of elevators and cut down the wide, carpeted hall past the Starbucks and the bar, headed towards an unmarked door tucked into one corner. He balanced one of the pizzas against his hip long enough to open the door to the fire stairs and slipped inside with a last glance around to see if anyone noticed him. No one he could see did. Inside and up five flights and out again, an exertion that would have left him breathless a year or two earlier. Down the hall to the right, and three quiet knocks on the door. He saw someone's head block the thin trickle of light through the peephole and he shook his head slowly to the left and then the right. Latches unlocked on the other side and the door opened. Chloe smiled and ushered him and the pizzas inside.

He scanned the suite for some empty, pizza-box sized surface, but found no likely candidates, so he placed them on top of the stacked luggage in the corner to his right. The others didn't look up from their various pressing tasks, and Paul didn't want to distract them. The food would be there for them when they remembered they needed to eat.

"What'd I miss?" he asked Chloe, who apparently needed to eat right now judging by the way she scooted past him and flipped open a box. She was wearing a smartly tailored gray skirt-suit combo that showed a little more thigh than might be considered strictly professional. Then again, the bright pink, short cropped hair clashed with the jacket's stylish cut in an even less business-like manner. But Paul knew there was a brown wig in a conservative cut lying on their bed that completed the disguise.

"Which one's mushroom?" Chloe asked.

"On the bottom I think."

"Not much. Things are finally up and running downstairs so we've got c1sman back with us. Their network's up. Ours is up. The outside connection is, and I quote, 'mostly up,' whatever that means."

"And the hotel connection?"

"Waiting for the hotel IT guy to get slightly less paranoid or a lot more tired. Are these mushrooms from a can?"

"Probably."

"That sucks."

Chloe took two slices anyway, and Paul turned to the rest of the room just to make sure they realized food was here. "Pizza," he said in a loud clear voice. At the desk across the room a slightly pudgy, Asian woman sporting a practical ponytail and jeans bent over a soldering iron and cheap digital camera that she'd taken apart. Bee didn't look up. Sandee, a lithe, athletic man with soft, strong features, a silk kimono, and just enough make-up on his nut brown skin to make him beautiful, reclined in the chair in the corner behind her, He smiled up from behind his laptop at Paul and nodded, but he never ate pizza. Spread out on the couch in front of three flat panel displays on the coffee table and the rack of computers on the floor beside him was a pear shaped man with a scraggly light brown beard and a black t-shirt. His eyes flicked up to Paul, back to the screen, up to Paul, back to the screen, towards the pizza, and then rested on the screen. "Um, thanks," he said. "Cool." He typed. "Thanks."

Paul could see how nervous he was. This was all new to him. Well not *all* new. The hacking was old hat. Hacking as part of an elaborate scheme to ruin someone's life was the new part. He glanced at Chloe and she twisted her mouth into unspoken agreement with his analysis. Paul went over and took a seat on the couch. "Alright, c1sman, walk me through this. Where are we at?"

"We're in the weeds, buddy," c1sman said. He had a mild southern accent to his deep voice, and Paul thought he sensed a slight quavering. He was tired of course. He probably hadn't slept for two, maybe three very busy days.

"It's not the weeds," Paul assured him. "It's the tall grass. We're in the tall grass and they don't see us coming. So walk me through it. Where we at?"

C1sman dragged his top teeth across his bottom lip, pulling on some stray beard hairs and then turned back to the screen. "Well, it took longer to get the con's wireless up and running and the other volunteers and me got into a little bit of a tussle over some setup issues but then we figured it out. It was like you said, they were so busy dealing with all the real problems of setting up a massive open network in a couple days that they didn't notice my little additions. And really we were almost totally screwed because for, like, two or three hours, even I wasn't sure we'd get it up running. And then I thought it was my stuff—our stuff, the thing for our thing, I mean, that was screwing things up, but it wasn't. It was something that should've been just obvious because we're all tired, right? So anyway, it wasn't me. Us. And I've just checked on it and we're up and running piggybacked on the con's connection and running through the new TOR clusters that we—the con staff I mean—set up for the demo tomorrow."

"So we're set," said Paul, wanting to be sure that The Onion Router (TOR) set-up was working right since it was crucial to their plans. An onion router is a cluster of computers that users can connect to the internet through, routing the signal around various machines in a way that makes it almost impossible to trace them back to their origin. Almost impossible, and c1sman had come up with some innovations for making it even closer to impossible, even if someone was monitoring the traffic as it came in and out of the the TOR.

"We're set on the anonymizer front, yeah. And we've got about half the bandwidth I'd want to really spread things out a little more than that. My little beasties are all in place and as of my last check… well, let's see here…" c1sman—pronounced sis-man, as in system admin—typed on one of the console windows open on the middle screen in front of him. A table of numbers and letters streamed past and Paul saw what he recognized as a long list of IP addresses flowing by. These were the addresses of the computers in the botnet that c1sman had built up over the last month, computers all around the world with software hidden in their root directories that allowed the Crew to control them remotely and use them without the owners' knowledge. Coupled with the new version of The Onion Router anonymizer network being shown off in the hotel that weekend and the other precautions C1sman had taken, their actions should be more than adequately hidden from anyone trying to track them down. Of course with a little luck, no one would ever realize there was anything that needed to be tracked down until it was too late.

"6,328 and counting," c1sman said, nodding his head slowly up and down. "More than enough to do the job."

"Well then," Paul said, "Let's get started doing the job, shall we?"

Paul knew exactly what c1sman was going through right now, or at least he suspected he did. He'd felt it himself often enough: that stomach sloshing, rising tide of doubt and panic that came when you were about to do something incredibly illegal for the first time. Or the second. Or the fifth. Paul had lost count at this point, and for him the fear now came as less of a tidal shift and more of an intestinal simmering. Most of the time. Right now he was so much more worried about all the complicated pieces he'd set in motion coming together in sync that he had little anxiety left for the potential legal consequences. But he knew c1sman felt he'd not broken the law in any serious way before. The RIAA and MPAA would no doubt differ if they could somehow look at his bit-torrent history, as would the people whose machines he now owned through what he called his "beasties." But they were faceless corporations or clueless losers who weren't out anything more than a little CPU processing time or profits they never would have earned from him in the first place. This time the target was a real person and the damage would, if all went according to plan, be quite devastating indeed.

So Paul looked for ways to distract the Crew's new recruit, keeping him focused on the area he was most comfortable with in the whole wide world: hacking. Ever since he'd agreed to come on board as a full member six months ago, c1sman had been working on this one project for them. He was a meticulous planner and very careful in his approach to any problem. Not that Paul found his style conservative. C1sman was quite inventive and innovative, but he always wanted to make sure that every little detail was just right before proceeding. So far that cautious approach had served the Crew's needs just fine, but now that D-Day had arrived, Paul doubted that circumstances would allow for such consistent circumspection.

When Paul and Chloe had revealed the target's true identity and crimes to c1sman the previous Fall, he'd been as outraged as they'd hoped and expected. Then they just turned him loose with the time and resources he needed. When they checked back in with him a few weeks later, he'd reported that it was by no means going to be as easy as he'd hoped it would be. He wondered if there might be an alternate target, someone less well protected, but that part of the plan wasn't fungible. It had to be this target, and it had to happen by February. C1sman had grumbled a bit, but only a bit, and got back down to work on his reconnaissance. Paul decided to "help" him as best he could and took a couple weeks to leave the Crew's home base in Key West and drove up to Athens, Georgia to sit at c1sman's right hand and watch the master at work. Paul ended up having more fun than he would have imagined, and Chloe would have been appalled at the amount of gaming they indulged in if he'd told her the truth, but mostly he learned a hell of a lot about how hacking a system works.

Those weeks in Georgia, in the long hours crammed into his tiny second bedroom they spent between games, c1sman had begun with what he called Recon on the target Paul had given him. "Before we even start to actually try and break into a system, we need to find out as much as we possibly can about our target," c1sman had explained to Paul. "Most people make the mistake of thinking only about their files and how they're going to keep them out of some hacker's stealthy grip. This is not thinking like a hacker. Hackers don't start with their focus on the data they're after, they focus on the applications they can break. Software is so complicated that the more you have, the more potential vulnerabilities there are. Kickin butt as a hacker really means finding out how these applications break and then exploiting them, and reconnaissance can tell you a butt-load about what software the target network is running.

"We've gotta be as thorough in our Recon as possible. In most cases reconnaissance should comprise something on the order of 70% of a hacker's effort, because the fact is, the more we know about our target, the less time we'll have to spend actually hacking their system and therefore the less likely we are to get nailed. We want to answer as many questions about the target as we can before we start." Paul always found it intriguing to watch c1sman slip in and out of teaching mode. One on one, most of the time, he was just your average gamer dude. In groups he quieted down a lot, although still threw in the occasional funny zinger or useful insight. When he was stressed and working he sounded scattered and often repeated himself. But when he was in his element, explaining the facts about something he knew backwards and forwards, he was as clear-spoken and talented a teacher as Paul had ever seen. OK, maybe a little pedantic sometimes, but still, he exuded the quiet confidence not of someone boastful of their abilities, but rather someone who takes their own expert knowledge as a given fact, no more notable or less true than the sky being blue or the laws of thermodynamics. When it came to network security hacking, c1sman's knowledge was unassailable. Or so Paul hoped.

The goal of their Recon Mission was to answer as many questions about the target as they could, starting with such simple things as figuring out what operating system its servers were running, which patch level they're at and so forth. C1sman pointed out that the biggest source of security holes is human errors, especially not keeping software updated with the latest security patches from the manufacturers. If they could find information about which version of the software the target's using without having to directly probe the target network, then they'd know where to start looking for likely vulnerabilities.

Paul had been surprised to see that c1sman's starting tool of choice was Google. As far as c1sman was concerned, the best place to start looking is Google, which he referred to half-jokingly as an "uber leet hacking tool." But c1sman was talking about the skillful use of Google to its fullest capabilities, not just typing the target company's name into the main search page and seeing what comes up (although that's in fact what he did to start). As he explained it to Paul, there's a vast potential reservoir of useful data waiting in places like Google Groups, where there are various tech support and software discussion groups. Company employees often post requests for help solving technical problems they're having with their networks and applications. Such posts sometimes include info about what version of software they're running, what problems they're having and even things like user IDs and passwords. Google is also a source for locating branch offices, information about the company's officers and executives, and other hints that might lead you to a weak spot in the company's security. The security at the corporate HQ might be top notch, but if the CEO is logging into the network from his unsecured home wireless network, an informed hacker can take easy advantage of the situation.

C1sman didn't find any obvious, easy to exploit holes in the target's security through Google, but he hadn't expected to. He got some of the information he needed about what software the target network ran and some especially juicy info about what patches they had installed in a few cases. He cross-referenced those with several databases of known exploits, but didn't come up with anything he could use right away. C1sman also used perfectly legal and passive (and therefore undetectable) tools to map out the Domain Name System (DNS) of the target's various websites. Searching through corporate records, openly available DNS registration info and using tools like samespade.org, they were able to uncover the full extent of the various sub-pages and hidden sections of the target's site that they otherwise wouldn't have found just by browsing the company website. These records provided c1sman with several dozen new possible points of entry when it came time to finally try and hack into the target network.

The searching took days, mostly because c1sman liked to leave no stone unturned and wanted to give his own mind time to refresh and come up with new search strategies after he'd had some time to go over the results he'd already gathered. Paul missed Chloe and Key West, and would have liked to go out and at least see some of the sites of Athens, Georgia, but c1sman was more of a stay at home and drink beer kind of fellow. So Paul improved his Halo and Call of Duty skills and in turn introduced c1sman to the online game he'd helped create, Metropolis 2.0. Paul still played the game, despite the painful associations he felt, because it was a good game. Which is not to say that when c1sman suggested a few possible hacks that might allow them to exploit the game, Paul's interest wasn't piqued. But that was for later—right now he wanted all c1smans skills focused on the primary target.

In the second week, they started breaking laws. Everything so far had been both passive and legal—there was no way the target could know that they'd been investigating it because they hadn't done anything intrusive or possibly illegal. But now it was time to cross the Rubicon and start actively probing the target's network, and that was why Paul had spent all this time with c1sman. Although he'd done this exact thing before, most of the time it had either been out of curiosity with no other malevolent intent or, more rarely, on behalf of someone who'd given him permission to test their network's security. Paul had feared his new recruit might back out, but no, he was too excited to follow up the leads he'd found during Recon and more than ready to start doing some real hacking.

With all that build up, Paul was a little let down when he realized how small and simple and, well, boring, that initial shift into criminal territory was. C1sman's first step had been a single "ping," a super short message sent from one computer to another to see if a particular port on that network is active. He assured Paul that the ping was "totally one of the most underestimated tools in the hacking arsenal." A series of pings would tell them about what servers were live and working on the network as intended, but it could also reveal data about the operating system type, the existence of firewalls, and other vital data. A Traceroute command (which traces the route the ping takes through the internet) gave them an idea as to where in the US the target network was physically located by calculating how long the packets took to travel. Although there were many tools that he liked for this task, c1sman described himself as "old school" and liked to use the classic hacker tool nMap for his personal pinging needs.

"The thing about port scanning," c1sman explained to Paul, "Is that, since the whole point is to send out packets and see how the target network responds, the target obviously knows it's getting pinged. A sudden series of rapid pings across the network is a sure sign that something fishy is going down, and a good sys admin will know something's up. Lots of firewalls and other security software packages are triggered based on the timing of events and will automatically respond to such scans." In order to avoid this fate, they did what amounted to stealth port scanning. C1sman set nMap to run a very slow scan, allowing their probing pings to get lost in the general background noise of regular Internet activity. They also coordinated their scan from several different computers using different scanning techniques so that there was no discernible pattern for the target's security programs to pick up on.

All this pinging took a patience-trying long time. Paul burned through four different disposable phones keeping in touch with Chloe while she and Sandee were still following up on their own recruiting efforts. Well, that and a couple sessions of text-sex. Meanwhile, c1sman's set-up pinged away, enumerating the target network. This enumeration process revealed the target network's layout, confirming what kinds of software the servers were using, how they were set up, and most importantly what their firewall was like. The firewall was the main bastion between the target network and the big bad world of the Internet, and the more they knew about it, the easier their job became. C1sman's meticulous port scan managed to find the sweet spot between efficiency and speed (or so he claimed, Paul had to take his word for it), eventually producing a network map that not only enumerated the firewall but also mapped all the individual computers (or "boxes" as c1sman referred to them) in the network. They also knew the most important piece of information—which ports accepted connections from the outside and what those ports were used for. Their particular target, while generally well defended and maintained, was not breaking any new ground when it came to usage or security. Like most, it used Port 80 for Web servers and Port 3306 for MySQL connections to its databases, along with a few other ports, some of which c1sman felt sure were going to provide them access through which they could launch an attack.

Launching the final attack was going to have to wait, though. It needed to be timed with everything else, and everything else wouldn't be ready until they'd all got set up in Washington D.C. But there was one stage left before D-Day, and Paul wanted to make sure c1sman saw it through while he was watching. A lot of the basics of network security hacking were freely available online, and Paul had done his best to bone up on them in preparation for his "quality time" in Georgia. But even with c1sman explaining things as he went along, Paul still only had a vague idea that things were going as planned. He had hoped to know enough to double check c1sman's work, but that turned out to have been some crazy pipe dream. He'd have to trust c1sman's word that things were going to go the way they were supposed to, so Paul had quickly shifted gears from looking over the hacker's shoulder to patting him on it. He'd heaped praise and support on the man, along with a healthy dose of friendship and camaraderie. Plus he'd paid all the bills and cleared some of c1sman's more pressing debt (particularly the back child support that the unemployed hacker had fallen behind on). It helped that he actually did like the guy, even if he was pretty dull at times. Hopefully all that together was enough to ensure that the new recruit really was being on the up and up with him and Chloe and the rest of the Crew.

"Most good attacks are designed to get control in some way, but the real skill comes in taking control without being noticed by the network's system administrators or intrusion detection software," c1sman had explained when they began their ping session. "Finding the exploit is just the beginning. Retrieving something of value from the system we've penetrated is the whole point. And, yeah, in some cases it's possible to just smash and grab, just break into the system and steal whatever data you can get your hands on. But there's no art to that kinda attack and, really just as important, they're less efficient. Ideally, we want to leave no trace that we were ever there. A loud, frontal attack will alert the network administrator, who will then do everything in his or her power to boot us off the network. But if we never trip any alarms, we'll be able to take our time and find what we want. Plus, you know, if the target doesn't know their data's been compromised, then they won't take any measures to minimize damage. Once the network's owners realize they've lost data they'll start changing passwords, rewriting code, and generally covering their losses and all our work won't mean crap."

C1sman had written his own arsenal of exploits that used shellcode to take advantage of specific vulnerabilities that he'd identified in the various software and hardware configurations of the target network. He could have downloaded "off the shelf" code from places like metasploit. com or shellcode.org, but he preferred to use his own versions since the target system was less likely to have a defense against them. C1sman had identified a few different approaches that he thought might work, but he decided to go with a traditional buffer overflow attack since he'd found a few points in the target network where these might work. "I love me some buffer overflows," he'd said once he realized he could use them in this instance. "They're my ultimate power-up—I can do anything with them."

Understanding exactly how a buffer overflow works required several explanations from c1sman, even though Paul had read all about them on his own. It was one of those things that was surprisingly difficult for a non-programmer to understand. C1sman's simplest explanation was, "Every program sets aside a certain block of memory to receive the input of data, right? Like, for example, a database entry might have a certain amount of memory set aside to receive social security numbers. As long as the amount of data entered is equal to the amount of data the program is expecting (enough for nine digits of an SSN) then everything is fine. But in some programs, if you enter more than nine digits worth of data, the program starts overwriting memory space normally reserved for other data. This can cause some serious problems in normal circumstances. But when someone like me finds something like that, it's like handing me the house keys and the security code. I can insert my shellcode right into the space, and BAM! My shellcode overwrites good data and then gets executed as if it were part of the normal program! The shell runs, it opens a door for me from the outside and wham, bam, thank you ma'am, I own the box."

When Paul had asked him how common it was to find such buffer overflow vulnerabilities, c1sman had shook his head in disgust. "It shouldn't happen at all, except people are lazy. It's entirely possible to write software that has no buffer overflow vulnerabilities in it. It just requires the programmers to be very security conscious as they code. But all the crap today's so huge and bloated and manager driven, with the work of multiple software engineers all trying to make their code work together, it just gets sloppy and messy. Besides, most programmers aren't security people and don't write code that's good for security—it's hard enough to get these things working in the first place without worrying about leaving buffer overflow holes."

C1sman writing his custom shellcode seemed to Paul like more work than was necessary. He'd started to suspect that the hacker was delaying, either because he was afraid of breaking the law or didn't want Paul to leave. As delays mounted and days passed, Paul grew restless. Chloe needed his help with other parts of the plan and he was getting sick of Athens and c1sman. They needed to move. The original plan had been for them to insert the shellcode, own the system's key boxes, and then sit and wait until it was time to grab the data they needed. C1sman would chill in Athens while Paul went back to Key West to help make final preparations before they all went to DC. Except at this rate he'd have to go straight to DC from here and Lord only knows what would be missed if he wasn't on hand to direct things. But c1sman insisted he wasn't stalling—that it was hard work and he wanted to make sure everything worked right. For all Paul knew, he was telling the truth. What Paul did know was that c1sman needed some extra motivation.

So during the down time, Paul started talking up Key West. The parties, the women, the relaxing atmosphere, the women. While he wasn't quite ready to let c1sman stay at the Crew house, he could easily find someplace for him to stay down there. A little bungalow with a private pool that was strip club adjacent maybe? And some spending money? C1sman eschewed the strippers, at least out loud, but Paul's temptations were getting to him. Or maybe he just really did happen to pull his code together the night after Paul promised to take him down to Key West as soon as they'd cracked the target network and owned the boxes they'd need to on D-Day. From Paul's point of view, watching c1sman work, he couldn't see the difference from one moment to the next. Numbers and letters changed on a screen and the hacker hooted with real, unreserved joy. Paul didn't think he had it in him to fake that kind of enthusiasm. They had root. They would be ready to go whenever Paul said the word.

Now, four weeks later, they were in a mini-suite in the Marriott and it was time. "All right c1s, you ready?" He dug his hand into the hacker's shoulder, massaging some tiny fraction of the tension out of him.

"Yeah. I think I am. Yeah. We're ready... ." he drifted off as he typed a few more commands into one of his machines. "OK. Now we're ready... Ready now."

"Your time to shine, buddy," Paul said. He looked around the room. Chloe was watching from the corner, wiping some pizza sauce from her lips. Sandee had looked up from his laptop. Bee kept doing whatever it was she was doing with her soldering iron, oblivious to the rest of them in her focus fugue. Chloe smiled and nodded and Paul patted c1sman's shoulder three times. "Let's get started."

Chapter 2

clsman • *before*

Chris had a love/hate relationship with hacker cons, but at this point in his life, any relationship with at least some love in it was worth clinging to as hard as he could. OK, things weren't that bad really. He'd wanted the divorce as much as Jessica had, if not more, and they'd been separated for almost two years now. What he hadn't expected was that she'd take Shawn and move to Arizona to live at her mom's, or that Athens without her and their child would be so, so empty. Whereas before he'd yearned constantly for a little more time for his projects, a little more privacy and silence so he could just think a problem through, now that was all he had. His college friends were long graduated and only slightly less long gone. His family was in Tennessee and, to be honest, bored him stiff anyway. Then his job had evaporated as well, leaving him home alone with no one to have a beer or catch a movie with. Of course his primary social circle on IRC remained as close as ever, and he was pretty sure that without them he'd have gone insane in some particularly depressing way. As it was, he could stay in touch with his friends, trade gossip and exploits, and always find some interesting project to throw a little bit of his coding expertise at. And just as important, those friends spread out all over the world could throw him freelance work from time to time, enough to keep him above water and in burritos and beer at least. Also enough, as a disappointed Jessica had pointed out, to make him think he didn't have to go out and find a real job. But he had a plan—his one-off contracts were starting to blossom into repeat clients and at this rate he'd have his own little computer security consulting company up and running within a year. Two at the most. He might even be able to hire on some help.

Until then though, the only quality time Chris was likely to get with any of his intellectual or social peers (i.e., hackers) was at conventions. But with his reduced available funds, he couldn't afford to attend anything he couldn't get to on a tank of gas, and where he had at least three people to split the hotel room with. That pretty much left CarolinaCon, one of his new favorites, and then the old warhorse, SECZone, which he'd been going to since it started. SECZone 5 was over in Atlanta, a venerable little hacker con that Chris had volunteered at for the past two years. This year he and a couple other guys were in charge of setting up the NOC and the con's wireless network. So right there he'd already broken his own rules on expenses because that had meant driving over to Atlanta every weekend for the month leading up to the con in order to get everything set up in the hotel. In exchange for helping the hotel upgrade its own network, the owners were allowing this extra access, and Lor3n, the guy who founded and ran SECZone, was paying Chris a small fee and comping his hotel room, which allowed Chris to write the whole thing off as a business expense. He'd have to remember to actually do that when tax time came. Despite all the perks, all this preliminary work was part of what he hated about hacker cons. It really was too much like real work, but he knew it had to be done and there was something to be said for the pleasures of working with other people face to face, like Lor3n and his old friend David, or "dmap" as his IRC handle read. He only knew the two men through hacker conferences and IRC, but that was more than enough for them to have formed a friendly bond that was what really made coming to these cons worthwhile for him. Besides, working on the NOC was a great way to get into the con for free. There was no way he was going to get up and give a talk, which was the other free-badge option.

All the major problems setting up the network were, if not surmounted, then at least identified. It was Thursday evening before the con started and he was confident that he and dmap would have things sorted out by Friday morning, maybe afternoon at the latest. Certainly they'd have it by the time the keynote speaker from BountySploit took the podium at 7:00 PM. Probably. Although he didn't think it would be the worst thing in the world if the BountySploit's talk didn't go well. He left Dave in the converted storage room they'd taken over as their network operations center and went up to the front desk to see if the fixes he'd just made had sorted out their latest set of network issues. The Cypress Estate hotel had been a Radisson until a few months ago, but the shift to a fancier name and private owners hadn't done much to spruce up the dull, cookie-cutter decor. Not that Chris cared much. It was mostly clean, there weren't any weird smells, and the air conditioner in his room didn't rattle, so he was happy. The quiet hotel sat near the highway and not much else—a strip mall with a Best Buy across the street, some banks and office buildings on their side of the 6 lane divided road. Sure they were technically in Atlanta, but the place could have been in any suburban ring highway sprawl in the country and Chris doubted he could tell the difference. He'd been to hacker cons in cities all over the country and seen nothing much more interesting than Cypress Estate (except for Def Con in Las Vegas of course). All the exciting stuff happened in the talks and presentations and inside people's heads anyway.

Most of the attendees would arrive tomorrow, but a few would come trickling in tonight. He wondered if Al was going to make it over from North Carolina, or Skydog down from Nashville. At the front desk he saw someone checking in who generally fit the profile: in his thirties, wearing jeans and a black t-shirt. In this case it had the Green Lantern logo on it and looked faded and well worn. He had shaggy brown hair, was unshaven and wore steel rimmed glasses. He looked up at Chris as he rounded the corner and gave him a quizzical look. Chris turned away, not liking the attention, and asked the manager if everything was OK with the hotel's network. It was. Good, one less problem to worry about. He turned to leave, but the Green Lantern dude called out to him.

"Hey, excuse me. Are you here for the hacker con?" he asked Chris. "I'm just guessing from your shirt."

Chris looked down at his stomach, which bulged under the too tight shirt. It had "AAAAAAAGH" in wild, red letters across the top of a grainy picture of a pony tailed man screaming into a microphone with the words "Bow To My Firewall" across it in bold, horror movie-style font. The man was Bruce Potter, who'd said the memorable phrase during a talk at Def Con several years earlier. His wife and friends, who helped him run Shmoocon in DC, had made the shirts and sold them at the first Shmoocon, much to his lasting annoyance. Chris's was a little too small since he'd put on weight, but he'd been in the audience at that talk and at Shmoocon when they distributed them, and it was one of his favorite hacker con mementos ever. He looked back up at the stranger, standing beside his purple suitcase. "Guilty as charged," he said.

"I thought so," the man replied, holding his hand out. "My name's Alan Denkins. I'm here to write a book about hackers and, well, this is my first con. So I'm just sort of feeling my way through."

Chris shook his hand. "A book about hackers? What kind of book?" There were lots of books about hackers. The ones for hackers by hackers were pretty good. The ones by outsiders were mixed. The ones by people looking for ridiculously sensational stories about high school kids supposedly cracking into the Pentagon were pretty much total bullshit. He wasn't sure which category this guy fit into.

"I don't really know yet. I'm still learning. I've been watching videos and reading stuff online about various other hacker cons and the scene in general and I just think it's so fascinating, you know? I guess like most folks I just thought hackers were criminals who attacked people's computers. But the more I learn about the scene, about what real hackers are really doing, the more interesting it all becomes. So I suppose what I want to do is dispel some of those media myths, you know? But I still have a lot to learn."

Chris at least appreciated the guy's perspective on things. He was tired of answering questions like, "Hackers have conventions? Isn't that illegal?" from friends and family all the time. Well, he had been tired of it when it was happening anyway. "OK," Chris said to the writer, "That all sounds interesting. Good luck. I think you'll learn a lot here."

He'd started to turn to go when the writer stopped him with another question. "Is there anything I can help out with? I came early to just kind of get the lay of the land, you know? Maybe I can buy you a drink later or something?"

Chris didn't know what to say. Normally help from attendees at hacker cons was welcome—they tended to run on shoestring budgets and volunteer energy—but this guy was basically a reporter and Chris didn't know anything about him. "You'll have to talk to Lor3n when he gets back from the airport. He's the guy in charge."

"Great, thanks, man. I'm Alan by the way. What's your name?" He held out his hand, smiling

"Oh, sorry, yeah" Chris said, shaking the offered hand. "I'm c1sman. Nice to meet you."

"You're the Sys Admin?"

"Spelled c-1-s-m-a-n."

"Got it, well, I'll see you around, yeah?"

Chris did see him around, that night and then a lot the next day. He'd apparently hit it off with Lor3n right away, and by that evening was helping set up chairs and tables and joined the group of a dozen or so volunteers and speakers when they went out to Dave & Busters for dinner that night. C1sman didn't get to talk to him much, but he listened in a lot. The writer listened a lot too, but he always had another question ready to fill any hint of a lull in the conversation, and he was more than happy to buy the table several rounds of drinks. He seemed to know a fair bit about the scene, and c1sman liked the kinds of questions he was asking and the things he was saying. When the book came out he might even buy a copy.

The next day the convention began in earnest, and Chris found himself spending more time than he'd planned in the NOC, because of course nothing was really working like it was supposed to, and people were already complaining. Ensconced in his converted storage room, he didn't notice when the mysterious fliers started appearing around the hotel. By 4:30, there were close to 200 attendees checked in, and the first three speaker sessions had come off without too many technical glitches. Chris turned the last few problems over to dmap and went out to get a Coke and see who was there and what was going on. First things first though, he needed to take a dump and didn't like using public bathrooms, so he decided to go up to the room he was sharing with dmap. As the elevator doors opened, he saw a bright pink flier taped to the wall opposite him.

> Tired of Corporate Sell Outs Giving Hackers a Bad Name?
> Disgusted with cons that are all about the money and the
> pay-day and not sharing the knowledge?
> Why pay more just to support the exploit exploiters?
> Why not try UnSECZone?!?!
> Room 346
> Free to attend. Free to learn.
> Free from Corporate Corruption.

Chris later learned that people had been leaving these fliers and similar cards all over the hotel and that Lor3n and the other SECZone volunteers had been tearing them down and throwing them away as fast as they could find them. It didn't occur to Chris at the moment to tear the flier down. He was just curious. He guessed that the flier was rooted in some sort of protest against the fact that BountySploit was the con's main sponsor. Not particularly happy with that turn of events himself, he pressed the button for floor three instead of two.

He heard them down the hall before he saw them. Room 346 was just like any other room in the hotel—two queen beds, a TV, a dresser, two night tables, and what looked like thirty hackers crammed into every available space. Chris heard the heated arguing from ten doors away, and as he looked in the door he was surprised to see that the speaker was H# (pronounced h-sharp, short for Henry Sharpe). He'd been a popular speaker at least year's SECZone, and Chris had really enjoyed his talk on cross site scripting vulnerabilities. It was weird to see someone of his caliber speaking in this hot, stuffed little room.

"What's going on?" he whispered to the man standing in the doorway while he tried to figure out what they were arguing about. Something to do with the NSA it seemed.

"As far as I can tell, they're hacking the hacker con," the man said. It was the writer, what's his name. Alan something.

"What?" Chris asked.

"They're pissed at Lor3n for, as they say, 'turning the con over to BountySploit' and so they're staging a counter-convention." The reporter's breath smelled like Altoids. "They've got speakers and badges and even t-shirts. They're trying to undermine SECZone with this whole UnSECZone thing. Pretty wild, eh?"

Chris just nodded. He'd never heard of such a thing, and yeah, it was pretty wild. Although it also made a whole lot of sense, at least it did if you were working from a hacker's mindset. Don't like the way something works? Find a way to change it so it does work the way you want it to.

"Can you explain to me what they're so mad about?" the writer asked. "What's the big deal about this BountySploit company?"

Several people in the room had noticed them talking and one woman (in fact the one, single woman) shot them a dirty look. Chris wondered if it was because of the talking, or his SECZone Staff t-shirt. Either way he felt embarrassed and stepped back from the doorway and out of line of sight. The writer followed him a few paces down the hall. "It's a touchy issue. It all has to do with ethical disclosure stuff."

"You mean like, when and how a hacker discloses to the world that he's found some kind of security hole?" He was pulling a small black moleskin notebook from his front pocket.

The writer did know some basics at least. "Yeah, so that's been an issue forever. Do you release the exploit to everyone so they can take the right precautions or do you just tell the people with the crappy software and give them time to fix it. I think you do something in between. But the way it's always been, releasing exploits is something hackers just do because, well, that's what we do. We find vulnerabilities and tell each other about them. That way software companies should, in theory anyway, make more secure software. If you don't publicize the exploits, then you gotta assume some other black hat clown has found it too but just isn't telling anyone. Instead he's taking advantage of it to do dirt on people, but the software maker doesn't know or doesn't care and so they don't fix the problem."

"And BountySploit," the writer said, jotting something in his notebook, "it's a company that does this disclosure stuff for a profit somehow, right? And somehow that helps them sell their security services to other companies. At least that's what I got from their website."

"Yeah, that's part of it, but here's what kinda sucks." Chris was warming to the subject—it was an issue that divided his friends and so wasn't something he could usually talk about without running the risk of igniting a flame war of some sort—and he liked the idea of having his views on the record with the reporter. It was nice to be able to cut loose with this guy who hadn't already made up his mind. That was the thing he really hated about the hacker scene sometimes—the little disputes that boiled over into insane feuds. "BountySploit and companies like them have kind of come along and screwed up the system. They pay hackers good money for their exploits, but they keep that information to themselves. Then they turn around and say to their corporate customers, 'Hey, we have leet hackers working for us finding the newest vulnerabilities so we can protect you from them better than anyone else can.' Now the exploits usually do get released, but maybe it's a month or two later than it would have been. Or maybe it never gets released until some hacker not working for a company like BountySploit discloses it. Or hell, for all I know maybe some of them never get released at all."

"So what's the problem exactly?" the writer asked. "It seems like by paying hackers to find these exploits you're both encouraging them to find these vulnerabilities more than they otherwise might have, and you're channeling their energies into legal ways of taking advantage of their hacking."

"That's the company line, sure," Chris said his lips curling up in what he thought of as a world-wise smirk. "It's probably even true, I guess. As far as it goes anyway. But it's totally against the hacker spirit and a lot of people—especially those people," Chris pointed down the hall towards the open doorway where the sounds of heated debate continued, "think that companies like BountySploit are destroying the scene. The whole point is that we share knowledge. It used to be that the reason we'd find exploits was as much so we could brag about being the ones that found them as anything else. To show how smart we were. That was one part. The other was to tweak the annoying, arrogant software makers who have the gall to both charge a bunch of money for their crapware and release it full of security holes."

"And now it's all getting closed up," the writer said, glancing back at the open door to the counter-con. "There's less information being shared and so it's eroding the hacker scene's influence as a whole. Dividing you up and sort of neutering you."

"Yeah, that's one way of looking at it anyway."

"And that seems to really piss you off," the writer said, looking back at Chris with what he took to be sympathy in his eyes.

"Yeah, I guess it does." And it did piss Chris off. He didn't like to think it or say it out loud much though, because then he might be forced to address some other questions he preferred to avoid.

"So why aren't you in that room with them instead of downstairs?" the writer said, asking exactly the question Chris didn't want to answer.

He didn't answer. He needed to take a dump. He needed to get back downstairs. He really didn't want Lor3n or anyone else from the con seeing him hanging out here. "Sorry, I gotta go," he said, turning his back on the writer.

"OK, well, I'll see you later then?" the writer asked him as he beat his retreat towards his room.

"Uh-uh," Chris replied, trying to be as noncommittal as possible.

The keynote went as predicted. Well not quite as predicted. There were fewer people there than Chris would have expected—maybe only a quarter of the registered attendees at most. The speech seemed pretty boiler-plate, a combination of BountySploit crowing about its successes and the good it was doing and pitching the assembled hackers about how much money they could make working for them. There were definitely some people in the audience, including friends of his, who were eating it all up. Chris tried to let it all just flow over him. He wasn't going to start selling exploits, even if he needed the money (which he kind of really did). There just wasn't any way he could see that as being a good idea. And normally he wouldn't have wanted to tell other people what they should or shouldn't do. Hacking was about freedom as much as anything else, and Chris always preferred things that maximized individual freedom. But the whole thing left him feeling a little sick to his stomach, and he couldn't for sure say why.

He went out to dinner with dmap and some of the other volunteers, going for pizza and beer at the Mellow Mushroom across the street, as was their tradition. No one talked much about the BountySploit key-note, since their crowd was evenly divided on the issue and everyone was too tired for a big in-person debate. There was however a lot of drink-ing and a lot of bitching about those guys who'd started UnSECZone. Even if they had a point about BountySploit and whatever personal shit they had with Lor3n, most of his friends agreed that having a counter convention was a cheap-ass, bullshit move. Chris wasn't sure he agreed anymore, but he kept his mouth shut and kept pouring more beer into his glass.

By the time they got back to the hotel, he hoped that the rest of them weren't as drunk as he was. Someone on con-staff needed to have their shit together when the inevitable idiocy broke out in the middle of the night and some attendee tried to do something stupid in the hotel. As he slowly levered himself out of dmap's back seat, he heard the sound of yelling from across the parking lot. Maybe the stupid wouldn't wait for the middle of the night. The commotion seemed to be centered around the rear entrance to the hotel, an area that had been a haven for smokers all day long as well as offering the easiest access to most of the parking spaces. As he approached the knot of people by the doorway, he saw that a few of them were standing around and smoking, but that most were clustered around a pair of large, angry, shouting men. Chris knew them both. Tall, lanky Lor3n and large, barrel-chested Intr00d. Since Intr00d was one of the guys behind UnSECZone (even though he hadn't been in the room when Chris was there), he knew what the shouting had to be about.

"It's got nothing to do with you, man," Intr00d boomed. "We're doing our own thing, our own way."

"Nothing to do with me?" Lor3n's face was bright red. "You may think I'm an idiot, but even you can't believe I'm that much of an idiot. Nothing to do with me? Bullshit!"

"Believe what you want. We're just doing our own thing."

"There's doing your own thing, and there's screwing up SECZone just because you're pissed at me."

"We're not the ones screwing up SECZone, man. You did that all on your own."

"That's your opinion."

"That's a fact!"

"Fuck you, Intr00d. You're such an asshole…"

"No, fuck you!"

Chris had reached the circle of people around the two screaming-mad hackers. They continued on in the same vein, exchanging slurs and curses without really saying anything. Everyone else just watched and, Chris assumed, enjoyed the nasty show. He on the other hand was sick of it. Another petty argument turned into real live douche-baggery. "They've been going at it for almost half an hour," said a voice from behind Chris. He turned to see the writer standing there, looking concerned. "Isn't anyone going to try and calm them down?"

"Probably not," Chris said, turning back towards the ridiculousness.

"They're about to boil over," the writer said. "Someone's going to hit someone."

"Nah." But Chris wasn't so sure. Hell, he wanted to hit both of them for being so stupid and not just letting everybody do their own thing. And it wasn't like either Lor3n or Intr00d were known for their calm, reasonable personalities. Intr00d was inching closer and closer to Lor3n with each spittle-laced epithet. It was getting as ugly as anything he'd ever seen.

"Should we call hotel security or something?" the writer asked. Boy, he sure was worried about shit for a writer. But security would be a bad idea, because there was no hotel security—just whoever was on duty at the front desk. So they'd call the cops. Cops would be jerks. Something might go real wrong and it could make the papers or whatever. That was another black eye the hacker image didn't need. Oh hell…

Lor3n was inching forward now, too. There weren't more than five inches between the screaming mouths, and some jerks in the crowd start egging them on, yelling "Fight!" and "Get him!" Idiots. Chris looked around. No one seemed about to jump in. The writer motioned with his chin and eyebrow in such a way as to suggest Chris should be the one to go in. Fine. Whatever. He was tired of this shit anyway.

He pushed his way through the crowd and inserted himself right between the two men, saying "Hey now, c'mon guys, let's just cool it off, OK?" But no one heard him over the yelling. Instead of calming them down, his intercession seemed to ignite their respective fuses. Lor3n started pushing his chest against Chris from one side and Intr00d grabbed his upper arm from the other to try and pull him out of the way. Jesus, what the fuck? They were both bigger than him, but they'd been screaming for a while and he had a fresh, beer infused set of lungs at his disposal.

"SHUT UP!" he shouted. No one did. In fact, some other people started yelling as well, although he wasn't sure if they were support-ing him or shouting back. "SHUT UP! SHUT UP! SHUT UP!" he repeated, loud enough and long enough that, try as they might, no one seemed able to ignore him anymore. Things grew quiet, aside from the low murmurs he ignored. "Come on guys! Cut it out. Chill out."

"Did you hear what they're saying about me, c1sman?" Lor3n said to him. "They're calling me all kinda of…"

"Nothing that's not true!" Intr00d interjected. "You're a goddamned…"

"SHUT UP! OK? Just shut the hell up. I'm stopping this. You hate each other OK. Let's all agree on that. And so you're never gonna convince the other of anything and you should just walk away."

"We're not stopping our con just because you tell us to," Intr00d said.

"What con?" Lor3n sneered. "You people are a fucking joke."

Chris gave up. He thought about shouting them down again. No, they wouldn't listen. They didn't care. Why should he? They weren't even fighting about the issues that were actually worth fighting about. No one was talking about whether or not BountySploit was good for the hacker community or how to best handle ethical disclosure. They were just calling each other "faggot."

"Faggot!" Intr00d hurled.

"Poser!" Lore3n retorted.

"Me a poser? That's rich coming from you, you fucking faggot ass poser."

"When was the last time you wrote any code at all you bloated, cocksucking over-hyped tech support lackey?"

"You're both such fucking IDIOTS!" Chris screamed, much to his surprise. "You know what? You're both posers. You're both fucking lame-ass script kiddie scene whores. You couldn't hack your way into your own pants. You know people and you talk big on IRC and you make a lot of goddamned noise but I've never seen either of you do anything worth talking about. So screw it all. Screw you both. I hope this goddamned fucking hotel falls down on both of you."

Now they both started yelling at him. The crowd started yelling too. "You fat little fuck… right on c1sman!… you've got some fucking nerve… who is that guy?… turn in your badge… you have no idea who the fuck I am!… this is lame… hit him!… what's going on?…" Chris just passed through it, forcing his way out of the circle and back towards the parking lot. Except his car keys were in his hotel room. Along with his stuff. Rather than go back through the crowd, which had now turned back in on itself, he decided to circle around the outside of the hotel to the front entrance. He couldn't believe these idiots could get so caught up in their own idiotic idiocy that they'd screw up everything so badly. All the work he'd done, and now… now… now he was going to throw up.

He vomited into an empty parking space next to a dumpster. Then a few steps later he threw up again, this time into an occupied parking space. He had had a lot of beer, but now a lot of it was in the back of someone's pickup truck. He leaned over, hands on his knees, breathing deep and trying not to think about throwing up again.

"Are you OK? Do you need some coffee or water or something?" someone asked. He looked up. It was the writer.

"No, I'm OK. I just need a second."

"Come on," the writer said, putting an arm around his shoulder and helping him as he tried to stand up. "Let's get you some water, all right?"

Water sounded good. "OK, fine. Thanks."

"And then maybe we can talk some. I've got something I want to run by you."

Surprisingly, talking sounded good too. The only intelligent conversation he'd had lately had been with this writer dude. "OK," he said. "Sure. But I don't want to talk about those two jerks."

"Neither do I. I want to talk about hacking."

"Oh thank God, finally," Chris said with a sigh, and leaned into the writer's shoulder as he led him away.

Chapter 3

Chloe

Chloe was having mixed feelings about Washington D.C. On the one hand it was so alive with ripe possibilities that she couldn't turn her head without seeing delicious new targets. On the other hand, it was ground zero for those nasty law enforcement agencies like the FBI and NSA that she'd spent the majority of her adult life avoiding at all costs. On the third hand, she was about to con a fucking Congressman, which was at once thrilling and terrifying as hell. Of course the strangest thing was that it wasn't even her first time conning a Congressman, although this time around he'd be much more personally involved in the chaos they were going to be bringing down.

She was glad to be out of the hotel room and on the streets, even though the February weather was, to say the very least, brisk. She'd never lived somewhere with real winters—mostly California and now Florida, and she'd been worried about the cold. But Paul had bought her some fur lined leather gloves that went well with her tailored, dark wool business suit and Bee had sewn some extra lining into her wig to provide added warmth. The thick, brown curls even kinda sorta worked like earmuffs. Except when the wind blew, which it did a lot. But she decided to let the cold invigorate rather than refrigerate her, and she marched down the busy street from the metro stop towards Capital Hill with a bounce in her step. She had to remind herself to calm down as she rounded the corner and saw the target Starbucks come into view. She was a bearer of bad news, a serious business woman with serious business to do. She took off her gloves for the last block, wanting her handshake to be chilled and maybe even off-putting when she met him.

Chloe slipped into the warm coffee shop, a nice older gentlemen holding the door for her. Inside, it was crowded with a line of seven impatient looking customers waiting to order and another half-dozen clustered around the pass-through, waiting for their lattes or whatever it was they'd ordered. Most of the tables and seats were taken, some with laptoppers, others with people peering at the tiny screens on their smart phones. One quaint woman was even reading the paper, bless her heart. She recognized two people in the room, although she pretended not to see either of them as she joined the line for hot caffeine. Only five minutes later, when she had her black coffee, did she start scanning the room in an obvious way, as if looking for someone.

He finally noticed her. Good, he wasn't that observant. Even better, he wasn't very observant because he'd been locked onto his Blackberry. As he stood up and smiled at her, he was still thumbing some e-mail or message into his phone. She smiled back and walked over to him, extending a hand. The long wait and the hot coffee had warmed it some, but her firm grip still got his attention, judging by the slight bulge of surprise in his eyes.

"Danny?" she said. "Nice to finally meet you in person." He looked like a high school kid, although she knew he was in his late twenties. Pudgy faced, and less than expertly shaven, he had short brown hair and dark bags under his eyes. His suit was about a size too small and fraying at the cuffs. She was pretty sure it was one of the two his credit cards showed he'd bought at Sears last year. The small smears of red paint on his shoes and the few droplets splattered on his cuffs were only hours old.

"Yeah, great to put a face to those e-mails and phone calls finally," he said. They sat down and he picked up his half-empty cup and sipped at it. "When did you get into town?"

"Early this morning," Chloe said. "I took the red eye in from LAX. I really need this coffee, I've been mainlining it all day as I run around the Hill."

"Lots of meetings, huh?"

"I'm afraid I've got a lot of bad news, and I prefer to give that in person. I don't know if I mentioned this, but I've dropped all my other clients at this point. There's just so much going on with my entertainment industry clients that I had to let my partners pick up my other consulting work. The industry is in freefall here and we're looking for some solutions from Congress." Chloe sighed and shook her head a couple inches left and right.

"Congressman Wolverton has always supported the film and music industries, I can assure you of that." Danny narrowed his eyes and nodded in rhythm with Chloe's shaking.

"We know he has, and that's why I wanted to make sure I got a chance to talk to you in person while I was in town."

"So, then, what's got your clients so worried? The DMCA revisions are in committee and are going to sail through with everything they asked for, including that college music service requirement we talked about."

"It's not that, it's something else that we're even more worried about. Something our investigators came up with recently that's really got everyone worried."

"Well if you're worried, I'm sure my boss will be worried too." Danny leaned back in his chair and held his palms up. "Hit me with what you've got."

"First of all we've got internal numbers—and these are very secret, very internal numbers that we can't let our clients' stockholders hear—that music sales are down by an additional 32% just in the last quarter. That's 32% on TOP of the steady decline we've seen in the past few years. It's a huge spike. Not a spike—the opposite of a spike. It's a plummet. And I'm talking all sales, CDs and downloads both. For the first time download sales are down as well. The bottom is falling out from under the industry. More and more artists are leaving their labels to sell direct to customers, which is bad enough, but there's something new at work here."

"That is bad," the aide told Chloe, moving his head slowly up and down and biting his lower lip in what she took for false empathy. She doubted he really cared at all about her fictional lost revenue beyond how it affected his ability to raise money and leverage influence on behalf of his boss. "But I'm not sure what else we can do to help from the Congressional end. We've raised fines and even jail time for piracy. The ipod tax is moving through the Senate right now, but it's got enough votes, so you guys will have that revenue coming in from every music player purchased. What more do you need?"

Chloe was well aware of just how much the Congress was already doing for the music industry, which was part of why they'd chosen this Congressman as the focus for their attack. The fact that the RIAA had managed to get so much ridiculous, anti-customer legislation through already made them the perfect cover for the Crew's plan. Why not one more ridiculous request? She felt her phone buzz in her coat pocket and pulled it out.

"Excuse me one second," she said, looking down at the text message on her screen from Sacco. "I need to take care of this quickly."

"No problem," he said. As she hoped, he took the opportunity to pick up his own Blackberry from the table and start doing some work of his own. Chloe keyed in some benign messages and waited for one of two pre-arranged replies from Sacco. She couldn't help but think of the time that Paul had e-mailed her while they were lying in bed together and how much shit she'd given him at the time for it. Sacco was only five feet away, sitting behind the target, eyes locked on his laptop. She knew he was trying to access the target's phone through its Bluetooth connection. Most people didn't bother to activate the Blackberry's built in security features, and even those might not be enough to stop Sacco from owning the guy's phone. If it went that easy, there was almost no point in her being here in person. It wasn't like they couldn't count on the guy using his phone.

It wasn't that easy. This was after all a Congressionally issued phone, and Sacco sent her a message letting her know that the target's shields were at full. Time for plan A. Chloe put her phone away and fixed her sights back on the target.

"Sorry about that," she said.

"No problem. I understand completely. So, what can I do for you today, Ms. Kross?"

"I mentioned that our investigators had uncovered something. When we saw the sudden drop, we went digging around for causes, and turned our investigative unit loose on the subject. Our agents in the field…"

"Agents in the field?" he asked, sounding surprised. Chloe had no reason to believe the RIAA had actual investigators or agents on staff, but she had no reason to believe that they didn't. Either way it sounded scary and impressive, and those were the impressions she wanted to leave in his mind.

"We've got investigators working online, trolling the message boards looking for places where people download music. We've got others out there in the streets checking up on bootlegs and so forth. We're in a battle to the death here, Danny, and it's win or die."

"Wow, OK. Well, what did they dig up?"

Chloe leaned in close towards him, lowering her voice. "There's a new piece of piracy software out there. It's called Mobbitt, and it's the new Napster. Maybe even worse than Napster in the long run, because it's impossible to trace. It's made for mobile phones—works on Iphones, Android phones, Blackberries, any kind of data enabled phone which, these days, is pretty much every phone. You put it on there and it broadcasts out your music and video library, stripping away any DRM in the process. Any DRM. And in return it downloads stuff from other people's phones near you. It's a mobile peer to peer network that's impossible for the phone companies to trace or stop. It's been spreading through Asia for the last six months and is hitting us here in the US and in Europe now. It's all over LA. I tell you, I installed it on my phone and it filled up with pirated music in just a few hours of normal driving around."

"That's amazing," Danny said. "And it just strips away the DRM without any problems?"

"It does. So anyone can copy the files freely. You need to see it in action to really understand it." She looked down at his phone on the table and acted as if an idea had just occurred to her. "Here, let me send it to you so you can see."

Danny picked up his phone and smiled. "Wouldn't that be violating the DMCA? We could go to jail," he joked. "Go ahead, are you going to send it via e-mail or Bluetooth it to me."

"On Blackberries it'll install right from the e-mail."

"Better not send it to my Congressional account. Send it to my RNC e-mail address instead. Those tend to have 'server problems' when needed."

Chloe had both addresses and the attachment already queued up and ready to go. Sacco had made the program small—smaller than something that did everything Chloe had described could probably be, but then again the scenario she'd described was pure fiction. Paul had come up with the cover story after reading some Cory Doctorow novel. It sounded plausible enough to her, and she was certainly more tech savvy than this guy was. She sent the e-mail and watched him as he opened it.

"OK, I've opened the attachment."

"It'll install itself on your phone. It might take a few minutes. In the meantime, let me tell you what we'd like to see happen here. First of all, even though this Mobbitt thing already violates the DMCA and a host of other laws, we would like some targeted enforcement. For starters we were thinking about a bill mandating that cell phone manufacturers install measures that prevent this software from working on their phones. Second we want them to monitor the data traffic between their phones, looking for any sign that this thing is running and then cancel the service if detected. Finally we want to make it a felony to even install the software on your phone in the first place." Chloe knew the requests were ridiculous, although not all that more ridiculous than some of the laws already in place.

"There will be resistance from the telecoms," Danny said, his gaze floating towards the ceiling as he seemed to mull over the implications of her requests. "They hate being told what to do."

"We considered that. We think you could sell it as an anti-terrorism measure as much as an anti-piracy one. We've already seen some traction on our campaign saying that piracy helps fund terrorism. In this case, we could argue that this kind of software enables terrorist cells to communicate and send files in secret without any way for law enforcement to effectively monitor them. But even so we know it's going to be an uphill fight. That's why I'm talking to you in particular, Danny. There's something you can do for us that no one else we work with can."

"What's that?" He smiled. This was a guy who liked to be needed.

"We know that the Congressman has worked closely with Ken Clover over at Clover and Associates, and right now he's not taking on any new clients."

"Clover, sure. He plays it very close. I've met him a few times. I didn't know he wasn't taking new clients though."

"Apparently he's very picky for a lobbyist. But my research shows that he can pull a lot of strings that would be helpful. Plus his pull with the Commerce Committee chairman might be crucial. Do you think the Congressman might be willing to extend a hand on our behalf in this matter? We'll certainly step up to the plate with regards to billables and backing of course."

"That might work. Clover and the Congressman are tight. I'll take it to the Congressman certainly."

"I appreciate it, Danny. Obviously he's not the only person we're talking with, and I have meetings with Senate staff later today, so there should be some added cover for you there as well. This is a top priority for us, and we're willing to throw all our support and resources behind the effort. But it's important for now that we keep it as quiet as possible. This Mobbitt thing is still mostly in the hands of nerds and techies right now—it hasn't gone mainstream. We don't want any publicity at all that might drive more users to it before we find a way to shut it down. I'm thinking maybe we can attach it to another bill or get it added in during conference. Something like that. So keep it on the QT, just your staff and your trusted allies. I know there are people on the other side of the aisle who would leak this whole thing just to fuck with my clients. We're counting on our old friends like the Congressman."

"Of course," said Danny. "I agree completely. We'll keep it off the floor, no problem." He looked at his phone. "So how does this thing work now?"

"There should be a start icon in your expanded menu now. See that? Activate it and it'll bring up the interface and start matching with other phones in the area. Hopefully mine is the only one." Of course hers was the only one—the program was designed to do three things—connect with her phone and download three songs to his phone, return the favor by downloading anything in his music folder to her phone, and of course own the phone completely so that Sacco sitting behind her could take over his Blackberry, access his passwords and files, and clone the phone so they could use it without his knowledge. Five minutes later it had done all three, impressing the target with the two functions he was aware of, and driving home her point that Mobbitt was the greatest threat to western civilization since Al Quaeda.

As they stood up and shook hands to part ways, Chloe looked down at the target's shoes. "Did you step in some paint, Danny?"

"Damn protesters," he said, leaning over and picking at the dried paint with his fingernail. "I don't even know what the hell they were upset about this time, but they were outside my apartment building and were yelling at all the staffers who live there as we came out."

"Cretins," Chloe said. "You'd think they would've learned by now that none of that nonsense makes a difference."

"Ohhh, they never learn. How smart can they be, standing outside all morning in this cold?"

They both laughed and went their separate ways. Chloe promised to check in with him that evening. Sacco had already slipped out ahead of them, his work here complete. She put her gloves back on and headed back towards the Metro a few blocks away. Everything seemed to have gone as planned and thus she was nervous. No battle plan survives contact with the enemy. At least his Blackberry had been secure— that would have been so easy she might have really been freaked out. As it was, the months of e-mail correspondence, campaign donations, and background work establishing her false identity as Lisa Kross, Los Angeles based lobbyist for shadowy recording industry interests had paid off. She didn't claim to work for the RIAA or the MPAA, but she had actually done some real lobbying in their interests. That fact alone had made some in the Crew, including Paul, feel dirty, but Chloe didn't mind. To be honest it wasn't a big issue to her—people would pirate music and there was no stopping them. If the RIAA wanted to waste money fighting it, that was their problem. She figured the whole industry would be dead in a decade anyway. In the meantime their bull in a china shop tactics provided cover for their real agenda. The target hadn't seemed to doubt she was who she said she was for even a moment and once he got in touch with Clover directly, they'd be in business. Assuming c1sman delivered of course, but Paul was on top of that.

She ducked into a drug store and found Sacco in the cold remedies aisle, where they could quickly debrief. He was almost too good looking for this kind of covert stuff. Sandee had literally dressed him down in ill-fitting cheap chinos and a baggy sweater and baseball cap to hide his better features. Standing there he looked like a handsome, dashing guy who was hung over and grungy, but could bounce back to ladykiller looks with just 15 minutes in the bathroom and a change of clothes. She sidled up next to him and started reading cough medicine labels.

"Got it," he said. "We own his phone."

"You just like saying that cuz it rhymes," she said.

"It rhymes and it's true. Double bonus."

"And your kids are in place and ready? I saw they got some paint on him this morning."

"They're good like that. Yeah, they're ready to go."

"And you're wishing you could be out there with them. But you can't. They're a distraction, we need to keep you behind the scenes."

"I always prefer to be where the action is."

"I know, that's why it was so easy for me to find you." She picked a bottle and turned towards the front of the store. "Besides, you should know by now, I'm where the action is."

"Well then, I'll stick close to you."

She smiled. "Of course you will."

Chapter 4

Sacco • *before*

S acco loved HOPE. He wished it came every year instead of every
other. As much as he hated midtown Manhattan and all its bour-
geois nonsense, he loved the creative, anarchic energy of the con, the
weird juxtaposition of the chipped and faded majesty of the Hotel
Pennsylvania mixed with the bodged together wiring and haphazard
organization of the volunteer staff running things, all combining to
provide a social petri-dish for hacker memes with a purpose, cutting
edge technology that could actually cut, and a wildness of mind that he
adored. Not that there weren't lots of things to hate. The smell would be
ripe by Saturday night, with the shower-phobic hackers' odors boosted
by the sticky, clinging July heat outside. There would be idiots doing
stupid shit, as always, and ill-prepared talks that went nowhere and
had no point. And the lack of organization would drive him crazy
sometimes—like now, where somehow he'd ended up as the only person
responsible for unloading a half-ton of t-shirts and old issues of *2600
Magazine* and transporting them up 18 floors through two different sets
of loading elevators. Or the fact that, even at this late hour, the NOC
still didn't have the network up and running. But that was all surface
bullshit and didn't speak ill of the soul of the event—rebellion, freedom,
and technology wrapped into one adorable anarchic ball. Hackers On
Planet Earth might not be the most poetic name out there, but HOPE
couldn't be beat as an idea.

He didn't even bother going to any other hacker cons in the US anymore. Germany was another story—those guys in the Chaos Computer

Club had their shit together and their priorities in line. But over here in the States, a big chunk of the so-called hacker scene totally eschewed anything to do with politics, which was, quite obviously, total bullshit. Hacking was, as much as anything, a political action, and anyone who ignored that fact was either living with their head buried in the sand or was part of the freaking problem. Def Con used to be cool, but now it'd become it's own for-profit company and not only welcomed the Feds, but actually had them as invited fucking speakers. That'd been it as far as Sacco and a lot of his friends were concerned. And most of the smaller cons were the same—corporate security professional types mostly, holding out the lure of big blood money to young kids who didn't know any better. Where was the rebellion in any of that? How the hell was that making the world any better?

Some of his friends tried to straddle the fence and keep a foot in both worlds, and it was something they argued about a lot. It might work for old timers like Simple Nomad, but he was his own thing for the most part, and none of the guys in Sacco's group, Hacks of Rebellion, had his cred or rep or, aside from maybe Sacco himself and one or two others, the skills. That left Sacco in the odd but exciting position of being the most radical member of a self-described radical group. Well, someone had to be the conscience of the team, and no one else was willing to step up to the plate, so he was it. It had taken him he didn't know how many hours on encrypted IRC channels arguing that they should in fact release their newest creation to the public in this most public of hacker venues. They were scared, they'd argued against him, but he'd taken the moral high ground and defended it tooth and claw. Saturday night they'd all see that he'd been right all along.

As he heaved another dolly-load of boxes out of the service elevator and onto the eighteenth floor, Sacco grunted in exasperation. He wasn't even halfway done. He'd just seen another dolly in one of the service halls on his way up here, so he decided that he needed to press some other volunteer into service right away, if he was going to get this shit done in time to grab a shower before opening ceremonies. He wondered what the hell the organizers had planned on doing about this truckload of crap if he hadn't shown up. No doubt some other eager volunteer would've done it. That right there was what he loved about hacker conventions, especially this one. People just pitched in and got shit done, maybe not in the most efficient way possible, but it got done.

He took the public elevators down to the ground floor and wheeled his dolly through the marble hotel lobby full of black t-shirt clad throngs waiting in the painfully slow check-in line. At some point the hotel had bought out the department store next door and turned it into a rather dingy but serviceable convention center. Here attendees picked up their badges, registered to be volunteers, and bought junk food and energy drinks. Sacco didn't see any idle hands he could press into service, so he wrestled the dolly onto the escalator and took it up to the main "convention" level. The bare concrete floors, broken up at regular intervals by heavy, concrete pillars were in full chaos mode. To his left people were setting up tables and chairs for the open network area. To his right they were adjusting a large screen and laying out rented individual hammocks for the movie and vendors area. Beyond he saw someone zipping around the floor on a Segway at what looked like almost maximum speed. He'd definitely have to try that, maybe even before he found someone to help with the unloading.

He passed through the empty stretch of what would eventually be Lockpick Village, towards the vendor area. A few booksellers and one hardware vendor had already set up. And there she was, browsing the books. Not just browsing the books, but picking one up and actually asking questions about it. He moved closer to see if he could get an angle on what she was looking at. Ooooh, Kropotkin's *The Conquest of Bread*. Nice. She gave off the vibe of a certain rare type of hacker chick that he always sought but seldom found. She was hot as hell for one thing, with a great body. The pink hair was certainly punk, but the jeans and black t-shirt were understated enough to make him think the hair wasn't purely a poseur punk attitude thing, but maybe a real aesthetic choice. Plus she looked like she showered and, as he came up behind her she smelled good, too. He reached over and tapped the back of the Kropotkin book as she read it. "That's a classic."

She shifted away from him as she turned to see who was talking, but not in a panicked way. Plus as soon as she saw him, she smiled, which was usually a good sign. "Oh yeah? I don't know how much time I have for classics these days."

"I should have said timeless classic," Sacco said, smiling back and keeping his eyes focused on hers. "A great, great book."

"I wouldn't think 19th century Russian anarchists would have much to offer hackers." She fanned herself with the book, her tone challenging but light. "Their economic models are all based on industrial and pre-industrial systems and we're moving into a post-industrial world."

"And you and I are probably the only two people at this convention who'll realize or care about that, but I think that book will surprise you. There are some great lessons in there we can still apply—especially if you're a free software kind of girl."

"As it happens I am. I like my software free as in freedom and my beer free as in someone else is buying."

He laughed. Hot and she could riff on Richard Stallman quotes. Very nice. "Well, I'll have to buy you that beer later."

"Maybe you will." She looked at his dolly. "Are you on staff here?"

"No, I'm just helping out. I don't suppose you want to help me unload a truck full of t-shirts and truck them up to the 18th floor."

"I really don't," she said, smiling. "But thanks for the offer."

"Well then, you'll have to come to the Hacks of Rebellion talk on Saturday night then." He gestured towards the ceiling and, 18 stories up, the speakers' halls.

"I will?"

"It's only fair. Either help with the boxes or come to the talk. That's my final offer. Plus it's going to be awesome. We've got a major new release the whole con will be talking about."

"That does sound better than schlepping boxes. You've got yourself a deal. And I'll do you one better hotshot. If your release really is as awesome as you say, I'll let you buy me that beer." She winked at him. That was always a good sign.

"Then keep your calendar free, because it's a done deal."

"I hope so," she said, putting the book back down on the table and picking up another one as she turned away from him. "I'll let you get back to work."

Damn he loved HOPE.

"You're fucking kidding me!" Sacco shouted. He hated shouting, found it almost always counterproductive, and generally liked to be the cool, calm, collected cat in the room. "You. Are. FUCKING. KIDDING. ME!!!"

"Sacco, calm down, man. Calm down."

"And you guys just decided this without even talking to me."

"You were busy and…"

"I was unloading boxes of goddamned t-shirts. I had my cell phone. You could have called. I would've stopped."

"We were pretty sure how you'd vote."

"So you thought, 'Hey, we know Sacco will hate this idea, so let's just not hear his arguments on it.' Nice."

"We're listening now."

Sacco looked around the hotel room. The wheezing air conditioner was just paying lip service to the idea of cooling. The other main members of Hacks of Rebellion were there, Bryan, fawks, ck, and Dex. But it was Dex who was trying to calm him down. The other three just looked like they wanted to be anywhere else but here. Right now Sacco felt the same way—he wanted the rest of these cowardly fucks to be anywhere but here. The five of them had started Hacks of Rebellion four years ago. Inspired by famous and influential hacktivist groups like The Cult of the Dead Cow, they'd wanted to find a way to put their hacking abilities to a good cause while still maintaining the mischievous edge that had drawn them all into hacking in the first place. Sacco, Dex, and fawks had been over in Germany for a Chaos Computer Camp when they came up with the idea. And yes, the mushrooms they'd eaten probably helped, but in the sober light of morning it still seemed like a good idea. When they got back home they roped in Bryan and ck and started doing their thing. From the beginning most of the ideological basis for their actions came from Sacco. The others were political in a sort of nebulous, vaguely lefty, fight the man kind of way. They were coders and hackers and tinkerers first, who cared about politics only up until the moment when it came to do any serious reading or studying about the issues. A devoted anarchist since high school, Sacco had read his Bakunin and Kropotkin and Proudhon and Goldman cover to cover. He eschewed the Sex Pistols-inspired anarchy equals punk equals chaos aesthetic that most people associated with the word "anarchist." Instead he focused on the core, ultra-democratic foundations of anarchist theory along with its deep anti-capitalist, anti-plutocratic tenets. He also knew better than to lay all that heavy poli-sci shit on the other four, instead feeding them spoonfuls as needed.

For the others, it was enough that they felt they were acting with some sort of moral justification to their actions. If they were going to cut a few corners and break a few laws along the way, at least they could do so in good conscience. They all worked for money and hacked for good. Originally Sacco had argued against any kind of name or public presence to the group—those kinds of things just attract attention. But the others wanted to be able to brag a little about some of the things they did (the legal ones of course), and earn some kudos from the community. So they'd settled on the name Hacks of Rebellion, and from the beginning more than half of their time was spent on decidedly "white hat" endeavors. Or at the very worst gray hat. They cracked some DRM schemes; they revealed some exploits. They created some open source crypto apps that people could use to communicate securely with one another. That was the public side of Hacks of Rebellion, the one that went to cons and gave presentations and played (sometimes successfully, sometimes not at all) at being rock stars. In truth they weren't nearly as rebellious or rowdy as their reputations suggested, but that was fine with Sacco. Reputations were in and of themselves a kind of social engineering—hacking the hacking community.

All the while though, Sacco had pushed his political agenda from the inside, slipping in bits of ideology and education when he could, while working on his own, non-public projects. Not that the others didn't help with the secret stuff—they totally did, and without their expertise he probably wouldn't have gotten much finished. One of his favorites was a set of Quickbooks hacks that would allow employees to take a peek into their employers' books and see what everyone was getting paid. Sacco considered the American stigma against employees knowing each others' salaries to be one of the great scams perpetrated on the workers by the ownership class—keeping information like income inequality secret directly deflected one of the principal impetuses to organizing and revolt. Most of his early stuff had been in this vein— tools and attacks to help workers strike back against their oppressors. The problem was, no one in his target audience was getting his hacks— most of them never learned about them, and few of those who did had the technical skills to use them properly.

So Sacco had turned his energy towards easier and easier ways to use apps—stuff that any schmo could run on his home computer or even cell phone without needing to be a hard core hacker. And more and more, cell phones had become his target of choice. Saturday's release was the culmination of a year's worth of testing and work by Hacks of Rebellion—Listnin, an easy to run Bluetooth hack that would allow anyone out there to eavesdrop in on Bluetooth cell phone conversations. The hacking elements were well known and developed by others, and Sacco wasn't breaking any new ground there. His innovation was making it so easy to use and deploy that every worker in the world would be able to eavesdrop on their douche-bag bosses with their earpieces attached to the sides of their head. They had two thousand CDs burned with Listnin loaded on them, including versions for every major phone OS, and they'd set up a dozen servers in seven different countries for people to torrent the file from. By the time they'd finished their talk, Listnin would be all over the goddamned place and no phone would be safe if it wasn't properly secured (and very, very few of them were).

That had been the plan anyway. Now Dex and the rest of them were backing out. They were scared, afraid they'd gone too far and would get arrested. Sacco railed against their cowardice but met a wall of downcast, ashamed resilience to his pleas. The Hacks of Rebellion had voted and decided not to release Listnin, at least not at this time and not in this public way.

"Well, screw you guys. I fucking quit," Sacco said, and it felt so good. Scary, weird, but so good. He was tired of these guys, of their whining and worrying.

"Come on, man, don't be like that," said Dex. "We can still put it out there, but we'll do it quietly, like the other things we've done for you."

"For me? You mean with me."

"Yeah, of course. With you. We'll do it like the others. That's always worked before."

"By your inside baseball fucking standards maybe, but not by any rational metric! It hasn't worked at fucking all. No one uses them, because no one but some 'leet-ass' motherfucking hackers even know they exist. It's fucking masturbation and nothing more, man."

"This will be different." The pleading tone in Dex's voice disgusted Sacco. "We designed it to be easy to use. It'll catch on if it's as good as we think it is. But there's no reason to attach our names to it. That's just asking for trouble!"

Sacco swallowed the rejoinder before it escaped his mouth. They'd decided, and he wasn't going to change their minds. But he did have a window of opportunity to change the future if he acted right now. "Maybe you're right," he said, voice filled with conciliation he didn't feel. "I'm probably just freaking out for no reason. But you know what, maybe I'm right too. Let's all just take a breather OK, let's just calm down and think this through for a couple hours. Then we'll take one final vote—I won't even try to argue with you anymore. I'll think about what you've said, you think about what I've said. Meet back here in two hours?"

Some of them probably suspected something, but they couldn't deny he was being reasonable and fair. They hemmed and hawed a few minutes, but as soon as they agreed, Sacco excused himself and headed downstairs. He had to find two people and liberate a case of CDs.

He was glad they'd decided not to spend the time and money to get custom labels put on the CDs, another argument he'd lost by the way, and another decision that would come back to bite them in the ass. He was even more pleased that he'd copied Dex's car keys last year and never gotten around to telling him about it. For the rest of the day and all of Friday he'd played the good and loyal comrade, going along with the majority. He sulked and teased and taunted of course—if he hadn't they would definitely have suspected something—but not so much that they became resentful of him. They were all still too relieved that he hadn't done anything stupid. Except of course he had.

They followed the Saturday keynote, which was once again former Dead Kennedy's front man Jello Biafra. He'd spoken at several HOPEs in the past, usually on Sundays but he had a scheduling conflict this year, and he always got the crowd going with his mix of political rants, humor, and flat out visceral anger. He was even nice enough to give Hacks of Rebellion a plug before he left the stage. They entered with their usual fanfare (which was very unusual for HOPE): music blaring (Won't Be Fooled Again), and lots of yelling. They'd dressed up of course. Variations on business suits hacked into almost unrecognizable forms by the addition of LED screens, keyboards, speakers, and even a pair of angel wings with old data tape for feathers. It was quite a show, and for the first time Sacco was fully aware that this was really the only reason these other guys did this shit anymore—the fame and attention, the thousand yelling hackers chanting trite phrases in call and response fashion. They did it for the bullshit.

Sacco's original role in the presentation had been cut, but they'd thrown him a bone and asked him to present the info on a stupid little Microsoft Excel exploit that fawks had found. Fawks was the least adept public speaker anyway, and so had been (as usual) put in charge of the A/V stuff. Sacco smiled at him as he took the microphone up on stage and looked out over the crowd of a thousand or more hackers. If they'd drawn back the curtains, they'd have all been treated to a rather impressive view of Midtown Manhattan. Sacco idly wondered for just a moment how many of them had actually bothered to peak behind those heavy drapes and enjoy the view. He knew he hadn't. Without bothering to look over his shoulder at whatever bullshit image fawks was projecting onto the screen behind him, Sacco wrenched the mic from its stand and climbed up on top of the table. People cheered. His comrades on stage had nervous grins on their faces. They had to suspect he was up to something.

He looked to his left and saw a heavyset young man holding a card-board box full of CDs. He looked right and saw another, even more heavyset kid with another box. They both nodded to him, reaching into their boxes.

"Listen!" Sacco shouted into the mic. "Listen! Listen in on what I've got to say. I want you listenin' to the words comin' out of my mouth! I wand you to listen in on the secrets I'm about to spill." He lowered his voice to a whisper, amplified with a hiss through the audio system. "Lissssssten. Do you hear that? Do you hear what the douche bag with the Star Trek lookin' earpiece is hearing? Can you listen in on what the boss man is whispering about over his latte? Shhhh. Listen. What's that? Can't quite hear it?" Someone behind him, down on the stage, was tugging on his pants leg. Probably Dex. "Be real quiet now. Listen real hard. Can you hear him now?"

The room was quiet, and Sacco had no trouble hearing the angry whispers coming from his former friends. The next time Dex tugged at his cuff, he kicked back and then jumped down in front of the speaker's table, shouting, "LET ME HELP YOU HEAR!"

His two paid accomplices, New York college kids who'd worshiped Hacks of Rebellion since they were fifteen-year-old script kiddies, started tossing handfuls of CDs into the audience. Sacco had snatched the burned copies of Listnin from Dex's car and replaced them with blank CD's he'd bought up from every drug store within twenty blocks. He'd written labels on the top dozen or so in each box, just in case someone checked. If his co-conspirators online were holding up their end too, there were a dozen different torrents being seeded with the software right now. He pulled out some disks of his own from inside his jacket and spun them out in long, floating arcs towards the middle of the audience. Hackers ducked, jumped, and snatched for the silver disks. Some rose up and mobbed his paid helpers, but instead of stopping them they were reaching into the boxes and tossing out even more CDs. Fawks cut his mic, and the jerks on the stage behind him were screaming bloody murder. Sacco laughed and laughed and laughed, hopping down from the stage as he tossed the dead mic over his shoulder.

He made his way through the crowd towards the exit. He wasn't going to answer any questions or make any more speeches. The software would speak for itself (and listen too). Dex came running up behind him by the time he reached the bank of elevators. He started yelling all the things Sacco expected him to. They had a deal. There'd been a vote. He was a fucking asshole. They were kicking him out. How dare he break into Dex's car. Sacco stood there and took it for a while, just letting Dex vent and rage. He figured it would do the guy some good to get it all out, and there wasn't a thing he could say that would affect Sacco in the least. He missed the first elevator to come, but decided to get on the next one. Quite a crowd was lurking about them now, listening in, and Sacco wanted to get outside. He jumped on the already packed elevator at the last moment, leaving no time or room for Dex to join him. He thanked the others inside for their kind words and encouragement on the way down. Stepping into the hotel lobby, he took a moment to decide which way to exit, looking left, in the general direction of a bar he liked, and then right, towards the front entrance and… and the girl with the pink hair.

She was holding a CD, spinning it around on her raised middle finger and smiling at him. He walked over to her.

"Nice speech," she said.

"You liked it?"

"Just the end part. Most of the stuff before it was pretty lame."

He nodded to the spinning disk on her finger. "And you got one of my CDs."

"I got two of them," she said, winking. Oh that wink. "Now, are you going to buy me a beer and explain to me how this Listnin thing of yours works?"

"Absofuckinglutely."

She laughed with such genuine delight at that, that she almost seemed like a different person for a split second. "Well come on then, cowboy, let's go."

He followed her out the front door, thinking that this HOPE hadn't turned out so disastrous after all.

Chapter 5

Paul

Paul still wasn't used to this part. It thrilled him. He looked up and down the list of e-mails—two and a half years worth of e-mails—and clicked randomly on one of them. It was something about a piece of Florida State House legislation having to do with land use regulations, but as dull as it was, it still sent micro-currents of excitement coursing down the back of his neck. He was not supposed to be reading this, and yet he totally was. Next to him on the couch Chloe was going through another massive download. At the table Sacco and Sandee were going through others. Their Data Guy on the outside had it all too, and was running his password crackers and his analysis software on all of it. Clsman's painstaking hack had worked—they'd owned the target's network and, best of all, no one seemed to have noticed.

There was nothing in any of his former lives that compared to these thrills, this level of excitement. An aspiring and then mildly successful comic book artist for the first decade of adulthood, his life had been ink stained and scrabbling for attention at comic book conventions. Then he though he'd hit the big time when his childhood friend turned dot com millionaire agreed to finance his brilliant idea for a video game. The game had turned out pretty good, but Paul had turned out to be a pretty crappy video game designer, mostly in the area of working with others in his own company. They'd fired him and in a moment of despair and desperation he'd met this crazy-hot woman named Chloe who offered him a chance to get his revenge. If he was willing to break some walls. Considering the much nastier and less practical revenge plots that'd been romping through his mind, Chloe's plan had seemed practically reasonable. They ended up walking out of the meeting where he was supposed to get his ass handed to him with a check for $800,000. Of course then things got complicated.

In the end he lost the money, lost his friends, and was wanted by law enforcement for questioning on suspicion of fraud and kidnapping. But he'd gotten the girl, and that was worth something. That was, in fact, pretty much worth everything. Chloe'd sacrificed her friends to stay with him—everyone but Bee—and they'd set up a new life in Key West. They still stole from people, but Paul needed some good reason, some moral excuse that allowed him to sleep at night. He knew that, at least some of the time, he was just lying to himself. But he'd gotten really good at lying, even to himself. Still, when this opportunity to strike out against a genuine bad guy in the world had come along, Paul had been excited. As high as the tension was, as dangerous as things had gotten, he was sleeping better now than he had in years. Well, metaphorically sleeping. In reality there wasn't time to sleep much at all, but he felt good about that too.

Paul opened another random e-mail. Again it was inscrutable to him, full of legal jargon and inside politics talk. There was no way he was going to be able to parse anything useful out of this stuff, but he didn't expect to. This was pure voyeurism until the analyses came in from outside and they'd found the specific files and e-mails they needed. After he'd escalated privileges all the way and completed the data dump, c1sman had collapsed back onto the couch in an exhausted heap of frayed nerves. Paul had sent him downstairs to Shmoocon with Bee to have some fun and mingle with the nice law-abiding hackers and security professionals. He wanted c1sman's mind focused on the familiar, or better yet, distracted by the "secret" crush that everyone but Bee knew he had on Bee. Let them play and keep tabs on the network down there—as part of the NOC team, c1sman had full access—as long as no one noticed that they'd piggybacked in on the con's bandwidth and experimental TOR server set up, they were golden.

"Well, it's started, finally," Chloe said. She had a third laptop, a little ultra-portable, propped up on the armrest. It had a copy of Outlook on it that would mirror every action on the target's system. Yet another, identical ulta-portable next to that had a similar setup monitoring e-mails from the Congressman and his staffer. Between the Blackberry hack (which got them into the staff's Exchange server), and c1sman's network hack on the target's office, there wasn't any e-mail between the two of them that they weren't going to see. There had been a few moments setting it all up where Paul had held his breath in nervousness as they'd inserted the rest of their malicious code and hacks into the target computers. The malware on the Congressional aide's Blackberry had given them access to all his e-mail, but they wanted to do more than just monitor his messages—they needed to be able to write their own. But at the same time they needed to make sure he didn't notice that someone else was sending mail from his account, with the added complication that everything he sent was cc'd to both his laptop and his phone. Sacco's first move after owning the Blackberry was to upload more malware onto the phone to make sure Danny didn't notice the changes. Then they'd sent a false message from Danny to the Congressman that included the same piece of malware they'd used to infect the first phone. There'd been a lot of concern at this point, especially about whatever added security the US House of Reps IT department might have installed, but as far as they could tell it all went as planned. They then installed the same back doors and stealth measures on the Congressman's machines. Now it was time to start pressing their advantage and use their newly stolen Congressional influence to maximum effect.

While they waited for their outside analysis to dig up the dirt, they had other work to do. Chloe moved one of the ultra-portables over so Paul could read it. They'd built in a minute-long delay into both e-mail accounts so they'd have a chance to read the messages before they went out and either delete or change them as needed. Paul scanned an e-mail from Danny to the target and keyed F10, the hotkey they'd set up to intercept outgoing mail.

The original read:

From: Daniel@wolvertonforamerica.org
To: Ken.Clover@cloverandassociates.com
Subject: Referral

Hey Ken,

Wondering if you had some spare time for a referral. TC is working on some legislation to help entertainment industry protect their IP from a new piracy threat and has some ideas about inserting procurements to fund new enforcement efforts. Ent. Ind. will need support from multiple C's for this I'm sure, since they're fearing a big hit to their

bottom lines. Hoping you could do some coordinating for
us on this.

Thanks,
D

Paul wasn't sure what TC meant at first, but it clearly referred to
Congressman Wolverton. The e-mail showed that Danny and the target were well acquainted with one another and that the staffer wasn't
shy about asking for favors. Paul assumed that the line about support
from multiple C's (congressmen?) and the mention of the entertainment
industry's bottom line was Danny's way of saying there was plenty of
money to go around. That was good. It confirmed their supposition
that the target was in it for the money first and foremost, and as long
as Paul kept the promise of a profit in his forged e-mails, he would be
speaking the right language. He was a little worried that Danny and
the target were so familiar with each other though—that meant he had
to be extra careful with the forgeries to not write anything the target
might find out of character. He dumped the e-mail into a folder on his
desktop and prevented it from being passed on to Clover. If everything
went as planned, Clover would never even know that the Congressman's
aide had been sending him any e-mails at all.

Paul sat back and waited what seemed like a reasonable amount of time
before readying his "reply" from Clover. Danny was e-mailing a lot, and
Paul was keeping up with it as best he could. The target was e-mailing
too, although not as much. Everything else seemed pretty business as
usual as far as Paul could tell—lots of scheduling issues and fund raising talk, but mostly details about meetings, pending legislation, and
more meetings. Then he sent his e-mail along, posing as Clover.

From: Ken.Clover@cloverandassociates.com
To: Daniel@wolvertonforamerica.org
Subject: RE: Referral

Danny,

Busy beyond belief right this moment, but I should be able

to help. Let's talk on Monday or Tuesday when things have
settled down a bit.

Ken

A few minutes later, Danny replied that Monday would be fine, and
Paul diverted it to his own machine. Hopefully Danny would put any
thoughts about the target out of his mind until they needed him again.
In the meantime, Paul could take over his e-mail duties just fine.

"Everything's rocking along," Paul announced to the room. Chloe,
Sacco, and Sandee all looked up at him. "Sacco?"

"All set with the earmark to insert," Sacco said, his voice a little
louder than necessary as usual. "It looks good. Hell, it might even be
decent legislation, but hopefully actually doing some good won't raise
any alarms with these fucks."

"I think we'll be fine," said Paul. "Give it an hour or so and then
we'll shoot the procurement language on over to him. Should give
him a couple hours to shoehorn it in but not enough time to dig too
deep."

Sacco checked something on his laptop, which also had all the data
from the Congressman's phone. "Yeah, the Congressman's calendar
confirms that the conference committee's meeting through the night
so they can get everything wrapped up over the weekend and signed
and passed on Monday morning for the big press event."

They'd had their pick of bills they could have inserted the earmark
into—a dedicated budget item that provided funding for a specific
program. In this case it was being inserted into a large infrastructure
bill that had been lingering around for several months but had recently
been fast tracked after an overpass in Georgia had collapsed two weeks
earlier. Sacco, who watched all the Congressional machinations for the
Crew, decided this was better than the federal land use bill they'd
originally planned on using, since the sudden fast tracking would mean
all kinds of congress critters would be inserting earmarks into it and
there'd be more chaff disguising their activities.

Paul turned his attention to Sandee. "How's Mr. Data doing?"

"He's plugging away, says everything's running the way he thought
it would. Should have something soon," he said. Sandee had a direct
link over an encrypted IRC channel with the Crew's data analyst. As
soon as he was done he could throw up some names for them and they
could formulate their earmark request perfectly. He'd been a real find,
although they still felt the need to keep him in the dark about most of

the details of the con. But that was partly his own choice—he knew enough to know he didn't want to know anything else.

Paul sat back on the couch and reached over to give Chloe's leg a squeeze. She smiled at him. "Do you think we should check on Bee and c1sman?" he asked.

"Let them have their fun. We don't need them on this right now, and they're in their element."

"Do you think Bee will ever get a clue about his crush on her?"

"Maybe," she said. "But this is a hacker con, and Bee's a single woman with an incredible mind for gadgets and hardware hacking who's outnumbered 5 to 1 by horny, mostly single geeks. Poor c1sman's gonna have a lot of competition down there. I'd be surprised if he summoned up the courage to make a move. I hope he does, but I'll be really surprised."

"I hope he does too," said Paul. And not just because he'd like to see Bee finally with someone. C1sman was in a weird place mentally, and Paul wasn't at all sure he was adjusting to the hardcore criminal hacking life very well. Paul had suffered similar doubts when he started of course, but he had a lot less choice and Chloe was dragging him along into it. C1sman's motivations weren't nearly as clear-cut and he had a lot more options, even if he didn't see them yet. Bee would bind him to the Crew, which would be great. They could use him.

Downstairs it was almost time for the keynote. He figured Bruce Potter, one of Shmoocon's founders, would be taking the stage to introduce the speaker, an academic-based hacker who'd led a project exposing some nasty vulnerabilities in electronic voting machines. Paul sort of wished he could be there, but he knew the video would be online in a month or less. Shmoocon was an interesting kind of hacker convention, mid-sized and extremely popular. The attendees and speakers constituted what Paul had come to think of as the upper middle class of the hacking community. Most of them were security or network professionals of some sort, some of whom no doubt got into a lot of mischief in their younger years but who had grown into well paying jobs and familial responsibilities. There was an undercurrent of youth as well—college students or twenty-somethings who were still searching for their place in the world. The vendors and sponsors tended to be security companies and publishers, all legit, all trying to make a buck. Despite the con's home in Washington DC, the talks mostly steered clear of politics except in either the most general or specific of cases. Privacy rights and personal freedom were always big topics of concern, but issues like social justice or political activism on non-technology issues seldom got much attention. And of course, like any con, the social aspect was just as much a draw as the talks, if not more so. The large hotel bar and lounge area would be full in the evenings, and Saturday night Shmoocon rented out an entire nightclub over in Dupont Circle to accommodate attendees. Paul and Chloe would be skipping those events of course, but Bee and c1sman might be able to take advantage.

The idea of running a complicated con from a hacker convention had been a calculated risk. Paul had gone back and forth on the idea, as had Chloe. At one time or another both of them had argued vociferously for both points of view. As it turned out, the first time they both agreed happened when they were both on the "pro" side of the argument, so they'd gone with the plan. Using Shmoocon as cover gave them a lot of advantages. They were able to get c1sman well positioned to let them piggyback on the convention's bandwidth, and once they'd decided on using the con, he'd submitted his plans for running a TOR server at the convention, one modified with new improvements of c1sman's own devising. The TOR worked in concert with other computers to help make the user's internet activity anonymous. Users logged into TOR would have their activities routed through layers of anonymous servers before proceeding on to wherever they were headed on the internet. This process masked the user's IP Address, making it very difficult to trace back the packet to its original point. The newer, more robust TOR server c1sman and his hacker friends had set up worked in conjunction with computers all over the country and in Germany. The whole point of the display at the convention was to stress test the arrangement, so they were encouraging as many con attendees as possible to hop on and give the setup a try. Hopefully all that activity and bandwidth would provide more than enough cover for the rather risky attacks the Crew was launching this weekend.

And if things went wrong, Shmoocon also offered perfect camouflage. There were over 1300 attendees at the event, any of whom was theoretically a suspect if law enforcement somehow got involved. Paul thought the odds of that happening during the actual weekend of the convention were pretty slim. Their plan should cover their tracks very well. But the almost inevitable investigation after the fact was another matter. Smart people would start digging around, trying to figure out just what the hell had happened. If they figured it out and managed to trace it back to Shmoocon, that still left them with over a thousand suspects. Beyond the fact that a sizable fraction of the attendees registered under pseudonyms, the real culprits, aside from Bee and c1sman, weren't even actually attending the convention. Paul, Chloe, Sacco, and Sandee were in the hotel under fake identities and often looked the part of hackers, but they weren't doing any socializing or interacting with the rest of the convention. Even the most diligent investigator would have a hard time finding any trace of them.

Paul watched and read strangers' e-mails for the next hour and a half. It was both boring and thrilling. Again and again temptation pulled at him to change a word or two just because he could, but of course he didn't. It was a real high, and he wondered how people who worked at places like the NSA dealt with the temptations to pry into everything. Maybe they didn't, or maybe they just got used to it. Maybe both. All Paul knew was that he loved the power that having Sacco, c1sman, and Mr. Data in the Crew gave him.

"Oooh!" said Sandee. "Good news everybody. We've got some names from Mr. Data. He seems very excited. Either that or he accidentally hit Caps Lock." Sandee worked the keyboard for a few seconds and then pulled a small USB drive from the side of his laptop and brought it across the room to Paul. He plugged it into his own machine and copied the list of names to his desktop.

"Here we go," said Paul. "Time to give the target his marching orders." Then he started to write legislation.

Chapter 6

Oliver loved his job. Well, Oliver HAD loved his job. Now he was looking for a new one, but there were plenty of offers on the table, and there was some level of potential for love in all of them. But he needed to clear his head, take a break, and put things in perspective before he made any big decisions. Plus his current, previously lovable job, wasn't aware that the feelings weren't mutual anymore and so still had no qualms about paying his way to a hacker convention all the way out in San Diego just because he said he needed to go. He didn't even feel guilty about it. There was still some slight chance he'd stay with the company, although with his friends jumping ship and the new government mandated changes in testing procedure going into effect next month, it didn't seem very likely. Still, there was a chance, and if he did stay, the stuff he learned at Toor Con could theoretically come in handy at work. Or at his next place of employment for that matter.

Ollie stretched out on his king sized bed 22 floors above downtown San Diego. He'd just been staring out the window down onto the field where the Padres play. Great seats if there'd been a home game that weekend. Even so, it was cool. Outside, the September evening was crisp and clear and breezy, a far cry from the heat that still suffused St. Louis. It was good to be away, on his own. He'd even turned his cell phone's ringer off so he'd only have to answer calls if he wanted. A nap would be nice, then maybe a free beer or two up at the Marriott's hospitality suite. Then he could head over to the convention center and see what was going on.

He woke up around 7:00 PM, trudged into the shower and threw on a t-shirt from last year's Toor Con that featured an ASCII design, just like every other year. He liked the old school sensibilities Toor Con tried to espouse. Even though he wasn't yet thirty, he still felt more of a connection to the original hackers than to the modern scene. Of course the flip side was that it was the modern scene that afforded him plenty of lucrative and exciting work as a full time penetration tester, so he wasn't going to complain too much. He just sort of wished people didn't take everything quite so seriously these days. It seemed like being a hacker must have been more fun back in the 80's and early 90's.

Ollie had been to the San Diego Convention center twice before. Once for a Toor Con, and once for San Diego ComicCon. The differences and similarities between the two amused him as he crossed the train tracks and made his way inside the sole open doorway. During ComicCon, the place was FLOODED with people. Flooded. It took up what seemed like 10 city blocks—the entire main floor of the hall plus more in the annex across the street—and by mid-day the place was packed solid with fans. Toor Con occupied just three small ballrooms on the second floor that could hold a couple hundred people each. He walked down the wide, white, hallway that seemed to him like something out of Logan's Run or some other 70's sci-fi version of the future. It was empty except for a cluster of a few dozen people around some tables and chairs two thirds of the way down the hall. He definitely recognized some faces and thought he might recognize a few others, but no one he knew very well. His old work friends who were supposed to be coming by weren't due in until later that night, so he'd have to make the opening night cocktail circuit on his own. That was fine.

He picked up his badge—he used his real name, not some silly hacker handle—and went into the middle ballroom, which had about fifty or sixty people in it. There was a mobile bar tucked into one corner, with a bartender serving a limited drink selection and charging somewhat inflated prices. Ollie got a Coke and started mingling. It was time to get some solid networking in, and he loosened his business card holder in his jeans pocket for some quick-draw action when he needed it. He'd brought along some work cards, but most of them were his personal ones—the one's with the private e-mail and the non-corporate phone numbers on them.

People were generally happy to talk. There were a couple individuals who were what passed for celebs in the hacker scene that always had a few people coming up to them and saying something or another. Ollie didn't bother with them. He'd read that the best way to get something from someone was to make them feel special. Those guys already felt special enough without him blowing smoke up their butts. He went over his opening conversational gambits again. He had them on his phone if he needed to check, but he'd gone over them enough on the plane that, along with the mnemonic device he'd come up with to help him, there was no way he'd forget. He'd put together the list from a couple dozen different books he'd read on ice breaking, networking, socializing, and dating. This would be his first time trying them in action, and he was eager to see how the conversational gambits would pay off.

He started by moving in front of another guy who was standing there alone, looking a little lost. He was beefy, with an unbuttoned, un-tucked gray and red shirt worn over a black t-shirt for what Ollie assumed was a band named Whole Wheat Bread. Ollie asked how the man was doing, introduced himself, commented on one of the more interesting looking people in the room, and asked the fellow what he did. And the guy was happy to talk about himself, especially once Ollie got him going. He was a sys admin at a university in California. He had lots of opinions that Ollie mostly shared. He never asked once about what Ollie did, and soon got distracted by his need for another drink and an obvious disinterest in talking anymore after he'd told his own life's story.

The next two people he talked to behaved in much the same way. Neither of them had jobs that were in fields Ollie had any interest in, so he didn't feel like he was missing any opportunities when he decided to experiment and see how long it would take for anyone to actually ask him about himself. None of them did. Funny. The books had assumed that most people would be at least polite enough to return one of Ollie's gambits with something like, "And what about you?" But no, not these guys. Was it that hackers were self-involved or socially inept? Could be both.

He'd just watched his fourth conversational gambit falter, this time because the guy's friends showed up and they left for dinner before Ollie could ask him much of anything. He turned around and surveyed the room, his gaze settling almost at once on a woman he hadn't noticed before. She was tall, dark skinned, and ridiculously pretty. She was wearing a form fitting skirt/suit combo that struck Ollie as very professional and yet still pretty hot. She looked like she might be Indian to him. Some kind of Asian possibly. She was talking to another woman Ollie recognized as a tech reporter from *Wired*, but the Indian woman caught Ollie staring at her and gave him a wink.

He waved back, deciding that winking back felt too unnatural. Two minutes later she was walking by him, offering to get him a drink. He asked for a Coke as she passed, and waited in anticipation of he didn't even know what until she returned with two Cokes a couple minutes later. "Hi, I'm Toni," she said, after handing him his drink.

"I'm, Oliver. It's a pleasure to meet you." They shook hands. She had soft hands of course, with a light but firm grip.

"So what do you do, Oliver?" She asked, leaning one arm against the high top table beside them and cocking her head slightly to the left.

"I'm a penetration tester," he said with some pride. He could see her eyes flash for a moment and her mouth curl up into a half-smile. Was she impressed?

"Really? How interesting. And who do you pen test for?"

"Oh, it's for a private firm. I'm not really supposed to say who, for security reasons. We do a lot of government contract work, you know, testing at government facilities and highly secure locations, that type of thing."

She moved a few inches closer to him, still smiling. "That must be interesting. And you live around here?"

"No, no, I'm from St. Louis." Ollie fought the urge to back away a few inches. The books said this was a good sign. "I flew in for the con. My company pays for it even though they're not really super happy that I go to these things because they're all afraid it will somehow make them look bad to the government auditors or something, which doesn't make any sense at all anymore if you think about it, because there are feds speaking at these things all the time now."

"I know what you mean. It's hard to get people to understand what a hacker con is really about. Are you giving a talk here this weekend?"

He shook his head. Should he move towards her now? He didn't. "Not this time, no. But I have before. I've presented at a couple of cons. I spoke at Def Con two years ago and was on a panel at Black Hat and did something at Notacon too. I like giving talks, but since I can't talk too much about my work…"

"It's probably hard to find things to talk about," she said, completing his thought for him. She was really paying attention to what he was saying! "That must be frustrating, right? I mean, part of what's so great about cons is that we're supposed to share what we know with each other."

"Exactly!" She'd hit the nail right on the button. That was one reason he wanted a new job—so he could release all his cool exploits and discoveries which, for now anyway, he wasn't allowed to do at all because of his employment contract. "I'd really like to participate a lot more. There's things I could tell these guys that would blow their minds, let me tell you. I'm serious. But I'm not supposed to and so I guess I won't."

"Not yet anyway," Toni said. "Someday maybe?" She sounded hopeful, like maybe she wanted that someday to be soon.

He smiled and felt a little warm. "Nothing lasts forever, it's true. Someday maybe."

"So tell me some gross generalizations then. Don't give me any details that will get you in trouble or anything, just some good stories."

"What do you mean?"

Toni patted his arm. "You've got to have some good stories. Every penetration tester I've ever met does. Change the names to protect the incompetent as necessary, but tell me a story."

Ollie thought for a moment. He had some great stories, most of which he'd never told to anyone but his coworkers because, well, aside from the fact that he didn't talk to anyone else very much, it was all supposed to be secret stuff. But Toni was right, he could easily leave out the sensitive facts and give her the gist of it. "All right, sure," he said. "I've got a great one that happened just a couple weeks ago in fact. Wait'll you hear this."

He launched into the redacted details of his latest red team assignment working on contract for the Department of Energy, explaining to her in more detail than maybe he should have if he were following the letter of his contract, but nothing that could identify the facility or the personnel or even the type of database he'd managed to corrupt with such efficient ease. Well, ease for him anyway. As he explained to Toni, databases were kind of his specialty. One of his specialties that is. She loved the first story and asked for a second and then a third, and by the time he was done with that one, digging deep into his past for something he thought might impress her, Toor Con's opening night cocktail hour had drawn to a close.

She laughed at his last joke, which he didn't think was that funny, but he wasn't going to complain if she thought it was. As they were ushered out of the small ballroom, she said. "Oliver, it was really nice to meet you. Thanks for sharing your tales of adventure with me."

"Not a problem," he said, butterflies in his stomach all of a sudden. She sounded like she was getting ready to say goodbye. He knew that he needed to do something now to stop that. Now. NOW! "Hey, I was wondering, I know it's kind of late, but would you like to get something to eat?"

Toni smiled at him, "Thanks, but I'm afraid I've got to go meet some people. But can I take a rain check? Maybe tomorrow night or the next? When are you flying out?"

"Monday morning."

"And you're staying…"

"At the Marriott."

"Great, great. Lucky you. Do you have a room that overlooks the stadium?"

"I do!" he said, and caught himself from inviting her to come see it.

"Let's exchange numbers, although I'm sure I'll see you at the con here bright and early tomorrow morning, right?"

"Definitely." They traded numbers, him giving her a card and her scribbling her number on the back of one of his cards. They said their goodbyes and he pretended to need to use the restroom so he wouldn't have to walk with or just behind her down the long hallway after they'd officially ended the conversation.

As he stood in the bathroom, washing his hands so at least he wasn't just standing there, he replayed his whole meeting with Toni in his mind, focusing mostly on any clues that she might really be interested in him. It took him a minute to realize she'd broken the trend and actually asked him about himself and another five minutes before it dawned on him that he hadn't asked her a thing about herself. Well, that would give him something to talk to her about next time they met! Ollie walked out of the restroom and down the long, empty hall towards the escalators, going over in his mind what questions he'd ask Toni first.

He saw Toni around the con throughout the next day quite a bit. She smiled and said hi every time their paths crossed, but she was always either on the move or already in conversation with someone and Ollie didn't want to intrude on her time. She went to a few talks that he was in, but usually she stood at the back, coming in late and ducking out early. For a few hours in the middle of the day, she was nowhere to be seen at all. He continued with his own experiment in conversation, meeting new people and seeing who would ask him about himself. The statistics started to even out a little, but not all the way. Two-thirds of the people he talked to still mostly just talked about themselves. Of those who did inquire about him, most were pretty nice, but none of them seemed like the kind of contacts that could help him find a new job. By Saturday night he was starting to wonder if maybe finding a lead on some new career opportunities here might not be as easy as he'd first assumed.

The Saturday night party was held outside the convention center, at a bar on the edge of San Diego's tourist-friendly Gaslamp Quarter. From experience, Ollie knew to get there early because the place was too small to hold even half the attendees and many of the people trying to get in would be left outside. Besides, he didn't feel like going out to dinner with anyone (Toni was nowhere to be found). He needed to cool down, and calm his head. He didn't want to go into the evening angry.

A trio of total yahoos had given a talk earlier in the day. Ollie didn't know them, but found their talk description, which promised "outstanding o-days" and "mind-ripping exploits" to be tacky and probably ridiculous. If the guys really did have anything worth talking about, he could watch the video of the talk later. Instead he'd gone to a much more interesting talk about the historical development of technology and hacker conventions. It was good, and he wanted to talk it over with some of his fellow attendees afterwards, but out in the vast hallway, everyone was discussing the talk he'd skipped. Apparently the speakers had revealed all sorts of alleged vulnerabilities in Firefox and Open Office and had been slamming open source and Linux programmers left and right for writing unsecure code.

As an open source contributor himself, Ollie naturally bristled, and once he'd heard some of the total bull hockey that those clowns had been spouting, his ire raised even more. Apparently at least half the things they were talking about weren't exploits but just crash bugs they were presenting as vulnerabilities, and Ollie wouldn't have been surprised if the rest turned out to be bogus too. He decided to approach one of the speakers, a hacker named Rstr, and politely confront him about one of the more egregious claims he'd made.

Ollie tried to be civil. He tried to give the guy the benefit of the doubt. But Rstr was having none of it, and as soon as Ollie started to ask his question, the jerk just laid into him. Called him a fat, know-nothing geek who couldn't hack is way into a Tiajuana stripper's panties. Ollie recoiled at first and started to turn away, but the guy kept at him. Ollie wasn't fat first of all. He was beefy. He was big. He also lifted weights in his garage and could run five miles. Rstr kept gabbing so Ollie stopped, turned back around and pulled the guy up by his shirt collar.

He had no intention of hitting the guy, or hurting him. But he did want to make him listen. He did want the little jerk to understand that he wasn't some fat ass sys admin who sat around all day eating donuts and deleting spam. He was a freaking penetration tester for the U.S. government and he knew his freaking shit!

"I have top secret clearance. I go to training sessions run by the NSA. I make a living breaking into military grade hardened systems. And you know what I know? I know a lame-ass crash bug when I see one. I know a lazy mind that can only tear down and never build up when I see one. And I know someone who couldn't hack his own dick out of his pants when I see one." Ollie let go of the gobsmacked weasel and headed out to get some fresh air. Behind him people were whispering. Someone cheered. Then a bunch of people laughed. No one said anything to him.

A half-hour wandering by the water and a shower and shave in his hotel room and Ollie felt like his heart was almost back to normal. He hated to lose control like that, to confront people like that. It was just lame and it did no more good than arguing with some troll online. He doubted he'd accomplished anything with that Rstr guy besides pissing him off and no doubt making him hate Ollie forever, and Ollie hated it when people hated him. He hoped the guy and his friends wouldn't show up here at the party tonight, but he didn't think they would. He was far from the only one who hadn't liked their talk.

Ollie sat at the bar and watched as the place filled up. It was, he supposed, kind of a dive bar, but it was trying to be cool with its red lights and avant-garde paintings on the walls. And he supposed it probably was pretty cool. He wasn't much of a bar aficionado. He decided to have a beer, which was unusual, as he didn't much like beer. But he'd discovered that people in bars were more comfortable talking to him when he had a drink, and he felt like this was his last big chance to do some real networking.

The place filled up pretty quick, with no sign or the three jerks (yay!) or Toni (boo!). He nodded and said hi to people he recognized, and caught up with a few old acquaintances he hadn't had a chance to chat with yet. He bought more than his share of drinks for them, which was fine since two hours later he was nursing his second beer. Everything was fine, if not thrilling, and the place was packed. Then they walked in, all four of them, together.

Toni had Rstr on her arm. She was taller than him, maybe even heavier too, and he looked like he was just lucky to be with her. She wore a cocktail dress he could only describe as slinky black, while he still had on the t-shirt and jeans he'd been wearing when he gave his talk. They got a lot of looks as they walked through the door, Rstr's two friends trailing along behind. Ollie finally gasped for air once he realized he'd been holding his breath. Well fine, if that's what she was interested in. Then fine. Just fine.

He tried to ignore them as best he could, but they were loud and obnoxious, and ended up forcing their way to the bar only about five feet from where Ollie had sat perched since he arrived. If Rstr had noticed him, he was pretending he hadn't. Ollie decided to do the same. Now that they were close, he could hear their conversation, and for the first time he smiled. Rstr was trying to impress Toni; that was clear enough. But Ollie recognized the patter he was laying out—they were the kinds of pick-up lines he'd read about in books on seducing women like *The Game*. Toni was having none of it, turning almost everything Rstr said into a joke, most of the time at the jerk's own expense. But he laughed along anyway, either clueless or, more likely, too fixated on getting in Toni's pants to let her know he was offended.

"These guys are all intimidated by me in here," Rstr said, leaning with his back against the bar, elbows propped on the edge in a way that might have been cool if he was five inches taller.

"Intimidated by sweet, little you?" Toni said, sipping a red drink from a martini glass. "That just doesn't seem possible."

"I told you, we kicked ass today. I'll buy you a DVD of it tomorrow."

"Won't they be free online soon? You should save your money, dear."

"I get 'em free because I was a speaker. You can have it."

"Isn't that sweet of you. I am sorry I missed it though. Everyone seems to be talking about you guys."

"That they are," he said. Ollie couldn't stand the smugness in his voice. He wanted to point out that they were saying bad things mostly, but didn't trust himself not to lose his cool.

"Why I heard you almost got in a fight, people were so upset," Toni said. More like purred.

Ollie stared directly at Rstr, who studiously looked every other direction. "Nah, that was nothing. Just a little disagreement that got out of hand. Besides," he said, leaning towards Toni and touching her bare shoulder, "I'm a lover, not a fighter."

Toni laughed, and not in a way that sounded particularly appreciative of Rstr's claim. "I can't believe that's true."

"Why not?"

"Because you spent all afternoon picking fights."

"I did not!" Rstr protested. "I was releasing exploits. That's one of the reasons we have these cons in the first place isn't it? I'm holding people responsible for their shoddy, leaky code."

"Oh, and here I thought you were just trying to get everyone riled up. Wait. Are you telling me you were serious this afternoon?"

"Yeah, of course."

Toni laughed and laughed. She laughed long enough that Rstr started to laugh along uncomfortably. "Oh dear, that's just too precious. I watched the video you know. I swore to my friends that it was performance art—a prank designed to poke fun at self-righteous blow hards who come to these things and try and show off." She laughed some more. "But you were serious? Ohh, that's just too cute."

Ollie chuckled silently on his bar stool and watched. Rstr had nothing to say, although the look on his face indicated that he was mentally trying out a number of different comebacks. Finally he gave up and just turned his back on Toni and started talking to his friends, pretending that he didn't even know who she was. Toni looked away, flashing her bright white teeth at Ollie and smiling at him. He nodded at her, still laughing to himself. She came over and stood next to him, quite close in fact, since the bar was so crowded.

"What an asshole," she said.

"He is that," Ollie agreed. Her perfume was a little strong for his tastes, but he decided he didn't mind. It was worth her standing so close. "You really put him in his place."

"You think so? Thanks. Really, I was just sick of listening to him babble on and on. Plus he needs a shower."

Ollie was glad he'd showered again before going out. He'd figured out that not showering during a hacker con wasn't really a sign of hard coreness or dedication, but rather lazy and probably impolite. "So," he said, mentally pulling up the file with the questions he'd prepared for this occasion. "Have you been enjoying the con so far?"

"I have!" Toni replied with some genuine seeming enthusiasm. "I've met just tons of interesting folks and maybe even learned a thing or two along the way. How 'bout you?" She patted his knee. "You having a good time?"

"Oh, yeah, of course. It's a really great con. But what do you do? Why're you here?"

"I'm a consultant," Toni said. "My firm provides integrated solutions and risk assessment analyses for mid-sized light industrial, service, and financial service companies in the U.S. and overseas."

"And you work in computer security?"

"Not even a little bit. OK, maybe a teeny, tiny little bit. No, I'm tasked with recruitment."

"So, you're here looking for recruits?" Ollie had a wild mixture of excitement and disappointment. On the one hand he felt let down that Toni wasn't actually a hacker. It was always nice to meet girl hackers, especially because they were so rare. He'd kept track over the years and the number of girls at hacker cons was pretty universally between 5 and 7%, a huge chunk of which were somebody's significant others who had come along for the fun of it. On the other hand, she was hiring! "What kind of people are you looking for?"

"Ohhh, we're pretty flexible. No, that's not true. We're not flexible at all—our standards are very high and we only recruit the best of the best. But we're not tied to traditional 'good resumes' or work-experience patterns. The most important thing is massive talent that's firmly guided by a disciplined brain and solid work ethic. Do you know anyone like that?" She winked at him as she finished.

"Hmmmmm. I think I know a couple people like that. But I only know one of them who's thinking about making a career change. What kind of work does it entail?"

"The jobs vary from client to client and week to week. We specialize in troubleshooting and high-quality, hi-result testing and evaluation. Find out what's wrong, fix it if we can, or farm it off to another company if the fix is too long term or resource intensive for us."

"Do you do much pen testing?" Please say yes, please, please say yes…

"Well, a lot of companies these days are moving away from pen testing, the argument being that they don't provide realistic or comprehensive pictures of the company's true security vulnerabilities. But we disagree. Pen tests are a key part of our consulting packages." She grinned at him. "Plus they're a lot of fun."

"I agree with all of that. Not the first part I mean. But about being useful and fun."

"I should hope so. You're a pen tester after all."

"So you're hiring full time?"

"We don't quite work like that. It's a little more complicated at first."

"How do you work?"

Toni looked around the packed bar. "It's loud and crowded in here, and who knows who's listening in." She held out her hand and he took it, suddenly surprised that she was pulling him to his feet. "Why don't you show me that view of the stadium from your room and we can talk it over."

He laughed out of some heady mixture of nervousness, surprise, and elation. Not sure what to say, he just let her lead him out of the bar by the hand. Even Rstr couldn't help but notice them.

Chapter 7

Chloe

You would think a two thousand dollar cell phone would be able to get a signal inside, but in this case it just didn't. And it was easier to walk outside than dig the satellite phone out. And it gave her an excuse to escape the hotel room. Not that what was going on in the hotel room wasn't exciting—it was, but it was also nerve-wracking. Everything seemed to be working like they'd hoped it would. This wasn't much of a surprise though, since they'd tested and re-tested everything they could and c1sman really was as good as Paul said he was. Equally important, most of the targets were just as clueless as Chloe had assured everyone they would be. Live long enough with the kind of knowledge that's common in hacker circles, and you start to get paranoid about every possible vector for attack. Live out in the real world of Washington politics and you just take the fact that your Blackberry works as a given. Instead you become obsessed with vectors for political attack. Chloe and Paul had figured out a way to not only exploit that blind spot in the target's defenses, but also (hopefully) use their own political paranoia against them.

This whole con was the biggest, scariest thing she'd ever been a part of. Not in terms of physical danger or even risk of going to jail. She thought they'd planned well enough and had their outs ready enough that neither of those disasters was very likely. But in terms of the impact they were going to have, the chaos they were going to stir up, and the number of moving parts that could suddenly stop moving the right way, it was definitely at the top of the list. Also in terms of how much, how very, very much, she really wanted to pull this thing off. Before Paul, even under Winston, the cons had always been about the money. Sure, 85% of the time they were taking that money from jerks or faceless corporations or both, and some of the time she'd gone after someone just because she didn't like them. But this time around they were going after genuinely bad people. Bad, nasty people who fucked with the lives of thousands. If they pulled this off, the lives of those thousands might actually be better, at least for a while. Certainly the fucking bastards would be out of the picture anyway. That was awesome. It also meant that she felt responsible to them, even though they had no idea who she was (and they better not ever have any idea).

Chloe had leaped out of the role of typical, law-abiding citizen when she was still in college after being tricked into helping pull off a particularly complicated con. She still had no firm idea who was responsible for her baptism into a life unbound by law, but there'd been no going back. The life she'd jumped clear of as fast as she could had been slow, frustrating, stultifying, and the world she wormed her way into moved fast, was always exciting, mostly lucrative, and yes, still awfully frustrating some of the time. But she'd figured out you never got away from frustrating entirely, you just had to find ways to take control of the frustration and blast through it.

Her crew of cohorts had operated in Northern California for years and included Bee and a few dozen others, all of whom were out of her life now. She didn't miss most of them, which was good, because she'd basically traded all of them for Paul one very tough night in San Jose. So instead of stealing Paul blind as originally intended, she'd ended up fighting by his side against certain former friends who had other ideas about what should happen to Paul and his money. Stupid love, makes you do stupid things, but she was definitely in love, so what're you gonna do? Apparently, in her case anyway, you make a run for Florida and set up shop in Key West because the love of your life has a pirate fetish and can't stand the cold.

It was no secret that she didn't like Key West very much—too small, too isolated, too touristy. But she, Bee, and Paul had scratched out a workman like con-artist living there as they built up their network of contacts, influences, and hidden cameras. They'd sucked a drag queen bad ass extraordinaire into their little circle, and that had both given them some local expertise and also made life a lot more fun. Still, she'd been clawing at the walls when her old mentor Winston arrived on the island and invited her and Paul to a meeting of other Crews from all over who were trying to plan some big score.

That's when she met Isaiah, the creepy-cool, intimidating as hell leader of a big New York Crew who was trying to organize a kind of shadow corporation as a tool to fight the man or whatever. Isaiah's politics were radically left and devilishly organized, while Chloe's were nascent and mostly gut level. But she and Paul recognized someone who had their shit together when they saw him, and she'd been interested in working with him. Then someone went and got murdered and the whole thing went to hell. Really, truly fucked up shit happened, but they came out alive and still together in the end. They'd opted out of joining Isaiah's shadow corporation, but times had changed, and while they weren't exactly members of the secret group, they had formed a sort of mutual aid pact. Now it was time to check in and make sure everyone was getting the aid they needed in this weekend's battle royale.

Outside the hotel, Chloe pulled out her special phone. OK, one of her special phones. The German-made cryptophone looked like a normal flip phone, if a relatively styleless, mundane one. And it worked like a normal phone too, plus a few key features. They'd gotten a half dozen of the things, and even with Sacco pulling some favors with some of the Cyrptophone founders he knew through the German Hacker scene, they still cost close to $2000 a piece. But they were operating in Washington DC and going up against some potentially very nasty and savvy foes. Plus they had to coordinate with their friends down in Florida. Secure communications were an absolute necessity. The cryptopohone uses custom software to encrypt calls with 4,096 bit Diffie-Hellman key exchange and SHA256 hash function AES 256 and Twofish. Chloe knew what half those words meant, and Bee explained the rest, assuring her that it was "pretty good." That level of encryption ensured that no known technology could intercept and decrypt the telephone calls, although as Sacco and Bee had both pointed out, you never knew what the NSA was really capable of. The trick was that the conversation had to be between two cryptophones for it to work, so setting up a secure communications setup was pricey. The hackers who'd started the company stayed true to their roots by making all the software open source, and Bee had claimed she could probably make her own versions of the phones given enough time, but they needed Bee's talents elsewhere and both Paul and Chloe agreed that when it came to secure communications, they preferred to trust in tested and hacker-approved hardware.

Chloe stood outside the hotel entrance, a hundred or so feet down the sidewalk from the porte-cochere and out of earshot from anyone, including Sacco, who was standing by the door and smoking. It was cold out, and she'd forgotten her gloves again, so she wanted to make the call to Florida as quickly as possible. She'd sent an encrypted text message ten minutes ago setting up the time for the call, and as soon as the clock tipped over to 3:24 she dialed the number from memory.

Isaiah picked up on the first ring. "Hello," he said, his voice patient and even as always.

"Hi," Chloe said, biting back an instinct to say something playful. Isaiah never seemed to appreciate the playful banter. He waited for her to continue.

"We've checked into our rooms and everything is great. It's a really nice hotel." That was code of course. Just because the call was encrypted didn't mean she or Isaiah were crazy enough to talk about what they were really doing in the open.

"I'm glad to hear it. Things are busy down south. The cousins are in town, so everyone's getting a little wild."

Uh-oh. That wasn't good. It meant Isaiah and his Crew were encountering some unexpected resistance or complications or what have you. "Sounds like quite a party. Do you have enough food for all of them."

"Oh, I think we'll be fine."

"Well, good. Listen, I was hoping to ask you a favor."

"Of course."

"Can you pick up my mail for me? I'm expecting a package and UPS will just leave it at the door."

"No problem, just let me know when it's supposed to arrive."

"Sometime this week. Everything's packed up and almost ready to go. I should have a tracking number for you soon." There was no package. She was letting Isaiah know that she was sending him some important data from the target's computer in the very near future.

"I'm happy to help."

"Just let me know when you've got time to pick it up."

"I will."

"Ok, bye."

"Goodbye."

That was the easiest, least argumentative, least condescending conversation she'd ever had with Isaiah. Any worries that his whole "tolerant wise uncle" shtick would be annoying during the actual operation began to evaporate. She knew intellectually that he and his Crew hadn't gotten so successful by being disorganized or inefficient, but the hours spent debating in the goddamned Brooklyn loft and on IRC and on the cryptophones had just about driven her up the wall. It was the exact opposite of what working with Winston had been like, but of course that was exactly why she was doing it. Still, there had been times when she was about ready to tear her hair out dealing with the man, and she had no one to blame but herself. It had, after all, been her idea.

Paul had been against it, which was weird, because he actually liked and tolerated Isaiah more than she did. But he didn't want to be saddled with a partner they had little or no control or even influence over. Once they'd rejected his offer to join his shadow corporation, Paul had wanted to cut all ties and branch out on their own, and in the beginning they'd done just that.

But their experiences with Isaiah had made it clear that they needed a top-notch hacker in their Crew, something they hadn't had since leaving California. Paul, Chloe and Bee had made the trip out to the country's biggest hacker convention—Def Con in Las Vegas. The scene had been overwhelming—more than 8000 hackers, a sea of black t-shirts and scraggly ponytails, occupying a Las Vegas hotel. It had been a crash course in hacker culture for all of them (even Chloe had never been to a hacker con), and they got the feel for the community and the kinds of people in it. Paul had also decided that Def Con was way too huge, chaotic, and uncontrollable for him to operate in comfortably, and so they'd decided to work within some smaller cons first and see if they found anyone there. They did.

But it turned out that even with their ranks swelled with new recruits, striking out on their own while simultaneously trying to strike against really bad targets was tough. Isaiah knew the targets, knew their weaknesses. She and Paul didn't. Not that the world lacked for bad guys, but they were having a hard time focusing their efforts, so hard in fact that they'd both let themselves concentrate almost exclusively on bringing in the new recruits without any real clear idea about who they were going after. Only when she'd brought Sacco in and he started pressing for some real action against legitimate targets had they been forced to confront their lack of direction. Chloe still had Isaiah's contact info in the back of her head, and they'd seen some signs that he and Marco's Crew were up to something in Florida. She tried to ask him what, if only so they wouldn't step on each other's toes. He ignored her, so she contacted Marco and asked him. He talked to her at least, but wouldn't tell her anything. Isaiah had sworn him to silence. Fine. She got even more interested and started digging on her own, flexing some of the new muscles that having c1sman and Sacco and the others on board had given her. Isaiah was careful and she still didn't know much about his power base, but she knew Marco worked mostly out of the cruise ship industry and so started tracing things from there. When she showed up at a Starbucks in Miami where Isaiah was sitting reading the paper, he'd been pissed. Or at least she assumed/hoped he'd been pissed. It was hard to tell with him.

So they'd gone outside and found a quiet, hot bench to have a talk. She hinted at her Crew's expanded capabilities and desire to do something meaningful. He'd re-affirmed that she and Paul were no longer invited to participate in his shadow corporation. She'd said that was fine, but, hey, no one can do everything on their own. Everybody could use some help sometimes. He'd agreed to think about it, and she walked away just happy that she'd been able to surprise him like that. When he contacted her five days later with a tip off and an offer, she'd been the surprised one, and she took the idea to Paul and the rest of the Crew.

OK, she probably should've taken it to just Paul first, but they were already having a planning meeting that night, and the topic of what to actually fucking finally do was the one and only thing on the agenda. Sacco had some ideas about going after big corporations or banks, but it all seemed either small fry hacker-pranks or incredibly unfeasible. The one area where he seemed both passionate, and to have some decent ideas, was something to do with labor or working conditions. Isaiah had told Paul that his chosen big bad victim for the shadow corporation's machinations was involved in modern slavery in some way, and both Paul and Chloe had thought that doing something in that arena seemed like a great idea, if only they could figure out how exactly.

Paul had come up with a simple test scam that they'd tried out just as a way to sort of get all the new guys working well together. They'd hacked into the payroll records of a number of different businesses in Miami, based solely on c1sman's analyses of the targets who had the most security holes he could find (mostly in the form of unpatched servers or firewalls). They'd pulled the payroll records, including salaries, benefits, and reimbursed expenses and then e-mailed the data to everyone working at the companies and everyone on the contact lists of every e-mail account in the company. Paul had written an accompanying cover letter explaining that they should use the information to make sure they were being fairly compensated for their labor compared to their fellow employees. Watching the ensuing e-mails flurry, they'd been successful in stirring up some serious shitstorms in at least a couple of the targets, plus encouraging all of them to improve their network security. But that was small-fry stuff, just a proof of concept for them. Coming off that, everyone, even c1sman, wanted to do something bigger and better.

So she'd pitched Isaiah's idea to the group. Paul had been miffed at being blindsided by the idea and was wary. The others had been fine with it. Sacco was really excited about it and wanted to know who the heck this Isaiah person was. Chloe hadn't been ready to tell him that much, but his enthusiasm was contagious and soon Paul had bought into the plan as well. Especially once she told everyone who the target really was. And now here they were, deep into the actual action after months and months of planning. Planning that so far was paying off.

The other phone in her pocket buzzed and she pulled it out while putting the cryptophone she'd used with Isaiah away. They had their own cryptophones for internal communications within the Crew—no sense letting Isaiah have too much information about their infrastructure. This one was a smart phone/pda model with a full qwerty keyboard. She saw a message from Paul asking her to find c1sman and bring him upstairs. Apparently there was some sort of problem. She was almost grateful that something was finally going wrong. As she walked back inside, Sacco fell into step beside her, tossing his half-finished cigarette into the bushes.

"How's everything?" he asked.

"Good."

"I wish I was down there." His breath smelled like cigarettes as he leaned in close to speak just above a whisper.

"I thought you wanted to be here."

"I do want to be here. I wish I could be both places at once. Did he say how those guys I intro'd him to are working out?"

"He did not." Sacco had provided Isaiah with some links to labor organizers in South Florida. Or rather, he provided them to Chloe who passed them on to Isaiah. "We were just checking in, seeing how things are going."

"And things are going good down there?"

She really didn't want to get into it with Sacco on this subject. While Isaiah had warned of complications, he apparently felt he had everything well in hand. She didn't want Sacco obsessing over anything else besides what she needed him obsessing about here in DC. "He says he's got everything under control. As soon as Mr. Data pulls it together and c1sman makes sure our tracks are covered, we'll send him the package."

"It's going to be awesome. I wish I could see their faces."

"It will be awesome, but you hardly ever get to see their faces at the moment it dawns on them."

"We should've set up a camera," Sacco said, probably only half joking.

"We should still be reading their e-mail and text messages. That'll have to do." She thought she sounded like an indulgent mother, which was sort of how she felt.

"I can't wait."

"There's much to do between now and then. How're your pet protesters doing?"

"They'd hate to be called pets," Sacco said with a frown as they wove through the lobby, Chloe by instinct steering them clear of any people who might overhear them.

"That's why I didn't say it to them. How're they doing?"

"They're good. They're raising a fucking ruckus, that's for sure. Nothing the mainstream media will notice of course, but we're getting plenty of video and the website's up and the press releases are all out to the blogs. When it hits, the accelerant will be there to light up big."

Chloe nodded, smiling on the inside. She'd found it best not to encourage Sacco too openly—it tended to go to his head. Always leave him wanting just a little more validation. "I need to go round up Bee and c1sman. Can you head back upstairs and see if Paul and Sandee need anything?"

They parted ways, Sacco heading for the fire stairs and Chloe heading for the escalators up to the second floor where Shmoocon was being held. She stopped herself from adjusting her wig and unbuttoned her coat to reveal a two year old over sized Shmoocon shirt she'd borrowed from c1sman that she had on over her sweater. She pulled the badge from her inside coat pocket and hung it around her neck.

The nice thing about hacker con badges was that they were incredibly difficult to counterfeit and thus the con organizers never really cared who was wearing it, as long as they were wearing one. The Crew had bought three memberships, plus they had the one c1sman got for being on staff. The badges changed every year, and this time they were hard, clear tinted plastic rectangles modeled after old computer punch cards, with holes in them and the Shmoocon name and logo etched into the surface. Since no one outside the staff knew what they'd look like before the day of the con, creating one on your own, while not impossible, was pretty impractical, and Chloe was willing to bet that if someone did make a solid forgery, the organizers would be impressed enough not to care. But they'd paid for theirs, and now Chloe was wearing one.

She planned to spend as little time on the con floor as possible, and she'd dressed down as much as she could. Mousy brown, scraggly wig with some gray highlights in it and dumpy clothes that hid her figure and made her look twenty pounds heavier. No makeup at all (she cleaned it off after meeting with Danny). She'd thought about taking a page out of Sandee's book and cross-dressing, but it was more trouble than it was worth. As it was she got a few looks, but not many, and she didn't think people would remember her passing through.

The volunteer watching the door barely glanced at her badge as she walked into the Shmoocon area, head down, eyes on a crumpled speakers schedule she'd pulled out. Since it was in the middle of one of the sessions, there were only a couple dozen people filtering through the main hallway. To her right were the doors leading into the speaker rooms, each holding a few hundred people plus a podium, stage, and screen for the speakers to project their Power Point presentations onto. To her left were the registration area and the NOC, both of them off limits to people with her badge. Tables for vendors lined the hall, most of them hawking security services or recruiting potential employees or promoting some new software suite. There was one lonely guy with a shaved head hawking some novels he'd written that she assumed had something to do with hackers. She ignored them all and followed the hall to the end and turned right, which took her through a short hallway that circumvented the speakers' rooms and led to the area with the fun stuff. It was another hall, parallel to the one she'd come in, with more vendors and doors that led into the speakers areas from the other side of the rooms. But there were other doors leading into smaller rooms, including the hacker arcade, the hardware hacking labs, and her destination: Lockpick Village.

Chloe had taught herself to pick locks from a book when she was in her early twenties. It had taken a lot of trial and error and practice to figure out the important little details that the book was leaving out and to get a feel for it. Now she was pretty good, and could spring handcuffs or a standard door or padlock in a lot less than a minute. That was nothing compared to how fast some of the people she'd seen at hacker cons were. In the hacker scene, lockpicking had become a competitive sport. She'd once watched one guy pick 12 master locks in under two minutes. It was an odd little adjunct to hacker culture—nothing to do with computers really, and nothing very technical about it, but from the point of view that it had to do with security and was also totally cool, she understood the appeal.

Lockpick Village was just a meeting room with some tables with a wide variety of locks on them. There were a number of partial doors set up on stands on the tables where you could practice picking deadbolts and doorknob locks from a variety of manufacturers. There were also padlocks, combination locks, bicycle locks, and even handcuffs on display. Behind the tables sat or stood helpful volunteers from TOOOL, The Open Organization Of Lockpickers, who were showing people the basics and would be judging a lockpicking contest later in the weekend. Standing in front of one of the tables were Bee, c1sman, and some hacker kid she didn't recognize.

Chloe would have been wary about talking to c1sman in public even with no one else nearby, but there was no way she was going to even nod in his direction while this kid was around. Bee had turned and looked right through her when Chloe entered the room, while the two men by her side were concentrating on learning how to pick the doorknob locks mounted in front of them. They both seemed to be struggling, and from the awkward way they held their picks, Chloe guessed neither guy had much experience with them. Chloe pretended to idly browse some of the other displays while watching the body language of the trio, and soon figured out what was going on. The two boys were doing their best to impress Bee. The kid was ten years younger and thirty pounds lighter than c1sman, and pretty clearly a little douche bag. But a cute douche bag. C1sman on the other hand was looking pretty flustered and the dew of perspiration had broken out on his forehead.

The douche-bag picked his lock first and made some joke about being good at putting things in holes that Bee actually laughed at. She was clearly enjoying the attention, and looked awfully cute with her hair in pigtails held in place with ethernet cable and a flattering red skirt and black tights combo that accented and obscured her figure in all the right ways. It wasn't subtle, but it didn't need to be. Bee's job was to both watch over c1sman and establish herself under the hacker name EtherOr as a member of the hacker community. The plan was for her to be the Crew's face with the hacker scene, someone who could maybe arrange one-time contract jobs and generally keep them apprised of new developments in the community. A cute little Asian chick in this crowd could open a lot of doors if she applied herself.

Right now though, she was letting c1sman get freaked out by the competition for her affection, and that was bad, because they needed him upstairs and concentrating. The fact that for whatever reason he hadn't responded to Paul's text meant he already wasn't focusing on the task at hand. Chloe sidled up next to the trio without saying anything to any of them. She rudely snaked her hand between the douche-bag and Bee and took a flyer for TOOOL from the table. "Can I take an extra one of these for my friend Caroline Green back home?" She asked the man behind the table. He nodded. She hoped c1sman wasn't showing too much surprise on his face at her sudden appearance.

She turned and left with the papers. The Caroline code was something Paul had come up with from his youth when he'd had a summer job at K-Mart. It was a way the store made emergency calls over the PA system without actually alarming the customers. You always said something about Caroline, but used a different color for the last name depending on the message. In this case, Green meant some sort of important but not emergency level problem. Brown would have meant a serious problem, and Red would have been an all out emergency. The reference to home referred to the hotel room they were using as home base. Chloe knew Bee had gotten the message,

Chloe made an unhurried stroll back through the convention and towards the exits. She lingered at one of the vendor tables and made sure that Bee and c1sman were following orders. She saw the whole trio come around the corner and cursed under her breath, but Bee knew what she was doing and said something to the douche-bag that made him stop tagging along and left him with a disappointed look on his face. Chloe suppressed a smile as she watched him curse to himself behind Bee and c1sman's backs as they walked away from him. She let them pass her, listened for a couple more minutes to the woman behind the table's sales pitch for security software, and then followed them out. They took the elevators, she took the stairs, and they met back up at the room to find out what the trouble was.

Chapter 8

clsman • *before*

If he hadn't met that writer Alan Denkins, the con would've been a complete disaster. Back home in Athens, Georgia, he was going through his usual post-convention decompression, which meant downloading torrents of all the new TV he'd missed over the weekend and eating a cake. But this time he felt different. This time he didn't have a job to go to on Monday morning and didn't have much in the way of pleasant memories to rehash in his mind as he drifted off to sleep. This time he was mourning the death of SecZone. Things had gone from bad to worse, as the hallway confrontations got more heated and both convention's networks got taken down. It never came to blows of course, but it was embarrassing and awkward and mortifying and a bunch of other words he couldn't summon up at the moment. It had just sucked. He'd wanted to walk away and probably would have except half the gear in the network room belonged to him and he wasn't going to be a jerk about it. So he'd waited and even hid in his room for a while until Sunday morning came and he could start pulling his stuff and going home.

Alan had been the one good thing. He was cool, and nice, and really interested in hacking. Not interested in hacker politics or rivalries or bullshit. He wanted to learn about hacking for the book he was writing, and Chris had been happy to tell him all about it. And he wasn't just listening to be polite. He was actually listening and asking questions and seemed to be absorbing what was being said. And he asked good questions too. Stuff that made you think. They'd stayed up late that night and Alan asked him all kinds of questions about how you'd actually hack into a company's network and why you'd do it and what you could do once you got in. Chris had even told him some stuff— all off the record of course—about some of his own exploits when he was younger. And later he might have mentioned something about some of his more recent exploits too, although he'd attributed those achievements to "friends" and "this guy" he knew. But there was a wink and a nod and he was pretty sure Alan knew what was what and who was who.

So when that first e-mail arrived from Alan on Monday morning, Chris was happy to see it. The writer had said he might have some more questions, and Chris was looking forward to the distraction of answering them, but when he opened the e-mail he was surprised to see just one line: "I'm in Athens. Can I stop by?" That was a surprise. It was maybe even kind of weird. He was a little wary in his response, but the two chatted briefly on IRC and Alan explained he was interviewing someone at University of Georgia anyway and wondered if he could come by in the evening and ask some follow-up questions. Chris agreed, and then spent the rest of the afternoon making his apartment something approaching presentable to the outside world.

Three big trash bags full of cans and frozen dinner trays later, he was still wishing he'd actually been able to fix his vacuum cleaner when he'd taken it apart six months ago. Ah well. If Alan had survived a hacker convention, he could probably stand a hacker's apartment for a few hours. He showed up promptly at 7 PM, as promised, and nothing in his demeanor showed any signs of recoiling at Chris's stained carpet or undecorated walls. He was much more interested in seeing the home network and office he had set up. Chris ran an open wireless hotspot as a favor to his neighbors, but that was entirely walled off from everything he did online. He'd never taken advantage of his ownership of the hotspot to snoop or sniff his neighbor's internet habits, but it was nice to know he could if he needed to for some reason. Owning all of their machines would be trivial. His main set up took up all of the second bedroom, with three computers on folding tables and a hardware store's worth of spare parts, tools, and electronic detritus covering all the free space. He had to pull in one of the seldom-used kitchen table chairs so Alan would have someplace to sit.

"So how're you feeling post con?" Alan asked as he sat, sipping on a Coke Chris had given him.

"Pretty crappy to tell you the truth. It wasn't good. My last one."

"Your last hacker con period?"

"No, just SecZone. I think I'm done with that. I'll still go to others, but I'm tired of working on staff. It just takes too much out of me. I'm gonna stick with being just an attendee. Or maybe a speaker sometime." He'd never given a talk at a con and generally the thought of being up behind the podium filled his stomach with angry squirrels, but it would be a way to stay involved and not be just another attendee.

"You're a good teacher," Alan said, seeming to mean it. "I think you could probably give some killer talks."

"We'll see if I come up with anything worth talking about. I have some free time, so I'm sure I'll come up with some sort of interesting exploit or vulnerability that'd make for a good talk."

"Working on anything now?"

"Not really, but like I said, I've got some time. I'll play around a little." Chris stopped himself from diverging off-track into musings about some of the potential avenues he might explore and focused on Alan. "But you drove all this way and you've got questions. What can I do for you?"

"Well, I don't have any specific questions right now. What I had in mind was some sort of demonstration. I was wondering if I could watch over your shoulder while you did some hacking. I've heard your explanations and I think I understand the basic theory and practice of it all, but I'm still fuzzy on the details of what it really looks like. I was hoping that maybe you could give me a live demo and really help me understand."

"Sure, I could do that I think." Chris said, although he was unsure if he really could. It seemed like it would be really boring for Alan. Plus there was another question. "But what would I hack into?"

"Whatever you want I suppose, although I don't want you to get in any trouble."

"Anything you do with a computer these days that's worth doing will get you into trouble with somebody. But there's trouble and then there's real trouble."

"We don't want any real trouble."

"Definitely not. But I'm not sure what I can show you without risking real trouble. I mean, there's some honey pot sites I know about we could mess around with. Some hacker sites that invite attacks to test security protocols, but that's not really what you're looking for."

Alan sat and thought for a minute. "What about the paper I do some freelancing for? If we had their permission."

"Sure, that would be fine. If we had their permission everything would be cool."

"Let me make a couple calls."

Alan stepped outside to make the calls. Chris watched him through a slit in the blinds as he paced around the parking lot, talking on his cell phone. Ten minutes later he had his permission and they were setting up in his office and snooping around the website for the South Florida-based *Weekly Voice*.

They started really digging in around 9 PM. Because he was explaining everything to Alan, it was much, much slower than Chris was used to, but also a hell of a lot more fun. Alan asked just the right number of questions, and never the same thing twice, so it was fun teaching and explaining. The newspaper's network was all standard, off the shelf stuff, set up competently enough but with nothing beyond his abilities to overcome. Some deep Google searching turned up a useful question tagged with the paper's sys admin's e-mail address on a help forum that let Chris know enough details about their firewall setup that he could start probing the network in the right ways. He took things slow and careful and so it took until just after one in the morning before they were in the paper's network and had escalated their privileges all the way to admin level.

"So we could do whatever we wanted on their network now?" Alan asked.

"Sure. Read and send e-mails, read and copy and change files. Let's see… looks like this is the layout for next week's paper. We could change a headline if we wanted."

"Let's not do that. I have permission to poke around, not to mess around," Alan said. He didn't seem tired at all. He was just utterly fascinated by the whole process. "If you want, I can e-mail the sys admin about the security holes we found so he can plug them."

"Why don't you just send that to me and then I can go over them with him in person. I think I want to give him a chance to cover his ass a little before I tell my editors how easy this was."

"OK, but don't let them be too hard on him. He's doing an OK job, just not nearly good enough to stop someone like me. But the truth is, if he was good enough to stop someone like me, I hate to say it, but he wouldn't be running IT for a weekly newspaper."

Alan laughed. "You're probably right." He stretched, and yawned. "Well, thanks c1sman. This has been awesome of you. I really appreciate it, especially staying up so late and all."

"Oh, I'd have been up late and in front of these screens whether you were here or not, so it's no big deal. I had fun showing off."

"You should be proud of those skills, man. It's scary stuff. This is all off the record of course, as I told you."

Chris had actually forgotten about that. He'd sort of assumed since they had permission, he and his exploits would be in the article or book that Alan was writing. Oh well, secrecy was probably better in this case anyway. No need to attract unwanted attention. He thanked Alan again for being such a nice guy at the con and said they should stay in touch and that he should feel free to contact him anytime he had any hacker questions. Alan promised he'd do just that, and then disappeared into the night.

He got some e-mails from Alan over the next few weeks, usually simple but very specific questions about some aspect of hacking or about what they'd done that night. Before he answered any of them he had Alan set up a PGP encrypted e-mail account so they could converse in privacy, and he was pleased that the writer seemed to have no problems doing that on his own. The e-mails became bright points in otherwise dull days as he looked for some sort of work that he might find interesting. He had plenty to keep him busy, but it was all boring and none of it paid very well and he needed money. His ex-wife was being sort of cool about the whole child support thing and not filing any formal complaints yet, but because of that he found it kind of hard to press her when she did things like switch the week that Shawn was supposed to come visit him from Arizona and then cancel the trip entirely because apparently his son would rather go on a trip with his new friends to than come hang out in his dad's dingy little apartment. He couldn't really blame him, and started looking into flights out to Arizona and places to stay when he got there. His ex's folks had never much cared for him, so there was no way he was staying there.

Then, three and a half weeks after he'd been in Athens, Alan pinged him on IRC and they started a private, encrypted chat. He wanted to know if Chris was free to fly down to Florida for a weekend and do some contract work. Some hacking. All expenses paid. Chris wasn't even sure what to think of the request at first, and asked what kind of work it was. Alan was vague, saying it was similar to what he'd done with the newspaper thing and that he could make $5000 for the weekend's work, but he had to do it on site. He couldn't think of any reasons that made sense to say no, and the thought of that money outweighed his natural laziness and hatred of flying. He said yes.

Three days later he was stepping off the plane in Miami and an hour later he and Alan were ensconced in an almost empty one bedroom apartment in Miami Beach. It had a bare mattress with fresh sheets and two pillows in the bedroom and a desk and two chairs in the living room that held a cable modem and some ethernet cable and not much else. Alan, who'd picked him up from the airport and kept a tour-guide style constant patter about Miami going for the whole drive out to the apartment, told him this would be his office for the weekend.

"What is this place?"

"Just a friend's apartment. She moved to Ft. Lauderdale and she's letting me use it until she can rent it out. Nice and quiet, plenty of bandwidth and air conditioning. You've got everything you need on your laptop, right?"

Actually he'd brought two laptops and three portable hard drives, but he did have everything he needed, or at least he assumed he did. "What is it I'm doing exactly?"

"I'll give you all the details once you get unpacked and set up and are comfortable. There's someone I want you to meet and then we'll go over everything. And if you aren't cool with it, that's fine. We'll pay you and you can spend the weekend on the beach and then head back to Georgia."

It didn't take long to settle in, so while he waited for Alan to return with his friend, he hooked up a router he'd brought along and plugged in his two computers. There were also three wireless networks within the building, two of them open, so he played around with those for a while and started sniffing at the closed one in case he wanted to access it for some reason down the line. Half an hour later, Alan returned with two women.

The taller woman, Alan introduced her as Sarah, had a killer figure and was, quite frankly, kinda intimidating. She was a harsh kind of beautiful, but her eyes were red and she looked on the verge of tears and her eye makeup had smudged. Even in such a bedraggled state she was obviously way out of Chris's league, and so he wrote her off as any kind of potential love/sex interest and filed her under "Unattainable and therefore A-Sexual." The other woman though, short, a little pudgy maybe (but who was he to talk), Asian with dyed blond streaks in her shoulder length black hair was another story. She had a shirt on that had a pair of red slippers and the phrase "There's no place like 10.0.0.0." He probably loved her at that moment, and would've laughed if the other woman weren't crying. Alan introduced her as Kim.

He had to concentrate on listening to Sarah's story, especially because Kim was occupying herself setting up all kinds of interesting hardware on the table next to his laptops, but it was a compelling story. Sarah was an old friend of Alan's (Chris guessed more than just a friend), and she'd recently been forced out of her job. Not just fired or laid off, but fired and accused of some truly nasty stuff, like stealing corporate funds and selling company data to competitors. She hadn't done anything of the sort—wouldn't even know how to do those things, but they were setting her up as some kind of scapegoat for their own mismanagement or misdeeds or whatever. They were "being nice" and saying they weren't going to press charges if she just admitted to doing the things she didn't do. It was all total bullshit. And her friend Alan had said that maybe c1sman could help her.

"I thought of you, c1sman. I thought maybe you could help us get something on these guys, some proof that Sarah is innocent or that they're guilty or whatever. Both, maybe. Something we can fight back against their blackmail bullshit with."

"So you want to hack your old company?" he asked. He could see the appeal. When he'd been laid off, he'd hacked his old company, although just to confirm that the financial situation really was as bad as they'd claimed it was. It was true, which meant he wasn't surprised when it went out of business four weeks later.

"Is that possible?" Sarah asked. "Could you do something like that? Maybe find an e-mail where they talk about setting me up or something?"

"Sarah and Kim and I scraped together some of our savings to fly you down here," Alan said. "It's that important to us."

Chris looked over at Kim, whose back was to him. She was setting up some sort of cell phone based device that looked quite intriguing. Of course he would help them. He needed the money sure, but now he felt kind of bad about taking their savings. But since he had no savings of his own and it definitely seemed like a good cause, of course he'd help. "We can do that." Kim turned around and smiled at him, just as Sarah started thanking him profusely. "We can do that, no problem at all."

The company, which turned out to be some sort of venture capital firm that controlled what seemed like dozens but turned out to be hundreds of other corporations, had pretty good security, and it had taken more than just the weekend. He waived any additional fee, though. He was deep in the hunt now, and working side by side with Kim, who soon had him start calling her Bee after the fifth or sixth time she failed to respond to Kim. It was an old childhood nickname, she said. Bee knew the electronics and mechanics side of things back to front, and was good with the basics on network security. They worked mostly together, with

Sarah and Alan coming and going at odd hours, bringing food and, one time, sheaves of papers and disks they'd liberated from the garbage bins at Sarah's old company.

Since they absolutely did not have permission this time, Alan had urged Chris to be extra careful and not get caught. Like he needed to tell him that, but Chris appreciated the concern. They took their time, found their hole, and slipped in nice and easy. Well, it seemed nice and easy at first. But then Chris had trouble escalating his network privileges beyond a basic user level. The internal security was tighter than he'd expected and he couldn't get into the executive's files or get root access. Then he and Bee came up with a plan. He mused about how much easier it would be if they just had a machine they controlled on the inside. A day later and Bee had built the thing—a computer in the shell of a power strip that would plug into a printer access point Chris had identified. All they needed to do was get it inside.

Sarah said she had a friend who'd do it for her. She and Alan disappeared late that night. Bee got a text message that told them he should be able to access the little trojan power strip. They could and he did, and by the end of business the next day he had root access and pulled down all the files Sarah needed to prove her case, and a lot more besides. He left it to the others to sort through the data and find the useful stuff. He'd done his part.

He offered to take Bee out to dinner and celebrate. Well, he actually offered to take them all out, but Sarah and Alan begged off, intent on digesting their ill-gotten data. Bee came along, taking him to a fancy crab place on South Beach. It had been a wonderful evening and if he'd thought about it he would've asked her to walk on the beach and then who knows what would have happened. OK, to be fair, he had thought about it, it was just that the words never quite made their way past his lips. Still, it was a great evening. They laughed and drank wine and got messy eating butter-soaked crab. When they got back to the apartment, Alan and Sarah were still at it, but they left with Bee an hour later, everyone thanking Chris up and down.

The next morning he found an envelope with $10,000 in cash sitting on his laptop and the print-out for a boarding pass on a Delta flight that afternoon to Atlanta. There was an e-mail from Alan, thanking him again for all his help, and one from Bee thanking him for a wonderful night out. He thought about staying, but didn't think he should stay in this stranger's apartment anymore. Besides, he had to deposit the money and pay some bills. Send Jessica some money for Shawn. Get back to real life.

*
**

In the weeks after he got home, Chris watched for news on the investment company he'd hacked, but never saw anything. Nor anything
about Sarah for that matter. Alan would drop him a note occasionally,
and he and Bee started up a nice e-mail thread that stayed friendly and
fun, although she either ignored or deflected his few, tentative forays
into flirting. Still, it was nice to have new friends, and apparently everything had gone well for Sarah. She was very happy with the results.
Good. He'd done his good deed for the year.

When Alan showed up outside his house one night, Chris was startled, but secretly thrilled too. "Alan, what the heck, man! Great to see
you."

"Good to see you too, c1sman. Can I come in?"

They sat down at the kitchen table, beers in hand, a few pleasantries exchanged. "I have another job offer for you, c1sman, if you're
interested."

"I am, sure." He was too. He'd sent most of the 10k to Jessica, and
paid off credit cards with the rest. And bought some RAM and two
new hard drives.

"Good, good. I'm glad to hear it. You were amazing on the Miami
thing, really. But there are some things you need to know."

That didn't sound good. "What kind of things?"

"Well, first of all, my name's not Alan. It's Paul."

Chris listened to the whole spiel, which even then turned out to
only be about one fifth of the whole story. He'd been secretly courted
by Paul and Chloe and Bee (she really was Bee!) from the beginning,
and he'd passed every test. They not only wanted him on board, they
needed him. He could work mostly from home. They could provide
documentation to make the money look legit. He'd never have to do
anything he wasn't comfortable with. No, it wasn't even a little legal,
but they weren't planning on getting caught. Never had been caught
before either. He wanted time to think about it first, and Paul understood that, but he had a job for him that needed attending to right
away—tracing the origin point of some e-mails Paul had somehow
intercepted. Could he help them?

"Of course I can," he heard himself say. "Of course I'll help."

Chapter 9

Paul

"Where's your phone?" Paul asked as soon as c1sman and Bee came through the door, trying to keep the anger out of his voice.

"In my bag?" c1sman replied, slipping the backpack off his shoulder. He dug around inside and pulled it out. "I had it on vibrate and I guess I couldn't feel it."

"I need you to have that where you can feel it," said Paul. C1sman just nodded. "But that's OK. You're here now. I need you to look at something for me. We're having what seems like a weird delay between when the e-mails are time stamped as being received and when we actually see them. And then another big delay when we send mail out. I'm worried stuff might be slipping through without us seeing it."

"No, I know what the problem is. Don't worry, I can fix it, but nothing's slipping through." C1sman sat down on the couch where Paul had been perched and started working at once.

Paul didn't need to give c1sman any other instructions. The hacker was prone to worry and distraction and second guessing when he didn't have something else to occupy his mind, but give him a well-defined goal and he was off to the races. Plus the Adderall seemed to be helping a lot too. Paul went over to Bee and talked to her in a low whisper. "And what about your phone?"

"It's not getting any signal in this hotel. I'm going to switch to one of the other ones. A stupid one. I'll forward everything to that." Bee sat down at the desk next to Sandee and started messing with her phone and another one she took from the box on the table.

Chloe knocked and then let herself in a few minutes later. Paul assumed that, as usual, she'd moved through the halls and waited until no one else was around before she stepped inside their suite. She pulled off the wig as she shut the door behind her, sighing in relief. He stepped up next to her and ran his hand through her short, pink hair and then down to the back of her neck. He rubbed there for a while and the two of them watched the others at work. Sandee was monitoring e-mails now, while Sacco looked over his shoulder. Bee and c1sman were hard at work on their projects. They had, he hoped, a moment to catch their breaths and relax.

"Care to follow me into the bedroom?" Chloe asked.

"Absolutely," he replied.

"Don't go too crazy in their kiddies," Sandee called from across the room as they started to close the door behind them. "One quickie and then back to work, OK?"

"Yes, mom," Chloe said, and closed the door.

The two of them collapsed onto the bed together and stretched out on their backs.

"How's Isaiah?" Paul asked.

"He seems good. Who can tell. Sounds like he ran into some kind of minor hiccup, but he's handling it. Any word from Mr. Data?"

"We're all good to go there too. He's sorted through everything on the accounts front and pulled it all together with the database Sacco sent him."

"So we're about ready to go?"

"As soon as c1sman sorts out that weird delay issue and assures me there's no problem, then yeah, I'd say so. Isaiah should be able to start printing tonight and then do envelope stuffing and distribution over the next twenty-four hours."

"And Monday morning the shit hits the fan," Chloe said. She sounded tired but also very pleased with herself, with all of them. "This is really big."

"They won't know what hit 'em," Paul said. They left unspoken all the worries about hitting a target this big, with this many connections. No, the bastard would have no idea what hit him, but after he'd been hit, he'd do everything he could to find out. And it was the kind of thing that, if they didn't play it just right, would attract a lot of law enforcement attention, something they'd been good about avoiding up until now. They'd thought all about that of course, planned and fall back planned, and emergency contingency planned for months. But there was always... always something that if you thought about it too much, you'd drive yourself nuts. He moved on to other topics. "How's Sacco holding up?"

"He's good. Way into it all, like you'd expect. Wants to be doing everything, everywhere, all at once, also like you'd expect. But he's good. Has his shit together. It'll be interesting to see his anarchists in action."

"Did you end up meeting any of them?"

"I changed my mind at the last minute. I listened in on Sacco's phone call with them last night and I can just tell that some of those guys are gonna get arrested, no doubt about it. They're itching for it. I decided it was best that they never had any idea at all that Sacco had a woman friend who knew something about what they were doing."

"Good," said Paul. They'd fought about that one, and Chloe had decided to meet them in heavy disguise. She had good reasons—review the troops, make sure they knew the rules of engagement, sniff out any weak links or possible undercovers in their midst. But Paul always liked to err on the side of caution with people from outside the Crew, and these black bloc cats were way, way outside.

"Yeah, yeah, you were right, I was wrong. But I wasn't wrong about c1sman was I? Did he forget his phone somewhere or just ignore it?"

"Claims he couldn't feel the vibration in his bag."

"Which is no doubt why he put it in his bag in the first place. He's freaking out a little."

"Just a little. Bee keeps him focused. The work keeps him even more focused."

"Bee needs to keep her focus on him then, because there are some cutie little hacker snots down there with their eyes on her."

"Oh yeah? Good for her." Bee had come out of her shell quite a bit since they'd dived into this uber-complex caper of theirs. Part of that was time and distance from past events, part of it was her newfound role as third in command and mentor/leader to c1sman, Sacco, and Mr. Data. Some cute boys lusting after her would only boost her confidence even more.

"It's good for her, maybe, but it's bad for c1sman. He's probably the jealous type."

"You'll…"

"I'll have a talk with her. Although a little competition is probably just what c1sman needs. I don't want him taking Bee for granted."

"As far as I know, they haven't even kissed, I doubt he's taking anything for granted."

"Well then, I don't want him thinking he's got 'dibs' or some bullshit like that. Like I said, it'll keep him on his toes, and give him something to focus on, as long as he doesn't get discouraged or give up on her."

"Sounds like a plan to me," said Paul, closing his eyes. He wondered if they could squeeze in a quickie. Then he wondered if he could squeeze in a fifteen minute nap. Then c1sman knocked on the door and he and Bee and Sandee all came piling in. The delay was fixed, Bee's phone was working, Mr. Data was ready with the package. Time to get back to work.

While downstairs the Friday night dinner outings and hacker competitions had begun, in their suite it was all work. Counter to the standard caricatures of government wastefulness and sloth, Danny, the congressman, and the target all worked late into Friday night. Most of it had to do with pretty arcane matters of legislation and/or fund raising. The target didn't attempt any more contact with the congressman or his staff that night, so Paul was left in the role of passive voyeur, letting all the mail and text messages go through as written. The congressman stopped sending mail and making calls around 9:00 PM and the lobbyist knocked off work around 8:00. Judging from the data from the GPS in his blackberry, Danny the aide didn't leave the Capital Hill office until 11:18. It was only when he was sure he was halfway through his walk home that Paul sent a wholly fabricated e-mail to Danny.

> From: Ken.Clover@cloverandassociates.com
> To: Daniel@wolvertonforamerica.org
> Subject: Heads Up
>
> Danny,
>
> Just wanted to let you know, I got a tip from a media friend who says there's something brewing out there about our man. Someone's digging into a story about the Congressman's record on national security issues. Border security stuff. I don't know what exactly, but thought you might want a heads up. I'm with the wife this weekend and won't be answering phones, but text or e-mail me if you have any questions or need a hand and I'll get back to you as soon as spousal harassment permits.
>
> K

Paul watched on his remote mirror of Danny's phone as he opened the e-mail, and presumably read it. Ten minutes later, by which time Paul could see on the GPS that Danny was back at his apartment, he started sending out e-mails and even making phone calls of his own. Paul let them all go through as written, since they served his purposes just fine. Danny was putting out feelers to his own media contacts, looking to see if anyone out there had heard any rumors about this supposed investigation into Congressman Wolverton's record on border security, which he assured them was spotless and above reproach. Just by asking the question, Danny was laying the groundwork for what they planned to unleash the following day. When reporters heard rumors of a story, the assumption was that there must be something there. Even if the story turned out to be bogus, the rumor still meant that someone out there at least thought they had a story worth investigating. And when Paul and Chloe and the rest of the Crew provided that story to them, they'd already be primed to jump all over it.

Danny stopped sending and answering e-mails at 1:30 AM, and there'd been nothing from the congressman or the target in hours. Paul checked in with Chloe and confirmed that the package had gone out to Isaiah as planned and that he'd started printing down in Florida, also as planned. Bee and c1sman were out in the hotel somewhere, hopefully having fun, and hopefully with their phones on. Sandee had passed out on his bed on the other side of the suite, and Sacco was snoring away in his chair. He and Chloe set up a watch schedule. She agreed to take the first shift, watching the e-mails to make sure nothing happened during the night with any of the phones or e-mail accounts they were tapped into. Paul would take over at 5 AM and let her get some sleep. He kissed her goodnight, leaving her with a Red Bull and the laptops and Sacco's snoring.

Paul took the early morning shift, fished out a Red Bull from the water-filled cooler that used to have ice in it, and started pulling up the e-mails he'd pre-written to go out to internet media figures and bloggers that he hoped would put some pressure on the congressman starting today, building up to a crescendo come Monday morning. The gist of all the e-mails pointed to a series of posts and articles spread around the Web that Paul and Mr. Data had dug up or fabricated/enhanced in the last month. They were based on a solid core of truth, namely that Congressman Wolverton had been a strong opponent of changes to labor policies in the U.S. controlled Mariana Islands. He hadn't been on the forefront of the issue, nor had he taken any paid-for-by-lobbyist junkets to play golf or otherwise enjoy the islands' offerings. But he'd voted straight down the line over the years against any kind of tightening of restrictions or even investigation into labor conditions on the islands, and had gone on record a couple times to reporters opposing any such changes.

The fabrications came in the form of a couple of pieces of gossip that the Crew had seeded out on blogs and various sites, including a rather risky hack into one of the newspaper websites from Wolverton's home town in Missouri. C1sman hadn't had much difficulty making the switch in the paper's online archives, but if anyone searched either the physical archives or the Way Back Machine for the original web pages, they'd find the change. The charade only had to last through a couple of days anyway, and there would be enough else going on that Paul doubted anyone would have interest in checking right away. Even the Congressman wouldn't necessarily have cause to doubt he'd said the fabricated quote, since, as Paul had suspected based on the man's record, it was totally in line with his actual beliefs as expressed in the private e-mails Paul had been reading through in the past sixteen hours.

Paul started by posting links to some of the articles in comment threads on Daily Kos and the Huffington Post and some other sites, using screen names that he'd established and cultivated for months, some of them even dating back to his first big scam in San Jose. Then he set up a series of time delayed posts to launch on the handful of blogs he'd been running as well, with alerts in his e-mail to remind him to post links to those blog entries back in those comment threads. Then he started refining the e-mails he'd send out to the more mainstream press and big time bloggers and news sites. He made quite a few changes, mostly incorporating a few choice facts he'd gleaned from the Congressman's e-mails about his general opposition to immigration reform that focused on local enforcement instead of showy, make-work projects like the border fence. There wasn't a lot there, but it was enough for Paul to build a really smoky, if not very hot rhetorical fire.

His kindling in place, Paul moved back to the big issue: the legislative changes. He and Sacco had worked hard researching and coming up with the perfect and legal wording for the budget earmark, and then Paul had spent a good chunk of the early morning hours going over the other e-mails that Mr. Data's search program had pulled from the target's servers about exactly how he worded such requests. When he'd composed his first draft of the bogus earmark request he'd used circumspect language full of euphemisms, and so he was surprised to see that the target tended to be very straightforward with his requests, especially when dealing with someone like Rep. Wolverton with whom he had a long history. The quid pro quo that would get everyone in trouble was never quite spelled out, but the camouflage was the bare minimum.

The target's bread and butter was a very specific kind of lobbying. It was Isaiah who'd first turned them on to Ken Clover, lobbyist. He'd worked in the Department of the Interior during the first president Bush's term in office and before that had been on staff for a couple of Republican Congressmen. During the Clinton years he'd cashed paychecks from several different conservative think tanks before setting up on K Street. He had no particular issues and no huge industry clients that he specialized in. Indeed, unlike many lobbyists, he did not stay on retainer for specific clients. Instead he was a kind of lobbying consultant, brought in when others couldn't get the job done or needed a little extra something. He was, in short, a deal maker, and for the past seven years he'd become known (within a very small circle of trusted clients) as a procurement trader.

Budget procurements, or earmarks as they were more commonly referred to in the media, were the best way going for a representative or senator to bring some money home to their district or state. The more money that came in, the more likely they were to get re-elected, or at least so went the conventional wisdom. But inserting earmarks often left fingerprints and could be used by political opponents or media critics to paint a very unflattering picture, so the fewer of these earmarks that could be specifically tied to electioneering greed and/or lobbyist paybacks, the better. If a congressman like Wolverton put in an earmark for something from which he would not benefit personally and that brought no particular benefit to his home district, then the assumption had to be that he was doing it because he honestly believed it was good policy.

Ken Clover and his firm offered what Paul considered a money laundering service to the members of Congress who paid his rather stiff fees. Chloe had approached Rep. Wolverton's aide with a classic deal. She, as a supposed lobbyist for the entertainment industry, wanted an earmark to provide funds for enforcement of new anti-piracy measures. Wolverton took in a fair amount of money from entertainment lobbyists because of his committee assignments, but he didn't want to be seen as being so obviously in their pocket. At the same time, there were other members of Congress who took no money from those lobbyists, but owed favors to other industries, like say Florida agricultural interests. Both sides worked through Clover, who arranged for the two representatives to swap earmark responsibilities. Clover would have the Florida

Congressman insert the procurement for the anti-piracy measure and in return Rep. Wolverton would insert the earmark for whatever farm-bill related procurement Clover told him to. Meanwhile, Clover would collect his money by charging a fee from the lobbyists on each side of the deal without ever having any direct monetary, and only minimum actual contact, with the two representatives.

That was how it was supposed to work, and how it did work week in and week out for Clover and Associates. Except that Chloe wasn't really a lobbyist and there wasn't any Congressman working to actually make a trade with Wolverton. From Wolverton's point of view, managed by Danny, he was making a trade on behalf of his MPAA and RIAA friends. In return he'd insert some earmark for Rep. Olivera in Florida, who would do his dirty work for him within a couple of weeks. Except Rep. Olivera didn't know a thing about it, nor in fact did anyone at Clover and Associates. Because plausible deniability was vital for the trading scheme to work, Wolverton would never talk directly to Olivera about the trade, certainly not before it was actually done. And since the two Congressmen didn't serve on any committees together or have many other points of contact, the odds of Wolverton saying something to Olivera that might tip the con were very slim.

So they'd hooked in Wolverton and his staff with Chloe and the forged e-mails from Clover's account. The agriculture bill was in conference this weekend, scheduled for a vote on Monday. Now was the time to insert earmarks, during the last minute wheeling and dealing as the Senate and House worked out their differences on the bill. Paul looked over his language once again, still nervous that he'd made some very obvious mistake that would set off alarm bells in the Congressman's mind when he saw it. Paranoid, Paul had re-written the entire thing from scratch, choosing to use a similar e-mail from Clover's archives as a template and then inserting his own legalese where needed. It seemed appropriately obscure and legislative to him, but who knew. Only one way to find out: send it.

But he couldn't send it. Not yet. He had to wait for the right moment—once the staffers from the House and Senate had gotten together and started horse-trading, so Danny would only have a window of a few hours to pass the new earmark along for inclusion in the bill. That wouldn't be until this afternoon at the earliest. In the meantime, all he could do was wait, watch, and intercept any e-mails or text messages or phone calls that could screw them up.

The phone calls were the biggest worry, since there was no way to fake those. They had one safeguard in place though: any call from Danny or the congressman or the congressman's office to any of Clover's phones would be automatically blocked and forwarded to voice mail, which they could then erase. The same was true in reverse. If the target tried to call Danny or Wolverton, his call would also go straight to voice mail. If they used other lines though, or somehow ran into each other on the streets, things could go very wrong. The key, then, was to keep them busy worrying about other things.

Saturday morning crept by, the others waking and setting about their tasks. Chloe offered to spell him at the watch, but he was still going over his e-mails and tweaking, so she went and got everyone breakfast instead. Bee and c1sman hadn't come in last night, and Paul assumed they'd stayed in c1sman's room. She showed up mid-morning looking more tired and grumpy than morning after bliss, so he doubted anything too exciting had happened between the pair. C1sman was on duty in the NOC downstairs and then planning on attending some talks and generally presenting himself as a solid, upstanding member of the Shmoocon staff. Shortly after noon, Sacco left to go meet up with his anarchists and coordinate the coming assault. Sandee had gone for a jog. Danny was busy doing the congressman's bidding and failing to get any confirmation about the alleged brewing investigation. The target remained largely quiet, apparently enjoying a nice weekend with his family. Time seemed to crawl by.

Then, all of a sudden, the moment was upon him. It happened in the space of a few minutes. Paul sent out the e-mail to Danny, who received it and jumped into action, forwarding it on to his fellow staffer who was in the conference committee meeting and telling him it was very important. The staffer texted back and said not to worry, it was a done deal. It was that easy. Months of planning, and thousands of man hours and dollars came down to that moment and Paul had managed to insert a $50 million earmark into the federal budget. Boom! Just like that.

He should have felt something more, he thought. He should feel different somehow, more excited, more charged. He just blinked, and rubbed his eyes. There was still so much more to do. The bill hadn't been signed yet, and the big score against the real target still hadn't come off. But hey, he'd just spent fifty million taxpayer dollars. "We're officially earmarked," he called out to the room.

"Really?" Chloe said. "Just like that?"

"Just like that."

"That's fucking awesome!" she sounded as excited as he was supposed to feel.

"It really is."

"So, time for Sacco to start some serious shit." She pulled her crypto-phone from her pocket and dialed. "Hey screwball, let's get this party started, yeah?" She hung up without waiting long enough for him to answer.

"I'm going to go get Sandee," Paul said. "Make sure the camera batteries are charged. I don't want to miss any moment of chaos."

Chapter 10

"Oh, come on, what the fuck? Seriously?"

"It's just not feasible, Sacco. I'm sorry, but it's just not."

"Fine, we can make some goddamned big puppets if you want. It won't make any sense, but…"

"That's not the point. The point is the target just doesn't seem like a high priority to us. We were thinking something with a much higher profile like the IMF or the World Bank. An enemy worthy of our attentions."

Sacco felt his eyes bulge with frustration. He probably should have tried to constrain himself, but he totally didn't. "Are you nuts or just a fucking idiot? What on earth do you think you can do to the IMF that will make a damn bit of difference to them?"

"Raise awareness. Embarrass them. Bring attention to…"

"The fact that anarchists hate the IMF? Wow, that'll be a freaking front page story. Wow, yeah, crazy hippie liberals hate the IMF and the World Bank and say they're evil and bad and stupid and smell funny. Who doesn't know that already, and more importantly, who the hell cares?"

"But with your plan no one will know we've accomplished anything!" Trevor countered.

"Yes, but we will in fact have accomplished something. We'll have made life better for people living in that fucking slum apartment building and we'll have fucked over the bullshit capitalist property owners in the process."

"Sacco, we've already voted, and I'm sorry, but it's not a priority for us. Now, we'd be happy to have you along at the anti-G8 protest in the Fall, but until then I don't see that there's much we can do together."

"Oh, and you're kicking me out too?"

"I suppose. We assumed you'd quit."

"Why would you assume that?"

"Well, last night you said, 'if we don't do this I'm going to fucking quit,' and we took you at your word."

Sacco had to laugh. He didn't remember saying that, but it sure sounded like him and he'd said so much last night at the planning session that he absolutely could've said something like that. "Well, I'm a man of my fucking word, so yeah, I quit." He stood up, tossed a sheaf of papers up into the air and walked out of the Brooklyn loft apartment in what could only be called a huff.

That was the second group he'd failed to properly motivate with his vision, not counting the Hacks of Revolution cowards. That was fine in theory—he wanted to be as choosy with his new allies as they were with him. But there was a clock running on things. The residents of the Polaris Hotel were being slowly but surely driven into homelessness by squalid conditions and predatory landlords. It was time to do something now, and the housing authority was never going to be the one to do it.

He was already hacked into all of the landlord's phones and e-mail. He knew just what kind of shit they were up to. But they were also old-school shit bags. They weren't in the digital age in any meaningful way and handled everything with face to face conversations and sometimes even written instructions. Taking them down meant manpower, and he didn't have it. He thought this last Crew of black bloc activists would be on board, but they had visions of the Battle of Seattle from a decade ago dancing before their twenty-something eyes, and so couldn't actually get behind doing real good for real people. Now what the fuck was he going to do?

Back in his own room in Brooklyn, Sacco logged on out of sheer instinct and started fiddling around online. He'd gained a lot of fame and notoriety in hacker circles for his little stunt at HOPE, and Listnin had been a huge hit. Lots of people wanted to work with him on lots of different projects, not a single one of which held much interest. He supposed he should have been more excited about some of those possibilities, but quite frankly the idea of slaving away on coding new apps and tools just bored him now. In Hacks of Rebellion he'd been the idea guy, and the others had done a lot of the implementation and, if he was honest with himself, the hard work. Or at least the grunt work. The boring work.

Now he wanted to be out there doing something, especially since the whole Polaris Hotel thing had come to his attention. He'd met Monique, a sweet, older Puerto Rican woman who worked at the coffee shop he frequented and lived with her sister and nephews at The Polaris. They'd got to talking, mostly so Sacco could practice his Spanish, but also because she was funny and liked to mother him about what he ate. So when she started dropping off-hand comments about her truly shitty living conditions—the broken elevators and chained shut fire doors and roaches and rats and dirty water and then no water at all—Sacco started asking more questions. And when he tried to stop by and see her one evening and bring her some clothing for her nephew and the burly, steroid ridden security guard refused to let him in because he thought Sacco was a housing rights advocate of some sort, Sacco's interest had really piqued. Anyone trying to hide something that hard needed to have all their secrets aired in public.

He talked with Monique, and learned the details of the violations and the threats and the lack of effective enforcement by the city. About the pay-offs to inspectors and the intimidation tactics used against tenant rights advocates. Sticking it to telecoms and global banking consortia started to seem a whole lot less interesting than making sure Monique and her family and friends had clean water and vermin-free homes. Having dug into KJL Properties, who owned the building, and discerned that they really were the scumbags he suspected and that they owned a dozen other slum properties as well, Sacco proceeded to own every phone and computer they had. It wasn't hard—they didn't give a fuck about computer security—but it also wasn't very useful. Now though, now he had his plan, and while it might not let him air out any dirty secrets, it would let him force the bastards to fix up The Polaris.

He was calling it Blackmail Blitz, and he planned to hit the owners, particularly the main dude, Frank Keller, with a barrage of problems so fast and so thick that he'd be driven to his metaphorical knees and left begging for some relief. But he needed help to pull it off in the rapid-fire time needed, and he needed a lot of one-time assistance from people who couldn't be tied too closely to him. There was the off chance (maybe better than off chance) that Keller had some mob connections, and he didn't want any of that OC bullshit coming back on him. So he needed cash, and gear, and operatives. He had exactly none of that.

Sacco turned to his newfound fans online, sending out some vaguely worded, innuendo laden calls for assistance. Contacting each one individually with separate, encrypted e-mail accounts and choosing only those he felt he had some reason to believe had a decent head on their shoulders, he told them that he needed donations and volunteers for a "radical operation" that would "force some good" down some people's throats. He never mentioned anything illegal and never even hinted at the target, but anyone who knew anything could guess he was up to something that was, at least, outside the bounds of the law. More people responded positively than he'd anticipated, at least at first, but when he was cagey with the specifics and exacting with his tech and cash needs, a lot of them stopped e-mailing him back and avoided him on IRC. Then he heard from her, the HOPE girl.

He'd bought her a few beers the night he quit Hacks of Rebellion, and she'd bought him a few more, all the while listening to him go on and on about the group and what it had meant to him and how his friends had failed him. She knew how to listen, that was for sure, and she seemed like she was really interested. Her name was Anne, and she kept asking him questions, wanting to know more, and he kept talking. It was great to vent to a kind ear who didn't have any ties to or interest in all the other fucking bullshitters and haters in his world right now, and as long as she let him go, he kept talking.

A few hours later, he was trying to figure out how to move things back to his place or her room. She was staying in the Hotel Pennsylvania where the con was being held, and that was a lot closer. She'd been flirty all evening, although in a sort of cutting way that left him scrambling to keep up with her. And then she got a call on her phone and took it outside. Just because he was drunk and curious and feeling full of himself, he took out his own phone and tried to see if any of the tools he'd loaded on there would let him pick up anything from her phone, but no luck. When she came back she said she had to go, that she was meeting some friends at the party over at Hacker Halfway House. She asked if he wanted to come along, but he knew the other guys from Hacks of Rebellion would be there and also he was pretty sure that the hostess, B9 Punk, was pissed at him after that thing he'd said to her at Notacon (which, in retrospect, had been pretty stupid). He tied to convince Anne to stay with him, but she was having none of it, although she rejected him with a smile and they exchanged e-mail and PGP keys.

Since then they'd sent some mail back and forth. She'd been trying out Listnin and liked it a lot, but had some questions about particular applications and he'd given her some friendly tech support. She was based somewhere down south, otherwise he might have tried to help her in person, but the conversations back and forth were cool, and she usually inquired as to how he was doing and what he was up to. He'd included her on the list of people he sent out e-mails to asking for help, but wasn't surprised when she didn't respond. But now, a few days later, there was the e-mail from her, offering to help. Awesome. They set up a time to chat over encrypted IRC for later that night.

Sacco: What's shakin' pinky
Ann3: Same as always, trying to take over the world
Sacco: Me too! What a coincidence
Ann3: So you need some monies
Sacco: yup
Ann3: Monies I got. Gear I got.
Sacco: rly?
Ann3: People you need to get.
Ann3: rly
Sacco: K
Ann3: There's a catch
Sacco: always is
Ann3: I wanna watch
Sacco: you wanna help?
Ann3: probably not. But I wanna watch.
Ann3: Assuming its cool
Sacco: its cool with me, yeah
Ann3: no, i mean assuming what ur doing is cool
Sacco: oh, it's fucking cool
Ann3: ?
Sacco: ? what?
Ann3: ? what is it. Tell me
Ann3: Do it.
Sacco: it's a secret
Ann3: so's the location of me cash and gear.
Sacco: it's a slum lord here in NY. I'm gonna take em down
Ann3: oh yeah
Sacco: haven't you heard? Property is theft. And property
        owners? Biggest thieves around
Ann3: Nothing wrong with stealing from a thief.
Sacco: Nothing at all. Not that I'm stealing anything
Ann3: Of course not.
Sacco: Im really not.
Ann3: ok
Sacco: I'm not!

Ann3: OK!
Sacco: I'm making him do good.
Ann3: ?
Sacco: Forcing him to be human. To do good.
Ann3: Will that work?
Sacco: of course it will. It's my plan.
Ann3: We'll see.
Sacco: So you'll help
Ann3: How else will I see if I don't help?
Ann3: Remember, I'm gonna be watching you
Sacco: I'll show you anything you wanna see
Ann3: uh-huh, I'll bet
Sacco: :)
Ann3: Show me what and how much you need.
Sacco: How much you got?
Ann3: I asked you first.

He ended up asking for $7500 plus some phones, three computers, and a whole lot of bugs and hidden cameras, stuff Anne apparently just had lying around because it arrived on his doorstop in a FedEx box two days later. He was impressed. With the money he could hire on some guys he could trust to do the work, and the rest was just a matter of digging in and getting it done. Anne didn't want to come up until the blessed day itself, which was fine with him. He hadn't been too thrilled about the idea of her looking over his shoulder the whole time, and he was still trying to figure out how to keep as much as possible from her when she did show up. The money and gear were great, but the fact that she'd been so free with it all kind of freaked him out. Freaked him out in the way leather and whips did—both exciting and scary at the same time.

The thing he never admitted to anyone was that he got the idea for his plan from an episode of *Veronica Mars* that he'd bit torrented. He didn't even watch much TV, but he'd appreciated both the tech-fetishism the show expressed for gadgets and the fact that Kristen Bell was super cute and smart. But, TV or no TV, the theory seemed sound to him. Find some total jerk who relishes being a prick to other people and has no interest in dealing with you in a reasonable manner (in this case, the Polaris landlords). Then overwhelm them with so much bad shit from so many different angles that he comes to realize that it was better to do the right thing than keep being a jerk. Originally his plan had been to hit KJL Properties directly, but that seemed beyond his abilities, even with Anne's helpful cash and gear. They were rich fucks who could hire their own private security and private eyes to come back on him. It would take someone in law enforcement or some sort of class action lawsuit thingy to take them on in any way that would really threaten them. Instead Sacco decided to focus his attention on the KJL minions who made day-to-day life at the Polaris basically unlivable. They were poorly paid slobs and petty tyrants, used to taking orders and giving in to threats from above.

So Sacco launched into an investigation of the three head security guys (who basically ran the building, supplemented by occasional part-timers they brought in to cover the odd shift), and the building superintendent and his son, who were responsible for the upkeep. Dirtbags each and every one of them, so digging up dirt on them was a breeze. Sacco paid some of his local activist friends, mostly college kids or kids who should've been in college, to follow them around with cameras, place GPS enabled phones under their cars, and Listnin on their phone calls. They got their drug deals and their hooker hook-ups and their general ass-hattery all on video, and Sacco learned their patterns. Through Monique, Sacco also got some of Anne's hidden cameras inserted into the public areas of The Polaris, where they could catch the bastards in the act of hurling abusive language at residents and intimidating social workers and housing rights advocates who attempted to gain entry, while letting drug dealer friends and prostitutes in to use vacants for their various business dealings.

On their own, the videos could probably have gotten the five fucks fired, but that wasn't Sacco's goal. He wanted them right where they were, but he wanted them to do what he told them, not what the owners ordered. When he'd gotten all the video and info he needed and had everything in place, he e-mailed Anne and told her it was time to come up to NY. He offered to let her stay at his place, but she declined. So instead she arranged to meet him at the squat he'd set up in as his command center for the crucial couple of days when he planned on putting the five fucks' balls in a vice.

"Nice place," she said as he let her in the door of the fifth floor walk-up. It wasn't a nice place at all, and the drafty, dusty, decrepit apartment would be unlivable in any kind of serious inclement weather, mostly because it was on the top floor and the roof was getting close to an even split between ceiling and holes. He had friends squatting in the apartment one floor down, and they'd made that much more livable, including stealing power and internet from the building next door. He in turn was borrowing some of both from them. "And I'm not being bitchy. I mean it. It's a nice place to run your thing from."

He looked her over, just to be sure she wasn't fucking with him. She looked good of course, like he remembered, although she seemed to have let her hair grow out and dyed it black. She wore jeans and work boots, a t-shirt and a dark, heavy sweater. No nonsense, plain Jane clothes. He hardly recognized her. "It's all I need and it's close to the Polaris. Let me show you around." He gave her the free tour, pointing out the sleeping bags piled in one corner, and the piss-bucket stashed away in the non-functioning bathroom. In a corner by boarded up windows and under one of the most hole-free sections of the ceiling sat his command center: three laptops and seven cell phones, each labeled and tied to one of his operatives out in the field. From here he could watch everything unfold and give instructions before his final showdown with the head fuck.

"None of the people on the other end of those cell phones know about each other," Sacco explained. "They each think they're doing one act of vandalism or whatever, and none of them know each other, at least not well. I use them for one, maybe two things, and then I cut them loose. It's as simple as that."

"So they're hired help," Anne said. "OK, nice, I can see that working. No one but you has the big picture or knows what the real goal is?"

"No one. Some of the people in the Polaris know someone's out there trying to help them, but only Monique, my friend on the inside, knows it's me, and she doesn't even really know who I am or where I'm from."

Anne nodded, pursing her lips in a way that Sacco interpreted as thoughtful approval. "So, you ready to get things going?" he asked.

"I'm just along for the ride and here to collect any gear you don't manage to lose or ruin. It's your dance, sport."

It all started with tire slashing and window breaking. He'd have liked to have been more subtle, like stealing the wheels and leaving the cars up on blocks or filling them with cement, but he was working with enthusiastic but untrained radical provocateurs. The simpler the task, the better. So the two security guys who had cars, both of which they parked in a secure garage nearby, had their tires slashed. Tiny little explosive devices, engineered from firecrackers with a shaped charge, were placed on all the windows and exploded on timers after Sacco's hirelings were safely out of the garage. Crack, crash, screech of alarms. Sacco laughed as he listened in on the phone calls from the garage, reporting the damage to the two cars.

This got the guards pissed off and riled up and looking for trouble, but there was nothing much they could do at the moment. Meanwhile Sacco started doing the simple stuff he could manage from his own computers: fucking with their credit cards, canceling their power, phone, cable, and water, changing their PIN numbers and their e-mail passwords. Nothing too debilitating on its own, but all of it extremely aggravating, especially when taken together. For the security guards, he sent in his second wave of hirelings, who approached the guards' usual drug dealers as if they were the lamest undercover cops in the world, dropping the guards' names as references and telling them all kinds of details about past drug transactions that you just didn't share with other people. As a result, when one of the infuriated guards came around that afternoon looking for a little mid-day bump to take the edge off, he was turned away and even threatened as a narc. The day kept getting worse and worse for these guys.

Then process servers started showing up, or rather people posing as servers, with paternity claims and lawsuits for child support and other baseless, but no doubt infuriating claims. These didn't go down very well either. The building superintendent and his son were getting these as well, even as they tried to figure out why they had no cable or phone or money in their bank accounts. The father went down to the bank to complain, only to have some young guy with a black bandanna over his face hurl a balloon full of red liquid at him before running off, leaving him covered in blood-red latex paint. Half an hour later he'd changed and showered only to be hit again three blocks down the street, along with his son who'd accompanied him. They gave chase, but the attacker slipped away into a waiting car with no license plate. By the time he was cleaned once more, the bank was closed for the evening, but the ATM told him he and his son were both overdrawn on their accounts.

Inside, the security guard at the front desk was dealing with a UPS package that exploded in white powder after the delivery man dropped it off. UPS deliveries were unheard of these days at the Polaris, so the guard had been suspicious already. It still didn't stop him from getting freaked out. If the phones had worked he probably would have called for some kind of help from his bosses, but they didn't and he was at a loss. The tenants, not sure exactly what was going on, but knowing they liked seeing their tormentors tormented, laughed and jeered and teased the fucks. The guards tried to intimidate them, to scream and throw things at them, but they were a little too freaked out to really vent their anger. If it was the tenants behind it, they must have begun to realize how outnumbered they were. When they came off shift they went home only discover the locks changed, the power out, and the water turned off. Sacco wished he could have seen their reactions, but he could extrapolate from how angry they were when they showed up back at The Polaris and demanded to see the super.

All five of them crammed into the super's ground floor apartment for a conference that one of Anne's bugs placed in the window allowed them to listen in on. They were angry and confused, but none of them had a working phone and were forced to talk by candle light as they debated whether to report to the bosses or not. That's when Sacco called Monique and had her do her part. While they argued inside, she snuck downstairs and left a phone in front of the super's door. Once she was safely clear, Sacco called it.

The negotiations went pretty well at that point. Sacco and the super talked. Well, after he cursed and threatened and yelled for a few minutes, Sacco got him to start talking terms. He had the man watch the videos he'd saved onto the phone—the guards buying drugs, the super and his son breaking housing and health codes and stealing from tenants. They knew their jobs and their freedom were on the line here. And when Sacco gave them a way out—a way to get their money back, and their utilities back online, and the harassment stopped, they relented. They agreed to Sacco's demands, that he was the new boss and that they were to start fixing the place up, hire some hard core exterminators, stop harassing the residents, and allow the renter's rights activists free access to the building. Once they'd done all that—ALL of that—their shitty lives would start returning to normal. By 1 A.M. it was over. Sacco had won the day.

"Well that was a fucking hoot," Anne said. She'd been laughing and cheering him on all day. "Nice work, man. Nice fucking work."

"Thank you, thank you. I'm pretty pleased. Couldn't have pulled it off without your gear and cash."

"You know it'll never work long term, right?"

Sacco looked at her, annoyed and surprised. "Don't be too excited for me," he said.

"I mean, those guys aren't gonna do what you say forever."

"Oh really? How long do you think they'll play nice?"

"A week, maybe two at most. Then you'll have to either do this all over again or the bosses will have found someone to replace them."

"And how long do you think it will take the renter's rights advocates Monique has on speed dial to document the atrocities there and bring a huge-ass lawsuit against those bosses?" Sacco asked.

Anne nodded. "It was never about making them your bitches."

"Never just about that. It was about buying some space for the activists and the lawyers to get the evidence they need without interference. They could probably win just on an hour's worth of investigation."

"And now they have a week."

"Maybe two," Sacco said, sticking his tongue out at her playfully. "Plus, that super will actually fix some shit in there, maybe."

"Well, Sacco, that all really works for me. That's some clever shit you pulled together."

"Worth your investment?"

"Definitely worth our investment."

"Our?" Sacco had never had any hint that Anne had told anyone else about the operation or her role in funding it. "Who're we talking about here?"

"My friends and me. The folks who donated the gear and the cash. It's not just me that's interested."

Sacco felt his heart beat rise. Anne was bringing the scary vibe again. "So, um, do I get to meet these friends of yours sometime?" Did he want to meet them? He thought probably that he did. Maybe.

"We'll see. Like I said, I'm impressed, but I have to make my report back to the group."

"You guys vote on stuff like this?" Sacco asked. That sounded familiar.

"Stuff like what?" Anne asked.

"I don't even know. Helping guys like me do things like this? That kind of thing?"

"Mostly we do the 'stuff' on our own, only on a bigger scale." She winked at him. Winking wasn't usually that scary, although it was often that exciting.

"Oooh, tell me more."

"Not tonight, sport. Tonight I'm going back to my hotel and tomorrow I'm flying home." She stood up and started walking towards the door. "And next week I'll let you know."

"Let me know what?"

"Let you know whatever it is I want to tell you."

He couldn't think of a rejoinder or which question she wanted to ask next before she got to the door. All he had in him was a lame, "Um, OK, thanks…"

"You're welcome," she said, and then she was out the door with a little, friendly wave. "I'll come back for the gear some other time."

Sacco grinned, no doubt like an idiot. He couldn't wait for her to come back, even if she was really kinda scary.

Chapter 11

Chloe

Chloe blew Sandee a kiss as he walked out the door looking like just about the sexiest woman reporter you've ever seen. A smart, tight, gray pin-striped skirt-suit with a red silk blouse and a brightly patterned scarf that could only be described as sassy. Chloe's own wardrobe options had expanded significantly since Sandee joined the Crew, not only because they could share some clothes, but because Sandee had a much better eye for fashion as a disguise than even Chloe did. Before, Chloe had always used changes of clothes and different wigs as a way to trick people into thinking she was someone else. Sandee taught her how to use outfits as a tool for inhabiting a whole new persona so that she not only dressed the part, but thought about what she wore as an extension of the life and mindset of the person she was pretending to be. It was a neat trick.

But there was no disguise she could wear that would make going out to watch the protests a good idea. Danny might be there at some point, and Chloe wasn't going to do anything at all to risk him making some connection between her and the protest. Besides, this was Sacco's part of the show, and he was in charge. He didn't need Chloe looking over his shoulder again, which was why she was sending Sandee to look over his shoulder for her. Not that Sacco's role in this afternoon's event required a ton of oversight. He was just there to make sure that things with the protesters really did get out of hand. If those black bloc anarchists of his ended up being wimpy little peaceniks who waved signs and chanted slogans instead of stirring up some serious shit, Chloe was going to be fucking pissed. Sacco was there to egg them on if need be.

Sandee was there to watch and record the whole thing, posing as an independent media blogger with a Nokia phone that could stream live video to the web. Paul had set up a site to host the live video stream as it came in, and had his cadre of fake online identities ready to start pushing the link out to his blogger and activist media contacts. From there they hoped it would hit the mainstream liberal blogs and through them the mainstream media. Saturday being an otherwise slow news day, and nothing too exciting going on in DC today as far as she could tell, they hoped to get some real traction with their stunt.

Chloe got the call half an hour after Sandee left. He'd taken the metro and was just coming up the escalator when he called in on his cryptophone. Chloe knew he had a hands-free ear piece dangling from his left ear, much to his dismay—and Chloe couldn't deny it looked tacky—but it was necessary.

"Two blocks north and then make a left?" Sandee said.

"You got it, babe," Chloe replied, a map open on her laptop so she could confirm the directions.

"I'm seeing a lot of dingy, faded black clothes and odd facial piercings around here," Sandee said. "I could probably just follow the gathering crowds."

"Yeah, but…"

"Don't be so obvious, I know, I know, of course not. But this is a pretty nice neighborhood. Not Georgetown nice, but you know, nice. I'm not the one drawing all the sidelong looks from the rich, white folks walking their dogs and strolling their kids."

"No one said this would be subtle."

"No one was right," said Sandee. "It is nice to get out of that horrible little room. Yes, yes, it's not very little and not actually horrible, but still, my dear, you've got to admit, it's getting mighty stuffy in there."

"No denying it. Another necessary evil."

"It used to be all my necessary evils involved drinking, dancing, and men with large muscles or women with large cocks. How did I ever let you madcap pranksters seduce me into this life of crime?"

"Well, technically…"

"OK, yes, technically I was already leading a life of crime and I seduced the pair of you, but you're missing my point."

"Which is?"

"That it's really cold out here and I know for a fact that it is wonderful and sunny and warm back home."

Chloe paused for a moment to look it up. "71 degrees and sunny."

"Now that was just mean!"

"You said you knew it for a fact."

"That doesn't mean I wanted the fact thrown in my face like some free, adorable kitten who just wants a home."

"Wait, now we're having the cat conversation again? Paul's allergic."

"They do make drugs for that you know."

"Fine, we'll talk about it when we get home," Chloe said, putting on her most motherly tone of voice.

"Thanks mama! You're so good to me. So listen, the anarcho-whatchamacalits are starting to get thick on the ground and I've discovered something else."

"What's that?"

"Whoever said these tights I'm wearing would keep my legs warm was a fucking liar."

"I told you to wear pants."

"I know, I know. Didn't I just admit I'm a fucking liar? OK, hey, there's something going on up there. I'm going to go ahead and whip out my phone."

"Great," Chloe said, clicking away from the weather in Key West back to the bookmark for Cap City Critiqual, the blog Paul had set up months ago in prep for this moment. The site was "run" by Sandee's persona for the day, a freelance reporter with an acid tongue and a nose for dirt named Talia Tailes. Paul and Sacco had done most of the actual blogging up to this point, and had written the talking points for the dozen previous video casts that Sandee had performed with his head back lit and the image fuzzed to preserve "her" identity as an investigative reporter who "had worked for the AP" (according to the site any way). Paul had kept her scripted commentary even-handed in its choice of political targets left and right, although the content of the critiques was never less than biting and usually quite unfair.

As she watched, the video from Sandee's phone started streaming video live onto the website. Chloe let Paul know it was time to get started and he readied his link bots and online sock puppets to start Digging and linking to the event once it got going. C1sman had a couple hundred computers out in the wide world that he'd taken over using trojans or malware of some kind, and these zombies would unknowingly serve up the comments and links on the Crew's behalf. The video was jumbled and blurry at first as Sandee brought the camera to bear on the scene, but once the object of its attention was in frame, it steadied immediately.

The scene was a row of recently gentrified and restored townhouses along a street crowded with mid-priced to low-end luxury vehicles, perfectly manicured micro-lawns, and well-swept stoops. Things were already starting to get a little washed out in the mid-afternoon sun, and the lengthening shadows looked cold and in some corners still preserved week old ice and snow. A knot of people were milling around about halfway up the block, most of them in their teens or twenties and wearing worn, oft-mended jackets or coats festooned with angry-looking buttons, pins, and patches. Some of them had knit caps pulled down close over their brows, others thick scarves or bandannas pulled up tight above their chins. Almost all of them wore scuffed, heavy boots of one kind or another. These weren't flashy, flimsy clothing that wannabe punks might pick up at Hot Topic. They were real second hand and refurbished gear, real work and combat boots, real serious cats.

"Well, well, well, what have we here?" Sandee said over the Nokia, not talking to Chloe but to Talia Tailes' audience. "These are some unsavory sorts, gathered in a neighborhood more typically home to Washington's lawyers, lobbyists, doctors, and yes, even Congress-critters. Looks like the kind of display of buttons and black that's going to lead to some serious shouting."

The cluster of disaffected youth began to cohere into action at this point. Chloe was happy to see that Sacco was nowhere in the picture. From within their coats came cloth banners wrapped around plastic or wooden rods. Nothing huge, but there were lots of them. Of the thirty or so protesters on the sidewalk and spilling into the street a third of them had signs saying things like "Free The Marianas!" and "End US Slavery Now!" and "Made by American Slave Labor." Their attention was firmly fixed on a townhouse in the center of the block, one with outward facing security cameras above the door and bars on the first floor windows.

Sandee focused the camera on the front of the house. So far none of the protesters had crossed the waist-high fence and entered the ten foot long front lawn, but they were pressing up against it hard. The video showed the address and was lucky enough to pick up someone inside pushing aside a curtain enough to peek out. "Now this is interesting, interesting, interesting," said Sandee/Talia. "Whoever in the world could be drawing the wrath of these very seriously pissed off people. Lucky for you, Talia Tailes has a database of Washington DC stars homes in her phone." The view tilted wildly, showing the ground for thirty or forty seconds as Sandee pretended to access something, then swung back to the protesters again who were acquiring new members from every direction. They now blocked one whole lane of traffic and had clogged the sidewalk entirely.

"Welly, welly, well, according to my reckoning, this is the home of none other than Representative Tom Wolverton, Republican from Missouri. A modest home for a modest Midwesterner. His wife and son live back in the home district if memory serves. Now whatever in the world could this salt of the earth, heart of America guy ever have done to piss off these scary people. Let's find out."

The camera moved forward until it was right behind one of the protesters. "Hey there, you're being broadcast live to the internet," he said. "Care to comment on what's going on here?"

The protester, a skinny dude with a thick beard and a torn, black baseball cap pulled down low over his eyes turned to Sandee in mid-yell, screaming "FREE THE SLAVES!" into the camera.

"Didn't we do that in 1865?" Sandee asked.

"Not if you're a textile worker in the Marianas Islands! There you can be locked into your sweatshop, forced to have sex with Japanese tourists, and forced to have an abortion if you get pregnant. And every pair of jeans you sew has a made in the US label on it. That's slavery, and it's in American controlled territory and that rat-fuck congressman in there supports it 100%! FREE THE SLAVES!" He shouted again, joining in with the whole crowd this time.

Sandee backed away to take in the whole tableau. "Still slaves in US territory! Who knew? According to these angry people, Congressman Wolverton knew. That doesn't sound good at all." The video now showed the angry protesters raising their fists and shaking them forward and back as if they were all hammering some invisible nails above their heads while chanting for the ending of slavery in the Marianas Islands. Pressure from those in the back to make way for a truck that showed no interest in slowing down was transferred forward so that the people up front had to step or clamber over the fence or be crushed against it. Once the first few had crossed onto private property, the ones behind were emboldened, and suddenly everyone was pressing forward. From somewhere in the crowd people started throwing bottles and cans.

Chloe, caught up in the video in front of her, didn't hear Paul the first two times he said something to her. Finally she looked up to him. "What did you say?"

"I said the congressman's in there and he's calling Danny right now." Paul had an earphone in his left ear and could listen in on any conversations made on either of the phones they'd hacked. "He's already called the cops. Or his wife has, on the house phone."

"I thought his wife was back in Missouri?" Chloe said.

"Not this weekend. I think she's here to go to the fundraiser with him tonight."

Chloe nodded and went back to the video. Sandee was too busy capturing all the action to answer a warning call about the cops coming and besides, that was pretty clearly going to happen no matter what. A bottle shattered against the bars on one of the windows by the front door. The shouting had gone from organized to calamitous at this point, and Sandee swept the video around the street to show both how large the group had gotten and how scared the few remaining bystanders on the street looked. When she went back and looked at the logs of the video and the phone calls, she would see just how impressive the DC police response time really was. The first car arrived within a couple of minutes, with the second and third cars not more than a minute behind those.

The cops leaped out of their vehicles as Sandee recorded them, their nightsticks drawn. At least they had the good sense not to pull firearms, which had been a real worry. Sacco was supposed to have briefed the protesters to scatter when police arrived, and most of them started to do just that as soon as the patrol cars screeched to a halt. The five cops (one was in his car alone) didn't bother too much with the first to flee, concentrating instead on those still menacing the front of the congressman's home.

"The cops have arrived now," Sandee was saying over the yelling. "And they do not look happy. I wonder if there are enough of them, but I'm betting there are many more on the way. This flash protest seems to be breaking up as soon as it... oh! Damn!" She got a close-up of a cop banging away on the back of a protester's head as he in turn was banging on the front door of the house. The poor kid went down in a flash, bleeding. "Things are ugly here. Real ugly."

The five cops had fought their way to the front and rallied on the steps before turning and facing the protesters in a unified phalanx of blue-clad menace. Only a dozen or so foolhardy stalwarts remained, one of whom was ripping a decorative cabbage from the front lawn and preparing to throw it at the cops. At that point one of the fleeing protesters knocked into Sandee hard, sending the phone/camera reeling to the ground. "Hey!" she heard Sandee shout.

A second later he picked the phone up and two other protesters slammed into him as well. The video was a blur of swinging, Blair Witch style motion. "Gimme that!" someone shouted at Sandee.

"Fuck off!" Sandee shouted back, and Chloe and the rest of the viewers got a camera eye view of a knuckle punch to the throat. The grabby protester went down and Sandee started to backpedal, bringing the camera back up and watching as more cops arrived and those who hadn't run in the beginning ended up in handcuffs or pinned to the ground by angry law enforcement. The guy Sandee had punched lay on the ground, holding his balls and neck, curled up in a fetal position.

"I think that's my cue to cut out of here," Sandee said, sweeping the camera back and forth across the whole street scene one last time. "This is Talia Tailes reporting live from Congressman Wolverton's own private protest party. Out." The video went dark.

Chloe sat back in her seat and blew out some air through her lips in a low whistle. She turned over to Paul, who was still listening intently to his tap on the Congressman or Danny's phone. "Are they still talking about it?"

"Now he's calling someone in the Secret Service apparently. He's still too pissed off about them trampling his front lawn to have even noticed what the signs said." Paul paused to listen to something. "He's maybe calming down some now. But I'm gonna start hitting Danny with some tips and questions from media sources in the next couple hours, and that should get them thinking about the right shit by the fundraiser tonight."

Chloe was happy with how things had gone, although a little surprised at how fast it had all happened. It was the kind of quick crackdown that pre-internet no one would have ever seen because TV wouldn't have gotten there in time. Now one lone drag queen with a camera could broadcast it live to the world. Sandee called in ten minutes later to report that he'd made it clear of the rigmarole and was on his way back to home base. Chloe had been slightly worried that the cops would try and hold him as a witness if they'd noticed him videotaping the event, but they'd obviously had bigger issues occupying their attention. Once the video was online, they'd have no way of tracing them back to Sandee, since the fictitious Talia Tailes was entirely anonymous, as was her site (no easy feat that, in this modern day).

An hour later he was back, and Sacco had called in to report that a dozen of his one-time recruits had been arrested, but there wasn't anyone who could lead the authorities back to him. His liaisons with the protesters had all been smart enough to split when they heard sirens, per the plan, and were preparing for the night's more peaceful but still important follow up. Paul reported from across the room that his campaign to drum up views for the protest video was bearing fruit and that the media outreach plan was reaching its first critical mass where they could get some real traction on Digg, Reddit, and the other social networking news sites. Then came the emergency text message from Bee, asking Chloe to come downstairs RIGHT NOW.

"What the fuck?" Chloe said. "Shit." She texted back, ignoring for a moment Paul's questions. Bee just reiterated her need to see Chloe in the lobby, and texted their pre-arranged code word for "it's not safe for me to come home."

Sandee walked in at that moment, a smile on his face. "Well, that was nothing but shocking and awesome," he said, and then saw Chloe's worried face.

"Is something going on downstairs?" Chloe asked.

"Bunch of nerds having a convention," he said. "Nothing out of the ordinary or even remotely exciting that I saw."

"What's going on?" Paul called across the room.

"I'm not sure," said Chloe, picking her mousy-brown wig off the table. "But you guys might want to start packing shit up, just in case we need to leave here really fast." Hopefully they wouldn't have to lower the rope they'd brought out the window, but it was nice to know the option was there. "I'm going downstairs."

Chapter 12

Oliver • *now*

O liver wasn't entirely satisfied with how the con was going so far. There was a hell of a lot of stuff to do, but he wasn't quite sure what the point of it all was anymore. He'd gone through much of Friday evening grumpy because work was making him put in a full day's worth of work even though he was supposedly here at the convention on their dime and for his job. Stupid job. And so he'd been stuck up in his room VPNing into the office for the first half of Friday and then by the time he got downstairs everyone he knew had already gone to dinner somewhere and there was just a hotel bar full of hackers he didn't know and he just didn't have the mental energy to try introducing himself to people. He idly sat at one of the pay-to-surf internet kiosks in the lobby and hacked it so it would be free, wondering what to do with the rest of his evening.

In the end he'd done what people often do in this situation: he hung around the outskirts of other people's conversations and waited for a chance to insert himself into one of them. After a few failed attempts it even worked, and he ended up talking Linux kernel stuff with a group of guys for a while, which was fine, but nothing he couldn't have done on a forum or listserv from home. Saturday he decided to throw himself into the talks, and that had proved a mixed bag as well. Everyone seemed stupid and boring and he wasn't learning anything. At least a couple of them were funny, like Johnny Long's talk which he'd seen a version of before but went to anyway knowing he'd at least have a good time. Coming out of it late Saturday afternoon he was seriously thinking about starting drinking. OK, not too seriously. Instead he decided to go up to his room and chill out for a little while, relieve some stress. Then maybe he'd buy a hundred dollars worth of shmoo balls and just hurl them at everyone who pissed him off.

As he stood waiting for the elevator in the lobby, the real reason for his discontent, the person who'd made it impossible for him to actually enjoy a hacker con ever since, came striding in through the side door as if she didn't have a care in the world. Ollie's eye's widened in surprise. She was dressed much more conservatively this time, in a suit/skirt outfit and with her hair tied back, but there was no mistaking her face, one that was locked tight in his imagination and which he kept coming back to again and again, sometimes at the most awkward moments. It was Toni.

He started to move towards her but then didn't know what to say. He wanted to confront her of course, make her admit what she'd done and tell him who she really was, but that wasn't going to happen. Even as he failed to take that step after her as she walked down the hall away from him, he knew he was scared to actually face her. She'd just deny everything, or pretend not to know who he was, or somehow humiliate him. Ollie had seen how she could cut a man down with her words, and see right through to their weaknesses and insecurities. He just couldn't face that, not on his own.

Only once she'd disappeared around the corner did his logical brain kick into gear again and start focusing on something besides his gut emotional response. If she was here at Shmoocon, it was probably for the very same reason she'd been at Toor Con—not to learn or network, but to recruit people for whatever sinister plan she had going this time. Ollie realized at once what he had to do. He had to warn someone.

He spun around and not-quite-jogged towards the escalators up to the convention area, making a bee-line straight for the front registration desk. With the con well under way, only late comers and people buying t-shirts needed the desk attendant's attention, so he was able to rush right up to the counter and say (not shout like he almost did), "I need to talk to Heidi!"

The guy behind the counter said, "She's around here somewhere. What do you need?"

"It's kind of... a security issue maybe," Ollie said, looking around behind the counter to make sure Heidi wasn't there.

"Should I call security then?" the guy asked, starting to sound anxious.

"No, it's not an emergency exactly. It's just there's this woman... Listen, I think I need to explain it to her myself."

"OK, OK, lemme get on the radio and see where she is." He produced a radio headset and said into it, "Does anyone have eyes on Heidi?" Ollie couldn't hear the responses, but after asking two more times, he finally got a response. "Could you send her to registration? Someone needs to see her about something. OK. Yeah, thanks." He turned to Ollie. "You're sure this is important right, she's really busy and you do not want to piss her off right now."

Ollie just nodded. He was sure it was important, but he was less sure of his ability to convince anyone else of that fact. Heidi, as everyone who knew anything about Shmoocon knew, was in charge of Shmoocon, and the wife of renowned security expert Bruce Potter. The fact that she not only managed Shmoocon and was super cool but was also a half-Norwegian, half-Fillipina MILF only made her more intimidating as far as Ollie was concerned. He'd seen her around of course, mostly on stage during events or prowling the halls putting out fires, but he'd never actually talked to her. Hopefully she would understand how important what he had to tell her was. What was he going to tell her exactly? He knew he wanted to warn everyone about Toni, but he hadn't quite thought through the details of how to make that warning make sense without making him look like an idiot or a sucker. He certainly wasn't going to tell anyone the whole story.

That night at Toor Con they'd gone back to his hotel room. Because he was never sure of these kinds of things, he wasn't at all sure he was going to get lucky, but he had his hopes. She'd admired the view of the stadium below and asked for one of the mini-vodkas from the mini-bar. She sat on the bed, curled up against the headboard with her shoes off while he sat in a chair and talked about penetration testing and hacking and all the other things he spent most of his waking hours thinking about. She wanted to know every detail of how his job worked, which was normal for someone who didn't know the details of his rather exotic line of work. He'd told versions (usually shorter versions) of all these stories before. But Toni had pressed into unusual territory, asking him not just about the things he did but the reasons he did them and what he found satisfying about them. And from the topic of satisfaction they turned to the topic of dissatisfaction, and why he was looking for a new job (short answer, he was bored with his current one because all his friends were gone and the bosses sucked since the buyout last year). Toni had a few more mini-bottles and he even had the two Heinekens that'd been in there for Lord only knows how long.

By 4 AM he was talked hoarse and she'd passed out on the bed. He tucked her in beneath the covers and slept beside her with his clothes on above the covers. Well, he tried to sleep, but mostly he just lay there willing her to wake up and turn towards him and put her arms around him. He'd passed out at some point and woke up to the sounds of her in the bathroom. She came out still wearing her dress from the night before, smiling and chipper. She'd apologized for nodding off and thanked him for his hospitality. She had a plane to catch, but wanted to stay in touch. She gave him her private phone and personal e-mail and told him to contact her on Monday so they could talk more. He fumbled about, rubbing the sleep from his eyes and swallowing again and again to lubricate his mouth, which was desert dry, indicating he'd been doing some serious snoring. He was, of course, mortified.

He e-mailed her the next day, not expecting a reply. But one came within an hour, and the two started a lovely little e-mail correspondence. Then after a few weeks, Toni sent him a job reference. She said a company she did some consulting for was looking to hire an outside pen tester for some insurance compliance and she thought he might be interested. Technically Ollie wasn't supposed to do that kind of moonlighting, but Toni said she could work things so the billing went through her company and she could pay him as a consultant to her and no one would ever know he'd gotten paid to do pen testing. They'd think he was just giving his expertise on general security matters for a court case, working as a kind of expert witness, which was fine under his contract.

Although he didn't see himself as ever working freelance on a regular basis—he much preferred the stability of a regular paycheck and someone else finding jobs for him to do—he saw no harm in doing it once in a while. Plus, he was happy to do a favor for Toni. He called the number she'd given him and talked to a guy named Steven from a construction company in Miami. He'd looked at Sun State Construction's website before calling, and wasn't too impressed. It was pretty simple and bare bones. A little googling and he started to see that there was more to the company than its off the shelf site. They were a big company, doing a lot of retail and industrial jobs all over South Florida. Family owned and operated with hundreds of employees and dozens of jobs going at once. Why they cared so much about network security that they needed an outside pen tester was unclear to him, but Steven answered that question on the phone.

"It's an insurance thing. My wife's cousin, Emmanuel, he says he can save us a bunch on premiums and he knows this techno junk so he convinced my wife we need it. So that's why I'm talking to you." He sounded tired and uninterested, although Ollie thought he had an odd voice that didn't quite match his picture on the website. "But are you saying maybe I don't need this testing thing you do?"

"I'm not saying that at all, no sir," Ollie replied, scared his questions had somehow screwed up the job. "No, no, not at all. I'm just trying to get an idea what kind of vulnerabilities you're looking for me to test for."

"The whole package I guess, top to bottom inspection. Whatever's your top of the line."

This was obviously a man more used to buying heavy equipment than computer security services. "Um, OK. Sure. I'll run a full test then."

"Sounds good, sounds good. How much is that going to run me?"

"I was told that the billing will be through…"

"Oh yeah, my cousin's little consultant friend. Right, right." Ollie heard yelling with a thick Spanish accent in the background. "My wife just reminded me." More yelling, although Ollie couldn't quite make out any of the actual words.

"I just need you to sign the waiver I e-mailed giving me…"

"My wife's putting it in the fax machine right now. Do whatever you need to do, but don't screw up the e-mail alright? She'll have my balls and yours if she can't get her e-mail from her sister in Caracas, and we don't want that." More yelling.

"No problem, sir. Hopefully you'll never know I was there until you get my report."

"If I never know you're there, how will I know you did any damned work at all?" The man sounded genuinely annoyed, although Ollie wasn't sure if it was at him or the world in general.

"Oh, don't you worry about that. I think when you see my report you'll know for sure." He'd already done some passive snooping and he didn't think he'd have much trouble at all penetrating right on through the company's network, and the waiver Toni had written up for him gave him all the carte blanche of a real Red Team to do whatever he needed to.

He got started the next day, but soon found that it was more of a challenge than he'd at first suspected. Compromising their company website was dirt simple, but also largely pointless. The site was obviously an afterthought for them and had no connections to their larger network or any interesting or sensitive data. So Ollie had to work through other channels and started poking around at the company's actual e-mail server. Here the number of employees worked in his favor, especially those who checked corporate e-mail through personal, less than fully-patched and secured machines. He found his hook and pried open an entry for himself. Within a week he'd compromised the entire system and filled out all the requirements that Toni had sent him for completion of the pen test.

He pulled down payroll and bank records, employee information files, telephone and cell phone billing records, and even some internet browsing histories. He got passwords to every machine in the network as well. He wrote his report and handed everything over to Toni who would handle billing with Sun State and sent it over to her. She reported back the next day with the good news—the clients were pleased but also dutifully alarmed at what he'd found and had paid the full fee right away. Toni transferred Ollie's payment to his account along with a little 10% bonus she said was, "for doing such a bang-up great job." He told her how much fun he'd had and when she asked said he'd be happy to do some more consulting for her anytime.

The two of them continued to e-mail, and after proving his abilities to her, his own self-confidence grew, and the back and forth got more and more flirtatious between them. A few weeks later he was bored, bored, bored after a long boring day at work, and decided to poke around Sun State again and see if they'd gone ahead and patched any of the security flaws he'd found. He was annoyed but not actually too surprised to see that they hadn't done a thing. As he was just scanning through, no real intention of snooping, honest, he noticed some e-mail threads shooting around inside the company about some sort of financial crisis. Maybe they were too distracted by their bigger problems to worry about security? Driven by curiosity, he looked a little closer. The company had been swamped in a chaotic flurry of seemingly unrelated troubles. Orders not getting placed for raw materials, bills not getting paid, employee payroll information being leaked.

Oh shit, he thought. Oh shit, oh shit, oh shit. It was starting to dawn on him then, what had actually happened. He read some more e-mails, especially from the company owners. There was no mention in any of them of the penetration testing, but lots of complaints about recent problems, including computer related ones. He pulled up the company's internal directory and got Steven's direct office and cell phone numbers. Ollie dialed and hung up three times before he made himself call Steven's office. He heard the voice mail message and it didn't sound anything like the man he'd talked to. He called the cell phone and got the real Steven on the phone and confirmed it—this, rough, old, accented voice did not belong to the person who'd given him the OK to run his pen test. He hung up. Not a pen test, but a hack. He'd hacked the company under false pretenses.

He should have thought his next move through, but he was angry and even scared. He could lose his job if anyone found out what he'd done. Hell, he could go to jail. He touch-typed a 60 word per minute angry screed directed at Toni, railing against her for sucking him into this madness under false pretenses. He demanded explanations and apologies and assurances. He threatened retribution and hinted at going to the cops. He fired it off, waited five minutes, and then called her phone number. It went right to voice mail and he hung up, calling again every fifteen minutes for the rest of the day. He started running IP traces on the e-mails she'd sent him, but they were either spoofed or dead-ended into anonymizers. The mail server for her personal e-mail account yielded no clues, nor did he get anywhere tracing the phone numbers. Nothing led anywhere. He couldn't find her. The only fact he knew for sure was that he'd hacked the Sun State Construction network and sent all the proof anyone would need to convict him of that crime to a strange, seductive woman who called herself Toni.

Ollie called in sick the next two days and suffered through three sleepless nights waiting for some sort of resolution, some sort of consequences for his action, but none came. He even tried to get the bank to trace where his payment had come from, but it had simply been a cash deposit into his bank account from an ATM in Miami. So yeah, he knew Toni or someone—who had he really talked to on the phone if not Steven?—had been in Miami a few weeks ago. That did him zero good. Even when he went back to work, his heart wasn't in it. He kept looking over his shoulder, expecting them to fire him or revoke his security clearance or something. One sleep-deprived Saturday night he pulled out all his hard drives and drilled holes through them before driving them out to the dump himself early Monday morning. He put the money they'd paid him in a separate savings account and let it sit there in case he ever got a chance to pay it back. Eventually he started to calm down, but the anger and resentment at being used so poorly never went away, never even receded very far from the front of his thoughts. He told himself that this must be what it's like to be shell-shocked or have Post Traumatic Stress Disorder, and it sucked.

When he'd seen Toni walking through the Shmoocon lobby it all came flooding back, but faced with an actual opportunity to take revenge on his tormentors, he was frozen with fear and doubt. What if he tried and failed to get his revenge? What could she do to him in return? Doubts, doubts, doubts. But there were other people here who could do something, people in a position of some authority and influences. Warning them might be enough.

"Can I help you?" asked Heidi, smiling but looking a little wary. "There's some sort of emergency?"

It all came out in a torrent, one word tumbling over the next. He ended up just telling her everything.

Chapter 13

Chloe

Back in her nerd un-chic persona, Chloe headed upstairs and then caught an elevator back down. She found Bee loitering by the entrance to the hotel's fine dining restaurant, pretending to peruse the menu. Chloe walked on by and headed out the door and down the sloping driveway to the street below, trusting that Bee was following her. She turned into a drugstore and started reading greeting cards. Bee arrived two minutes later and started looking at cards as well.

"Sandee's been spotted," Bee said.

"What? By who?"

"That failed recruit ended up showing up here anyway."

"Oliver. I thought we checked on that."

"We did, as best we could, but he hasn't been online in his normal haunts. He posted that he probably wasn't coming."

Chloe sighed and picked up another card. She wanted to be outraged and tell someone that she'd told them so, but the truth was she hadn't. Just like the others, she assumed that the odds of Oliver both being there and recognizing Sandee were negligible. She was still smarting about how badly they'd misread Oliver and the likelihood of recruiting him into the Crew. "What happened?"

"He came to Heidi Potter and told her the whole story."

"You're kidding me. Everything?"

"I think so. I'm getting this second hand through c1sman, which I guess makes it third hand. Oliver went to Heidi and she listened and thought he was probably a little nutty, except he's got an OK rep in the community and so she took him seriously enough to want to be safe rather than sorry. She told Bruce and then they pulled in some of the other Shmoo Group people and talked to them about it in the NOC, and c1sman was one of the people that got called in. Well, he was already in there and they let him stay."

"And they believe him?"

"It sounds like they don't believe it all, but they're curious."

"Curious is bad," said Chloe. The last thing they wanted was all these hackers getting curious about them.

"So they have a description and they're pretty sure she's staying in the hotel. The word is that she's some sort of black hat recruiter who's looking for people to suborn into a life of crime. People are supposed to keep an eye out for her in the con areas and Heidi asked some of the Shmoo Group to do some subtle poking around."

"Well, that's not the end of the world, I guess. They think Sandee's a she, so we can solve that problem easily. And they don't have any idea what we're really up to. But still, we're going to have to get him out of the hotel for good."

"If they get real curious they might go to the security tapes," Bee said. "Heidi said she wasn't going to go to hotel security unless something actually happened in the part of the hotel Shmoocon was responsible for, and obviously nothing like that has happened."

"Except us piggy-backing on their network to hack into Clover's network."

"But c1sman's in charge of that."

"Not so in charge that he could keep one of the others from poking around because they're curious. And just because Heidi's not going to security doesn't mean one of the other Shmoos won't go poking around in the security tapes on their own."

"You're saying we have to leave."

"Oh, there's no question we have to leave," said Chloe. "The question is, do we have to do something else besides just leave."

"How do we explain c1sman leaving early? And if he leaves then we lose our person on the inside," said Bee. Chloe agreed with the point, but suspected that Bee just didn't want to leave the con yet or freak out c1sman too much by doing a full scale emergency bug out. There was only half a day of convention on Sunday anyway, so c1sman sticking it out might not be such a bad idea, and keeping Bee on top of him only made sense. "You and c1s can hole up in his room while the rest of us skedadle. The only thing is we need to make sure they don't somehow connect you two to our room in case they ever connect Sandee to us."

"So what's the plan?"

"I need to talk to Paul and then get to some hardcore misdirecting."

The key to making this work was to find the right person. She'd managed to get c1sman on a cryptophone while he was in a private place and debriefed him on exactly which of the curious investigators to focus her attention on. C1sman was freaked out and scared of all of them, and wasn't very helpful at first, but eventually she got what she needed from him—someone smart (that part was easy, they were all smart) with a good rep in the community who was willing to take matters into his own hands to do a little investigating and if he was the type who could be distracted by a pair of tits, all the better.

He was a big guy, well over six feet, and barrel-chested with a heavy, solid gut. A formidable presence but a friendly face, and he smiled down at her and said, "Yes, how can I help you?" when she asked if he was part of the security for the convention. He twisted and turned his broad back to her to show the word "SECURITY" stenciled on the back by way of presenting his credentials.

Chloe gave him an embarrassed, shy smile and said, "Something weird's been happening to me and I thought maybe I should tell somebody about it."

"I'm definitely somebody. What's up?"

"Well here's the deal, and I know it sounds weird or whatever, but I've been talking to this lady who I think might be an undercover fed." Although they didn't formally play the game at Shmoocon, Chloe knew that at other conventions "Spot the Fed" was a serious contest with prizes and special t-shirts if you successfully spotted the undercover federal agent in their midst. She was betting that the security guy's curiosity would be roused sufficiently to want to look into it, if only because he could then share in the bragging rights for having uncovered the undercover.

"Oh yeah? Interesting, interesting. What makes you think this lady is a fed?" He looked around to see if the person Chloe was talking about might be nearby.

"Well, she seemed all cool and whatever at first, you know just kind of curious. I thought maybe she was a reporter or something. I guess she could be a reporter, but I don't really get that kinda vibe off her, you know? Plus she's like wicked smart on hacking stuff. Knows things and technical terms and stuff the way reporters just really don't, you know?"

"OK, sure. But you think she's a fed why?"

"Well I was out last night with some friends from the con at this bar in Adams Morgan, right, and she was there. A bunch of people were there from the con. And I had some drinks and whatever and I think maybe I got all too talky and stuff. Maybe, you know, bragged a little."

"Gotcha," he said, nodding and smiling. "Don't tell me anything I shouldn't know, right?"

"Exactly, yeah, sure. Right, but the thing is, I kinda did tell her some stuff. I didn't, like, actually admit to anything specific, right? But we both knew what I was talking about. And she kept asking more questions and stuff, and buying drinks and I kept talking. Then she starts saying, like maybe she could hire me or get me a job when I finish school and that sounded really great and all. So this afternoon I get this text message from her and she wants to meet with me and talk things over, but she wants to do it not here but in her room which isn't even in this hotel but over across the way at the Omni."

"Hey, tell me something, what does this lady look like?" he asked.

"She's real pretty, kind of exotic looking you know? Like maybe she's part Indian—Indian like from India—and dresses really nice. Suits and stuff. But she's fun too, not all serious. I was kind of flattered she was talking to me since there were like dudes all over her. That's also kinda why I think she might be a fed or something, she wasn't paying no mind to the other guys and people once she heard me say some stuff I shouldn't have."

Chloe could almost see the thoughts and hints clicking into place behind his eyes. According to c1sman, Heidi had passed on the basics of Oliver's warning to the trusted Shmoos and Chloe's description matched the general stats they had for Sandee, or Toni as they were thinking of her. "Interesting," he said. "And so you think she might be a fed, OK, sounds like maybe you should avoid her."

"But she might not be a fed, right? And if she can actually hook me up with a job, that would be awesome. So I want to meet her, but I'm scared to sort of, even though, honestly, I didn't really do half the stuff I sort of hinted to her that I did do. So I was wondering if, like, the feds check in with you guys or whatever and if there was some way you could look up if she was legit?"

"No feds have checked in that I know of," he said. "Not that they usually would unless they were on a panel. Now, you said she's staying over at the Omni, not here?"

"That's what she said, yeah. I'm supposed to go over there and ask for her at the front desk."

"And what did you say her name was?"

"Terri Robinson, she said she's a security consultant of some sort, but that could be anything right?"

"Well, I'm not sure what to tell you. I've got no idea if she's a fed or not, and there are some strange people out there, so if you don't feel comfortable with it, I'd just forget the whole thing. If she's not here actually at the con, I don't think there's much we can do about it."

"I was just hoping someone might know her or something." Chloe was hoping he'd suggest the next move, but he didn't. She wasn't even sure if the thought had occurred to him, so she tried to throw a hint his way. "I'd like to talk to her and be sure, but I'm a little freaked out about seeing her over there by myself." Nothing from him, he just nodded in sympathy. Fine, she'd just ask. "Is there any way maybe you could come over there with me, just to make sure, like, she's not crazy or whatever? Or maybe find out if she's a fed or an undercover reporter or something. Like that woman from Def Con a couple years ago?" A reporter had tried to pose as a hacker and get people attending Def Con to go on record saying or bragging about black hat types of things, but she'd been outed almost at once and in a very public and embarrassing manner that was all over YouTube within hours. Chloe hoped that maybe the allure of outing another such infiltrator might appeal to the man. Just to help matters, she stuck out her chest a little too, and stopped just short of batting her eyelashes at him.

"Hmmm, I don't know what good it would do, but if it'll make you feel more comfortable, I suppose I could come along. Maybe snap a picture of her and see if anyone else on staff recognizes her as a fed." Chloe imagined he was hoping to show the picture to Heidi or Oliver and see if this mystery woman was indeed the same as Oliver's mystery woman. At least that's what she hoped he was hoping.

He used his radio to tell his fellow security staffers that he was going on break, and then the two of them walked the block down the street to the Omni. Chloe kept up an amiable chatter with him as they went, talking about the con and Washington DC and other innocuous topics. She marched him up to the front desk and asked for Terri Robinson. The woman behind the counter returned with an envelope with the name of Chloe's alias, Penny, on it. It contained a room key and a slip of paper with a room number and instructions to come on up. They both agreed that this was pretty weird behavior for a fed or anyone else, but they took the elevator up to the fifth floor and went to the room. Chloe knocked first, but got no answer. She waited, knocked again, then finally used the key card to open the door.

Inside they found a normal looking hotel room with a single king sized bed and a small disposable cell phone sitting in the center of it. Ten seconds after they'd closed the door, it rang. They both stared at it, surprised. It rang three times before he said, "Maybe you should answer it?" She looked nervously at him and picked it up on the fourth ring.

"Hello, Penny," said the voice on the other end, a woman's voice.

"Hi, um, Terri. How are you?"

"Sorry I had to run out for a meeting, but I wanted to talk and it had to be secure, so I left you this phone." Chloe was holding the handset so both of them could lean forward and listen.

"Um, OK," said Chloe, mouthing to him, "This is really weird."

"We talked about you doing some work for us last night, are you still interested?"

"What, um, what kind of work are we talking about?"

"Oh, things like you were talking about last night. The kind of jobs you said…"

Chloe punched the off button and tossed the phone on the bed. "Jesus!"

"What?" he asked, "Why'd you hang up?"

"Are you kidding? This whole set up is weird. I'm getting out of here. You were right. I should have left it alone." She headed for the door and turned back when she saw he wasn't following. He was reaching for the phone. "Leave it!"

"Why?"

"Because she might want it back or she might have it bugged or it might be trapped or who knows what!" Chloe raised the pitch of her voice, almost screeching by the end. "Are you not freaked the fuck out by all this?"

"I guess it's pretty weird," he said, drifting towards the doorway where she stood.

"So she's a fed and it's creepy, or she's not a fed and it's even creepier. Whichever one it's got nothing to do with me anymore. Come on, come on, come on." She reached in and grabbed him by the arm and pulled him back out with her. Then she slammed the door shut, leaving the phone and the room key locked inside on the bed. "We're leaving."

"I really don't think she was any kind of fed," he said as they walked back.

"Why not?"

"Feds don't need to be that sneaky and, well, weird."

"They do if they're trying to entrap you in some sting or something. If they were trying to get me to be all hackery and evil or whatever, then they might be all strange like that."

"Maybe, but I think it's something else. We got word that there was some woman matching your description of this lady who talked to you who's been going to hacker cons and trying to trick people into doing black hat style jobs for her. I'm pretty sure this was her."

"You're serious? Really? What the hell is that all about?"

He told her the whole story, or at least a fourth-hand version of it that got most of the details wrong but still contained the core truth about what had happened with Oliver. If he was telling her that easily, the whole story would be spread throughout the hacker community by the end of the convention. And now they'd added their own little chapter of misdirection to the mix, hopefully giving any curious Shmoos plenty of false leads to chew on. The hotel room they'd rented as a back up three nights earlier in case they needed some place close to stay or retreat to. Sacco had checked in under a false ID and no one but him and Bee had been in since, and she'd only been there long enough to drop off the phone and the key. There was nothing that would lead back to the Crew.

When they got back to the hotel driveway, Chloe thanked him for escorting her and said she was going to go into McDonald's and get something to eat and try and calm down. He said he needed to report in but would be happy to talk with her about it some more later if she was still freaked out. She said she might take him up on that, then went into Mickey D's long enough for him to walk up the driveway. Then she ducked back outside and took the escalator down into the Woodley Park Metro stop and left the hotel and Shmoocon far, far behind her with no plans of ever stepping foot inside again. Hopefully Paul had gotten everyone and everything else out without any difficulty.

Chapter 14

Paul

It was a bad time to bug out. Not the worst possible time, but certainly a bad time. Saturday evening would be a high-traffic period for the hotel lobby, with the last talks wrapping up around 7 PM and people milling about the bar area trying to decide where to go to dinner and which room parties might be fun and whether to take a cab or walk all the way over to the dance club in Adams Morgan that was hosting the Saturday night party. Plus Sandee couldn't help. As soon as Chloe reported back what had happened, Sandee changed into boy clothes, pinned his hair up under a baseball cap, and got the hell out of the hotel. And since Chloe said she needed the Omni room for her scheme, that meant he'd had to go all the way to fall back position two, a Days Inn out in Maryland.

That left Paul and Sacco to try and clear out a room full of computers and other gear without attracting too much attention, since their emergency protocol dictated no one who had had any contact with anyone in the Shmoocon staff could now return to their HQ suite for fear of drawing some unwanted attention or cementing some future connection between them in a hypothetical investigation. So that ruled out Bee, c1sman, and now Chloe, and Sacco only had two hours to help before he had to go back out in the field to oversee tonight's candlelight vigil/protest at Wolverton's fundraiser. The two of them scrambled around the room, stuffing everyone's clothes into whatever suitcase they fit in and trying to pack up electronics gear such that it both wouldn't break and wouldn't attract attention as it traveled through the lobby. All the while Paul kept checking the two laptops that were mirroring the targets' email and phones to make sure nothing unexpected happened. It took them three trips to load up the cars, and he knew that he'd gotten at least one curious look from a hotel staff member even though he used a different exit each time. But they got everything packed up and out the door in under an hour, giving Sacco enough time to get on over to Georgetown.

As he drove towards the Bethesda Days Inn to meet Sandee and wait for Chloe, Paul kept checking the one laptop he had a mobile internet connection for, hoping that nothing transpired that needed his attention. But at this point all the wheels that they'd set in motion were spinning on their own momentum, and most of it he couldn't stop even if he wanted to. He'd followed up the afternoon's dramatic protest with links and tips via e-mail and even a couple of calls to help stir the media plot, and the story was now out there at places like Daily Kos and Firedog Lake, waiting for the papers, cable shows, and networks to start Googling when the night's protests hit the wires. One gang of rowdy, disaffected youth was a minor event. Two obviously coordinated protests in one twelve hour period smacked of pre-mediation, planning, and a bigger story.

And the story wasn't new, it had just largely been ignored by the mainstream media. The U.S. protectorate of the Marianas Islands was a haven for sweat shops and forced labor. Clothing companies with factories there operated outside the reach or interest of U.S. labor laws but still got to print "Made in the USA" on their labels. The owners not only kept their laboring class in slave-like conditions, they often imported them from other countries, trapping them on the island with no support network and no recourse. And working in the factories wasn't the sole dehumanizing endeavor on the island. Many of the women were forced into prostitution in the island's bars and nightclubs, and if some slimeball sex tourist should get one of them pregnant, well, forced abortions were the order of the day. This was horrible news, but it wasn't new news, and it had gone on not just under the noses of Congress, but with their explicit consent and support. While back in the day the defrocked Tom Delay might have been the slavers' main champion, along with felonious lobbyist Jack Abramoff, he was not the only one who'd repeatedly voted against any kind of change or enforcement of decency and humanity in the Marianas. Congressman Wolverton had voted straight down the lobbyist line on the issue too.

Was Wolverton the worst offender? By no means, which was part of why Paul and the Crew had chosen him. The other part was his connection to their real target, lobbyist scumbag Ken Clover. Clover's earmark trading scheme had found a reliable client in Rep. Wolverton, and a lot of those trades had been for votes that included protecting the status of the Marianas as a tropical US forced labor camp. As far as Sacco and Paul could determine, there'd been no direct contributions from any of the Marianas-associated lobbyists and Wolverton. Instead, as their analysis of the e-mails c1sman had hacked free for them confirmed, he'd voted in return for other favors from other Congress critters. Paul doubted that he'd actually even given what was happening on the islands much thought, if indeed he knew about it at all. Wolverton's sin was one of thoughtless, depraved disregard for human life, which made him an asshole. But it didn't make him quite as bad as people like Clover, who knew exactly what they were doing and for whom the Marianas was just one small part of a much larger rap sheet of shame. Thus, Wolverton would be left with a way out, a path to avoid punishment, but only so that the real target's fall would be all the harder when it came on Monday.

Pulling into the hotel parking lot, Paul regretted being forced out of Shmoocon prematurely like this. Now they were farther away from the action and the team had been split, with c1sman having to stay at the con to make sure all traces of their secretly using the con's resources were erased and now to keep tabs on Oliver and whatever shit storm he'd managed to stir up after seeing Sandee. And Paul had been so sure about him. C1sman had pointed him out to them as a good possible recruit, although the two men didn't know each other beyond saying "hi" at cons and irregular exchanges online. They'd done their research on the guy and he seemed ideal—headstrong, disaffected, lonely, mischievous, with more than a couple axes to grind. And Sandee had hooked him in perfectly. Maybe if they'd gotten a chance to really suck him in the way they'd planned, more gradually, he might have worked out, but once he figured out how they'd conned him, he just went ballistic (not that Paul could blame him).

Afterwards, they'd been much more careful with the guy they got instead, the hacker they called Mr. Data. Although the name was almost too geeky for words, it was the guy's own choice and it was an apt description. He tore through data in efficient, sometimes dazzling ways, coming up with nuggets and patterns and hidden files like he had some sixth sense for that shit. He didn't of course—just a good set of algorithms and the know-how to use them. Mr. Data remained isolated from the group, had never met any of them in person and only dealt directly with Paul. They fed him data and cash, which helped with both his gambling debts and his medical bills, and he didn't make any complaints or ask any questions about where the data was coming from. His distance (he was in Germany) meant that he was all the less likely to be in a position to do the Crew any harm. The only real problem was that they had to pay him in Euros.

Paul slung a laptop bag over each shoulder and went through the hotel's back door, up the stairs, and knocked on the door of their new HQ. Sandee, wearing jeans and a sweatshirt and the baseball cap, let him in. "Welcome to our little hidey-hole, one third the size of our last place, as ordered." Two queen sized beds, one half-sized table, and a dresser greeted Paul as he walked in dropping the bags on the bed.

"It's only for a day, two at most," Paul said.

"Plus," said Sandee, "I've called down to the front desk for extra pillows, so, you know, pajama pillow fight is on the agenda."

"Can't wait. But you're not having them…"

"Just waiting for you to arrive, sweetie. I'm going down to the front desk to pick them up right now."

Paul saw that Sandee's laptop was already set up on the dresser and plugged into the hotel's network. He'd thoughtfully left the undersized table for Paul, who occupied it at once, firing up both his computers and using cellular modems to get online and set up a VPN connection to their secure network back in Key West, through which he could monitor the calls, the e-mails, and all the rest. There'd been nothing critical on any front. Danny was still working his ass off on other issues related to the conference committee's approval of the farm bill, but it all seemed like routine politics stuff. Wolverton and Clover were both dark, and for a horrified moment Paul imagined that Clover might be attending the same fundraiser as the Congressman. He checked the GPS locater on the target's phone and saw that he was in a restaurant off Dupont Circle, and nowhere near Georgetown. He sighed with relief and kept unpacking.

Chloe arrived a little over an hour later, reporting success. She'd talked with Bee on the cryptophone on the way over to see what the reaction had been. According to Bee's version of c1sman's account, the security guy had reported the whole story to the rest of the Shmoo group. Heidi had decided that whatever it was, it wasn't Shmoocon's problem and unless the strange woman showed up at a con event, she didn't want to hear about it. The others in the group split between being intrigued by the story and those who thought of it as just one more of those crazy things that sometimes happened at hacker cons. The few who'd been intrigued seemed to have turned their focus towards the

Omni as a source of more clues, and the general theory seemed to be that the whole affair was some kind of botched attempt at a sting by the feds or maybe some media outlet. No one had seen Oliver since he'd spilled his guts to Heidi.

"I think we're out of the woods on that one then," Paul said, after he'd heard Chloe's report.

"I think so, yeah," Chloe agreed. "The only question is, what do we do about Oliver?"

"I'm so sorry about that," Sandee said. "I feel like I blew this whole thing."

"It's not your fault, San," Paul said. "It's really not. We checked as best we could about him being here, and to be honest I'm shocked that he remembered you at all. You look totally different in your reporter outfit."

"I suppose so, but I shouldn't have come back through the lobby. I should have stayed clear of the whole convention area. I know you guys told me that, but I'd lost track of which door to use when and all that. I'm just an island girl at heart, you know. This big-city spycraft business is a little beyond me."

"San, really, don't worry about it. We're cool."

"We're definitely cool," Chloe agreed. "I'm not at all worried about getting caught in the here and now. What I'm worried about is Oliver in the long term. We all screwed up on him, underestimated or over-estimated or mis-underestimated him. Whichever. The point is, he's out there, we know he's smart, and he's got two pieces of the puzzle that is us."

"What are you thinking?" asked Paul. He'd been kind of hoping that Oliver would just disappear from their lives as long as they steered clear of hacker cons in the future. He hadn't imagined that they needed to do anything.

"I don't know, which is why I'm asking. It's a tricky situation, right? I mean, he's out there and he knows Sandee was operating at two different hacker cons, and he thinks she is up to serious no good. He also probably knows Sandee's not alone, since he talked to you on the phone and heard me playing your Columbian wife in the background. All I'm saying is, he's got some puzzle pieces. Not nearly enough to see the big picture. Hell, the picture he's probably trying to put together is nothing at all like reality, but my point is, this isn't something we can safely ignore."

"That all sounds pretty bad when you put it like that," Sandee said, sounding dispirited. "But what can we do?"

"I'm not sure. Maybe try and put some pressure on him. Let him know we've got dirt on him and could take it to the police if he keeps blabbing to people."

"But that's not fair," Sandee said. "I mean, yeah, he's screwed things up for us this time, but only because he did the right thing! I mean, we conned him. We're criminals for Christ's sake. All he did was point out to the authorities, well, the con authorities anyway, that there was a criminal in the building. And you know what, he was right to do it. I'm not down with punishing him for that. That ain't right."

Paul agreed with Sandee. It wasn't right. He felt ashamed for a moment that he'd been ready to go along with Chloe's suggestion of trying to intimidate or scare Oliver off. Living in their world, doing what they did, it was easy to view everyone as part of the game, pieces to be moved around. And yeah, they were part of the game. Paul accepted that, but he tried to play fairly when he could, and in this case, he could. All he had to do was give Chloe a slight nod and she understood that he agreed with Sandee.

"Yeah, OK," Chloe said. "You're right. It would be a shitty thing to do to the poor guy. It's our mistake. We shouldn't make him pay for it."

"Besides," said Paul, "I'm not sure we'd do much good intimidating him. It might make him more interested, not less."

"Oh, I'm pretty sure I could intimidate him. Oliver's smart, but he's also careful and conservative. We've seen how he reacts under pressure now—he caves right in when there's something serious like his job on the line. But you guys are right, let's not find out. Besides, he already blubbered the whole story to everyone on staff. We can't intimidate all of them."

"I'm not sure that's better," said Paul. "That means the pieces are out there for everyone to put together."

"It's not better, no. But Oliver's still the only one who'd be able to recognize Sandee in a line up or put a voice to a face. And this evening I spread enough fear, uncertainty, and doubt that the others will hope-fully start making up their own pieces or working off their own made up pictures or... fuck, I think I broke that metaphor. My point is this: we'll probably be OK. I think. Maybe."

"Either way, we're not going to do anything about it now," Paul said. "And Sacco's candle-light thingy should be coming online in the next hour. You guys ready to watch?"

Chloe and Sandee curled up on one of the beds with a pair of laptops while Paul stayed at the table. This time around the protesters them-selves would be streaming pics and audio onto the Web, a technique

Sacco had introduced to them. All Paul had to do was start exploiting his online sock-puppet personas to direct traffic towards the protesters' sites, and since this time around there (hopefully) wouldn't be any craziness or violence, they could sit back and watch and wait.

The candle-light protest was organized well in advance of almost everything else that had happened this weekend. Conventional wisdom within the protest circles had decided (thanks to Sacco's suggestions) that the afternoon's flash mob assault on the Congressman's house was simply a spin-off splinter group of those who'd been involved in the planning of the more peaceful, evening event. Sacco had worked with several east coast labor rights and anarcho-friendly NGO's to pull the march together. Taking some cues from the anonymous anti-Scientology protests, the whole thing was organized over the Internet, mostly through Craig's List and other free community sites. The protesters came armed with signs and explicit instructions on how not to cross over the line from peaceful demonstration to unlawful gathering.

Paul watched the grainy, night vision enhanced footage as it streamed online. They'd gotten about 200 people together, most of them carrying candles or lanterns or small electric lights. Some were using their cell phones or ipods. They marched in silence, carrying signs similar to those at the earlier protest: END CORPORATE SLAVERY; EMANCIPATE THE MARIANAS; RAPE IS NOT AN AMERICAN VALUE. They had pamphlets they were handing out that explained the whole issue, with citations to mainstream media reporting on the subject and websites to go to for more information. None of them said anything, and many had put tape over their mouths to symbolize the silent suffering of the workers on the islands and their lack of representation in Congress. They marched in single file past the posh Georgetown townhouse, making a block-long circle of light and silent accusation without ever blocking traffic or taking up the whole sidewalk. Tip offs from the NGOs and legitimate groups that had helped organize the protests had brought out TV camera crews from two of the local stations, along with a *Washington Post* reporter and journalists from a few political magazines and websites. Combined with the online streaming video, the protest was sure to get some solid airtime on the local news on what was an otherwise slow Saturday news night.

As the pamphlets explained, inside the townhouse at the epicenter of the march a fundraiser for Rep. Wolverton and several other Republican congressmen was underway. It was a standard Washington D.C. kind of affair, and there were probably two or three others going on that very night within a twenty-block radius. They contrasted the well-dressed, well-fed, wined and dined Congressman and his $500 a plate supporters with the plight of textile industry slaves in the Marianas. It was not a flattering comparison, and the congressman remained holed up in the townhouse until well after the marchers had dispersed of their own accord, which happened to coincide with both 11:30 and the last opportunity for any of the local news teams to run a live feed. One reporter stuck around long enough to get Wolverton's official "no comment" on tape as he ducked into a waiting limo with his wife by his side.

Sacco stumbled into the crowded hotel room after 3 AM, drunk and high and happy as hell, waking up the three of them. As grumpy as that made the rest of them, his enthusiasm was contagious as he recounted the night's events. They all agreed that it was great that the protesters could actually make a difference, even if it took their Crew breaking a bunch of laws and manipulating events behind the scenes to actually make their work pay real world dividends. Paul wondered how the well-meaning, good-hearted civilians who'd gone out on a cold night to march in silence would feel if they knew the truth of their role. He liked to think that if there were any way to let them know what was really going on (and, oh hell, there was no way that could happen), they'd approve.

Paul's hope that the Sunday morning talking head news shows would pick up the story didn't work out, but there were stories in both *The Washington Post* and *The New York Times* as well as mentions on CNN and all the major news blogs. C1sman's Digg bots moved the story up to front-page news there as well. The story was getting some real traction, as Rep. Wolverton, heretofore hardly known at all in national circles, became a much-discussed figure. Especially once bloggers and reporters picked up the threads Paul had laid out connecting him to big time classic scandal names like Jack Abramoff and Tom Delay. Their scandals might be years in the past, but they weren't forgotten by policy wonks and political junkies.

He'd planned to pass on an anonymous tip to Danny for the Congressman, but there wasn't any need. All he was talking about the next morning in both e-mails and on his phone was what to do about the bad press and protesting that it had materialized out of nowhere. As Paul had suspected, Wolverton was only dimly aware of the Marianas situation and what exactly he'd been voting for when he came out against bills and funding for reform. He'd certainly never heard the words "slavery," "prostitution," or "abortion" used in conjunction with his name before and he didn't like it one bit. His initial instinct was to deny, decry, and divert attention from the issue, and Danny started working up some language and strategies to do just that, putting off any official comment from the Congressman's office until Monday morning.

Paul didn't let Danny flounder too long. Using Clover's e-mail, he sent the harried aide an email:

From: Ken.Clover@cloverandassociates.com
To: Daniel@wolvertonforamerica.org
Subject: RE: Referral

Danny,

Couldn't help but notice our boy is having a little trouble in the papers this morning. Never fear though, you're in luck. I've got just the solution to all his bad press, and best of all he doesn't have to do anything but crow about what he's already done.

The procurement on the Farm Bill includes funding for new enforcement measures on labor violations. It calls for direct enforcement of laws on the books that will crack down on abusive labor practices and all that. Just have our friend trumpet his efforts to fight the very abuses these yahoos are yelling about and he should be fine. I'll send you a link to the DOJ site that details the programs the procurement funds.

hope that helps
ken

Danny read the e-mail minutes after it arrived and sent a big thanks to Ken (which Paul deleted). Then he e-mailed the Congressman, telling him all about the great opportunity the earmark in the farm bill offered him. Paul got a kick out of the fact that Danny took full credit for coming up with this strategy, not mentioning Clover, even in passing. The Congressman ordered up a full position paper on the procurement along with a press release and talking points for him to run with come Monday morning.

Holy shit, thought Paul, this shit's really going to work. He had really passed through legislation and conned a United States Congressman into doing his dirty work for him. He wanted to shout for fucking joy, except Sacco and Sandee were passed out on the bed beside his table. Instead, he jumped up, ran over and kissed Chloe on the back of her neck as she leaned over her laptop, headphones on while she read a thread on Daily Kos. She yelped in surprise.

"What?" she laughed. "What's up?"

"This is really, really going to work isn't it?"

"Did you ever doubt it?"

"Every minute of the day."

"Me too, but yeah, I think it just might."

"That's fucking nuts."

"I did the math last night, I'm not entirely sure it wouldn't have been cheaper to pay a lobbyist to just push the earmark through."

"But then we'd be supporting some dirtbag lobbyist, not ruining one's life forever."

"I was more pointing out the irony of it all," she said. "Did you get any sleep at all last night? You were tossing and turning."

"A little maybe."

"Me neither. You know what would perk me right up? A shower," she looked at the clock on her computer. It was 12:42 PM. "Shmoocon's about over, but Bee and c1sman won't be here for hours yet. There's a whole hotel's worth of hot water. Care to join me, Congressman Reynolds?"

"Absolutely Madame Speaker. Absofuckinglutely."

Their clothes were off before the water got hot. Paul came running out a minute later with a wet towel wrapped around him and woke up Sandee, who looked very startled to see a nearly nude and obviously excited Paul. "I need you to watch the e-mails while we're…"

"Fucking in the shower?" Sandee said.

"Come get me if anything exciting happens."

"Oh yeah, the e-mail is where the interesting stuff will be happening I'm sure. Well if you two are going to leave me alone with a snoring anarchist and a keyboard while you have steamy hotel shower sex, fine. But you owe me one serious party when we get back to Key West."

"Deal!" said Paul, pointing him towards the laptop and rushing back into the warm, wet embrace of the bathroom.

Chapter 15

Chloe

Slow to anger, slow to forgive, that's how Chloe liked to think of herself. OK, sometimes she was really quite quick to get pissed off, or annoyed, or irked, but those were just responses to negative stimuli, and she did a good job of never letting those fleeting feelings dictate her actions. But real, honest to God anger, now that was something that could motivate a woman to get some shit done. We're talking the rage of Achilles here; deep, deep anger at how fucked up the world is treating you or someone else. Anger that leads to abolitionist movements, civil rights marches, anti-war protests, and getting out and changing things for the better (OK, yeah, or the worse, but those people weren't just angry, they were angry assholes).

Aside from some very notable and very personal affronts to her and her loved ones, Chloe hadn't ever gotten mad at the great big forces at work in the world that were constantly screwing people over. Railing against the hurricane just wasn't her thing—there was no upside in it, no angle she could see to make a shit's worth of difference. So she had ignored those big picture issues and focused on other things. Then Paul came along and fucked everything up with his Robin Hood fetish and insistence on doing some good with their bad. And, damn him, it worked—she started to care and even enjoy the whole helping the helpless shtick; it made the victories sweeter and the takedowns more satisfying because the fuck being taken down really deserved it. OK, their profit margins were tighter, but it seemed all good.

They added new Crewmembers and racked up some lovely scores

against nasty-ass developers and bankers and the like. Then Isaiah came back into their lives and fucked everything up yet again. Granted, she'd been the one who approached him, but only because it was clear he was up to something big and she couldn't ignore it. It was clear to Chloe at least that Isaiah and whoever else he was working with had bitten off more than they could chew. She'd seen echoes of their activities in the greater Miami area, signs that they'd committed heavily to a zone of operations far from their native New York. She had to admit, she'd been all kinds of curious about what he was up to (Paul said she was obsessed), so when she asked for a face to face meeting to pitch his plot, he'd agreed, and even came down to Key West to do it.

The man could talk. Not just talk, but inspire. And in Chloe and Paul's case, he inspired them to be angry. The target Isaiah had in mind was a multinational conglomerate of agriculture and manufacturing concerns, which sounded dull as dirt. But in fact they were, quite simply, modern day slavers. They oversaw a network of scumbags that formed every link in the chain that brought in penniless illegal workers from places like Mexico and China, set them up in labor camps or locked factories where they worked off their "debt" under unregulated, inhuman conditions. And those were just their operations in the US. Look abroad, to the Caribbean and Africa, and things got much, much worse. Slavery, without even the pretense of calling itself anything else. Isaiah called this Gordian Knot of nastiness The Enemy, since there was no single, easily identifiable corporation that seemed to control it all. Isaiah and his Crew had spent the better part of two years untangling the connections and levers of control until they identified the handful of assholes in charge. Now that he had, now that he was able to lay a bill of charges as long as a dictionary at their feet, now he was ready to move, and he wanted to move on all of them at once.

Isaiah, Marco, and whoever else, were concentrating all their efforts in the tropics, home base to most of what they were going after. But there was one piece on the board safely ensconced in Washington DC, and they needed some help with him. He was a plump prize pig asshole and Isaiah's research would give them a nice head start on taking him down. How they did it was up to them, all he asked in return was that they coordinate the timing with his Crew. Paul and Chloe had taken the night to talk it over with the others, but it hadn't been a hard sell. They all felt ready for something bigger, and Isaiah's speeches (along with the photos and the videos and the rest) had worked their magic and made them angry. They agreed to help, and as the plan unfolded and they decided to attack under the cover of Shmoocon, it ended up that they were the ones determining the timing of today's final blow. And now the time had come, and the ax was falling fast towards a whole mess of heads.

Monday morning Paul had them up and watching the computers early. There was no more street work to be done, no more face-to-face cons to be pulled. Just send the e-mails and tip the dominoes and make sure nothing interfered with the falling, sprawling mess that was about to ensue. Sandee had gone out and, wonder of wonders, brought back both bagels and donuts. He didn't approve of donuts at all, but the rest of them had pounced on them. Sacco was still bleary-eyed but focused, becoming even more-so as the coffee kicked in. Paul was in the sort of trance-like state he would always get when things got complicated and tricky, seeming to look with almost autistic fervor from one screen to the next, constantly shifting views and re-arranging things on the desktops to get a different perspective and maybe tease out some previously unseen opportunity. Chloe wanted to pace, but knew that would drive the others nuts, so she made herself lie on one of the beds and focus her attention on Danny's e-mail mirror on her laptop.

The boy got started early, hitting up his many media contacts and trying to both get a sense of what they were writing about the protests against Rep. Wolverton, and at the same time doing his best to assuage them of any doubts or criticisms they might have. He said off the record over and over again that the Congressman had something to announce that morning that would clear all of this nonsense up and confirm his commitment to a safe, secure, protected and productive American work force. Meanwhile, Paul got in a message from Isaiah that he passed on to the room, "He says they're starting to head into the banks and check cashing places now. Everything went out late last night or early this morning. So tell Jamie and the others we can start, too."

Chloe got up and dug one of the previously unused cryptophones out of her bag and called Jamie down in Key West. He helped run The Party for them, which, of necessity, was no longer running 24/7 but still popped up somewhere every week. Since it wasn't anywhere near noon yet and he answered on the first ring, she assumed he hadn't slept last night. "Hey hot pants," she said. "It's pay day. You and the boys can start cashing those checks. How's Miami?"

"Miami is, as always, too fun for it's own good. But we've got our checks in our hands and a fist full of fake IDs."

"Go get paid, and spend some of it for me," said Chloe, hanging up. She made several follow-up calls to other contacts with other phones, and half an hour later the stopper on the drain of Ken Clover's personal and business bank accounts had been pulled.

The great innovation for businesses, and the people who want to steal from them in this modern era, was the ability to print your own checks. For companies like Clover & Associates that cut a lot of checks to employees, vendors, and sometimes even clients, it just made sense to order thousands of blanks and then print the information as needed. Stealing that information from the company's network had been at the top of their list when they hacked the Clover network, although they already knew the bank account numbers and routing information before that. They'd sent all the data to Isaiah on day one, and since that time he'd been printing and distributing checks all over South Florida. Almost all of the checks were made out to people with some of the most common Hispanic surnames and just a first initial, so there were a lot of J. Hernandez, J. Rodriguez, P. Garcia checks for $2000 being distributed almost at random to day laborers and workers of all stripes. She wasn't sure exactly how Isaiah was getting the checks out, but she knew Sacco had put him in touch with some worker's rights organizers down there and that they were told it was part of a settlement in a class action lawsuit of some kind. That was certainly what Paul had told the Bank of America representatives when posing as Clover's accountant. Thus forewarned, the bank should refrain from putting any holds on the accounts when money started to evacuate from them in a torrent of $2000 drops.

Meanwhile, Chloe and her Crew had siphoned off some of the cash for themselves, which were the checks that Jaimie would be cashing today and would account for another $50,000. All told, the hit would suck about $1.5 million dollars from the accounts, which was as much cash as Clover kept on hand between his personal and business accounts. The wonderful thing about distributing all those checks was that, once they'd been cashed, the money was pretty much untraceable. The people receiving them were the very victims of Clover's clients, people who were probably here illegally and had no bank accounts or even permanent addresses. Once they'd cashed the check at one of the thousands of check cashing places in South Florida, there was no way Clover would be able to recover the money.

His money tied up in stocks, bonds, and real estate was harder for them to get at. They could order some sell-offs electronically, and they were doing just that, but there was a good chance he'd be able to recoup some of his losses or cancel the trades. Maybe. But in the meantime, they would transfer funds to offshore electronic accounts that Isaiah's co-conspirator Marco had set up for them. Chloe wasn't counting on getting that money any time soon, if ever, since Marco would have to move it through a series of Caribbean-based accounts and take his cut before it became cash in her pocket. The important part was that Clover wouldn't have access to it either, and figuring out what the fuck was happening to his money was only one of the problems he would be facing in a few hours.

Just to add a little insult to injury, Paul had come up with the idea of paying off all of Clover's debt as well. Clover & Associates carried mortgages on their offices and several other properties, along with leases for cars, various corporate credit cards, and several lines of credit from companies like caterers, private plane and car services, and even security and legal bills. All of these could be paid electronically, and so they went ahead and did that, costing Clover another couple hundred thousand dollars in the process. He would have a hard time getting those companies to refund the payments just because he didn't actually authorize the money, and it would continue to deplete his ready cash. Plus, it would just piss him off.

Having checked in on all her check cashers and transfers, Chloe got up off the bed and went over to peer over Paul's shoulder. "Danny's been on fire with the damage control," she said. "Any sign that Clover has noticed anything at all is going on?"

"Not yet," Paul said, "But not because people aren't trying to tell him something. He's gotten e-mails and calls from The Enemy down in Florida. Isaiah's bringing the heat down there. According to the messages they're sending, there were a series of break-ins and acts of sabotage across a dozen different agricultural sites and five different industrial sites, and the workers seem to have gone on some sort of general strike. Shit's on fire down there, in some cases literally. They're looking for law enforcement help or something, because the cops they normally buy off are all out of commission—either out of town or on suspension for sudden revelations of misbehavior. Some are just plain missing. Isaiah's Crew is tearing them to pieces and they're freaked the fuck out. I'm not answering calls—just text messages and e-mails. As far as they know, Clover is trapped inside a closed-door Congressional hearing this morning and can't make a call, but he swears he's doing his best to help them. Well, rather, I swear he's helping them."

Chloe whistled and shook her head from side to side. "Isaiah must have a hundred people on this with him. It's so cool it's scary."

"It's also just plain scary," Paul said. "Although I think he's got fewer than that. He's just making it look like he's got a hundred guys. Which, now that I say it out loud, might even be scarier."

"How much do you think he'll make?" Chloe asked. "About three million?"

"I guess. It's hard to say. I know they're taking checks and stealing cash and transferring a lot of money. But yeah, three to five million for them to take away. But probably a couple hundred million in damage to The Enemy, plus jail time or deportation for a lot of 'em."

"Fuckin' hell," said Chloe, blinking a few times to refocus on the task at hand. "OK, so are we ready to feed Danny his next lines?"

"As soon as the strikes and fires and raids hit the AP wires," Paul said, tapping a screen on one of the laptops that showed a news feed. "They did dawn raids in a lot of the camps that Isaiah set up for the feds to take down, so news should be coming soon."

It was 10:30 before the news wires started pumping out the headlines about "ARRESTS MADE IN SE FLORIDA ILLEGAL WORK CAMPS." The stories, as predicted, focused more on the angle that the raided places employed illegal immigrants and framed the story as part of the larger immigration debate. One key difference from the normal version of such stories was that these didn't list how many immigrant workers the feds had rounded up because they hadn't gotten any. All the raids, as per Isaiah's plan, focused on the employers for once.

With these as ammo, Chloe got everything ready to send Danny the tip off he needed to add a little punch to Rep. Wolverton's press conference. She sent the file over to Paul, who composed the final message:

From: Ken.Clover@cloverandassociates.com
To: Daniel@wolvertonforamerica.org
Subject: Ammo

Danny,

Check out the links below. This is exactly what I was talking about last night. The task force in Florida pulling these raids is using funding that the procurement our boy added in will not only continue to provide, but expand. Talk about enhanced surveillance, increased enforcement, securing our nation's vital food supply from terrorist threats, and all the rest. If he runs with this, he runs all the way to free and clear.

K

Attached below were links to the AP stories along with a file containing more information about the Special Labor Enforcement task force that Isaiah was manipulating into being his unwitting weapon.

An hour later, Congressman Wolverton went before the press, and included a live stream of the press conference on his campaign website. Chloe watched with the other three, laughing and yes, she'd admit it, giggling with no small amount of glee as a United States Congressman delivered their talking points almost verbatim. He stood there, smooth, distinguished, and polished with his flat, fatherly Midwestern accent. "Nothing matters more to me than the integrity, power, and freedom that come from decent, patriotic Americans who put in a good hard day's work," he began, sliding into a five minute paen to the non-immigrant laboring class that his union-busting voting record made laughable. This in turn transformed into a short but pointed screed against the "sweat shop tactics" and "inhumane working conditions" in other countries (read China) and how American Workers should never be subjected to such indignities and how "The label Made in the USA inspires pride of workmanship and the promise of freedom to everyone who buys it," whatever that meant.

As expected, the slimeball slid on into typical anti-immigrant bashing that would have made Lou Dobbs proud before moving to the material they'd given him through Danny. "But we don't need new laws, and border fences are expensive and inefficient wastes of resources. Illegals won't come here if there are no jobs, and there won't be any jobs if employers follow the law. That's why I'm proud to be a proponent of increased funding for programs like the Special Labor Enforcement multi-agency task force, a program that just today has made some stunning raids on the kind of vile, exploiting employers who not only drive off American jobs, but also use and abuse the workers they illegally employ. When we improve the value of a man's hard work and treat it with the respect it deserves, we improve all of America. When we arrest those who break the law, those who harbor illegals and flout our national security. When we put those criminals behind bars and leave jobs for law-abiding citizens, then and only then will we be as strong as we can be."

Wolverton went on to praise some of the specific triumphs of law enforcement against factory and industrial farm owners and touted projections from the SLE task force that promised even greater results if they got the full funding they were asking for to not only investigate but also to prosecute law-breaking employers. With his speech and the formal statement on his website that went with it, Wolverton had gone a long way towards both controlling the damage of the weekend's protests and tying himself very much on the record to funding the task force and supporting the arrests that Isaiah had engineered in Florida.

In the Q&A from reporters that followed, Wolverton adeptly brushed aside any references to the weekend protests or to his connection to the Mariana Islands, promising that the new task force would be looking into those issues he was sure. "I'm unaware of the specifics of any such abuses, but these are exactly the sorts of things this task force is designed to end forever, and that's what I support." Only at the end did one question come out that the Congressman didn't seem quite prepared for. It was a question Paul had taken a great deal of time and effort to plant, something from Kal Petersen, a low-level *Washington Post* reporter/blogger who was second or third string covering the House of Representatives and looking for a break.

"Congressman, what about your connections to lobbyist Ken Clover? Were you aware of his connections to the Mariana Islands textile manufacturers or part of his so-called 'earmark market' of votes trading in Congress? Have you ever worked with Mr. Clover?"

To his credit, Wolverton's only sign of dismay was a slight narrowing of the eyes and lips. "I know Mr. Clover, yes, but I'm unaware of whatever it is you're talking about. If you have some specific questions, send them over to my office and we'll get back to you." He looked up at the rest of the audience. "I'm due in a committee meeting now, so I want to thank you all for coming out and if you have any follow-up questions, address them to my office, thanks." The live feed on the website stopped there, cutting off an attempt by Kal Petersen to shout out another question.

It only took ten minutes for the word to get back to Ken Clover that something to do with him was going on, and for the first time their target began to realize that his life was turning to shit. "Wow, he's upset," said Paul, watching the stream of text messages and e-mails flood out of Clover's computer and listening in on his calls. They shunted anything directed at the Congressman or Danny to voice mail. "Really, really fucking upset. He's calling everyone. I don't think we're going to keep a lid on him for long."

"Then let's send Danny the rest now," said Chloe.

"You don't think it'll make him suspicious?" Paul asked.

She knew Paul seldom felt comfortable deviating from the plan unless necessary. "It's plan B for us. We hit him with all of it and keep him thinking about how bad it would be if he weren't so lucky and then hopefully he'll never get around to feeling suspicious about how lucky he is. At least this way he's not already suspicious, which is what he will be if Clover decides he's tired of voice mail and gets up off his butt and walks over to see Wolverton in person."

Paul thought about it for what seemed like a full minute, time she'd learned to give him in these instances. "Yeah, yeah, I see that. OK. Lemme just change a few things in the e-mail." He was already pulling it up, ready to go. "Yeah, this could work. Absolutely."

Ten minutes later he launched the attachment laden info bomb from the e-mail account of one of the assistants in Clover's office, aimed straight at Danny. Posing as a disgruntled employee who'd become disgusted with what his boss was doing and who he was working for, the e-mail laid out everything. It was confidential material taken from the Clover & Associates computers that detailed vote-trading transactions, payments, and connections between Clover and the slavers Isaiah had been hitting, including links to the Marianas groups. It was a lot of data, but Paul had composed a summary cover letter and included a sort of table of contents that Mr. Data had come up with that summarized the most damaging tidbits from each of the attached documents. Paul changed the letter some to incorporate some new material explaining that the assistant had been planning to send the files to contacts in the media, but after seeing Wolverton's courageous stand he thought that the congressman might be able to do some real good with the documents. Just in case though, he would be sending the documents on to the media in six hours no matter what.

The six hours gave Wolverton a final out—one more hoop to jump through. Chloe honestly didn't think it would matter a whole lot if he took their bait or not. Just releasing all that confidential data from the Clover servers would cause the lobbyist an immense amount of trouble for both himself and his clients. But if Wolverton decided to get in front of the coming trouble he could both ensure he was safe from most of the fallout and score some points for himself as a kind of crusader for honest government. In the process it would also go a long way towards sealing Clover's fate even more dramatically. None of his allies in Congress would be able to publicly come to his aid, and even privately they'd be hard pressed to do him any favors. Any association with him would become poisonous, just like any association with Jack Abramoff had been. And while Clover's crimes were more subtle than Abramoff's, he was still potentially radioactive. Just to spur Wolverton on towards making the right decision, the files that Paul sent him had been scrubbed of anything that might incriminate the Congressman himself. The version they'd release to the media on the other hand, would have some more incriminating material in them. Although Paul's e-mail didn't mention this fact, Chloe was betting that the Congressman knew full well how in bed he was with Clover and would probably take the opportunity to jump clear of the sinking ship.

Things went dark for both Wolverton and Danny in the hour that followed. Presumably the two of them and maybe some of the rest of the senior staff were discussing options. Meanwhile Clover was going more and more ballistic. "What the hell is that fucker up to?!?!" he screamed into his phone to one of the other congressmen on Wolverton's committee. No one seemed to know, and since none of his direct calls or e-mails were getting through to the congressman, the lobbyist began to assume that he'd been frozen out in preparation for being thrown under the bus. Meanwhile, representatives from The Enemy down in Florida kept asking for help from Clover as their situation collapsed around them, but he wasn't receiving any of them, making his biggest clients just as angry at him as he was with Wolverton. Chloe reveled in all the anger she'd helped sow between these utter assholes.

At 3:30 they learned about the Congressman's decision. Danny sent an e-mail to Kal Petersen from *The Washington Post*, offering him an exclusive head start. Kal could have the documents and be the one to make them widely available, but Wolverton's name had to be kept out of it. In effect, Danny was becoming a deep-throat style source, never to be revealed. Petersen would have all the evidence he needed to go after Clover and some of his clients with front-page worthy material and plenty of Pulitzer-level follow-ups to come after. Kal took the deal and Danny sent him the documents. That night he would be teasing the story on Countdown with Keith Olbermann and Tuesday morning it would run on the front page.

"He's so fucked," said Chloe. "I mean, we did it right? We fucking won?"

"I really think we did, yeah," said Paul. Clover had gone silent just after 5:00 pm. No e-mails, no phones, nothing. The GPS on his Blackberry showed that he'd gone home early from the office. He seemed like a beaten man. "I think so."

"Name one way we didn't win?" said Sacco, who'd been practically bouncing off the walls for the last hour, he was so excited. "Did we ruin his political connections? Oh yes. Did we steal a shit load of his money and give it to some deserving workers? Hell yes! Is the Washington fucking Post digging into every aspect of his dirty life? My God are they fucking ever! Did Isaiah and those guys take down his biggest fucking client? They took them down in motherfucking flames! How is that not winning?"

"That's winning," said Chloe. "That ain't nothing but winning."

"We should get really drunk," said Sandee, rising to the occasion finally as the victory settled in on him.

"Oh yeah," said Paul. "I'm ready for that."

"We should get out of this city and then get fucking drunk," Chloe said, looking around the stuffy, hot, computer-filled motel room. "Let's pack up and go somewhere nice. Somewhere with silk sheets and hot tubs and room service and private rooms for all of us. Let's get out of this cesspool capital city and spend some hard stolen cash on ourselves. Our work here is fucking done!"

Paul called Bee and c1sman and gave them the all clear. Sandee and Sacco and Chloe started packing shit up. Twenty minutes later they were on the road and headed south, Googling the nicest hotel they could find in Richmond that wasn't named after a Confederate president (Sacco had his standards). They all really did think their work was done.

Interlude

"Hello? May I speak to Ms. Marsh please?"

"Speaking."

"Ms. Marsh? This is, um, this is Ken Clover calling. Mickey Walters gave me your number."

"Yes, Ambassador Walters said you would be getting in contact. How can I help you?"

"Yeah, this is… I'm the Ken Clover from the papers. Here in DC. I'm sure you've seen the news."

"I have. What is it you're hoping I can do for you? I'm not a publicist or the kind of lawyer it sounds like you need."

"I know that. I've got those other guys… I've got a lawyer. I've done nothing wrong. But something very wrong has been done to me. I've been framed, I think. Certainly attacked."

"And you don't wish to go to the police or the FBI?"

"I can't. I mean, I don't think it would be a good idea. A conflict of interest for them, right? I mean, they're already investigating me, they can't also investigate whoever attacked me without maybe me having to tell them some stuff that they could, well, misinterpret. In their zeal, you understand."

"Yes. So you were attacked?"

"Hacked I think. Someone hacked into my bank accounts and issued a couple million dollars worth of checks to a few thousand illegal workers down in Florida."

"Really? How odd. Why would someone do that?"

"I've got no idea. But they did, and took all my cash reserves with them. Both my business and my personal accounts, all gone in the space of twenty-four hours and I never got a word of warning. According to my bank, I told them the checks were going out, warned them to be ready."

"But of course you did no such thing, and with so many different people cashing the checks, tracing down who's responsible will be even more difficult."

"I'm sure whoever did this fucked me... sorry... screwed me in different ways too. There's some weirdness in my stock portfolio and with my credit cards."

"But you're still capable of paying my fees?"

"The money, yeah. They didn't get everything. I've got the second house on Martha's Vineyard if it comes to that. As for the other, well, only if you can help me get out from under this other stuff."

"I assume your recent troubles in the press and in the bank are linked. Who would do this to you?"

"I've no idea. I never saw anything like this coming. It's fu... it's crazy."

"I'll look into it and see what I can do. One of my people will be coming by tomorrow morning first thing to look at your computers. He'll require full, unquestioning access."

"Yeah, yeah, sure. Anything you need."

"All that's left is the matter of my retainer. Once that's settled then I assure you, I'll find whoever did this to you."

"Thank you so much. Thank you."

"You're quite welcome, Mr. Clover."

Chapter 16

Paul

It was soooo good to be home. Back in Key West in early March, where the weather was warm and wonderful and the Spring Break hordes were still a week or two away. They'd stayed over at c1sman's place in Athens for a day, most of which Bee spent trying to convince him to come down to Key West and most of which c1sman spent trying to convince her to come out West to visit his son (the mere thought of which obviously freaked Bee out). Sacco was coming down to the Crew's home base for the very first time, and Sandee's tales of island excess had him fired up and ready for some serious neuron blasting fun. Word had come in from Marco that their share of the money had moved on through all the appropriate hoops and that their cash delivery would be coming in with the next cruise ship to dock at Mallory Square. Even Chloe seemed psyched to be home, judging by the upbeat head bopping as she drove down Highway One towards mile zero listening to some obscure ska band he couldn't remember the name of.

He was still monitoring the e-mails back and forth between Danny, Wolverton, and Clover, although he'd stopped intercepting them and checked in only every couple of hours instead of every few minutes. Not that the Congressman or his staff were having anything to do with Clover, and the lobbyist had in turn given up on trying to contact them. The follow-up stories in *The Post* and then other papers continued to unravel the man's dastardly dealings, airing all kinds of dirty laundry for the world to see. After a few days of constantly sending out e-mails and calls asking for help, Clover had left the city for points unknown, leaving his phone off and not using any of the company machines or e-mail accounts. Paul assumed that he'd figured out that somehow he'd been hacked, which wasn't unexpected. Once he discovered the bank losses and checks it would be the only logical conclusion.

Reading the Congressman's e-mails remained interesting, although there were so many of them, especially from Danny, that he usually only skimmed through them looking for anything relevant. There were a few early on from other lobbyists who were trying to get Wolverton to back off his support of the new task force funding, but the last thing an embattled elected official wanted in this climate was to be branded a flip flopper by his opponents. Since internal polling (which Paul got to see when Danny forwarded it to another aide) showed strong support in the home district for the tough enforcement stance, there was no way he was backing away from it. Paul felt a twinge of guilt that they'd effectively given the Republican a winning re-election issue, but the trade-off was worth it.

Their home by the cemetery looked just like they'd left it—boarded up and locked tight as if another hurricane might come barreling through any minute. Just undoing all the locks and seals on the front door took five minutes and opening all the windows took an hour (which was vital considering how stuffy six weeks being locked up had left the place). Sandee gave Sacco the grand tour while Bee went up into her top floor lair and started firing up their island-wide network of cameras and RFID scanners. By evening Chloe and Paul had restocked the kitchen with food and booze and the whole place was up and running at full capacity. For the first time in months Paul felt calm and safe and relaxed at the same time.

The next night they took Sacco to his first Party. Before they'd embarked on the DC job, The Party had been a 24/7 money-maker for them, but once they'd moved their focus to bigger things, they'd had to cut back to just special occasions, maybe a few times a month. In truth that had been for the better, as the upkeep on a constantly moving 24-hour underground party was pretty high. Now that the events were rarer, it was easier to fill them up with people willing to drop a lot of money and have a crazy good time for a day or two straight. Paul hadn't given much thought to when the next Party would be, but Sandee had apparently given it a lot of thought since he'd been quietly organizing an event for the past week or so. This was Sandee's domain in any case, so if Paul had thought of it he probably would've just asked San to take care of it anyway, but it was a nice surprise to have a real live Key West style bacchanal to celebrate their success.

"This is an empty house?" Sacco asked as they walked up to the front door. "Not what I think of when I think of a squat."

"It is not in any way, shape, or form a squat," said Sandee. He was dressed in full regalia—a tight, black micro-dress, five-inch heels, and a lustrous red auburn wig. "This is a classic Key West home that's languishing in legal limbo, a fine stately home that's proud to play host to some serious enjoyment in these otherwise sad, recession ridden days and nights."

"OK, OK, I stand corrected."

"You can stand, sit, or lie corrected as long as you're having fun," said Sandee, winking at him. "And if anyone asks, tell them you're with me and they'll treat you more than right."

Sacco smiled and nodded, eyes alight with anticipation. Paul glanced over at Chloe and squeezed her hand as they exchanged knowing glances. She was nearly as dressed up as Sandee, wearing black vinyl pants and red and black corset top, along with a platinum blond pageboy cut wig. Paul, who felt reliably ridiculous in anything too costumey, had opted for loose linen pants and a black silk t-shirt. They'd tried to get Bee to come along too, and Sandee almost had her convinced when c1sman called and she decided she'd rather chat with him than come to The Party. She said she'd be watching them on the cameras though, so she'd be there in spirit.

Inside the eighty-year old Victorian style house on the edge of Key West's Old Town, The Party was well under way. Sandee served as hostess and tour guide for Sacco, and Paul and Chloe tagged along to see the sights. The large living room area at the front of the house was the dance floor, with Jaimie spinning records at one end and their old friend and pot dealer Bert at the other. There were about a dozen people in there, a mixture of genders and backgrounds, the music thumping loud enough to make casual conversation impossible. In the dining room/ kitchen area was a sort of lounge space, with pillows and rugs artfully cast about the floor, a four-person hookah in one corner and a video screen with a console and rock band-style simulator set up. The adjacent kitchen had booze, beer, and food for sale with one of Jaimie's friends as bartender. The former rear porch had been enclosed to make a Florida room, where two tables hosted a large-stakes poker game that showed every sign of having been going on for hours upon hours. Upstairs the bedrooms had been converted into more private lounges, each with its own compliment of cushions, carpets, and condoms along with sound and video equipment. Three of the four rooms were occupied by small clusters of people, some simply lounging and drinking, one group singing topless karaoke, and one with two couples engaged in some rather vigorous public sex while a well dressed woman in her 50s wearing an evening gown videoed them.

They ended their circuit tour back in the downstairs lounge area where Sandee produced a bottle of champagne and four glasses. They drank the whole bottle, before Sandee dragged them on the dance floor for an hour of grinding, gyrating, and sweaty shaking. Hot, tired, and damp, they retired upstairs, commandeering a room along with two more bottles. They lounged in the room, reliving their recent triumphs in exaggerated details and working half a bottle of vodka in the process. They laughed and giggled at the cries of excitement and the cracking of a whip from across the hall, then laughed some more as Sandee sang a surprisingly sexy version of Ina Gada Da Vida on the karaoke machine. OK, maybe not sexy, but his movements, mostly directed at Sacco, were definitely sexual. Paul wasn't the only one in the room turned on. He could already see where this was going, and went downstairs just long enough to get some more ice and some treats from Bert. When he returned Chloe and Sandee were singing "I Touch Myself" as a duet, and Sacco had the stupidest grin on his face that Paul had ever seen. After the song ended and the ensuing giggle bout ended in a group collapse to the floor, Chloe took Paul in her arms and kissed him while Sandee sat straddling Sacco next to them.

"I sometimes forget you're not a woman."

"Sometimes I am a woman."

"Oh, Jesus, that feels good."

"Let's give the little man some room to breathe..."

"Oh yeah... do you mind if I..."

"Why else would I be wearing a skirt this short? Please."

"Sandee, you've got an amazing ass. I wish I had your ass."

"And I wish I could have breasts like yours, honey."

"These old things? Hey that's my nipple you're licking mister."

"What're boyfriends for?"

"Oh, fuck."

"My, my, this is nice and hefty. You don't mind do you?"

"Not if you don't mind this..."

"Not at all, honey, not at all. Now can you still reach if I'm down here?"

"Oh. OK, yeah, that works."

"Mmm hmm."

"Oh"

"These vinyl pants are too tight."

"You're just not trying hard enough. There, that's better."

"Free at last."

"Now you're the only one left. Strip on off sailor…"

"Yes ma'am."

"Oh. Oh. Wait, I'm going to…"

"Not yet you're not honey."

"You're amazing."

"Why don't I slip these off and see how you are."

"I've never…"

"But you want to. It's easy. Just do what I do."

"Oh…oh! OK."

"Now you try. Take it out for me."

"I didn't think it would be that smooth and soft. And hard."

"Just like yours."

"So I just… mmp!"

"Just like that."

"Watching them makes you so…"

"And you, too."

"Oh, shit yeah."

"Roll over. Can you still see?"

"Oh yes."

"And now?"

"Uh… uh…"

"Are you watching?"

"Uh… yeah…"

"That's it, baby. You're so sweet honey, so sweet."

"Mmm… ahh… wow, that's wild. I never…"

"Don't stop now, you're a quick little student."

"Yes ma'am. Sir."

"Whichever you desire."

"Oh fuck!"

"Oh damn, baby, oh damn."

"Come on. Up on your knees."

"You first…"

"Yeah, like that. Yeah… like… ahhhh."

"I think we're inspiring them now."

"Why're you stopping me?"

"Oh it's great, honey, you're doing great… but isn't this what you really want."

"My God, yes."

"Come on then. Slip one on and slip in."

"You guys are awesome."

"Fuck him, Sacco, come on…"

"Oh baby, you've got such a filthy mouth."

"You fuckin' love it."

"That's it… easy… ohhhhh shit…"

"Oh fuck. Uh. Uh."

"Slowly now… that's it."

"Jesus, look at them…"

"Now reach around and…"

"Don't fucking stop now…"

"That's it…"

"Jesus!"

"Fuck!"

"Omigod, yes!"

"…"

"Uh…"

"Mmm…"

"Wuh… wuh..eh,eh… wuh… wuh. Oh!"

"Ahhh…"

"Ohhh yeah…"

"Not yet… not yet… ok now! Now!"

"Like… ?"

"Yeah!"

"…"

"…"

"…"

"Holy shit."

Paul came, too, with the something vibrating under his ass. He assumed at first it was a vibrator from the night before. There had been a couple of them floating around. It was only as he began to shake off sleep and look around that he became aware that he was lying nude on top of his pants, Chloe's legs draped across his stomach as she slept perpendicular to him, also nude. He could hear Sacco snoring on the other side of the room, and when he sat up he saw that the guy was curled up around a big pillow. Sandee was nowhere to be seen, which meant it was probably pretty late in the morning. No matter how late the partying went, he was always up early to do yoga.

The phone had stopped buzzing for at least a minute before Paul was awake enough to extract himself from under Chloe's legs without waking her up and then extract the phone from his pants pocket. He'd missed a call from someone anonymous, probably Bee since everyone else but Sandee who knew the number was in the room with him. There was also a text message with a link to a web site. He followed the link to a blog called Thoughtful Insouciance which rang some bells. It was a simple blog, nothing special. Just some guy's rantings. Not just some guy though, it was Oliver. And he wasn't just ranting, he was ranting about Shmoocon. And he wasn't just ranting about Shmoocon, he was ranting about a con woman named Toni and how she was probably connected to another con man who tried to steal money from a bunch of Republican fundraisers a couple years ago in Los Gatos, California. He was ranting about Paul Reynolds.

Chapter 17

Chloe

Paul seemed to take his second outing as a criminal much better than he had the first occasion. No panic attack, no vomiting. No first thing in the morning sex like she'd been drowsily contemplating when his phone started buzzing, but that was OK. She wasn't that horny anymore either. While she re-read the blog post on his phone, Paul had already gone over it two curse-filled times, he was getting dressed and trying to wake up Sacco. The thing that bothered Chloe almost as much as the actual crisis at hand was the fact that Oliver was obviously so damn smart. They knew that of course—that's why they'd tried to recruit him—but for him to take just a few small data points and do all that research and then weave them together into what she hoped sounded to most people like a crazy conspiracy theory but was in fact the truth took some real mental cojones.

Oliver's post was titled "Former Game Designer Paul Reynolds: Black Hat Hacker Mastermind?" OK, so that wasn't quite right, but it might as well have been, and it was a catchy enough title that it was likely to catch the eyes of plenty of curious surfers. She saw the Digg and Reddit links along the side and saw it was already collecting links that would bring it to the front page and thus to the attention of millions within days if not hours. Right below the title was that goofy picture of Paul from his old company's website, looking like a goober. Ugh, that hair. He'd lost weight and filled out some since then, and his hair was shorter and a different color, but he still looked pretty much the same in all the important, identify him in a line-up kind of ways.

Oliver's post scrolled down for inches upon inches of screen real estate. Chloe guessed it was at least 8000 words long. He started off smart, with a lead line designed to keep the reader interested: "Wanted con man and former lead designer of the hit MMORPG *Metropolis 2.0* is linked to a ring of black hat hackers who've been recruiting at conventions for their criminal conspiracy." Not only engaging but entirely true. After that, Oliver went into his own story and told a version that was very much edited down from what he'd spilled to Heidi and the other Shmoo Groupers. In this public version someone named Toni approached him at Toor Con and offered him thousands of dollars to use his ace pen testing skills to hack into a private company's database. He'd of course refused, and the mysterious, beautiful woman disappeared. Then he'd seen her again at Shmoocon last week and of course immediately reported it to the security staff. After that, one of the other attendees reported being approached by the same mysterious woman, who tried to lure the attendee to her hotel room. The attendee brought along a Shmoocon security person, and the mystery woman was spooked and disappeared once again.

Once the con was over, Oliver decided to find out what had really happened. He started scouring the Web for other signs of these con artists, and before long he found them. They'd also been trying to recruit people in certain hacker IRC channels (Chloe laughed at this— it wasn't true, but maybe someone else was), offering high bounties for cracking systems. From there Oliver had used some of his connections from the pen testing profession to get a law enforcement friend of his to pull some of the security tapes from the Shmoocon hotel. This was where Chloe really started cursing. They'd done their best to avoid those cameras, always making sure to keep faces turned away from them when possible. Oliver said he wasn't allowed to look himself, but he'd given his friend a description of Toni and he came back with a couple of stills taken from the tapes. They showed her entering and leaving the hotel, but not any of her interacting with the con attendees. However, one clear shot in the hotel lobby showed her walking almost next to a figure that seemed very familiar to Oliver. He'd taken the still of both Toni and the guy who seemed familiar and run them through facial recognition software and started searching images from across Flikr and Google Image search using some choice key words to narrow the field. After a good long chunk of processing time he'd come up with a match: Paul Reynolds.

Then Oliver went into the whole sordid tale of the disastrous failed con they'd tried to pull in San Jose and the subsequent fall out. He not only tracked down all the media coverage from the time it happened, but then did some follow-up, contacting some of Paul's former co-workers. Although the CEO of Fear and Loading Games, Greg, refused to comment, the CTO Frank was more than happy to rant about what Paul had done, along with "that bitch" who he'd worked with. Oliver made the incorrect assumption that Paul's cohort was the same as the woman he knew as Toni, but that was hardly a comfort. The result was clear: Paul was a con man and generally horrible person who'd attacked Frank and tried to steal millions of dollars from conservative donors.

But what to make of all this? Oliver said he was going public with this information so hackers could be on guard against Paul and Toni and whoever else they were working with. He encouraged everyone to circulate their pictures and the whole story. He also set up a wiki devoted to Hunting Paul Reynolds that could serve as a focal point and central repository for any information anyone discovered about the mystery group. In the meantime, despite whatever personal danger or professional risks he might be taking, Oliver would continue his hunt for these "evil-doers" who were giving the hacking community a bad name.

"Well, that blows," Chloe announced to the room. Paul was on her phone talking to Bee, and Sacco was looking confused and pulling on his pants. "But I don't think it's the end of the world."

"Hold on, Bee," Paul said, covering the phone with his hand before answering. "There's a lot of fucking room between good and the end of the world, and this is definitely on the bad end of the spectrum. But right now I'm trying to convince Bee to not panic over the fact that c1sman's apparently panicking."

Great, thought Chloe, listening as Paul said all the right things to Bee. Sacco stared at her, confused, probably wondering what was going on. Or maybe just because she was stranding in the middle of the room without any clothes on. She explained what was going on while she got dressed and then the three of them headed back home. Bee was upstairs in her lair with Sandee, so the five of them crowded into the sealed, computer-stuffed room to plan strategy. In addition to mismatched monitors showing street scenes from all over Key West courtesy of their secret network of hidden cameras, Bee had thrown up Oliver's blog and then a dozen or so other sites that had linked to it or were discussing it.

"I'm famous again," said Paul, voice even and calm in a bitter kind of way.

"More famous than ever," said Sandee. "I'm sorry Chloe, you were right, we should've done something about Oliver."

"I don't know what we could've done to stop this," she said. "It happened fast and he's obviously got a bug up his ass about the whole damn thing. We would've had to really scare the fuck out of him in a serious way, and you were right, he doesn't deserve that. He hasn't done anything wrong."

"But I do deserve it," said Paul.

"I'm not saying that."

"No, I'm saying that. I do in fact deserve this. It's all true, or at least true enough."

She could sense him slipping into one of his dark moods, but she wasn't at all sure how to pull him out of it.

"Should we go after the site?" Sacco said. "Maybe not hack it, I mean the story's out there. But we could try discrediting it. Throw up some chaff. Maybe release the real details about what Oliver's done that's illegal. Or just make some shit up."

"It's going to be hard to fight truth with lies," said Paul as he scrolled through the comment thread on Digg.

"You've obviously never watched the evening news, then," Sacco countered. "Lies win out all the time. We just need to give them a better story to chew on."

"No, we really don't," said Paul.

"Are you giving up?" Chloe said, although the words didn't come out the way she meant them to.

He looked at her as if she'd accused him of something. "No, I'm being realistic. Think about it for a minute."

"Why don't you just tell me."

"Fine. Look, this doesn't change anything. It's awkward and fucked up and makes me look bad and is probably freaking out my family and old friends, or it will if they ever see it, but fine. Whatever. I haven't been able to talk to them in a couple years anyway, right? It's not like I ever forgot I was wanted on suspicion of kidnapping and felony fraud. I know that. Now a lot of other people know it too, and there's nothing we can do about it."

"Some kind of damage control might be in order," said Chloe, watching him slip into what he called his "slough of despond" right before her eyes. Whenever she got hit with a setback, her first instinct was to hit back.

"It will just make things worse," said Paul. "Listen, think about it, OK? Oliver is right in every detail that matters about me, but wrong on everything that has to do with why we were actually in Washington. We weren't really recruiting people and we weren't really screwing around with anything at Shmoocon besides piggy backing on their network and TOR set up. All this stuff of Oliver's, it's old news. Were we going to recruit new Crewmembers from other hacker cons? Maybe, I guess, but we don't need to. Oliver's drumming up a posse to come after me, but he's looking at where we've been, not where we're going. As long as we stay careful—OK, extra, super careful—and change things up, there won't be any trail for him to follow. It's an internet thing, a flash in the pan. We need to ride it out. We're flush with cash, so let's just take some time and let it all sort itself out."

Chloe nodded. She didn't want to argue with him and thought he was making sense, even if it wasn't what she wanted to do. Except she didn't know what she wanted to do exactly. Better to go with Paul's plan until she actually came up with something better. "OK, that works. I see your point. We'll watch this shit real close, track what happens as best we can, but take no active measures. Everyone good with that?"

She looked around the room. Paul was back to reading the comment thread, but Bee, Sacco, and Sandee all nodded in agreement. They broke the meeting up and went back down into the house, leaving Paul to follow up with c1sman and try and calm him down. Chloe noticed a little weirdness between Sandee and Sacco as they descended the stairs. In the sober light of morning, she imagined Sacco might be having some confused thoughts about the fun he'd had last night, while Sandee had been through this morning after thing often enough (including with Chloe and Paul) to know that he needed to stay friendly and casual but give Sacco his space. She hoped it didn't fuck things up between them. It certainly had been hella hot at the time. Back downstairs she made coffee and then went for a run, hoping that things would return to normal in the next couple days.

It got bad before other things got even worse. The story didn't just fade into obscurity after a few hours on the front page of various social networking news sites. A number of tech news and then some mainstream news sites picked it up, as did most of the video game sites. *Wired* had it too. Paul's face—that same stupid picture—went up all over the place. Then the podcasts of course had to mention it, and Paul and "Toni" became a topic of brief snark and mild curiosity on Buzz Out Loud, TWIT, and of course all the hacker 'casts. Paul listened to every one of them, despite Chloe's encouragement to avoid them. At least they didn't seem to make him any more angry or depressed, although they did a good job at holding his bleak mood at its current level.

Posts went up defending Paul in some of these stories too, and when the details (mostly wrong) about their exploits in San Jose came out, a certain subset started to view him as some kind of hero figure because he was an outlaw who was trying to stick it to the man in some way. Paul didn't like these posts either for whatever reason, but Chloe got kind of a kick out of them. That is until she overheard Sacco repeating some of the Paul-praising pretty much verbatim and forced him to admit that he'd started some of the pro-Paul movement (including, of all things, a fan page on Facebook) himself. "Just don't tell Paul, OK. And stop messing with it. We're just watching." Sacco agreed, but they both knew it didn't matter now: the movement had taken on a life of its own. Someone even started selling t-shirts with a heavily photoshopped version of that damn picture that put a beret on Paul and made him look like Che Guevara on it.

Laying low and watching might have been the smart move, but Chloe soon became desperate for some other form of distraction. Going to The Party was a bad idea according to Paul, who (probably wisely) decided that he shouldn't be seen in public at all for a while unless he was heavily disguised. Towards that end he'd started growing a beard, which was coming in patchy and scratchy and annoying the hell out of her, but she kept her mouth shut about that too. That left sitting around the house and trying to come up with a next move.

There was no obvious next move, though. They'd poured every ounce of everything into pulling off the Clover sting, and there'd been no point in planning much beyond the endgame. In the back of her mind Chloe had pretty much assumed that if things went well with Isaiah, then he'd probably want to partner with them again, which would have been fine with Chloe. But Isaiah was no doubt still wrapping up all the many loose (and sometimes burning) ends from his strike on the slavers, and with Paul in the news wouldn't be terribly inclined to have anything to do with them. Same for Marco and his Crew—they were being good about paying Chloe and the Crew's share, but beyond moving money, Marco claimed to have no leads on future plans or prospects.

Chloe ended up digging out the list of contacts they'd gotten from Winston before everything with him went to hell last year. They'd sent out a few feelers to the nearest and most promising Crews, and even got a few responses back, but they hadn't followed up much once Paul came up with the idea of recruiting new members from hacker cons. Then they'd focused in on going under cover to events and looking for likely candidates. Looking back over the list now, she allowed herself to consider some of the more far-flung options, like a contact name and drop box for someone named Henrik who operated out of Sweden and in Northern Europe in general. Although getting over there might be tough given Paul's wanted status, Chloe was pretty sure they could do it, especially with Marco's help. Maybe an expansion into the Old World was just what they needed—a sort of working vacation. She decided to put together a letter reaching out to him.

The whole process would take months, between sending untraceable letters back and forth and then encrypted messages and then whatever else was needed. Chloe wouldn't let on where she was really operating out of and then Henrik would probably be just as cagey about his situation. There would have to be an exchange of favors to show some good faith like gathering some intel on an American target for them or moving some item through customs or whatever. Establishing that kind of trust where they felt comfortable actually meeting could take a year or more, but it seemed to Chloe like a good use of their down time and it would be something to keep them occupied.

When she'd brought the idea to Paul (as she almost always did before presenting something to the whole group), he'd seemed down on it at first. But then he keyed in on the idea of establishing a base of operations abroad. She wasn't sure she liked the fact that he was so excited about the idea of what amounted to just running away. Then again, if they had to run, they might as well have some goal to run towards instead of just fleeing from the badness. Paul even tore himself away from watching his own infamy unfold online long enough to help her compose the original letter.

Chloe made the drive up to Miami to one of their letter drops. It was a middle-aged woman named Ignacia who served as a kind of underground, off the books Mailboxes Etc. She had extended family all over the United States, and she would send them large care packages filled with cookies and other people's mail, which her relatives would in turn send on from wherever they lived. Thus Chloe could send Henrik a message that, were it traced, would dead end back in Dearborn, Michigan. Likewise, Chloe could receive mail back where the sender was using an address for one of Chloe's aliases that was in Charleston or Austin. She had two such messages, one of which was from an alias she recognized as belonging to Isaiah. It contained nothing but a simple greeting card signed with a pseudonym. That was not a good sign. The only reason Isaiah wouldn't use one of the other secure means of communication they'd established was if he felt they were somehow compromised. Not a good sign at all.

Chapter 18

Paul

Paul had had better days.

OK, better weeks or months even. The feeling was like the horrible, dulling emptiness of loss that comes after a bad breakup with someone you love or, he assumed, when a loved one died. It sucked all the energy out of you, all the verve, and there was nothing you could do about it but lie there and let it wash over you, wash you away, until the nastiness started to recede. It wasn't unusual for Paul to have these memory moments every month or so where he flashed back to some really embarrassing or stupid incident from his life, like the time he'd thought he and Angela Lindel were dating in the 10th grade up until she made it clear they absolutely were not and never had been. Or the time he'd invested all his savings into a joint venture with a flaky partner to start their own comic book line. Or that time he got fired from his own company. These moments would arc across his brain and for just an instant he'd feel all the shame and awkwardness and regret, but then they'd pass just as quickly, he'd say to himself, "Fuck it, that's done and gone," and move on with his day as normal.

This was different because it was like having some of his greatest, most epic failures replaying in front of him in what amounted to slow motion. Websites, forums, and podcasts rehashing his former scandal, and speculating about his current ones. He couldn't just let the moment pass because the moment dragged on and on and on. Chloe said he should stop looking. So did Sandee and Bee and even Sacco. But how could he stop looking? What else was there to look at? There were the worried e-mails from his old friends and particularly his family. He'd never been close with his folks, not since he graduated from high school. But he didn't hate them or dislike them or anything like that. They disagreed on so many fundamental things, from religion to politics to what was funny or interesting, that going home had become a chore. A chore he soon stopped doing after he graduated college. There were phone calls and cards on holidays and birthdays, and his dad would include him on his periodic e-mail blasts to his whole mailing list. When he'd had to drop out of polite society a few years back, he'd sent them a single letter assuring them he was fine and not to believe the stories. Since then, no contact at all.

Giving up on his friends had been much harder. Although his world had largely shrunk down to Greg and the others at Fear and Loading Games while he'd been out in San Jose, he'd still kept in touch with a number of his old high school and college friends, especially guys like Conrad and Shelby and even Rick from the old gaming group. His freshman-year sweetheart and he were on good terms and would talk every month or so about life and love and the rest. But on Chloe's very solid advice he'd cut off all contact with all of them, and it had sucked. They'd all written him concerned e-mails in the wake of his sudden disappearance back in San Jose, and while he'd read them he hadn't been able to respond. He didn't even read their e-mails for months afterwards when he had Bee help him hack the accounts so he could blind forward everything from the mailbox without anyone knowing he was looking in case they were still trying to trace him. They'd been heartbreaking, and he wished he could respond.

The first time around, things had been local news and Web news but not national news. Now, thanks to the frenzied power of new media to actually drive a story into mass consciousness, his infamy had gone national. Tech bloggers from *Wired* and *Engadget* and *Valleywag* were digging up his old friends and family and interviewing them, asking them about what Paul Reynolds was really like and why he might have turned to a life of crime. Even his mother and father went on record with a tech reporter from *The Washington Post*. Paul learned that he'd always been a quiet kid who hated authority and was always getting into trouble. He'd also been a lazy, feckless worker, a pain in the ass to work with, an inattentive boyfriend, and a godless liberal. On the plus side, he'd been a creative genius and amazingly imaginative and either a hugely talented or massively overrated artist. It was like going to group therapy except he didn't get to do anything but listen to other people talk about him.

Sacco tried to assure him that, in retrospect, he'd relish his growing reputation as the new Kevin Mitnick. That might even be true as long as he didn't have to spend as much time in jail as Kevin had. Or any time for that matter. The stuff with the t-shirts and the fan sites was one of the few bright spots in it all, although they kind of irked him too. It wasn't like they were lauding him for the good and cool things he'd actually done. Instead they were just taking what Oliver had made up and running with it, attributing all kinds of interesting crimes and hacks to him. The fact that he had no measurable hacking skills at all made the whole thing all the more ironic.

But in the end, Paul remained confident that the whole thing would blow over, like it had before. In the short and medium run it meant that he'd have to pretty much withdraw entirely from the face to face aspect of any cons they pulled, but that was fine. Chloe and Sacco and Sandee could handle that. Paul had always been more comfortable on the planning side of things anyway. The idea of trying to set up shop somewhere in Europe was especially appealing. Paul had never been across the ocean, and the idea of a whole new continent where he'd committed no crimes and wasn't wanted or famous was pretty appealing. He'd begun spinning ideas around in the back of his mind about the kinds of things they might be capable of pulling off over there. Sacco spoke Spanish and Chloe knew a little French. Maybe he'd start learning Italian or German or hell, Swedish.

He'd been alternating tabs in his browser between a forum thread about him and an article about how Estonia was one of the most wired countries in the world when Chloe got back from Miami with the emergency letter from Isaiah. Or at least they assumed it was an emergency letter. Reading it you'd never guess anything was wrong: "Happy Anniversary, thinking of you and hoping you and yours are well. God Bless. Jake." Isaiah was using an emergency code that they'd established back when things were still in the planning stage. The message meant that somewhere along the line communications had been compromised and the normal ways of talking to each other, including their crypto-phones, couldn't be trusted.

"I went ahead and sent the reply while I was there," Chloe said. "He should have it in a day or two, so I set the meet for three days from now in the Boca Raton location."

"OK," said Paul, re-reading the letter just in case he might have missed something. By using "anniversary" in his message, Isaiah had sent his half of a list of suggested pre-arranged meeting places. Chloe's response had included the word "Love" which, when combined with "anniversary" signaled a Starbucks in Boca Raton. The time was pre-set to 3:00 PM. "Do you think he'll show up?" Paul asked.

"Why wouldn't he?"

"I dunno. Don't you think maybe he's just blowing us off because of all the heat on me? Maybe he's not compromised at all. Maybe he's just assuming we are."

"Could be, I guess, but then why call for a meeting at all? He could just throw away his phone and not respond to e-mails. Cutting each other off isn't hard."

"Maybe you're right. We'll see in three days."

"When we meet up with him…"

"When you meet up with him. I'm not going."

"Don't you want to know what's going on?"

"I do, but I'm not going anywhere I don't have to. You can handle this one. Take Sacco. He should meet Isaiah anyway. I'm going to hide in our little fortress of solicitude here."

"You're sure?"

"Nothing else makes sense."

It didn't take three days before Paul started to suspect that Isaiah was right to have hit the panic button. They'd expected some fallout from their high profile attack on Clover, but they'd covered their traces very well, and there was nothing that could lead back to them. When Sacco had originally put forward the idea of using some of his activist contacts as protesters against Wolverton, Paul had been skeptical about the idea. It was a lot of added moving pieces to put in play, and he'd felt confident he could stir up enough interest just through his online connections. But the others had liked the protest idea, and when was all laid out Paul had to admit it added a powerful punch to their attack. Stories of corruption and faceless labor abuses were one thing, but actual people out there yelling and throwing things and marching by candlelight were rare meat for the sensation-hungry media.

The inevitable consequence, especially of the first, flash mob style protest at the Congressman's home, was that the cops would detain some of their people. For those arrested and held on the day, it was nothing new. They couldn't name or even describe Sacco, because they'd never met him. They'd come because of anonymous postings on Craig's List and other sites, and because they wanted to fight injustice. They paid their fines or clocked their community service hours and maybe spent a few hours in a holding cell. Most of them had been there before. As for the second march, the peaceful one, there'd been a risk of arrest of if the cops freaked out, but Sacco had worked hard with the organizers to make sure that everybody was on their best behavior. They should have been fine.

Except now Sacco was getting reports that they weren't fine. There were three different activist groups that had been involved in organizing the candlelight march, all of them with relatively clean records of legal activism, all of them just getting by on donations, grants, and volunteer hours. In the past week, the federal government had come down on the trio with a combined arms assault. The FBI came by asking questions, the IRS notified them of audits and was threatening their non-profit status, and even INS came calling in search of any illegal aliens. Local city agencies got in on the game too, with OSHA and the DC fire marshal sending over investigators for spot checks on compliance. It was coordinated harassment of the most egregious kind, but the groups' complaints fell on deaf ears as their computers were hauled off to be gone over by FBI computer forensic experts and their books were combed through by forensic accountants.

Of course, the harassment only made the groups more outraged and more committed to their causes. From Paul's reading of public complaints and the private messages that were working their way back to Sacco, many in the groups were feeding on and even reveling in the attention: it confirmed what they already knew to be true. The government was made up of a bunch of fascist fucks who'd rather screw over the poor and helpless than actually do anything about social justice. Sacco shared their outrage, and Paul wasn't unsympathetic, but when the first reports came in he didn't worry about them too much. The assumption was that Congressman Wolverton was flexing his muscles a little and getting some payback. They'd expected some of that, although not to this level. Still, it would pass.

Then, a day later Paul saw in the news that federal investigators had shut down a number of check cashing businesses in the South Florida area. The big chains, like Amscott, managed to avoid being shut down, but a lot of the small businesses didn't have the clout. Their records were seized, their accounts frozen and their owners and clerks taken in for questioning. Paul knew it could only be for one reason: they were trying to follow the checks. One local news story reported that there had been massive check fraud and that the FBI was even going so far as to dust hundreds, possibly thousands of cashed checks for fingerprints. There were dozens of agents dedicated to the task, and as far as Paul could tell, no one in the media was making any connections between the raids in DC on the protesters and the raids on the check cashing places, but Paul felt certain they were connected. Here it seemed that Clover was flexing his muscles, although given all the negative attention he was still getting for his own scandals, Paul was very surprised that he could summon the political will to press for such a large scale crackdown.

The following day came the INS raids on migrant farm workers and day laborers all over the region. Hundreds of agents were sweeping through and rounding up thousands of immigrants, legal and illegal. The news showed school buses full of sad-faced workers being bussed to government owned warehouses for processing. The news and cretins like Lou Dobbs hailed it as a firm, forward step on the road to an illegals-free America, but there were no stated connections to either the check cashing investigation or the DC harassment. But the connection was there, and Paul began to understand why Isaiah might have been panicking a little bit. They thought they'd kneecapped the slavers and their political connections. They'd thought Wolverton and Clover would be too wrapped up in their own problems and commitments to strike back effectively against an enemy they couldn't see or even prove existed.

The morning Chloe and Sacco were planning to drive up to Boca Raton, the three of them met to figure out exactly what their situation was and how bad things were. Paul knew going into it that Sacco was pissed, angry at the way that the government was cracking down on innocents without doing anything about the people he saw as the real villains.

"Isn't there some way we can help them?" he asked.

"I don't see it," said Chloe. "We've flown close enough to that federal sun already—any more attention from them and we'll get burned."

"Right now we're insulated from the trouble," said Paul. "We stay put and they shouldn't be able to trace anything back to us. We try and interfere or do something—and I don't even have any idea what that something might be—and we get screwed."

"Some sort of diversionary tactic," Sacco suggested. "We set up some front group or fake activist cell to take responsibility for it all and draw off the heat. They'll stop detaining innocent workers if they think they've got a name for the enemy they're looking for."

"For it to really fool them it would need to be really convincing, and that would mean really risky," Paul said. "We can ride this out."

"Paul's right," said Chloe. "Let's just wait and see. We shouldn't be doing any serious planning until we hear Isaiah out anyway. Maybe this backlash is a result of some fuck up of his, not ours. Maybe he's already got a plan and wants our help."

"Then we should help him," said Sacco. "Because I don't believe for a minute this isn't at least partly our fault."

"We don't know," Chloe said. "That's my point. Let's find out more and then we'll act, OK?"

"If Isaiah does have a plan, we'll consider it," Paul added, wanting Sacco mollified. In truth, the last thing he wanted right now was to get sucked into another of Isaiah's big plans. He secretly hoped their ally was calling the meeting just to give them the heave-ho. Europe was looking nicer and nicer. "But like Chloe says, let's wait and see."

Sacco seemed satisfied, and Paul saw them to the door. These days he didn't like to step out the front during the day, just in case. You never knew who was looking. They'd activated some new disposable cell phones they'd had clsman ship them from Georgia. He patted his and said, "Call me when you're done."

Chloe gave him a quick goodbye kiss and squeezed his butt. "Will do. Be good."

"You too," he said. "Stay out of the sun." He went back upstairs to check on Bee and see if there was any more bad news. Of course, there was.

Chapter 19

Sacco

Sacco still hadn't decided if he liked Key West or not, but he was glad Chloe and Paul had agreed to let him go on the Boca trip. The island city was cool, sure, but the high concentration of both tourists and the idle rich made his skin itch. If it weren't for the Crew's amazing set up and surveillance network that secretly made fools of all of them, he didn't think he'd be able to handle it. Now granted, the party scene was pretty awesome, especially The Party that Sandee ran. And then there was the whole thing with Sandee. Not the first time a night of excess had led him down that particular path, although he'd never gone quite that far. But that was fun too, and thankfully Sandee was being cool about it and not making a big deal of things. If anything, he was the one kind of being weird about things, but it was kind of a weird situation—he'd never had to live and work with one of his hook ups the next day. He kept having these vivid fucking flashbacks to that night, and not just to him and Sandee, but to Chloe too—she'd been really into watching them, urging them on. And of course he'd thought Chloe was hot since the moment he laid eyes on her, so now that he knew about this side of her personality he wondered what else she might be open to. Looking over at her as she focused hard on the road ahead of them, Sacco just shook his head without even realizing he was doing it. Damn, she was kind of amazing.

"What?" she asked. Of course she'd noticed him staring.

"I was just thinking about how screwed up everything's gotten."

"It seems bad, but we're not sure yet. Let's wait and see what Isaiah has to say."

"No matter what he says, my contacts are getting fucked over by the feds."

"And Paul's wanted all over the internet," Chloe said. "I agree that both these things suck, but neither of them is unprecedented or disastrous. Your friends must be used to and prepared for this kind of fed bullshit."

"They are I guess, as much as anyone can be."

"And Paul's dealt with this wanted shit before too. We'll make it through. There's plenty of cash."

Sacco just nodded. Chloe had spoken and there was no sense debating the point any more right now. She and Paul both were stubborn as hell when they'd made up their mind, especially when they both agreed on something. The Crew was supposed to be one member, one vote, and it was, but he'd never seen anyone vote against Chloe and Paul when they presented a united front. That included him, too. When they agreed on something they seemed so certain, their arguments were so sound, that he'd always ended up voting with them. He never seemed to mind at the time, but he was starting to understand how his former comrades in Hacks of Revolution must have felt when he was the one whose voice always seemed to carry the day.

"Here's the thing about Isaiah," Chloe said, changing the subject. "He's a really serious dude."

"So I gathered."

"I mean, he doesn't like joking around, he doesn't like flippancy, he's all business."

"You're saying I should let you do all the talking."

"No. If I was saying that, I'd just say that. Talk when you want, I'm just telling you how to say it so he'll listen. The only thing I ask is that you hold to the party line on where we're at with Paul's publicity problem."

"It's not a huge deal. It will pass. We're not worried. Even though we totally are."

She glanced over at him. He thought she was pissed but she gave him the slightest upward curve of a smile. "Not totally."

"Why a Starbucks?" Sacco asked as they pulled into the parking lot. "Why not someplace independent?"

"Wasn't my choice," Chloe said as she scanned the parking lot. "Isaiah likes the anonymity of these chain joints. No one notices strangers because they get strangers all the time. A local joint has locals and workers more likely to pay attention to who comes in. Chain joints have higher turnover in staff too, less likely that some employee will still be there to answer question if someone comes asking later. Practicality over politics, Sacco. Gotta learn that shit."

He did know that shit, but sometimes his anti-corporate ethics drove his mouth before his brain could catch up. Slamming Starbucks was second nature, but he was kicking himself for playing into whatever preconceptions Chloe already had about him. They went inside, ordered two large coffees (Sacco refused to say Venti) and took a seat at a corner table. There were only four other people in the place, although a steady stream came in to get their caffeines to go. He assumed that one of the four was with Isaiah, probably one of the two with laptops, but he couldn't be sure. They'd been there almost twenty minutes before Isaiah showed up.

Isaiah slumped into the coffee shop, a tall, well-built African-American man in a wrinkled button down shirt and old jeans. He managed to give off an air of dejected defeat in his posture, pushing his thick-framed glasses up on his nose as he waited in line for his frappucino. Sacco was impressed with his unimpressiveness. When he sat down at the table with them, mumbling a greeting, Sacco could hardly hear him.

"Thank you for coming," he said. "It is urgent."

"What's up?" asked Chloe.

"We seem to have stirred up a hornet's nest and I'm not sure exactly how or where. Our target, The Enemy, is entirely defeated and driven from the field. Their offices are closed, their accounts empty, and many of them are either in jail or missing." The way he said "missing" made Sacco think that Isaiah knew exactly where they were, probably because he'd had them buried. Or maybe not. Hard to know for sure. "We do not believe that there is any way that they could have the financial or political pull to be bringing such concerted pressure to bear."

"OK," said Chloe. "I'll take your word on all of that. But what makes you think there is anyone exerting pull at all? Couldn't this just be the feds' natural reaction to all the shit we stirred up?"

"That no longer seems likely. While the various law enforcement agencies might well be interested on their own, the level of coordination they're displaying indicates some sort of prime mover. So we looked into it. Using some of our labor contacts who ended up being dragooned into helping the feds, we put out some feelers. Several different sources confirmed it for us. There is significant pressure coming down from on high. Someone is calling in favors, demanding fast results, and pushing the attack."

"Any idea who?"

"No, other than that they seem to have Washington connections across many federal agencies."

"So you think it's someone from our end," said Chloe. "Clover or Wolverton."

"That seems the most logical conclusion."

"We agree," said Chloe, much to Sacco's surprise. "Paul's been going over these events too, and it's obvious someone's behind these setbacks. The question is, do we really care? Can we just ride it out under the radar?"

"Paul is nowhere near under the radar right now," Isaiah said, voice low and flat. "He's dangerously exposed and it makes us nervous."

"It's not a big deal," Chloe insisted. "We can handle it."

"I see no evidence of that."

"Paul's handling it very well," Sacco put in. Isaiah's tone was worrying him. "He's keeping out of sight and we're watching things close. Nothing's in danger of coming back on us. This guy, this hacker Oliver, he just made some lucky guesses is all. There's nowhere left for him to run with it. Chloe's right, it's not a huge deal."

"We'll see. And until we see, this has to be our last interaction. There is just too much chaos and unpredictability surrounding your Crew. Until you figure out who's behind this new pressure and how to stop or avoid them, we're not interested. We need to seal ourselves off from you completely."

"I get that," said Chloe. "But it seems like we'd get to the bottom of things if we pooled our resources."

"As I'm trying to make clear, our resource pool is no longer at your disposal."

"You're just giving us the heave ho?" asked Sacco. "That doesn't make any sense. We're in this together, yeah?"

"No, we're not. I've taken losses in the past few days, some of them irreplaceable. I am done taking losses on your behalf, it is as simple as that."

"What about when we do solve it? What then?" Sacco asked. "What if we need your help solving the problem."

"You need to learn to solve problems without us."

"Yeah, but what if you can't solve the problem without us, huh? I mean, we find this problem guy or group or whatever, and maybe we can get out from under them and maybe doing that means throwing them you. What do you think of that plan?" Sacco knew he was letting his anger get the better of him, but he also knew he was right. They had started this together. Not finishing it together was fucking lame-ass bullshit. He did have the good sense not to say that aloud though.

"We'll all do what we have to do," said Isaiah, standing up.

"This line of communication will remain open though, right?" Chloe asked.

Isaiah started to shake his head no but then stopped mid shake. "Yes, alright. This one path, although on my end there will added layers of security so messages may take longer to arrive."

"Same on our end," said Chloe. "If you need us."

"We won't."

"If you do though. You'll know how to find us."

"Which is, I think, the root of your problems," Isaiah said, walking away from them.

"Well, he was kind of a dick," Sacco said as they wove their way through Boca Raton, making sure no one was following them. Sacco'd already used Bee's gadget to check and make sure there weren't any bugs or tracking devices on the borrowed car.

"He's a dick, but he's not wrong," Chloe said.

"I hope I wasn't out of line with him."

"No, you were fine. Said what I was thinking, which was nice, so I got to come off as the cool and collected one for once. Kinda why I brought you along."

Sacco suddenly felt slightly used. "You could've told me the play," he said, trying to keep the resentment out of his voice.

"It wasn't a play. It was just you being you so I didn't have to be me. You made him think twice and we kept our connection to him open, at least a little bit."

"And why aren't we saying 'screw you' right back at him?"

"Because, well, he's big and strong and helpful."

"Sounds like you've got a crush on him."

"I mean his Crew, dumbass."

"I know, I know. Just teasing. Shit. So now we figure out who's behind all the political pressure?"

"That's the plan. Paul should be working away on it right now with clsman and Mr. Data."

"Assuming he's come out of his funk."

"He's not in a funk," said Chloe, and Sacco detected more than a little defensiveness in her tone. "He's just pissed off. Wouldn't you be?"

"I dunno. I don't know that'd I'd really care, or mind. It's certainly doing wonders for his rep."

"Reputations suck, at least if they're public ones and they're for being a criminal. It's going to make things harder for us."

"For you and Paul?"

"For all of us. It's just going to be a pain in the ass. So you're going to have to step up, Sacco. You up to that? We need you to step up now, you and c1sman both probably. Paul can't be doing any of the face to face shit anymore."

"Seems like he's better at the behind the scenes and planning side anyway."

"He is, but that's only because he's so damn good at that side. He's great on the face stuff too. Believe it."

Sacco nodded and they rode in silence for a while. The truth was, although he'd never admit it to anyone else, Paul kind of scared him. Yeah, Sandee could physically beat the shit out of him and most people, and, yeah, Chloe was a tough, ruthless badass when she needed (or just wanted) to be. But Paul had that brooding anger thing going on. Even before this latest round of bullshit came on, he'd always had this quiet, simmering something that threw Sacco off. Maybe it was just the way he sometimes looked right through Sacco, or the way he could finish a sentence and sum up what you were thinking before you'd even figured it out yourself. Maybe it was just the fact that Chloe was so into him, so respectful of him that you just knew there were hidden depths there. Even after that night at The Party where he saw a whole helluva lot of Paul, he didn't feel he knew much more about what made the guy tick.

Whatever. It was what it was. Sacco tried to concentrate on the problem at hand. How to figure out who was behind the attacks on his friends and contacts? And assuming they did find out, what the hell could they do about it? Especially when compared to what the fucking feds could do to them, nothing much came to mind. But he was confident something would come to him. This was what it was all about after all, fighting the fucking Man. And as clichéd as that sounded, it was the truth—it was why he'd gotten into this life with these scary, wonderful, sexy people. He wasn't going to pass up the chance to hit back.

Chapter 20

Sandee

This wasn't a party anymore.

Sandee had never gotten into the... the whatever the hell it was you called his life now... for the money. Or the politics. And certainly not for the crime. It was for the fun, for the thrills, for Chloe and Paul. He'd met them their first week in Key West (he didn't even know they had a roomie named Bee for two months), and the three of them had got on like hot and bothered. What had been crimes for them started out as larks for him. Trick some poor suckers into believing ghosts were real? What a laugh! Foist off fake treasure maps on some cigar-chomping rube from New Jersey? The joke's on him! Set up free housing in empty guest houses for his friends? That wasn't stealing, it was just doing the right thing. And start a party that never ends? A private, exclusive roaming house party where drugs and sex and gambling were not just allowed but encouraged? He'd been breaking all those laws since he was fourteen. Weren't none of that a thug-life style life of crime. That was just getting by in proper Key West Conch Style.

When things started to get heavy, first with that woman getting murdered last year and then with everything that followed, Sandee found himself swept up in it with the rest of them. Sure it was serious, but man, oh, man was it thrilling. The close calls? They only made it more interesting, especially since Chloe and Paul always managed to think their way clear of any problem. And when the traveling started, going off to other cities and pretending to be tough, smart, sexy women for an audience of pussy-hungry nerds, well, that was like Fantasy Fest taken to a whole new, weird level. He hadn't traveled much, nowhere really, beyond Miami and one trip to New York. A couple cruises around the Caribbean. But now he had fake ID's and James Bond gadgets and gullible, googly-eyed men who didn't doubt he was a she for even a moment. It had been grand.

Then there'd been the whole stupid fucking Oliver fiasco, and now The Party was literally over. He watched on the screen in Bee's sanctum as cops and strange men with FBI on the back of their jackets came storming through the Crawford House and started pulling apart everything. Not that there was much to find. The guests were all gone, the once never-ending Party stalled out a couple days back when everyone else in the Crew became obsessed with bigger problems. Sandee'd meant to go back and get the other cameras today at some point, but it was such a chore to do it by himself that he'd been waiting for Bee to come with. A few hours later and they'd have been on those screens, with those nasty, brutish thugs and probably under arrest. He watched as they kicked down another door. They had guns drawn.

"Omigod," said Bee again. "Oh, oh... oh shit."

"Call Paul."

"OK," said Bee, reaching for a phone.

"I'll do it," said Sandee, putting a hand on hers. "PAUL! GET IN HERE!" he shouted down the stairs.

You didn't need to tell him twice, especially as high strung as he was. He heard Paul's steps come thundering up the stairs, taking them two at a time from the sound of it. He fairly slammed into the wall at the top, caroming off and stumbling into Bee's room. "What is it? Chloe?"

Sandee just pointed at the screen and watched awareness and then horror creep across Paul's features. The boy didn't need deeper worry lines, but he was getting them. To his enormous credit, Paul didn't panic, which Sandee thanked God for, because he was pretty close to peeing himself in terror. But Paul's show of strength kept his rising alarm and bladder in check. "We have to get out of here right now."

"They're across town," Sandee pointed out, wincing at how silly it sounded.

"This town is only a mile wide," Paul said. "If they're there, they're coming here. They can trace us through those cameras, right, Bee?"

"Maybe not..." Bee said. "It's wireless and there's the blind."

"Nope. Not good enough. This is it, we're done here."

"Done?" asked Bee clearly wondering if done meant what both she and Sandee thought it meant.

"Bye-bye. We're bugging out. I'll call Chloe and Sacco. You start hitting those kill switches."

"Oh…" said Bee. "Should I warn c1sman?"

Paul, who was almost out the door already, stopped, his back to them as he thought for a minute. "No. Not yet. We'll update him when we're gone. Right now we gotta go. Go!" He rushed downstairs and Chloe heard him yanking the door open to his room.

"Sandee, can you help me?" Bee asked, sounding small and far away.

"Sure, hon, what do you need?"

"My drill."

Bee's realm was always the part of the Party that Sandee understood the least. Not that he was computer illiterate by any means, but that didn't mean he understood how the things worked on the inside. And as for the electronics stuff—the wires and cameras and circuit boards—he'd just never paid any of that much mind at all. That was Bee's thing. So Sandee had never asked about the machine under the table in the corner that was always plugged in and ready to go. It was just one more humming metal box. But when Sandee shot back up the stairs with Bee's drill from the shed outside, he saw that Bee had pulled the thing into the center of the room and was putting something from inside the computer she'd just disassembled on top of it.

"I'm going to degauss these," Bee said. "I need you to then drill some holes in them."

"What?" Sandee asked, more out of reflex than actual confusion.

"The degausser erases the drives and the drill makes sure. Luckily I upgraded to some terabyte drives last month, so we have fewer to get through." Bee removed the hard drive from the degausser and handed it to him. "This one's ready."

Bee started taking apart another of the computers, while Sandee tried to figure out the best places to drill holes with the diamond tipped drill. On the screens the FBI agents were still poking around the empty Party scene, cutting open mattresses and cushions and generally making a mess of the place. Two of the cameras had gone dark. "Can they really trace us back here from there?" Sandee asked.

"I think so, yeah, now that I think about it."

"How long do we have?"

"I'm not sure. Half an hour seems reasonable. Maybe more?" She pulled out another hard drive and started degaussing it, then saw that Sandee hadn't drilled his first hole yet. She came over and showed him just where to drill. The screeching sound made further conversation impossible. A couple minutes later Paul came tumbling back in, his hands full of laptops for them to erase as well.

"We're taking one laptop and the backup drives. All encrypted right?" Paul asked.

"Yep," said Bee, handing him an external drive that she'd pulled out from under a table. "Here it is."

"How long?"

Bee degaussed a third drive as she looked around the room. "Ten minutes maybe?"

"And your go-bag's where?"

"In the closet."

Paul went to the closet and rooted around, pulling out a small black duffel bag. "Sandee, where's yours?"

"My go-bag? I don't have one."

Paul stared at him with a moment's confusion. "Shit, OK, well, I'll throw some of your clothes in a bag for you. We're leaving in fifteen minutes." Then he was out the door again.

"When were we supposed to pack go-bags?" Sandee asked Bee.

"I've had mine since we moved in. Well, since the last time we bugged out I guess."

"You've done this before?"

"Once with Chloe. Well, sort of with Chloe. And once on my own back before. Here, this one's ready to drill."

The repercussions of what was happening began to sink in on Sandee. They were going to leave and not come back. Because if the cops found their way here and already knew about The Party, they would have plenty to go on when they started asking questions. It was a small town, a small island. Everyone in the party scene on Key West knew Sandee—that was how they got such high attendance and spread to word to wealthy out-of-towners. Someone with a drug charge hanging over them would talk. He was going to have to leave or go down in flames. There was some small relief in the idea that most of those people knew him as a woman or at least a drag queen. He never interacted with that crowd in his boy form. But no matter what, that meant the woman Sandee wouldn't be able to live in Key West anymore. His heart sunk deep down, crashing into his stomach and bursting into butterflies. He wanted to cry and scream and hit something, maybe all at once.

Instead he drilled holes in a fucking hard drive and tried not to drill one in his hand.

By the time they finished with the drives, Paul had packed everyone's bags, including Sacco and Chloe's, and the feds had found all the cameras in the Party house. Bee's computers were all down now, but she still had a phone that could tap into her island-wide surveillance network. When she told them that was going down too, Bee was no longer in any doubt that they'd find their way to the house. It was only a matter of time.

Paul stood in the living room, looking around with an intensity just short of wild-eyed. He'd taken the SIM cards out of all the cell phones and Bee had degaussed them before putting them in the microwave on high for a few minutes. "Our fingerprints are all over the place, and I'm pretty sure there's nothing we can do about that, or the DNA, short of burning it down."

"We're not burning it down!" said Sandee. It wasn't even their house, for God's sake. They were renting it from some old gay couple who lived in Boston and couldn't come down anymore since one of them was put in a wheel chair.

"You're right, that would just draw more attention and I'm not sure we could stop it from spreading to the neighbors." Paul said, looking around the room again for the hundredth time. He'd taken the tear gas grenade out of the light fixture and they'd disconnected all the security measures. The last thing they wanted was to fry some fed and add even more reasons for the cops to be after them. "Bee, how long do you think it'll take 'em to get here."

"I'm assuming they'll be able to track down our blind. From there there's not obvious way to find this house in particular, so they're going to have to go door to door. We should take down the antenna though. It's a dead give away, if they know what they're looking for." The blind was a house down the block where they rented out the bottom floor. In the attic was the hub for all their internet access, which was then beamed wirelessly from to an antenna on their roof. Thus there were no wires going into their actual home, aside from electricity.

"Good idea. If they see it they might consider that probable cause," said Paul. "I'll get up there and take that thing down. If they don't have a warrant and no one's home and they've got no probable cause to enter, it could take them hours or even days before they get inside. That's a good head start."

"I'll do it," said Sandee.

"Do what?"

"Take down the antenna. Come on Paul, I know you hate the heights and I can be up and back inside via my bedroom window before you prop the ladder against the wall." Paul was many things, but he was no gymnast. All they needed right now was for him to slip on some loose shingle up on that shitty roof and break a leg.

They agreed that Bee would make one last pass through he house looking for anything vital and Paul would go get the getaway car—a ten year old Honda Civic registered to a dead-end name and paid for in cash, that they kept a couple blocks away. It looked like a junker, but ran like a dream. Sandee looked at the mess Paul had made of his room, at the dresses and wigs strewn about the floor, and sighed. There were probably ten thousand dollars worth of clothes there, and he hated to leave them all behind. He gave the dress he'd been wearing before Sacco stripped it off him one last lingering look before sliding out the window and shimmying up onto the roof. Two or three hours a day of yoga and martial arts combined with the healthiest diet someone who drank as much as he did could manage made it almost as easy as walking. He walked up the slope of the roof towards the peak where the tall antenna was secured about ten feet away from the much taller lightning rod.

As he got to the edge, he looked down and over to see Paul walking as nonchalantly as he could towards the car, one of the duffel bags (presumably the one with all their cash) slung over a shoulder. There was a hidden compartment up under the trunk that was only accessible from beneath the car, which is where he'd probably try and hide the money if they had time. Sandee took the screwdriver from where he'd tucked it at the small of his back and started unscrewing the antenna. Far up and away Sandee heard the faint thrumping of a helicopter in flight. That wasn't unusual of course—tourist and coast guard choppers flew over Key West all the time—but Sandee had seen *Goodfellas*. He looked up and watched as the aircraft made tight, slow circles over old town. That was unusual. That was a bad sign.

He'd gotten the second of the three clamps undone when Paul returned. He'd moved the car, probably somewhere closer, but he wasn't about to pull it up in front of the house, which was good. Sandee waved and hissed, trying to get his attention without drawing anyone else's. Paul finally looked up as he was crossing the street, and Sandee made throat slitting motions and waved him off, pointing up. Paul glanced casually towards the helicopter and kept walking down the street. Sandee worked hard on the final screw, and heard Bee's cell phone ring from downstairs. A minute later she walked out the front door, weighed down with a laptop bag and two duffels, headed in the opposite direction Paul had gone.

The antenna finally came free, and Sandee just tossed it off the roof, hoping against hope that the helicopter hadn't seen him. He slid back down the shingles towards the edge and then flipped down and through the window into his room in one smooth motion. He glanced over at his dresser and froze. Shit. Paul hadn't opened his hidey hole, which made sense, since Paul didn't know about it. Sandee ran over, pushed the dresser aside and used the screwdriver to pry it open. Inside were his extra party favors—an emergency supply of ecstasy, pot, and some coke for those unfortunate nights when Bernie couldn't come through for them and the Party guests were in need. With the hard drives destroyed and the money gone out the door with Paul, there wasn't anything else incriminating in the house, but when the cops found his drug stash, it was enough to lay on a felony distribution charge if they wanted. Sandee snatched the ziplock bags and ran to the bathroom. He started flushing the coke, then the acid, then the pills. There were only a dozen loose joints, which he saved for last. It took five, maybe ten minutes at most, during which time he knew Paul would be freaking out.

He flushed one last time for good measure and only as he was headed down the stairs did he hear the sound of car engines outside. Multiple engines, multiple cars. There weren't any sirens or flashing lights, but he knew what was going on. He looked through the peephole and saw dark haired men in suits that looked quite familiar from the earlier surveillance footage walking up the front porch steps. They knocked on the door with confidence and authority, not quite banging, but not banging either. "Federal agents, open the door!"

Sandee took a deep breath and let it out slowly through his nose, the tip of his tongue touching the roof of his mouth. He took two more breaths before he responded, shutting out the knocking and yelling, if only for a moment. "Who is it?" he called, trying his best to sound butch and tough.

"Federal agents, open the door."

He looked through the peephole again, and could tell they knew he was looking at them. He could probably beat the crap out of both of them before they could draw their weapons, but that wasn't any kind of solution. No, he knew what he needed to say.

"Where's your warrant?"

"We just want to ask some questions."

"Write this number down. It's my lawyer. Ask him any questions you've got and come back when you've got a warrant."

The two men looked at each other in obvious frustration and Sandee smiled, if only for a moment. He'd stymied them, bought the others some time, but that was all. The two men weren't about to give up, although they did retreat from the front door to discuss tactics. One of them made a phone call, while the other ordered his fellow agents to surround the house. There was no doubt in his mind that they'd get their warrant soon enough. Sandee started to go over the details of his story in his mind. The house was watched over by a rental company. The Crew controlled the rental company, and Sandee was a legal employee, with a right to be here. He had his own home apartment in New Town that he never spent time in, but which was his legal residence. He was just the property manager, he'd say. They were good tenants, always paid their rent on time, never caused any trouble. And then last night they'd just up and left, just left a note on the office door with the keys taped to it. He'd come by to look the place over and found the house in its current state. That was the story anyway. It might explain his fingerprints everywhere. It might be enough for his lawyer to work with. There was DNA though—all over all those dresses. He had some time, and hoped that bleach and water would erase the microscopic evidence. It would certainly ruin all his beautiful dresses. He walked upstairs, glad the windows were closed and the blinds drawn. If he had half an hour, it might just be enough time. Then maybe he wouldn't spend the rest of his life in jail. Maybe.

Chapter 21

Paul

Paul was relieved. He felt kind of guilty for feeling relieved, but he was. Not that Sandee had, well, whatever it was that Sandee done. Or had done to him. Arrested probably, although right now he had no way of knowing. But there was no mistaking the fact that the house was surrounded with feds and that Sandee missed the rendezvous at the car. Waiting any longer would've been insane, especially if they decided to close the bridge. Paul and Bee got in the car, the money and the encrypted hard drive hidden in the compartment under the trunk, and headed north. They checked ahead with a friend to make sure there wasn't any kind of blockade, and Paul hunkered down in the back while Bee drove them north. No police or federal attention that either of them noticed, and no sign that anyone was following them. Just in case the feds were sweeping the whole area for cell phone traffic, Paul kept off the phone, even the cryptophone. They might not be able to decrypt it, but the encryption alone would send up alarms. A couple hours later they left the car on Marathon Key and took the getaway boat from there, headed to Miami.

The relief came from finally letting the voice of doom in the back of his mind out of its cage. He'd been sure this moment was coming ever since he'd seen Oliver's blog post, and now that it had come he could ignore the niggling, chewing, nasty Doubt Monster and concentrate on the problem in front of him. Logically the odds of Oliver's post leading to an FBI raid on his house were pretty slim. He and Chloe had gone over those odds again and again, and there was no clear path from one to the other. Or at least no path they'd seen. The path clearly existed though, that much was obvious. Now he just had to get back together with Chloe, make sure she was OK, and move forward from there.

If they'd found the house, then who knows where else they'd found. On the one call that Paul had risked from the cryptophone to Chloe, he'd called an audible and picked a random letter and number out of the air. Using a simple transposition code and a AAA map of Miami both of them had in their cars, it named a map coordinate in Dade county and a time. They'd meet at whichever McDonald's happened to be nearest the center of that map grid at 3:30 the following afternoon. Until then, no contact, no calls, no e-mail, no texts, no nothing. Paul and Bee left the boat at a slip they rented, and took a bus to a motel for the night (fake ID, cash payment). Bee was quiet the whole time, folding in on herself like she usually did when they met some major setback. She knew better than to try to contact c1sman. Paul had sent him the emergency code via e-mail before leaving the house, which should have sent him scurrying offline and hunkering down in his house in Athens.

They killed the next day taking public transportation and slowly making their way to the shitty neighborhood Paul had randomly chosen for their meeting. They scoped out the McDonald's an hour early. As it turned out the only person they saw who approached looking suspicious was Sacco, and that was just because Paul knew he never really read the paper while lounging on the corner. They skipped the McDonald's meet and followed him back to the car where Chloe was waiting.

Chloe gave Paul a love-filled python of a hug, crushing him close. He was so relieved to see her, he could have cried. Then he did, but just a little. Wiping the moisture from his eyes, he kissed her, while Bee and Sacco sort of awkwardly shook hands. Chloe took the wheel and Paul slid in beside her, the other two in the back. There was no secret compartment in this car, but the only thing they had incriminating was a duffel bag with $300,000 in cash and some gold coins in it, which was pretty suspicious if anyone ever saw it, but there was no reason anyone should. They stowed it in the trunk. Driving the speed limit, they headed for the highway.

"Sandee's under arrest, or something like it," Chloe said.

"How do you know?" asked Paul, nervous that the call would be traced.

"Believe it or not, he put it on his MySpace page."

"What?"

"His actual MySpace page. The one under his real name where he keeps in touch with his family and old school friends and stuff."

"The one full of lies," Paul said. He hadn't thought the public page was a very good idea, but Sandee had insisted. If he disappeared from his family and friends, they'd be worried, they'd ask questions. He kept the page up and updated it often enough with believable lies about his life as a pretty boring Key West resident who worked for a property management company and took yoga classes. Nothing about being a drag queen, and certainly nothing about being any kind of anything illegal.

"Yeah, he just put up a brief thing about how some tenants were in trouble and he was being questioned about it and it's all a big misunderstanding, but his lawyer's on the case."

"Man, that might work," Paul said, although he had his doubts. It all depended on what the feds already knew. But at least Sandee had brought in the Key West Condos and Estates lawyer, who only knew Sandee as an upright citizen who occasionally hooked him up with some pot.

"Do you think so, really?" asked Bee from the back.

"Maybe," said Chloe. "I mean, if he's updating his MySpace page from his phone, at least we know he's not being interrogated at Guantanamo or some shit. Hopefully he can stall them until we figure out a way to get him free."

"We're going to get him free?" said Bee.

"Damn straight we are," said Sacco. Paul was surprised but pleased to hear the determination in his voice. "If we have to break him out of jail, we will."

"Hopefully it won't come to that," said Chloe. "First we go check in with c1sman, regroup, and figure out what the fuck just happened. Then we rescue Sandee."

Rescuing Sandee from the feds was way, way beyond anything they'd ever tried to do before, and Paul had not the slightest idea how they could do that. "Absolutely," he said to Bee, looking back over his shoulder. "Abso-fucking-lutely."

Whoever was after them, however they'd found their Key West operations, they didn't seem to know anything about c1sman. After driving straight through from Miami to Athens, the four of them arrived at c1sman's apartment complex, tired and cranky and happy to be out of the car. They dropped Bee off first, letting her make first contact and make sure everything was safe and sound. She signaled that it was, and the rest of them trudged across the parking lot and into the tiny townhouse.

It seemed like it was definitely safe—no signs of law enforcement anywhere—but Paul had his doubts about how sound it was. C1sman was in a mood. And really, even though the last thing he wanted to deal with after the over twelve hours in a car worrying about Sandee was calming the nervous hacker's worries, Paul couldn't blame him. As he kept telling them, this wasn't what he'd signed up for. Bee was supposed to be trying to keep him calm, but she was as tired and burned out as the rest of them and clearly didn't want his shit either. It was Sacco who stepped up, thanking c1sman profusely for letting them crash with him and assuring him that the law wasn't going to come crashing through the door or anything like that. Bee and c1sman retired to his room, while Chloe and Paul set out sleeping bags in the office and Sacco took the lone couch downstairs. If he hadn't been so exhausted Paul's worries would have kept him up, but he managed to get in a solid seven hours before waking up alert and anxious after a dream disturbing enough that he was happy to let it slip from his mind.

Things were calmer the next morning, and by things, he meant c1sman. Bee had filled him in on every detail, and while he was clearly still worried, he also understood how much more worried and upset the rest of them were about Sandee's arrest. He did his best with the role of host, going out early for Krispy Kremes and coffee and buying some air mattresses from WalMart for Chloe and Paul. By noon everyone was ready to concentrate on the task at hand. Paul stood in the center of the living room with a small white board taken from c1sman's office. The others sat perched around him, c1sman, Bee, and Sacco with laptops open and ready.

"So what do we think?" Paul asked. "What the hell happened?"

"Well, I've got one idea," said c1sman, "Although I've been dancing around confirming it because I don't want to fall into the same trap."

"What trap?"

"You know that wiki that Oliver set up about you? Did you look at it a lot?"

"Yeah," said Paul, seeing where c1sman was going. "But I was always running through a TOR proxy. They shouldn't have been able to trace my IP address, right?"

"Not usually no, unless they were able to monitor all the traffic going in and out of the TOR proxy you were using. If they could do that and then had some decent analytics and a really comprehensive look at the traffic going in and out, they might have been able to do it."

"Well, fuck. We saw feds at our door, so the FBI or NSA could do that?"

"I wouldn't be surprised."

"Well, fuck."

"That doesn't explain how they found everything else," Chloe said. "That might lead them to Southwest Florida or even Key West, right? But how did they find the party and then the house so fast?"

"Who knows," said c1sman. "Maybe some other clue we're not thinking of. Maybe just, you know, good police work or whatever."

"The point is," Paul said, "Whatever it is it boils down to the fact that we're dealing with a shit load of law enforcement involvement."

"And that jibes with what Isaiah told me," Chloe said. "He was seeing massive mobilization across state, local, and federal agencies. I think the general consensus is that the pressure's coming down from someone with real pull in Washington. Wolverton or Clover are the most likely culprits there."

"So what do we know about what they're up to?"

"Wolverton's been back to normal as far as we can tell," said Sacco. "The hooks we had into their computers and Blakberries got cleared out during the scheduled security upgrades, pretty much as expected. No sign that they ever realized they were there, but we've lost our monitors on them. The scandal we set up has pretty much passed by. Even the bloggers have let it go and are working on other shit. Now the Clover thing is different. He's basically gone into seclusion in his home in Virginia. Clover and Associates shut down and filed for bankruptcy and there's talk of an investigation working its way through the House. So he seems pretty fucked. The way *The Post* and then *The Times* and *The Wall Street Journal* raked him over the coals—I mean, even the Murdoch Journal, shit—he seems done to me. He hasn't been online, hasn't been on the phone. I wouldn't be surprised if he hangs himself."

"Sounds like you think it's the Congressman," said Chloe.

"He's got the pull, yeah, but we've got no reason to think that he suspects anything. Why would he bring down all that heat, call in all those favors, if he doesn't know something hinky is going on?"

"The obvious answer is that he does think something hinky is going on," replied Chloe. "Maybe it wasn't routine security sweeps that found our hooks, maybe it was some smart Capital Hill IT guy figuring out what was what."

"Maybe," said Sacco. "I suppose. But I don't think he would have sat on the information. This is a guy who never fails to play the victim given half a chance. I've read all his public statements since he came into office, and he's always whining about being persecuted for being white or a Christian or a conservative or a man or whatever. If he found trojans on his computers or phones he'd be blaming every political enemy in sight, especially the protesters and the bloggers who jumped all over him."

"But we don't know, do we. Maybe it was the FBI who found them or the NSA and they're making him keep it quiet for security reasons. We'd have no idea."

Paul couldn't argue with either of their positions. "If it is Wolverton, then there's really not a whole helluva lot we can do about it," he said. "I mean, if it is Wolverton then I think you're both right. He'd be shouting about it if he could, which means either he doesn't know or he knows and the feds are making him keep his mouth shut while they investigate. If that's the case, then they're watching him close and we can't do a thing about it."

"So either way we focus on Clover," said Chloe.

"I just don't see him having the pull anymore," Sacco countered. "He's done."

"He's down but not out," Chloe said. "But maybe this is some death throes thing."

"Or maybe we'll find he's still got some leverage on Wolverton that he's using to force him to help," said Paul. "I think he's the best place to start no matter what. We saved all the files we pulled down from his servers before we bugged out. Let' go through it all again and see if we can find anything at all. And start sniffing around him some more too see if we can get any inkling of what he's up to now."

"But carefully," said clsman. "Carefully. Nothing that leads back here."

"Absolutely. Carefully. But fast as we can. We've got to find some lever, something we can use to help Sandee, OK? Remember, the most important thing right now is getting him out."

Paul and Chloe had decided they had to cut Mr. Data out of the loop. They didn't think he was a leak, and their contact with him had been sequestered from all their other activities, so even if he was, it would have only been awful and not devastating. But he was still out of their direct control and thus just too risky. It was a shame because his data-fu would've come in handy at the moment, but it's not like the rest of them were idiots. They divided the Cloverfield files into five chunks and each of them started plowing through them. Then everybody switched chunks and started going over the files again just to make sure nobody missed anything. It took the rest of that day and most of the next, and at times felt as promising as panning for gold in a swimming pool, but then c1sman made the connection.

On her go through, Chloe had highlighted some phone numbers that appeared in e-mails but not in any of Clover's phone records. It was c1sman who had the idea of going through the records again and searching for numbers that were similar enough to be multiple lines going to the same home, office, or set of cell phones. And there was the match, a number one digit off from the number given in the e-mail Chloe had found. Paul re-read the e-mail, which was a note from a fellow lobbyist giving the contact information for "the person I was telling you about last night." At first blush Paul suspected it might be for an escort service or something like that, especially when c1sman started digging around and found that both numbers were unlisted. That wasn't going to stop him of course, and it was easy enough to discover that they in fact belonged to an offshore holding company, which told them nothing more than that they were an intriguing lead.

Looking at the timing on Clover's e-mails and phone records, there was no immediately obvious connection between the timing of the call and anything else. He'd called the number only once, and that was a day and a half before he went offline completely. But it was close enough to cause and effect that Paul went back through the e-mails from those last two days, looking closer at messages before and after the call. There was a difference. Before, Clover had been in emergency damage control mode, sending mail to everyone on his contact list looking for help and getting very little in response. After the call, most of his e-mails were either him dealing with responses from those original inquiries (none of which offered him much hope) or wrapping up other business matters by handing clients off to other lobbyists or lawyers. He'd pretty much stopped asking new people for help, although he did send out feelers when friends and allies asked if there was anything they could do (although when he came up with something they could do, they all found some way to say "sorry, I wish I could but I can't"). But it struck Paul that Clover was just going through the motions with these later e-mails. The stridency and urgency was gone, and his replies to those denials were sharper and even sometimes venomous than someone who really expected help would send. From one point of view they could be read as the writings of a bitter, angry man who'd lost hope, but Paul thought there was more to it than that. To him they seemed like they were from a bitter, angry man who'd already settled on a course of action and was just calling out "old friends" in a way that revealed how little they actually valued the supposed friendship. He was seeing who would stand by him in a fight, and it turned out to be nobody, or at least not anybody who was in a position to actually help him.

That number, and whoever was lurking on the other end, seemed to be the only piece that they couldn't place. Paul laid out his theory, and the others agreed, although he wasn't sure if it was because he'd actually been convincing or if it was because there simply weren't any other leads. It was a Washington DC exchange, and it was a cell phone registered to a International Business Company in Belize, meaning it was a shell corporation. Unless they went down to Belize and raided the IBC registry's files, that was a dead end. All that was left to do was call the number. Chloe, Bee, and Sacco ended up driving to Charleston, SC to make the call, taking along a tricked out laptop to record everything and buying a disposable cell phone once they got to town. They had to assume the phone was monitored and had a trap on the line. The number rang and went straight to a generic voice mail. They didn't leave a message and dropped the phone in the ocean before driving back. They tried again with another phone the next day from Raleigh and then the following day from Asheville. Same thing every time. Whoever it was, it seemed like they were only picking up when they knew the number, which wasn't really a surprise, but they'd been hoping for some voice or message at the other end that would give them a clue to work with.

When the traveling phone crew returned empty handed, they met again to discuss options. From Paul's point of view, there really weren't many. The number was their only lead, but they had no way of getting more info about it unless they hacked phone company records and got some GPS data on where the phone was being used, but c1sman assured them that was basically impossible. That left only one way of finding out who was on the other end of that phone, and thus (hopefully) who it was that was bringing all the pressure to bear on them: Clover himself.

Paul admitted from the outset that it had to be one of his crazier schemes. Chloe said it was definitely ballsy and probably insane. Sacco loved it. C1sman hated it. Bee voted for it. Chloe shook her head and smiled. "What the fuck else are we gonna do?"

Chapter 22

Chloe

Chloe missed having Paul by her side. Sure, he was in her ear on the other end of a phone that was less than a mile away, but that wasn't the same as having him right there next to her. For them, this kind of thing had become easy. They had an almost telepathic rapport and could riff and improv off each other without pausing to think. Together they'd been feuding married couples, hare-brained business partners, wild-eyed meth-dealers, suave business consultants, grizzled treasure hunters, and multiple variations on the theme of expert con artists. Paul had the imagination and the ability before they'd met, and she'd brought out his repressed wild abandon and helped hone his fast talk chops after they got together. And while this newest gambit came straight from that amazing fevered mind of his, he couldn't play one of the two key roles. She looked over at Sacco, who had cleaned up nice. Intellectually, Chloe knew he was up to it, but she wasn't really comfortable with him. Not that she would let him know that.

"You clean up nice," she said. They were driving a rented Mercedes along the winding, artificially picturesque streets of a Virginia bedroom community that was home to hundreds of wealthy DC commuters. Sacco wore a new, perfectly tailored Italian suit and had shaved his usual stubble into a pencil thin mustache that floated above his pursed lips. His hair was moussed back in a Gordon Gekko inspired look, shiny black and just a little wavy. With the subtle but expensive gold cross around his neck, the Rolex on his wrist, and the diamonds on his cuff links, there wasn't a sign of his inner, anarchic true self on display.

"You're too kind," he said, with a mild, indeterminable European accent that could be Spanish or Italian or something more exotic. Sacco called it his Euro-mutt voice. "And you, my dear, are looking as lovely as ever."

"Why thank you, Bernard," she said, rhyming his cover name with "herd" instead of "hard" as he preferred. She respected him for keeping in character, but it was another thing she and Paul never did. They fed off the energy of jumping right in at the last possible second. She and Paul would also keep going over their cover story again and again until that last second, but rehashing the plan only seemed to make Sacco more anxious, so she kept biting her tongue on that too. She had decided to go with a dress instead of suit. It was a business dress though, nothing with ridiculous cleavage or showing too much leg, but the blue fabric clung to hips and breast just enough to be flattering. She'd accented with black pearl earrings and a silk scarf that complimented her ridiculously expensive shoes. They aimed to present as representatives of powerful business interests, and she thought they passed remarkably well. But these were exactly the kind of people that Wolverton had dealt with all his professional life, and he would probably notice any mistakes they made. So the key was to not make any mistakes. Hah.

They pulled up into the driveway that matched the house number. They'd gotten lost a couple of times back here, but c1sman had made them all paranoid about how there could be someone at NSA or wherever tracking any GPS device that was using Clover's house as a destination and so, even though Chloe wasn't entirely convinced that was possible, let alone likely, they'd used good old-fashioned maps and pens instead of Google and GPS to figure out where they were going. As they pulled into the empty driveway of the multi-million dollar cookie-cutter McMansion that looked just like the ones to either side, Chloe took a breath in through her nose, the tip of her tongue on the roof of her mouth, and then slowly let it out. She waited for Sacco to get out and come around and open the door for her, taking two more breaths in the process, before grabbing her briefcase and stepping out of the car and into Maria Lanier.

Sacco let Chloe lead the way towards the front door, a frosted and beveled glass affair that was one of the structure's few distinct features. She pushed the doorbell and waited. She could see a shadowy figure moving in the foyer beyond, but whoever it was didn't come all the way to the door until the second time she pressed the button. "Who's there?" he called out from inside.

"Mr. Clover?" Chloe said, using a flat, all business accent that could've been polished at any top-tier MBA program in the country.

"Who's there?" the voice repeated, undeniable annoyed.

"My name is Maria Lanier and I'm here with my associate—"

"No reporters, solicitors, or evangelists." It was hard to hear him through the glass.

"We're none of those, sir. We'd like just a moment of your time."

"I don't know you," he said, and the shadowy figure started to recede back into the house.

"It's about what happened to you," Chloe not quite shouted. "We know you were hacked. We know you were conned."

The shadow grew close again. "You cops should be talking to my lawyer. You know better than this."

"We're not law enforcement, Mr. Clover. We're fellow victims. We work out of Florida. And the Caribbean."

The shadow stood there, his hand on the doorknob. Chloe let him sort through what she'd said on his own schedule, and he came to the right decision. He opened the door and looked out at her, face painted with skepticism. The real live Ken Clover looked good for someone whose life was falling apart. He wore a golf shirt and khakis, his feet were bare, his face tan and healthy. He was probably twenty pounds overweight, but he carried it well. His dark hair was graying at the temples and well-groomed, his gold-rimmed glasses the perfect size for his face. But he did look very tired, and there was no hiding the bags under his eyes or the drooping at the corners of his mouth.

"Who are you again?" he asked.

"Maria Lanier, and this is my associate, Mr.—"

"I heard that part. I meant who are you? Who are you with? What do you do?"

"We're consultants. Consultants for, among other companies, PWS Agricultural and Kore Construction, limited." These were names they'd gotten from the original briefing files that Isaiah had sent them when they were still in the planning stages. Both companies provided labor and management for their clients, and by labor they meant slaves and by management they meant guards. They were part of the extended Enemy empire and had been among the hardest hit in Isaiah's attack.

"I don't recognize your names," Clover said.

"We're recently promoted. I worked out of Miami and Mr. Orozco here is from our European office."

"How do you do," said Sacco. The accent sounded just right to Chloe; all that practice paying off.

Clover just nodded at him and fixed his eyes on Chloe again, not saying anything but clearly expecting more. "If you'll allow me," said Chloe, holding up her briefcase, "I have letters of reference from some of my partners who you are more familiar with. I realize you are involved in your own difficulties and may not have heard, but our organization has suffered some rather traumatic setbacks in the past month and many of our top-level executives are either indisposed at the hands of the U.S. government or are out of the country and entirely unavailable."

He thought over what she said and then stood aside, ushering them in. "Alright, let's see what you've got."

Only two groups of people could know everything that Chloe laid out on Clover's kitchen table as evidence of her identity: the real slavers or the people who'd conned them. Their whole plan counted on him never believing his enemies would be crazy, stupid, or daring enough to come see him face to face like this. Between his own records stolen from his server and the data they had from Isaiah, the Crew had been able to piece together the most important (or at least most often used) connections between Clover and his slaver clients. With both of them under heavy and public investigation, the odds of them continuing to contact one another by anything other than in-person proxy were pretty slim, or at least that's what Paul reasoned and what all of them were counting on.

"So what's the story with you guys?" he asked, once he'd gone over each piece of false evidence with diligence and care. "I'll admit, I've been distracted."

"It has been very bad," Sacco said, taking the cue he was waiting for. "Almost our entire Caribbean-centered operation lies in tatters and there is grave concern at home that these troubles will make their way across the Atlantic as well. At first we supposed it was some unfortunate combination of over-zealous, under-bribed law enforcement and Norte Americano incompetence and security lapses…"

"Which turns out to have been a faulty assumption," Chloe interjected, pretending some measure of pride in her alleged employers. "Our security measures met all the agreed upon parameters."

"And these parameters proved insufficient. As Maria says, it was not entirely their fault. The protocols were set up to protect our interests from a certain type of interference and attack. Governments, competitors, and so forth, you see? But this attack, this attack it comes from a direction unexpected. It comes from criminals, anarchists."

This revelation didn't seem to surprise Clover. "Yeah, I know."

"You do?" asks Chloe, feigning surprise. Well, maybe not entirely feigning. It was good confirmation about their assumptions that he was behind the attacks on their Crew, or at least in touch with those who were. "What do you know about them?"

"You show your cards first. Then I'll share."

Sacco shrugged as if it were no big deal and continued. "So, not the usual incompetence, but some criminal threat we never suspected. Nor, I think, that you ever suspected either, no? Otherwise you would not be so badly in shape as you seem to be, I think. Like you, our operations on this side of the ocean are all but extinct."

"We're not dead yet," Chloe said.

"Dying, then."

"Not dying either. But we're not good."

Clover gave a wan smile. "I know how that feels. What the hell happened to you all exactly anyway?"

"It was a multi-front attack," Chloe explained and then shot Sacco a dark look. "Totally unprecedented. There was a mass protest among core groups of workers spread out across a dozen different clients. Protesters and activists we can handle, of course, but we'd never seen it on this scale and with this kind of timing."

"Still, nothing you shouldn't have been able to handle," Sacco said.

"Nothing we couldn't have handled, I assure you, except that we suffered a massive communications breakdown across our entire network. Cell phones, landlines, and internet access all went down within hours, sometimes minutes of each other. Our clients couldn't contact us and we were focusing on our own problems and so remained unaware…"

"Tragically unaware," Sacco said with a sneer. "Tell him of the errand boy's radio."

Chloe shook her head, showing both annoyance at Sacco and sadness at her own tale. "It wasn't until one of our junior analysts was driving back with lunch for the office and listening to the radio that we learned three of our biggest clients had been arrested by the FBI, charged with harboring illegal aliens and violating anti-terrorism statutes. I should say that even the cable television in our office and in our homes had been shut off."

"Quite embarrassing, no?"

"Sounds pretty shitty," said Clover.

"From there things went from bad to worse. Workers on many of the farms set fire to offices and equipment, seized private computers and files, and made their contents public. Light industrial facilities were vandalized, managers attacked and in some cases beaten. Police coming to investigate found nothing but evidence they could use against the owners, the workers having fled the scene."

"And then those politicians we pay people like you to keep in our pockets," Sacco said, turning his gaze on Clover, "They took our difficulties as an excuse to solve their own political problems. This of course only made matters worse. More arrests, bigger investigations, public embarrassment. And the worst is yet to come. There will be the filing of more charges, the cutting of deals and the spilling of information. If there's any left to spill."

"He means the encrypted files. They were encrypted anyway, but someone got the passwords, and a whole lot of information that never should have seen the light of day suddenly is. There are names and account data in there that... well, like Mr. Orozco said, it's going to get worse."

Clover sighed and leaned back in his chair, biting his upper lip. "And I really am sorry for you folks, I am. I got caught up in the same web of shit, as you probably know. These are some bad fellas that came after me, and I'm doing what I can, I assure you."

"And what do you know about them?" Sacco asked. "Do you know who it is that attacked you?"

"Hackers. My whole company got hacked. They fucked over my private accounts and paid out checks to a bunch of illegals down your way in Florida. I'm having to get a divorce just so some of my assets will be protected by being only in my wife's name. It's not good. Especially if they do end up filing charges on me."

"But you have found a way to strike back at these people, have you not?" asked Sacco with a knowing smile.

"What makes you think that?"

"There have been signs. We are not inactive. We seek to strike back at those who have attacked us. We notice that there are federal agencies investigating others besides us—check cashing businesses, illegal immigrants, and so on. We see signs of pressure from on high, pressure we're not able to currently bring. But perhaps you are?"

"Perhaps, perhaps," Clover said, trying to hide a smile that was lighting up his eyes.

"You see, Maria! Did I not tell you as much? This man is not yet beaten."

"Mr. Orozco holds you in high esteem, Mr. Clover," Chloe said. "It was his suggestion that we come here."

"Well, I'm not sure I deserve all his praise, but I'm even less sure why you came here. Whatever it is I might be doing, I have to tell you, I'm doing it for me. I have to save my own skin."

"And we want to help you do just that!" Sacco said. "What's good for you is good for us. This has always been true, yes?"

"What Mr. Orozco is saying, is that we would like to try and pool our resources. You obviously know some facts about who's behind our mutual troubles that we do not. Likewise, we have information about the groups responsible for attacking us that you might not be aware of. I'm sure there's some connection there. If we share data, we both benefit."

"Possibly, possibly. I'll have to think about it. Why don't you give me what you got and I'll see if there's any connections I can see."

"Oh, come, come," Sacco purred. "This is not how business is done. We must both benefit."

"You can't fault me for asking. But I've got someone working for me on this you know, and they're not cheap. I paid good money for what I got, and if you want it, well, I might be willing to sell it to you for a fair price."

"This is not why we're here," said Sacco. "We're not here to pay you for information. Are you so blind you cannot see what is in your best interests?" Chloe wasn't sure that was the right tone to take with Clover. She in fact might have been perfectly happy to pay him, if the information was right and would lead them to what they needed to get Sandee out from under whatever charges were being laid on him. But Sacco, or at least Orozco, was on a roll. "Let us put aside petty concerns over money and think about the best strategy for all of us."

"My money concerns aren't any kind of petty," Clover said, and it was clear he was both angry and unafraid of letting them know it. "And I have put some real information out there for you and haven't heard anything but moaning and groaning from you. So you already owe me something by my calculation and I'm being up front with you. I need money. That's what I need strategically. And I've got plenty more to sell. My contact can help you, I'm sure, but you're going to have to go through me."

"What contact is this?" Sacco said, almost audibly scoffing. "I would be surprised if anyone was taking your calls, your face is so much in the papers."

"Like the lady said, I'm not dead yet. I have an ace up my sleeve."

"And who is this ace, then?"

"I told you, you want to use my contact, you have to go through me."

Sacco glanced over at Chloe for some sort of signal. She hoped Clover didn't think that was strange, given they'd gone in trying to sell this idea of Orozco being the sexist, dominant jerk that Clover could identify with. Whatever the case, Chloe felt pretty sure that Clover had tipped his hand on one crucial point—he was down to one single contact that was charging him an a shit load of cash but was getting results and there was no way he was going to give up that person's identity. Chloe didn't look at Sacco, but pressed forward with the play she'd decided to make and hoped Sacco would follow along like Paul would have.

"We could arrange to make a payment through you, of course," said Chloe. "That's a familiar arrangement for us. And naturally we'd mask the source of the funds, as always."

"Assuming you can produce the kinds of results that warrant such payments," Sacco added. Good, he was saying the right things.

"Oh, you'll get results. My contact gets results, for sure," Clover said, and Chloe could see him start to relax, no doubt seeing a way out of whatever financial hole he'd found himself in. Correction, that they'd put him in. If they did end up paying him, it would be with some of his own money. "I can get you the full file for $150,000. And I'm sure you'll want to have some follow-up from there. You let me know, and I'll price it with my contact."

"Can you give us the file now?" Chloe asked.

"You have $150,000 in your briefcase?"

"We could get it here in under an hour."

"You can have until tomorrow, and I don't want cash. I don't keep anything here, no computers, no files. There are too many search warrants with this address on them. No, you give me a number where I can reach you and I'll arrange to have someone make the exchange."

"Surely your phones are tapped," said Sacco, almost forgetting his accent.

"Maybe, but not when it comes to talking to my lawyers. You won't be paying me, you'll be hiring one of them."

"And they'll credit your account," said Chloe. Smart move.

"My accounts with my lawyers are complicated, I assure you. But you'll find them more than worth their fees. Sound good?"

Chloe looked to Sacco as if asking him to confirm the deal. He did. The three of them exchanged pleasantries, the mood much more convivial now that a mutually beneficial arrangement had been struck. Chloe glanced at the cordless phone on the kitchen wall and sighed with relief as she allowed herself to be shown to the door without having to make any unusual requests to use the bathroom or get a drink of water or, God forbid, make a call because her cell battery was dead. Thankfully the Clover home was like 82% of American homes when it came to its choice of home hand sets. She and Sacco drove off in the Mercedes, not even glancing towards the white plumbing van parked one street over with Paul and Bee in it.

Chapter 23

Paul

Paul was thankful that Clover was being pretty paranoid but not very smart about it. He'd given up using his cell phone apparently, having perhaps figured out it was hacked or warned off using it by whoever told him to stop going online. So he was using his landline, knowing that legally the government couldn't eavesdrop on his conversations with his lawyer. Of course this was the new golden age of illegal wiretapping, so Paul wasn't sure why he was so confident about his security, but perhaps all he was worried about was what they could use in court. His "landline" was only on the land up to the base station of his cordless phone. From there, it was broadcast through the air, and although the phone probably had a pretty sticker on it that claimed to be in the 5.8 Ghz spectrum (which was hard to scan without special gear), the base station's signal was sill in the 900 MHz range (which Bee, her scanner, and her large antenna could scan with relative ease). He waited all of three minutes after Chloe and Sacco left to make the call.

Bee would be able to figure out the number he was dialing from the sound of the tones that went flying by from his speed dial. Paul pressed the headphones close to his ears and he strained to hear every nuance of the static-laden signal. "Marsh, Dutton, and Hermann, how may I direct your call?" said a crisp, professional young man's voice.

"This is Ken Clover calling."

The receptionist or whoever paused for just a moment before replying. "Just a moment, Mr. Clover," he said, then put them on hold. Paul listened to Vivaldi for over a minute, wondering if perhaps this delay was designed to time out any feds listening in. Paul suspected that was just something from the movies though. He'd have to look it up. Either way, it was interesting that the receptionist knew just who Clover wanted to talk to without him saying.

"Ken, how are you?" a woman suddenly said in Paul's ear. She sounded older, with a friendly, almost motherly tone to her voice.

"I'm doing OK, Emily, I'm doing OK."

"I didn't know we had a phone conference scheduled."

"We don't, and I'm sorry for calling without an appointment, but there's been a development. I think I might have a referral for you."

"We're not taking new clients right now, Ken, I'm so sorry. I can give you some names if you'd like."

"No, no, I know that. It's not like that. These are people that are sort of connected with my case. Similar interests."

"Why don't you come by and you can tell me more about them. Let's see here, how about Thursday at 7 AM?"

"I'll be there."

"Wonderful. It's always a pleasure, Ken."

"Thanks, Emily. I really appreciate it."

By the time Paul had taken off the headphones, Bee had already pulled up Marsh, Dutton, and Hermann on Google. The biggest surprise was that the law firm didn't have a website at all. They were listed in various directories and mentioned in some other sites, but they had a very low exposure level. All Paul could learn from his quick scan was that they were a Washington DC based law firm with offices in Georgetown. There wasn't even any indicator as to what kinds of law they specialized in, although the few other places where their name came up were all related to political matters rather than lawsuits. On a hunch, Paul checked with a database for registered lobbyists and found all three of the named partners listed there, although there was no indication who their clients might be or even what kinds of issues they specialized in. He already knew that this firm was not the same one that was actually defending Clover against all the charges filed against him. That was one of the national mega-firms based out of New York. This was going to require more research.

They waited another half-hour to see if Clover was going to make any more calls, but he didn't, so Paul climbed up front and drove them back to the rendezvous point with Chloe and Sacco. The four of them made the long drive back to their base of operations up in the DC area. This time they were, unfortunately, all the way over in Baltimore, where Sacco had lined them up an empty apartment where some friends of his, who were doing aid work down in Ecuador right now, normally lived. It was kind of a dump in the way that hippified group homes often are, but it was a clean, secure, and untraceable dump that had neighbors whose wi-fi c1sman could hack, and that's what they needed. Any hotel they were likely to find that was quiet and secure enough was on the system somewhere, and they couldn't trust any of their fake-name credit lines or identities now that the Key West house had been blown. Even the van and the old Corolla they were using had been bought with cash using fake IDs in South Carolina, and they were paranoid enough that they'd destroyed those IDs once they'd driven the used vehicles off the lot.

Once they were back at the Baltimore base, they filled in c1sman on what they'd learned and then everyone started digging into this Emily Marsh person any way they could think. Chloe even went out and bought a new disposable phone, drove into DC, and pretended to be a reporter doing a story on lobbyists who wanted to interview her, but she never got past the receptionist's firm "Ms. Marsh doesn't do interviews." Not, apparently, even on deep background. Sacco suggested calling his DC area activist contacts, but those were the very people who were under heavy investigation, probably thanks to Marsh, so they decided any contact with them was too great a risk. That left hard core online searching, but even that didn't reveal much that they could do a lot with. That night they met around the house's third-hand wooden dinner table to assess their newly revealed foe.

"Emily Marsh, age 54, lobbyist and lawyer." said Paul from one end of the table. "What' the deal here?"

"The deal is," said Sacco. "We have no idea what the deal is. She's a registered lobbyist, but her only registered clients are other lobbyists. No direct ties to any corporate or policy groups, but plenty of money coming in from practically every firm on K Street. Including, of course, our friend Kenny-boy Clover. They're also a law firm, but we couldn't find any record of them representing anyone in any legal cases or any public records filings that we could dig up. In essence, she knows lots and lots of powerful people and they pay her firm money, but she doesn't have any firm positions or history of serving particular interests that I can see. Going through all the forms they file reporting their lobbying stuff is dense shit, and I can't be sure I'm reading it right though. But my general take is that it's a bunch of bureaucratic hand waving to cover up whatever it is she really."

Paul nodded and turned to Bee. "Yeah, OK. So, I went through the public records and stuff for her, you know finances and whatever. She owns a house with her husband in Georgetown, worth well over a million dollars, although they've lived there for 14 years, so I think the appraisal is, you know, low. She has great credit as you might imagine. Her husband doesn't seem to do much of anything as far as I can tell. No job record for him in forever, but he used to be a lawyer too. He's no longer a member of the bar. There are two kids, Milo who's 24 and attends Columbia for grad school in philosophy and Melinda who's 19 and is at UCLA in her freshman year. They own three cars, all of them Mercedes of different types. No criminal anything on them, not even parking tickets. No lawsuits filed against them. They sorta seem like a rich, white family and that's all."

Bee looked over at c1sman, who was fiddling with something on his laptop. She nudged him with an elbow. "Yeah, I know, hold on. I had an idea while you were… damn, never mind." He looked up. "OK, well, there's not much to say really. No corporate website or anything like that. It took me forever to even turn up an e-mail address. The mail server's beyond secure as far as I can tell from poking around a little. I could poke more, but I think it'd be useless. If you want to read her e-mail, you're going to have to get her to open up a trojan or something, and even then their system might sniff it out before it ever got to her. So that's that. And there's no home internet connection at all as far as I can tell. Maybe they're using some cellular wireless service or something, but nothing going into the house that I could find. I do have both her kids' e-mails though. They were easy. I gave them to Chloe."

Chloe nodded, "I looked through them. Nothing much there. Nothing at all about Emily Marsh. Neither of them e-mails their parents or talks about them much with their friends. Milo is pretentious and well-read and really likes latina-porn. Melinda spends a lot of time on Facebook and has a wicked music downloading habit, but again, nothing out of the ordinary. Both have a lot of friends but neither has a significant other. Neither seem to have been back home since Christmas. My attempt to call their mom at the office got me nowhere. It's by appointment only and you can only make an appointment if you either have a personal recommendation from another client or Ms. Marsh has invited you to do so personally. The Dutton and Hermann who're also on the firm name are both retired. Marsh joined the firm back in 1982 and was made partner in 1991. The others retired in 2000. I get the impression from reading between the lines in some of the minuscule coverage that she might have forced them out. Whatever, they're both off fishing or whatever. So she's the only one in the firm, aside from associates and aides and what not. Total of fifteen people working there."

"So, what do we think?" Paul asked the table. "Follow Clover to the meeting and make sure that we just spent all this time researching the right person. I guess there's an outside possibility that she's just a go-between for him and someone else, but I doubt it."

"I think that's right," said Chloe. "We follow him and we have a camera or someone waiting near her office—which is only five blocks from her home by the way—to confirm it. But then what? She's got no weaknesses that we can see, and I at least am certain she's got powerful friends."

Paul let out a breath and thought it over for a moment. Marsh was not, as far as they could tell, a criminal of any kind. That didn't matter to him in the least—she was behind the assault on their Key West home and Sandee's arrest, or at least he was pretty sure she was. Theoretically, then, she might hold the key to getting Sandee free. But with no obvious vices, secure phones and computers, and unknown but probably vast resources at her disposal, there was no obvious way to get any leverage on her. "Yeah, I got nothing," he said at last. "Let's do the follow her around thing and then see where things go from there. Maybe some obvious weakness will present itself. Or fuck, even some non-obvious one."

They started planning for the surveillance, and had everything ready bright and early the day of Clover's meeting. They had to, since they were operating out of Baltimore and had to get going before 4:00 AM to ensure they beat the DC area traffic and had their teams set up at both ends. Paul and Sacco took the van this time, while Chloe and Bee set up cameras outside Marsh's home and office back in the city. There were no surprises from Clover, and it didn't look like he'd noticed he was being followed. Once he parked in Georgetown, they took the opportunity of his car being on the street to plant a GPS device on it. He went in, had his meeting, and walked down the street to have some food at a nearby restaurant. Two hours later, they followed him home again, then fought their way back through traffic to meet up that night back in the Baltimore house.

"Well," said Chloe. "Everything went as planned, but there are a few wrinkles. Marsh walks to work, which is expected, but she's not alone. She walks her dog in the morning and then has her assistant or maid or housekeeper take it back home. I didn't catch them at first, but Bee spotted them when she walked back home for lunch. She's got at least two bodyguards that are doing a good job of keeping low key and at a distance. They were replaced by another pair in the evening when she came home. I'm betting three shifts total, 24-hour protection. That's expensive, so I'm betting it's not a normal thing for her, but rather a new precaution brought on by, well, us. So that means they're not bored with routine and used to no trouble. They're fucking looking for trouble. We took the cameras back rather than leaving them overnight like we'd planned because I was afraid they'd find them. That makes any thought of getting in the house or the office physically a lot more of a pain in the ass."

"Things just get worse and worse," said Paul, his frustration slowly slipping towards a kind of fatalism that would do no one any good.

"Maybe we just forget this whole thing," said c1sman. "I mean, listen, I've been following Sandee's blog like all of us, but I've been reading up on the charges. They really have no evidence and he's out on bail under house arrest. Maybe the whole thing will blow over if we give it time."

"Come on, man," said Sacco, "You know better than that. We both know hackers who the feds held for years without any real charges. It's what the fucking feds do. I'm honestly surprised Sandee's not already locked up somewhere."

"We have a good lawyer down there," Chloe said. "But Sandee's gonna run out of money to pay him soon, and he's under so much scrutiny I don't know how to get him more."

"My guess," said Paul "is that the only reason he's out at all is as a trap for us. They're hoping to lure us into making contact or making some other mistake. But actually I think c1sman maybe has a point." Chloe gave him a curious look. "Not about giving up exactly, but about giving up on Marsh. At least directly."

She nodded. "You're thinking Clover. We have plenty of leverage on him."

Paul smiled. "Hey, it worked once, I don't see why it won't work again. I mean the first thing, before anything else, is we need to figure out a way to find out everything Marsh actually knows about us and what kind of strings she's actually pulling. We need to know what we're actually up against. And if she and Clover are in it together, which they obviously are, then he's got to have some sort of in with her. We push through the door that way."

"I get what you're saying," said Chloe, "But I'm not sure I want to test my and Sacco's aliases against her security. Fooling lonely Ken Clover was one thing. This woman's something else entirely."

"I agree, on our own it'd be tough. But she must trust Kenny-boy, at least on some level. He's her trusted client. So we just need to fool him into fooling her for us. Get us in the door and show us her cards. It's not a solution, I know, but it's a step forward."

"And you have a plan on how to do this?"

Paul looked at c1sman. "I've got the beginnings of one. First we need to get c1sman a suit."

Chapter 24

clsman

The collar on his shirt was too tight, but that was probably his fault for refusing to try it on before buying it. He thought he had a 15 inch neck but apparently it was more like 16. Maybe he'd been putting on weight since he joined the Crew. His calorie intake had certainly risen, if only from the added energy drink consumption. And all that sugar couldn't be good for him. He slipped his finger into his shirt and tugged at it again and then came upon a perfect solution. He could undo the top button and relieve the pressure but keep his tie cinched up tight and no one would ever notice because the undone button would be behind the knot. He glanced over to make sure Bee wasn't looking—she was staring out the bus window as Georgetown passed by—and released his pinched neck from its agony. He sighed with relief, but then started to regret the change—now he was out of distractions to keep his fore brain occupied and so had to start worrying about, well, everything else.

His suit was blue and, he thought, looked pretty good. He hadn't owned one since high school. Chloe said it looked "appropriately off the rack," which he thought was meant to convey the idea that he was a man that didn't know or care a whole lot about fashion. That at least was true. He couldn't tell the difference between a good and a bad suit except that the ones in the weird colors were probably bad. His was dark blue, and heavy, almost like a suit of armor. If he balled his hands into fists and flexed his wrists, they disappeared into the coat sleeves, which made him look like some sort of robot. Bee told him to stop doing that.

Bee was wearing a suit as well, and he thought she looked even better. It was gray with pinstripes and she had on a yellow silk blouse underneath. She seemed even less comfortable in hers than he did in his and kept fidgeting and pulling on things. Unfortunately for her, there were no buttons she could undo to relieve whatever pressure she was feeling except ones that would make her indecent. He thought briefly about unbuttoning them himself later and wondered if that would be OK. When they were alone he could never tell when it was and when it wasn't anymore, especially not since Key West.

"Your suit doesn't fit either?" he asked.

She turned from the window and smiled. "No, it's not that. I just wish I had a bug on me. And a stun gun. And a hidden camera. Nothing but this stupid phone and clean laptop."

"Really? Why?" Chris had been relieved when Paul and Chloe had said that they weren't going to take any of the spy gadgets in because they didn't want to risk any kind of exposure, so there would be no listening devices hidden on their persons so the others could listen in from outside. "I think it's good that they won't hear me make an idiot of myself," he said, trying to make the truth sound like a joke.

"First of all, we're not going to make idiots of ourselves. Second of all, the whole point is that if we did make idiots of ourselves and they were listening in they could say something to help. But now they can't, so it's all on us."

Chris just nodded and looked past Bee out the window. All on them. That was what he really hated. But Paul couldn't do it for obvious reasons. Chloe and Sacco were already playing their parts. Sandee was… gone. That left him and Bee, the two people least skilled at whatever this was. Acting. Social Engineering. Lying.

They rode the rest of the way in silence, getting off in the center of Georgetown and walking the four blocks to Marsh's office. It was in an old looking building sandwiched between two other, nearly identical, brick and wrought iron old buildings. He'd never been to an office like it. It was like somebody's house or something. He double-checked the piece of paper with the address on it, but it was the right place. When he heard "office" he pictured glass and aluminum and cubicles and fluorescent lights shining down on crowded conference rooms. Inside this place it was quiet, thick carpet and wood paneled walls and a good-looking guy in a suit behind the front desk. They gave their names— fake names, he was John Cooper—and waited on the leather couch for five minutes before being ushered into a meeting room. More heavy wood and thick carpet, with thickly cushioned wheeled leather chairs. At least there was something he recognized—a large screen on one wall and an HD projector hanging from the ceiling. There was a USB port hub in the center of the table. The receptionist told him to go ahead and set up his presentation and that the others would be in shortly.

Chris couldn't help himself. As he plugged in his laptop he decided to take a peep around the network. There wasn't any wireless. The USB hub was only connected to the projector, nothing else. No snooping for him. He fiddled with getting his clean laptop working with the projector and brought up his power point slides. Neither he nor Bee said anything until they came in.

Emily Marsh looked like a man. No, that was his brain getting ahead of him again. This wasn't Emily Marsh, it was someone else. He was a younger guy, maybe around Chris' own age. He wasn't wearing a suit, just a button-downed shirt and black pants. He had long, frizzy red hair tied back in a pony tail and wore little round glasses. "Hello," he said, bearing straight down on Chris with his hand extended and a smile on his face, "I'm Roger Fitzpatrick."

"Oh, shit," slipped out past his lips before Chris could stop it. "Wow, hey, nice to meet you. I've read your stuff. I'm John Cooper."

"Great to meet you, John," said Roger. Chris knew him of course. Well, not personally. But he'd seen his talks at Black Hat and Def Con and he'd read his columns and articles. He was, in hacker circles anyway, pretty famous. He was known for his no-nonsense, call it like he saw it attitude and a particular fondness for going after the hacker community's sacred cows and preconceived notions of what's right and what isn't. His Black Hat talk from two years ago, "Why Microsoft Rules" was incredibly controversial but, once you ignored all the politics and bullshit, was in fact pretty smart. The question was, why was Roger Fitzpatrick in this room with him?

"I'm Trisha Kim," Bee said. "Nice to meet you." Chris was a little surprised at how completely different she sounded—quite clearly chipper and excited, neither of which had been true about her for days.

"So, Emily handed this meeting over to me. I'm a consultant for her on these kinds of things."

"I thought you were with Keller, Wilson?" Chris asked. It was one of those big security firms that did everything from info sec to hired bodyguards and private intelligence contractors.

"Left about six months ago and set up my own shop as a private consultant," he said, taking a seat and motioning for them to do the same.

"So, Emily tells me you guys are selling some sort of security service?"

Chris covered his rapidly rising panic by turning away from Roger and needlessly adjusting his laptop. His first instinct was that this was a disaster. They'd thought they would be giving a pitch to Marsh herself, who probably wasn't any kind of tech savvy person as far as they could tell. He'd been prepared to just steamroll over her with technical terms, impressing her with the apparent breadth and depth of his knowledge while Bee translated his techno-babble into sales talk. That had been the plan. But Roger would see through any bullshit right away. Roger knew his shit, cold. Oh Christ.

"It's OK," Bee whispered in his ear. "Do the presentation as written, it will be fine. Trust me."

"We could just—"

"Trust me." Bee turned to Roger and started the pitch, sounding just like every marketing person Chris had ever ignored when he was in the corporate world. He started punching through the slides in time with her words. According to Bee's story, they were a sort of start-up, a network of exploit hunters and hackers who'd met while selling exploits to Bountysploit for cash. They'd started to team up to maximize returns and discovered that there was even more money to be made as a team. They weren't incorporated as such, and liked to refer to themselves as The Post-Hoc Posse. Originally it was because they'd come in after a new software release and scour it for zero days and security holes, often claiming bounties within days, sometimes even hours.

"That's the background," said Bee. "But in the past four months we've created a new alliance called Propter Hoc. She pointed to a symbol with a cool logo of some sort of black-hat wearing spy that Paul had come up with. "This is a new service we're offering that specializes in preemptive or aggressive network defense. What we've learned over the past few years is that many times multiple attacks on a network can all be traced back to a single source. Look at what happened in Estonia. A single source practically took down a whole country's network. How was that lone, angry Russian able to do that? He had a bot net army the size of the 101st Airborne Division. But we've come up with a way to strike back. How? We've gone and recruited out own army. I'll let John explain."

Chris took a breath and retracted his sweaty left fist up into his coat. "Thanks, Trisha." He moved to the next slide, a complicated diagram showing links between dozens of systems and computers. "We call our covert army of battle bots Legion. Like most botnets, it runs hidden in the background of thousands of computers all over the world. Unlike most of them, we have permission. The bots come bundled with adult entertainment, video downloads, and some music downloads, all of which are sold at a discount in return for permission to install the Legion client on their machines."

"And people knowingly agree to this?" asked Roger.

"They do," Bee replied. "It's in the EULA."

Roger laughed at that, and nodded. Chris wasn't sure if it was approval or disapproval. "OK, I gotcha. So tell me how it works."

Chris launched into his description in considerable detail, maybe even more detail than he would have used with someone besides Roger. But Roger would be able to really understand what he was describing, even if it didn't actually exist. It was an idea Chris had been playing with for a number of years now, not just the aggressive defense thing, but also the idea of opt-in botnets. There were a number of opt-in distributed computing things out there, like SETI at home and the folding at home one to study protein folding using excess processor powers on PS3s. This was the same idea. Of course, just having the army wasn't enough. You also had to know what to do with it.

He explained to Roger that they'd developed a system for fingerprinting and tracing botnets that used a combination of massive databases they'd compiled of known bots and some proprietary code that would allow them to use their army of bots to counter attack against the enemy bots and, in many cases, trace them back to their point of origin. The Legion could serve many other uses as well, including distributed computing and, if necessary, launching DDOS attacks anonymously on behalf of their clients. And Legion was just one of the tools in Propter Hoc's arsenal. They also had custom software packages designed to secretly identify, track, and seize the boxes of anyone caught snooping around a protected network in a suspicious way. Oh! And they had a crack forensics team that was especially skilled at dissecting malware and recovering lost data.

Roger's face was unreadable. Had he bought any of this? Chris began to have serious doubts when he finished his pitch and Roger started asking technical questions. Lots and lots of questions. He hadn't been prepared for this kind of scrutiny, and he could feel what seemed like lakes of moisture pooling at the small of his back and under his arms. Maybe that was why businessmen wore suits—it hid the embarrassment from others. He answered as best he could. He just imagined what the answer would be if they had infinite resources at their disposal and, unlike most company's, were actually willing to do the smart thing rather than the cheap thing. The company he described would have been a dream place to work. Chris had to remind himself that it wasn't real. Then he began to worry that maybe he'd made it sound too good. Roger asked the next obvious question.

"How are you paying for all this? What's your revenue stream?"

Chris froze. Was he supposed to know this? Apparently not. Bee jumped in at once, spinning tales of silent investors and high-paying clients who wanted to keep a low profile. Lots of hints about European and Asian technology cartels. He couldn't imagine that Roger was satisfied with any of it, but if he had his doubts, he was keeping them to himself. They finished up meeting and Roger saw them to the door.

Inscrutable to the last, he said, "Thanks a lot for coming in. Really interesting stuff. I'll give Emily my report and I'm sure you'll be hearing something soon."

They caught a cab once they were back on the main street and headed for Union Station where they could jump on the subway and meet up with the others. Chris felt damp, exhausted, and beaten.

"You were awesome!" said Bee, as soon as they were in the cab and out of sight.

He was more than surprised to hear her say it, he was stunned. He couldn't tell if she was teasing him or not. "I just babbled on and on like a freaking idiot," he said.

"No, no. What? No, are you kidding? It was awesome. Really impressive. Roger obviously thought so, too."

"That's not what I saw at all."

She shook her head. "No, c1s, you were great. Really. I'm totally not just saying that, OK? You had him eating out of your hand. He was loving every minute of it, I swear. We did it!"

"Huh," said Chris, not wanting to argue. Who knew, maybe she was right. That would be nice. And hell, maybe she was. That was the biggest problem, intellectually speaking, that he had with being part of The Crew: he could never accept that the plans they came up with were going to work. When you knew the truth, it all seemed so obvious. Bee kept reminding him that the whole point was that no one else did know the truth, which was why it worked. Maybe she was right. They'd see.

A day later, back in Baltimore, it looked like things had worked out after all. Bee had sung his praises to the others, and they'd congratulated him, clapping him on the back and assuring him that they'd known he had it in him. All that praise felt pretty damn good, he had to admit. And when they got the call the following afternoon that Marsh wanted to meet with Chloe and Sacco's alter-egos to discuss using Propter Hoc, he felt awesome. They'd set up as much of a provenance as they could for the fake company, buying a Belize-based off the shelf International Business Company that had been in existence for over a year (just waiting for someone to buy it). Chris used some of the IDs he had on different hacker forums and sites to give some cred to the thing and they'd put up some testimonials. There was enough out there that a casual or even only moderately thorough investigation would find some real evidence that a fake cabal of hackers had gone into the security business together. Paul put him to work almost at once though, coming up with more fake activity and using scripts that he wrote for forum discussions about the new company. There was no time to slow down and enjoy the success. No time to stop and think about what had just happened. They had a plan and were committed to it 100%, which was fine with Chris, especially since he'd done the hard part. The rest was just hacking, no talking necessary.

Chapter 25

Chloe

Her and Sacco again, as Maria Lanier and Bernard Orozco. This time though, there was no time for banter or psyching themselves up, because they were sharing the back of the limo with Ken Clover. Ken was fidgeting in his seat and kept eying the bar, but it was only 10:00 in the morning, so apparently he at least had some sense of dignity and self-control left. Chloe was actually kind of disappointed. She wouldn't have minded the excuse to have a shot of whiskey herself right about then. Instead she pretended to play with her Blackberry so she wouldn't have to make too much small talk with him. Sacco was hiding behind the shield of his enigmatic Euro-mutt persona, just smiling with wise indulgence at everything Ken said.

Mostly Ken wanted to talk about how fucked up his life had gotten and how eager he was to get back at the fucking fucks who'd fucked him over. Ken really liked the word fuck, and now that he felt he knew Maria and Bernard he felt free to use it ceaselessly. They'd paid him $50,000 to introduce them to Marsh, and Chloe had hoped that would be the end of it. But he'd insisted on hearing what it was they were going to say to Marsh and how it would help them get their "mutual enemy." Once he heard Chloe's explanation of c1sman's fictitious botnet attack army, he was sold, entranced with the vision of taking revenge on the fucking hacker fucks who'd fucked everything up for him. He'd insisted on coming along for the final pitch to Marsh herself now that her tech guru had signed off on it. Chloe hadn't like the idea, but Paul had pointed out that having him in the room and on their side might go a long way towards easing any suspicions that Marsh might have. Maybe so. Chloe knew one thing for sure though; she was sending Ken home in the limo alone. She and Sacco could catch a cab.

"Now the thing is," said Ken. "Emily's very old school, right? You guys have to be totally fucking polite and fucking deferential around her. The fucking friends she has? Yeah, you be polite. Always call her Ms. Marsh. Don't try and talk over her. Let her ask the fucking questions."

"In other words," Sacco said in his Euro-drawl, "Common courtesy."

Ken looked at him, and Chloe thought he was trying to decide if Sacco was making fun of him or not. "Just respect her, OK? The woman's got some serious pull in this town."

They rode the rest of the way in relative silence, with only a few instances of Ken bragging about his former connections to politicians and media stars that came out whenever they passed some DC landmark or bar that reminded him of the time when... The limo stopped right in front of Marsh's office door, and the driver opened the door for them as they exited. Inside was exactly as Bee had described it to her, only they didn't have to wait in the reception area or pass muster in the conference room. The guy in reception showed them straight up the stairs to Marsh's office, which overlooked the street below.

Emily Marsh in person struck Chloe as vivacious and strong in a way her pictures could never convey. She was a small woman, but not frail or even delicate. Her meticulously tailored suit and subtle but expensive jewelry presented the woman of power and means that Chloe had been expecting, but the sparkle in her eyes and the way they seemed to lance across Chloe and Sacco like a laser was something else. Chloe felt like a boxer standing across the ring from the heavyweight champ, all the weaknesses in her game exposed. The two of them shook hands, smiling. Interesting that she'd come to Chloe first, not Sacco or Ken.

"Emily Marsh," she said. "Thanks for coming in."

"Maria Lanier. And this is my associate, Mr. Bernard Orozco."

"A pleasure to meet you both. And how are you Ken? A pleasure as always. Please, have a seat. Did Larry offer you something to drink?"

They settled into the three leather chairs arrayed before Marsh's desk. Chloe suspected there were usually only two, and that the third came from an empty space along one wall. Larry, the receptionist, brought them all coffee and then things got started.

"So," said Marsh, leaning forward in her chair and looking at each of them in turn. "What do you have for me?"

"Well, that depends," said Chloe, "On what you thought of the Propter Hoc presentation. We were pretty impressed with what they had to offer. What did you think?"

"According to my expert, they seem interesting. You must understand, I'm not much of a technology person, but I gather from his briefing that these Propter Hoc people might very well be capable of delivering on their promises."

"That was our assessment as well," said Sacco. "They come highly recommended by some of our associates in Germany."

Marsh nodded. "We all seem to agree on that then. The next item on the agenda is, what would you propose hiring them to do?"

"Well, to begin with, we'd like to go after the people responsible for the, um, difficulties my associates recently had down in Florida," said Chloe.

"Which are the same people who screwed me over," Ken said. "Or related to them."

"And how do we know the two groups are related?" asked Marsh. "I know law enforcement recently raided a hide-out of some sort in Key West and is holding one of the members of the group under house arrest. Those are the individuals responsible for your problems, Ken. I don't know of any connections between them and the problems Mr. Orozco and Ms. Lanier's associates may have been having. Problems that are, I must apologize here, outside of my interests."

"We believe there are connections," Chloe said. "And if you have only one person in custody, there are surely others still at large. The damage done to my... my friends was the work of dozens, maybe hundreds. And the fact that whatever the hideout the police raided was in South Florida should indicate to you, as it does to me, that there is some connection."

"Perhaps, perhaps," Marsh said. "It is certainly curious. But none of this answers why I should care."

Chloe looked to Ken, nodding for him to make the case. He got the signal. "It's like this, Ms. Marsh. I need to clear my name. I need to prove that I was set up. You've done great work for me already on this, great work. No doubt. But the thing is, I need this to wrap up fast. Every day I'm on the sidelines, my business suffers. If I'm not cleared, I'm out of the lobbying business forever, guaranteed. And again, I'm not complaining about what you've done so far, it's just that if these people can help things move forward faster, well, that's important."

"I take your point, Ken. And after all, you are the client. But I wouldn't be doing my duty to you if I didn't warn you against this plan.

I believe it could end up being more trouble for you than you think." Ken started to say something, but Marsh talked over him. "But I see that your mind is made up. Fine. Let us hear the proposal."

"For first," Sacco said. "We must to share information between our two groups. We know things. You know things. Until we are all knowing the same things, we cannot move forward."

When Marsh didn't immediately reply, Chloe jumped in. "If we pool our data and hand it over to the Post Hoc guys, they can start digging into it and hopefully come up with something new. And of course you and your people can go over everything and we'll comb through it on our end. Between us all, we should be able to come up with something."

"Maybe I'm just not up to date on all the technology these days, but I'm still not sure what you hope to accomplish."

Chloe felt her frustration mix with panic and grow inside her. Sacco tried to answer her question. "They say two heads are better than one, yes? Surely you see the advantage of working together."

Marsh smirked. "I'm not entirely sure I agree with you on the subject of heads. But what I'm looking for from you is some sort of concrete plan. Think of it from my point of view. I may or may not have information about the people who hurt you. Whatever information I do have, it came from private sources and/or law enforcement agencies who I would rather keep confidential. My reputation is at stake here, and I'm loathe to risk it without some firm idea where you're headed with it."

"We turn whatever information we have over to the police," said Chloe.

"I'm not entirely satisfied that any information we get would be useful to the police, as the methods Post Hoc employs are not, from my understanding, clearly legal."

"There are certainly other ways to use this information," Sacco said. "Fighting the fire with fire, yes?"

"You mean breaking the law to strike at lawbreakers?"

"It is—" Sacco started to say, but Chloe cut him off, sensing a trap.

"Nothing like that, of course not," she said. "We're confident in Post Hoc's legal status and would strictly work within the boundaries of the law, of course."

"Of course. Because your associates would never break the law."

"We would not. Are you implying otherwise?"

"I'll leave the sorting out of implications to you," Marsh said. "It would however be impossible for me to do business with admitted criminals."

"So you'll share what you have?" Chloe asked.

"Yes, yes, let's have a little show and tell, by all means." Marsh pulled open a desk drawer and laid a file in front of her. "After you."

Chloe opened her brief case and pulled out a file of her own. It contained a heavily edited version everything they knew about what Isaiah had done, plus Paul had added in some pretty enticing false leads. From the file's contents Marsh would understand the full breadth of the damage Isaiah had done to the slavers down in South Florida, from petty thefts and minor property damage all the way up to mass embezzlement and the arrests. And of course there was the one big piece that tied those responsible for Clover's problems with those behind the attacks on the slavers: the fake checks from Clover's account that were spread out amongst immigrant workers all over the state. The Crew had debated long and hard about putting that data in the file, but aside from the firm connection to Isaiah's Crew that their version of the story made clear, it wasn't anything Clover and Marsh probably didn't know already. "I think you'll find it interesting reading," said Chloe as she handed over the file.

Marsh took the file and handed her much slimmer one back to Chloe. "I have more than this of course, but I need a day or too to assemble everything I'm going to share with you. In the meantime, this should get you started."

Chloe opened the envelope and pulled out two pieces of paper—one a page long description of a "suspect" and the other a grainy picture of Isaiah. Chloe willed her eyes not to bulge and kept her breathing slow and steady.

"You should recognize him," said Marsh.

What the fuck did she mean by that? "I don't," said Chloe, looking up from the photo into Marsh's gaze. "Who is he?"

"The man responsible for the attacks on you and your friends," she said. "Find him, and you'll get your revenge."

"But who is he?" asked Chloe.

"I don't know yet. What I do know is in that file. I'm going to take a day to go over what you've given me here. In the meantime, why don't you find out what you can about that man. Then maybe we'll see if two heads really are better than one."

Chloe and Sacco made their thanks and Larry showed them out. She listened to an excited Ken Clover babble on about his revenge until the limo pulled up and she practically shoved him in it and just barely avoided slamming his fingers in the door. Then she and Sacco started looking for a cab. He started to say something but Chloe just walked on ahead, forcing him to almost jog to keep up. She took the second cab that presented itself and didn't say a word to Sacco until they were in the subway headed towards Maryland.

"Now what do we fucking do?" she asked at last. Sacco didn't have any answer.

Chapter 26

Paul

"It's not that bad," said Paul.

"Isaiah is going the freak the hell out," said Sacco.

"Not if we don't tell him," said Chloe.

"How can we not tell him? He's our ally, our comrade. We can't fuck him over like this!"

"I'm not saying we fuck him over, I'm just saying we haven't decided to tell him."

"Isn't that the same thing? I mean, she has his fucking picture. If we don't tell him, we are in fact fucking him over, yes or no?"

"It's not that fucking simple, is it?"

Paul wasn't sure what side he was on or even if Chloe and Sacco were on opposite sides or just yelling at each other because everyone was freaked out. "All right, all right, let's talk this through with some logic here, OK?" He looked around the dingy Baltimore room. There was one bare bulb hanging from the ceiling and the glow of three laptop monitors. C1sman had his head down, looking at one of the screens. Bee was next to him, looking at the floor. Chloe and Sacco were pacing around each other in the center of the room while Paul leaned against a peeling wall. If the tension were any thicker, they'd all suffocate. "Here is a fucked up situation, but we need to sort it out. We need to do something."

"What do you suggest?" asked Sacco. "Let me guess, you're with her, right?"

"He can't be with me," snapped Chloe. "I haven't even decided where I am yet."

"Nobody's anywhere yet," Paul said, doing his best to exude calm he didn't feel. "Let's just talk it through." Nobody made any objections, so he continued. "So, we know she's got a picture of Isaiah, but no name to go with it. At least not one that she's sharing with us. Now from the picture quality and angle, it looks like it was taken from some sort of security camera or maybe a hidden camera. Not high quality, not good lighting. That means she can probably place him at an exact time and place, and that time and place probably have some connection to his operations in Florida, otherwise Marsh probably wouldn't care. But that picture alone is not going to get her anywhere near Isaiah. He's in New York, not Miami. He has no criminal record as far as we can tell, and while Marsh no doubt has better connections in that area then we do, if she had found something like that I think she would've told us. Instead she just gives us a photo that she says connects him to the attacks on the slavers. So right now, Isaiah's pretty safe. Safer than me, for instance.

"And then there's Sandee. He's under house arrest in Key West, which sucks. And I think it's pretty likely that Marsh could pull some strings and have him released. The question is, how do we convince her to do that? She's not going to do it out of the goodness of her heart, she's going to want something in exchange. And right now the only thing we have that she wants is information on Isaiah."

"Then we should give it to her," said Bee. Paul looked at her in surprise. She hadn't spoken for half an hour. "Tell her everything we know about Isaiah if she lets Sandee go."

"Are you high?" asked Sacco. "We can't turn Isaiah over to her. She'll tear him and his Crew to pieces. Without him we wouldn't have pulled off any of this, right? I'm not going to betray him."

"But you'll betray Sandee?" asked Bee.

"We'll find some other way to get Sandee out."

"You're just too embarrassed because you slept with him and now you think you're gay."

Sacco opened his mouth but no words came out. He swallowed and tried again. "That's not it. It's not true."

"I saw the video of you four fucking!"

"I mean that's not why I don't want to rescue him! I do want to rescue him. But I don't want to screw over Isaiah. That's not right."

"The Crew comes first," said Bee. "Sandee matters the world to me and Isaiah can go to hell. He's not part of us. He used us. You weren't there when we met him. You don't know what he's like. He doesn't care about us and there's no way we should care about him. Especially not more than we care about Sandee."

"I'm not a traitor," Sacco insisted.

"You're betraying Sandee!"

"I'm fucking not! There's gotta be another way to do both!"

Paul was letting them just work it out. He'd sensed the tension between them building and hoped that if they cleared the air a little it would help. But Chloe had apparently had enough.

"Stop it, both of you," said Chloe. "Listen, Sacco, I think Bee's right. We need to focus on Sandee. He's in real danger. The cops fucking have him, OK? And we need to do something about that." Sacco started to say something, but Chloe wouldn't let him. "Hear me out. Isaiah's free, well-connected, and has a ton of resources. Sandee just has us. Isaiah's already on a super paranoid defense footing, and is probably already looking out for people like Marsh. It's not like they're going to take him by surprise. Wait, there's one more thing. We couldn't give up Isaiah if we wanted to. Do you know where he lives? I don't. I don't even know his real name, but I'll bet you a million bucks it's not Isaiah. So I say we give her what we've got, which is not much. Maybe we gin up some extra bits to fill out the file. We tell Marsh some shit she doesn't know and in exchange she pulls some strings for Sandee."

Sacco didn't seem happy with Chloe's take, but he didn't have any immediate rejoinder. C1sman however, did. "Why would Marsh pull strings for Sandee?" he asked.

"To get Isaiah," Bee said.

"No, yeah, I get that," c1sman said. "What I meant was, why would we as, you know, representatives of the slavers, why would we ask for Sandee to be freed? Why would we care?"

Now both Sacco and Chloe looked unhappy. "That's a good point, c1s," Paul said. "We'll have to think of something. I *will* think of something if that's what we decide to do. But first let's decide what we're for sure going to do. I think Chloe makes some good points, but I'm not sure it will be enough. I think in order to have enough leverage on her to free Sandee, we're going to have to give her some information that seems both recent and useful enough for her to find Isaiah."

"And you're willing to do that?" asked Sacco.

"If that's the way the vote goes. If that's what we decide to do. The question is, are you willing?"

Sacco looked at each of them in turn and then sighed. "Yeah. What else am I going to do?"

"All right then," said Paul. "Let's vote."

*
**

It was a careful balancing act, trying to look like you were hunting someone to your best efforts while at the same time hoping you didn't find them. But Paul knew that Marsh was definitely going to be a "show your work" kind of person. She'd want to know everything they did in order to smoke Isaiah out, and she'd want to see some real results. At the same time, they needed to build up some credibility for Post Hoc, so Paul and Chloe came up with a plan that looked like something Post Hoc would have come up with on their own. They decided to create a honey pot.

The honey pot was a trap meant to lure in a target and trap it. Honey pots designed to capture hackers were usually websites that gave the appearance of being easy to hack and which seemed to contain interesting or desirable data. Hackers would break in, not realizing there would be a host of hidden processes running that were ready to snatch them up and hopefully catch them in the act. In their case, they set up a Post Hoc-created website that was very much modeled after a kind of America's Most Wanted for the internet. The site featured descriptions of wanted hackers and then offered bounties of tens of thousands of dollars for information leading to their capture. Hackers could report leads through the site anonymously and receive payment anonymously too, just the way an outfit like BountySploit worked.

Of course the main target was Isaiah himself. Paul had debated long and hard with Sacco about whether or not to put Isaiah's picture up on the site. Weirdly, it had been Sacco who wanted the pic up and Paul who wanted to wait. Sacco felt that by putting the picture up right away, they would indirectly be warning Isaiah just how much danger he might be in. Paul agreed with that assessment, but was more concerned with ways to show that the site was working at generating leads about Isaiah over time. He wanted to save the picture for later and pass it off as a discovery made by one of their bounty hunters, along with an announcement that they'd paid the fictitious bounty hunter an award for such valuable information. That was the key, of course—making Isaiah think that the site had valuable information on him that he in turn would try to steal back. In the end, Paul's position carried the day and Sacco seemed to resign himself to the plan as they'd laid it out.

The description of the wanted hacker Paul put up included no personal information about Isaiah at first. It did however detail some of the crimes he was accused of committing, including some that Paul and the rest of the Crew were actually responsible for, like cashing the fake checks. It also included a list of some of the networks, websites, and bank accounts that Isaiah was believed to have compromised. They posted links to the site in various hacker forums online and Paul and c1sman spent some time talking it up on IRC. They got traffic almost immediately, and a steady stream of hits showed there was real interest within the community, but hopefully not too much outside. Paul didn't want a lot of tourists coming in from Digg or Slashdot just to poke around and so they encouraged people to keep the site to just hackers. Ostensibly this was because they didn't want newbies muddying the waters with false or ridiculous leads, but in fact Paul wanted to keep the number of users low so they would have less data to hunt through when they checked their trap for victims.

They worked mostly out of the Baltimore house, although Sacco and Chloe had taken separate cars and gone war driving around the city and suburbs looking for open wireless networks they could take over for added bandwidth. They'd built a pretty complete map after a few days, allowing c1sman to work out of a van moving from spot to spot and piggybacking on either open or ill-protected hotspots. Although their site was hosted through a German ISP and heavily protected, they didn't want anyone (especially Isaiah or Marsh) tracing traffic back to them in Baltimore. After the third day, Paul started adding in new information about Isaiah, simulating supposed leads that bounty hunters were turning in. The truth was, no one was actually giving them any useful leads at all. But that was OK. All they needed to do was give the impression that they were closing in on Isaiah. Then, hopefully, he'd get curious enough to try and hack in and leave some trace of his activities they could follow back to him.

C1sman put in the most hours, second only to Paul. Chloe continued to interface via e-mail with Marsh and Clover, forwarding them progress reports that were supposed to be from the Post Hoc crew. They'd decided not to tell her about the honey pot site directly, hoping she wouldn't have her security people try and hack it just to get more data on them. There was a good chance she might find it on her own, but no sense in stirring up problems for themselves unnecessarily. C1sman's main job was to pore over the traffic data for everything coming in and out of the honey pot. He had an array of traffic analysis tools set up, along with various scripts and cookies attached to the site that clung on to anyone who visited it. Most hackers would be protected against most of these bugs, but even the way they disabled them told c1sman something about the skills of those visiting him. Plus, there were other, more sophisticated pieces of malware that c1sman had created that were much harder to detect and only a handful of those visiting the site managed to remove them. The assumption was, if Isaiah was visiting the site regularly he'd be in this final, uber-skilled set of visitors who left practically no trace. Thus, tracking them down became priority one and they might, just might, find some clue to Isaiah's location.

It was on the fifth day, when Paul put up Isaiah's picture, that things started to fall into place. C1sman had identified some distinct patterns in the traffic data that pointed to someone who was both interested in what was being published on the site and who had (they suspected) tried to hack into the site on several occasions. They had even "succeeded" once, cracking into a portion of the site full of corrupted data meant to serve as trojan horses for the hacker who took them. Whoever it was caught on almost immediately though, and their malware was deactivated or destroyed before it could give them any useful information. But it was enough to give c1sman a thread to start weaving a pattern together from, and it eventually led them back to a physical location.

"It's a hacker space in New York," c1sman said when they'd all gathered in the Baltimore room once more. Sacco and Chloe looked as exhausted as Paul felt. They'd been out driving within a hundred mile radius buying disposable cell phones, hijacking open wi-fi spots, and getting supplies and food for the group. Paul had busied himself with the false posts and regular updates to the honey pot site, while Bee and c1sman had combed through the analytics. "It's called HackNY, and it's a non-profit set up by some NY hackers as a place for people to work on projects and stuff like that. It's all white hat stuff, a lot of fun hardware hacking and things like that. I was there when they were setting up right after the last HOPE. It's pretty cool."

"And you think Isaiah might be using it to connect to our honey pot?" Paul asked.

"I think someone there is, yeah. Or if not, they're using HackNY's big fat connection to connect to its TOR network. But yeah, they missed one of my little bugs from the honey pot and it popped up at HackNY twice."

"What's this hacker space like?" asked Chloe. "Who has access to their network?"

"According to their website they've got about 70 dues paying members—it's $65 a month. You gotta figure at least twice that many come through just to check it out or as friends of the members. And they have classes and demos that're open to the public, and so anyone could be coming through then."

"So he could probably slip in and not arouse any attention," said Paul. "It makes sense. You gotta figure a hacker space's network is super secure, right? And we know he's based out of New York. Isaiah could easily be using the space to do some digging into our honey pot. Even if we do trace it back to HackNY, that leaves us with dozens, maybe hundreds of possible targets. It's great camouflage."

"C1sman, you said you've been there?" asked Chloe.

"Yeah, the one time when they were just setting up."

"And they know you? The people who run it?"

"A little bit. From, you know, cons and stuff. Not well."

"Perfect," said Chloe. "We need you to go to NY and start hanging out there."

Paul saw her plan, and he liked it. All except one part.

"I don't think I can do that," said c1sman. Paul could see from the way he fidgeted and looked down at his keyboard that he wasn't happy with the idea at all.

"Of course you can," said Chloe. "You were great during the pitch to Marsh's security guy, and this is even easier. We're only asking you to be yourself. You go in there, start hanging out, and wait for Isaiah or someone you can identify as one of his followers to show up. We'll coordinate with you from somewhere nearby and let you know when we see someone poking around the honey pot. Then you ID the guy, unless it is Isaiah, in which case you can ID him right away. Either way we follow him when he leaves and track down Isaiah's home base."

"I don't think I could do all that. I really don't."

"It's not dangerous," Chloe insisted. "The thing is though, you're the only one in our Crew he hasn't met or even gotten a description of. Isaiah knows the rest of us by sight and will have briefed his followers about us in all likelihood. You're the only one who can do this for us. Do you see that?"

C1sman didn't answer, just kept looking at his laptop. Paul gave Bee an imploring look and nodded towards him. She moved up close and put her arm around his shoulders. "Chris, honey, please. Sandee needs this, she really does. And we'll be right outside. You did so well before. And this is much easier than last time."

They all waited in silence for a long time, at least a minute, but to Paul it seemed like ten. He was readying his own salvo of encouragement when c1sman finally nodded. "Yeah, OK. I'll give it a shot."

Chapter 27

Chloe

Chloe didn't like having to go into Marsh's den one more time, but the woman had insisted. Their dealings over the phone had been very professional and non-committal. Chloe as Maria would claim to have dug up some new fact about the target—they hadn't put the name Isaiah out there yet—and Marsh would ask to have a hard copy delivered by Fed Ex or private messenger. No e-mail or faxes. That meant driving somewhere far away from their Baltimore hideout before dropping a couple of pages into an envelope and paying twenty bucks to overnight it an hour's drive away. Still, that was safer than delivering it personally and then having to spend the next few hours shaking any tails she might have put on them. But today Marsh had asked for a face to face meeting, and that meant hiring a limo and driver again just to keep up appearances. It also meant buying new outfits for her and Sacco, since they didn't want to seem like they only had one suit apiece (which was true since the Key West house was lost). The dollars just kept adding up. They'd come out of the con with over a million in cash, but they'd spent over three hundred thousand since then.

It was worth it if they could get Sandee out, though, and Chloe was going to do her best to make a play for Sandee's release at this meeting. She and Paul had come up with an excuse that seemed reasonable enough—they would say they have information linking Sandee to Isaiah. If Marsh got him released, they could follow Sandee back to his friends and hopefully learn Isaiah's location. How could they do this? Well, Post Hoc had uncovered some secret e-mail and credit card accounts that Sandee used and would probably use again to contact Isaiah (or at least that's what they were going to tell Marsh). All they needed was for Sandee to be out from under house arrest long enough to make him disappear and then the rest of them could escape along with him, leaving Marsh and Clover and Isaiah far, far behind them.

Chloe and Sacco had to wait in reception this time, something that made her all the more nervous about this meeting. Was Marsh just playing power games with them or was she really busy? Or was it both? Or something else altogether? Chloe did her best to appear bored and unconcerned as she paged through a copy of *National Geographic*. Sacco played Tetris on his phone. When Larry the receptionist ushered them into Marsh's office twenty minutes after their appointment was supposed to begin, Chloe was expecting apologies or excuses. Instead, Marsh just motioned for them to have a seat.

"What do you have for me?" she asked, raking her gaze over each of them in turn.

Chloe looked over to Sacco, who dropped the big bombshell. "We've been having some great successes," he said. "We have, for instance, identified the man in the photograph you gave us. He is Isaiah, and he is head of a gang of confidence artists and computer hackers operating out of New York. We think that this is the gang responsible for both our problems and your Mr. Clover's difficulties."

Whatever she thought of that information, Marsh didn't show any reaction. "Go on, what else?"

"Well, this is important news isn't it? We've been able to establish a connection between this Isaiah person and one of the confidence artists based in Key West. A man named Sandeep Arsani. We think he could be the key to unraveling Isaiah's cloak of secrecy."

"Yes," Chloe said, "We think Arsani is the key. Currently he's being held under house arrest in Key West. If it were possible—"

"I'm afraid your information there is a little out of date," Marsh said, interrupting Chloe.

"Excuse me?"

"Mr. Arsani was taken into federal custody this morning and is currently in a holding cell awaiting trial." Marsh passed a sheet of paper across her desk to Chloe. It was a fax from a local FBI headquarters in Miami alerting Marsh to the arrest.

Chloe sucked in a breath through her nose. She sensed that Sacco had gone rigid next to her. "Oh, I see. That is unfortunate. We were hoping to—"

"Mr. Arsani is currently a person of great interest to the federal authorities, wanted in connection with a number of felonies, several of which run afoul of new anti-terrorism laws. He's in a very tough position, I'm afraid. I don't know what plans you might have had regarding him, but I believe it's time for you to rethink them."

"Yes," said Chloe, stalling for time. What now? "Do you have any other new information to share with us?"

"As a matter of fact, I do." Marsh opened up a file in front of her and started reading from it. "Paul Reynolds, born March 23rd, 1975, wanted for questioning in a felony fraud case in California. There's a picture here, would you like to see it?"

Chloe didn't trust her voice at that instant so she just nodded. Marsh passed over a print out of Paul's old California driver's license photo along with a still from the security camera footage that Oliver had put up on his site. Oh shit, oh shit, oh shit. Chloe focused on keeping her face still even as she mentally went over the available exits. "Who's he?" she asked, passing the photos over to Sacco. His face betrayed nothing but she could see sweat starting to bubble up at his temples and he looked a shade more pale than normal.

"He's another con artist that my investigators believe has ties to both Mr. Arsani and, we suspect, to the attacks on Ken Clover. That security camera picture was from a hotel here in Washington during the weekend that Ken came under assault. It was actually following his trail that eventually led us to Key West where we found Arsani. Subsequent investigations have shown that the two of them are part of a team of con artists that includes at least three other members. There's a white male in his mid-twenties with dark hair and a slim frame, a short, somewhat overweight Asian-American woman in her early thirties, and an attractive, Caucasian woman in her late twenties or early thirties. We don't have names or pictures yet for these other three, but I think it's only a matter of time before we either find Mr. Reynolds or Mr. Arsani starts talking. I don't think he'll adjust to prison life very well, not a man of his proclivities."

Chloe knew that Marsh was wrong about that last point—Sandee could kick anyone's ass—but that was small consolation when weighed against the other bombs that Marsh had just dropped. Holy shit, they were in trouble. Chloe struggled to find the right response, but Marsh continued.

"The case against Arsani is weak. He has alibis and excuses and a good lawyer, but I'm confident the federal prosecutor can load on enough charges that he'll plead out to something in the neighborhood of six years rather than face a potential decades long sentence. Part of any such plea agreement would of course entail a full disclosure of information about his accomplices."

"Sounds like you've been busy," Chloe said. "This is great stuff. Do you have any more?"

"No more specifics. Just that the group is very tech savvy and also prone to using disguises. You know, I went through a phase, when I was much younger, of wearing a wig quite often." Marsh gestured towards her carefully coiffed gray and brown hair. "It was fun, dressing up, pretending to be some other girl. But in the end it was more trouble than it was worth. I'd have to explain the sudden change the next time I went out with a young man or with new friends who only knew me as a blond or red head. It got tiresome, all that pretending, all that explaining. I'm sure you can imagine."

"Yes," said Chloe, painfully aware of her own wig. "I can imagine."

"I'm glad Ken didn't join us this time," Marsh said. "It allows us to talk business without his very serious emotional investment getting in the way."

Chloe nodded, thinking ahead to what her excuse for leaving suddenly might be. She considered reaching into her briefcase for her phone and claiming an important call. That might work.

"Ken thinks he wants revenge," Marsh continued. "He thinks what he really wants is to destroy those who have destroyed his life. And I'm sure he would be happy if that happened, at least for a short time. But in the end, his life would still be destroyed. No, what Ken wants is his old life back. He wants things to be the way they were before Paul Reynolds and Sandeep Arsani and their fellow gangsters snuck up behind him and took away everything. But Ken's a smart guy, he knows there's no going back. You can't change the past. So he's just about given up. If he stays out of jail and gets back at those responsible for his destruction, he thinks he'll be satisfied. He's wrong of course.

"Ken is my client. I honestly don't care about you and whoever it is exactly you represent. From what I can gather, the victims of this Isaiah person's attacks whom you claim to represent, deserved everything that happened to them. All evidence points to them being gangsters and proponents of what amounts to modern day slavery. I don't care what becomes of them. That Ken had dealings with them is on his conscience, not mine. But my job, the job I was hired to do, is to help Ken Clover. That is all. Do you understand?"

Chloe wasn't sure she did, or at least she didn't want to believe that she did. Was Marsh really saying what she thought she was saying? "I think so," Chloe said.

"Good. I think you do too. I can keep Ken out of jail. It will be costly and difficult, but I can do it. I can't, however, give him his life back. Not on my own. But perhaps you can help me. You see, what I need is a plausible scapegoat for all of Ken's alleged misdeeds. I need someone to take the fall, both in the courts and in the media, and that someone has to be seen as a credible threat. If I got a full confession or some other form of irrefutable evidence that exonerated Ken from the scurrilous charges against him, say proof that his e-mails had been doctored by a third party, his network compromised, and the evidence against him fabricated, why then I'd be able to restore Ken to some position at least comparable to his former life. Do you understand?"

"Yes," said Chloe.

"Now, I imagine you were going to offer me some sort of plan that involved releasing Mr. Arsani and somehow using him to find this mysterious Isaiah person. That's just not feasible right now, I'm sorry. But I could see it working the other way. No, what has to happen is that I need to exonerate Ken completely before any action can happen with Mr. Arsani. I need a plausible scapegoat. I'd use Mr. Arsani, but he's just not suited to it. No one would believe a drag queen from Key West orchestrated the downfall of a powerful Washington lobbyist. But I'll at least give it a try if no better options present themselves. Paul Reynolds comes to mind as a legitimate and believable alternative, but since you claim not to know him, you might have a hard time finding him. Or maybe not. But I imagine that since you have been looking into this Isaiah person, and given the tremendous damage he caused your supposed clients down in Florida, he would be a very believable alternative. Very believable. Bring me evidence that he's behind what happened to Ken, along with some guaranteed way to actually apprehend him, well then I think Mr. Arsani could be freed on probation with no more fuss or bother. Do you understand?"

Chloe hadn't wanted to believe it, but it was clearly true. Marsh knew everything, or at least all the important stuff. She was hiding it in double talk and insinuation, but she knew who Chloe and Sacco really were, along with Paul and Bee. The question was, why she wasn't just having them all arrested right here and now. If things were as bad as they seemed, what harm could come from asking? "I understand. But I have a question."

"Please."

"Why not have this Paul Reynolds person picked up yourself?"

Marsh leaned back in her seat and smiled. "You do understand. Good. The truth is, I don't know where Mr. Reynolds is. And while

I could lay hands on some of his cohorts with ease, that might not be enough. Secondly, once I put Reynolds in the hands of the FBI, my ability to make deals effectively vanishes. Whatever arrangements that Reynolds and his friends might make with federal prosecutors would probably do Ken very little good. On the other hand, if I can, on my own, gather rock solid evidence that not only proves that Ken's computers were tampered with but also casts serious doubts on other actions he might or might not have actually done in the past that have since come to light, well, all the better for Ken."

"You want the perfect deal for Ken, one that will clear his name with the feds and the media, which is not the kind of deal feds would be offering," Chloe said. "I get that. That seems doable."

"I'm glad you think so. I prefer to control the outcome precisely, but there are also issues of timing here. I need to do something soon, since the longer these charges linger, the worse things get for Ken. If no other option presents itself, I'll take what I can get. Or rather, I'll take whatever the FBI can get with my assistance. Do you understand?"

Chloe nodded. "Yes, I understand. What kind of time table are we talking here?"

Marsh looked at the calendar on her desk. "I would say, eight days seems about right. After that, I'll have moved on to other options."

Chloe stood up, and a moment later a stunned-looking Sacco did the same. She shook Marsh's hand, saying, "This has been interesting. I'll let you know what we come up with."

"Please do," said Marsh. "I look forward to seeing it. Can I show you to the door?"

"We know the way." Chloe did her best job of not running for the door, although Sacco twice bumped into her from behind. He was clearly spooked. So was she. The limo was waiting right out front, and they climbed in, sweat turning chill at the small of her back. Even with the privacy shield up between them and the driver, Chloe wouldn't let Sacco talk. There was no telling who might be listening now.

Chapter 28

Paul

The sudden lack of options can either give rise to panic or focus the mind on the task at hand. For Paul, who was by now growing more and more accustomed to having his entire life turned upside down without warning, Marsh's "deal" brought life into perfect focus. He knew exactly what he needed to do, he just wasn't quite sure how to do it yet. But he'd figure that part out later. Right now he needed to let his focus infect the others and stem the rising panic he saw in all of them. Chloe and Sacco had returned silent and shaken. When they explained what had happened, that Marsh was on to their little trick, probably right from the beginning, Bee and c1sman had both nearly passed out. Sacco wanted to run. C1sman was already halfway out the door. Bee curled up in her chair and kept reminding everyone that Sandee was still in jail and that it was all their fault. Even Chloe wasn't quite herself, seemingly lost in thought. He'd hugged her close for a long time until he finally whispered in her ear, "We have to go to New York."

Once he said it out loud she understood, and then the pair of them rallied the other three, putting them to work packing up their stuff in the Baltimore squat and arranging transportation—new vehicles, because none of the old ones were safe any more—to get to New York. Twelve hours later they were in a ten year old Honda and an eight year old Chevy van (both bought for cash off Craig's List), traveling back roads instead of highways as they worked their way to the big city. They found a motel in New Jersey that took cash and didn't look too close at their fake ID, and settled in as best they could. Exhaustion had overcome panic, at least for the time being.

Now Paul and Bee were in the van, which had no air conditioning or radio and practically bald tires, giving c1sman a little pep talk.

"These are you friends," Bee said. "Your hacker peoples."

"I don't even know them, really," c1sman protested. "They're just people I've met at cons."

"That's better," Bee said. "They'll leave you alone. Just stick to the story and keep an eye out. Keep looking around whenever anyone new comes in, but otherwise keep your head down, right?"

"I know, I know. Right."

"Remember, even Isaiah doesn't know about you. All you need to do is watch."

C1sman bit his lower lip and bobbed his head up and down six or seven times, rocking forward and back as he did. "OK, OK, OK."

Bee gave him a kiss and sent him on his way. Then she and Paul watched the video feed from the hidden camera in c1sman's glasses as he crossed the Brooklyn street and entered the four story, run down building down the block. They could hear through the hidden microphone in his MP3 player attached to his belt and could talk directly to him when he put the earphones in. Everything he said or saw they'd catch as well.

According to c1sman and its own website, HackNY was a relatively new hacker space modeled on what worked best in similar hacker spaces in the U.S. and Germany. Members each paid $65 a month in dues, which went towards rent and utilities. In exchange they got access to the hacker space and could participate in the various classes and activities that the space sponsored. HackNY was on the third floor and occupied a large loft space. It had its own high speed internet connection of course, along with a network to support it and a variety of tools for common use. Not only computer hackers, but hardware hackers, makers, artists, and general tech enthusiasts used the space as a combination social club, workshop, and office. There were people coming in and out at all hours, and with over a hundred members, there was always someone there.

C1sman had an appointment to meet Ray Poole, one of the founders, who he knew from the convention scene. His cover story was that he was in New York doing a contract job, but that he didn't like working out of the client's office because the client was way too pushy and annoying. He needed a place to work out of for a few weeks, some place where he could relax and think. Ray was fine with that, especially since c1sman offered to sign up for a full year's membership, claiming, "I'm going to be in and out of NY for the next eight months with this client." C1sman paid cash up front, Ray gave him the grand tour, and then left him to settle in at a corner table with his laptop to do some work. Outside, Paul and Bee settled in to wait.

C1sman, wearing glasses with a hidden video camera that broadcast to the van, stayed in the space for twelve or thirteen hours at a time for the next three days, working on coding some personal project of his the entire time. As nervous as he might have been, he at least had the ability to lose himself in his work. Whichever shift was on van duty at any given moment, was left with nothing but a couple of Nintendo DS's, a portable radio, and a really unpleasant smelling bottle. Halfway into day three, and Paul was starting to feel the slightest inkling of panic. Paul was about ready to put up some really incriminating information about Isaiah on the honey pot, details about what he'd done in South Florida, when a man walked in that he recognized.

He sat up straight and fumbled with the microphone so he could talk into c1sman's ear. "Who just came in?" C1sman whispered something back that Paul couldn't understand, but he started looking around the room. "There!" said Paul. "Hold on that guy."

He was African-American, early to mid-twenties, wearing a Transformers t-shirt and jeans. He unfolded a Mac at the big table in the center of the room and started powering up. Paul was sure he knew him from somewhere. "I need a closer look," he said. "Go to the bathroom and walk by him, OK?"

C1sman nodded, making the camera shake up and down. He stood up and walked across the room, looking at and then away from and then back at the newcomer. The closer he got, the more certain Paul became. "I swear that's one of Isaiah's people. I recognize him from Key West. Bee, take a look."

C1sman was in the bathroom now, staring at himself in the mirror. The low-quality image combined with the fluorescent lighting made him look almost corpse-like. Bee rewound the live feed they were recording to look at the man. "I don't recognize him," she said. "But I wasn't with you and Chloe when you met Isaiah's crew."

"I swear that's one of them. And that makes sense, right? It's not like we thought Isaiah would come here himself. He'd use one of his crew members. C1s, when you come out, just ignore the guy, don't show any interest, but be ready to leave as soon as he does. We want to follow him."

"OK," said c1sman, still whispering, but at least loud enough for Paul to hear him. Paul watched as c1sman flushed the toilet, washed his hands, and walked back out into the main room. Without looking at the target once, he took his seat and resumed working. Paul and Bee sat and waited an agonizing three and a half hours while both men sat at their computers and did whatever it was they were doing. Finally, c1sman got up. "He's leaving."

"Great, let him get ahead and then be ready to follow him. We'll be watching outside and tell you which way he went."

A couple minutes later, the target came out the front door of the building and headed to his left. Paul let Bee out to start following him at a safe distance. C1sman came down a couple minutes later, but instead of following the target, he came running down the block towards the van, tearing off his glasses as he did so. He banged on the side of the van once before Paul slid open the door.

"What're you doing?"

"I can't do this!" said c1sman, in a panic.

"You have to! Come on, Sandee needs your help. You have to."

"I can't," he repeated, trying to climb back into the van, but Paul wouldn't let him. "He'll see me."

"We need all three of us following. Bee has him now, so you stay back. Then we'll switch off. If he gets on a subway you need to follow, if he gets in a car, I'll follow him in the van. If he stays on foot, Bee will follow him. Come on!"

C1sman sucked in both his lips and flared his nostrils. "OK," he said. "I get it." He turned and headed off down the road after Bee.

Paul directed them both from the van, driving a couple blocks behind. When Bee said he was going into a subway station, Paul told c1sman to hurry up and join the two of them on the platform. The plan was for c1sman to stay back and get on the same train as the target and Bee. Bee would watch the target and stay on when he got off, but would tell c1sman, who would be in another car, to exit the train. Paul would do his best to keep up with them on the surface streets. Fortunately this part of Brooklyn had elevated trains, so he was able to keep in contact with them, at least until the train went underground.

Bee reported in as the target ascended the steps to the train station. Paul found a place to illegally park in a loading dock a block away and listened as Bee narrated events. The target was standing idle, waiting for the train. C1sman arrived five minutes later, and spent his time looking at the subway map. The train arrived, headed towards Manhattan. Bee got on in the same car as the target. C1sman kept looking at the map.

C1sman wasn't moving towards the train. C1sman waved goodbye to her as the train roared away. What the fuck?

Paul told Bee to keep following the guy, and he jumped out of the van and ran over towards the station. He went ahead and jumped the turnstile and ran up onto the platform, but a second train had already come and gone by the time he got up there. C1sman was nowhere to be seen.

He raced back to the van and tried to catch up with Bee's train, but it soon went underground and Paul got caught up in traffic trying to get across the river into Manhattan. He was still in Brooklyn when Bee came back into contact. The target had gotten off in the Lower East Side and she'd followed him to an apartment building where he went inside. She was waiting and worried about what had happened to c1sman. Paul called in Chloe and Sacco to give them the heads up, and then all four of them converged around the apartment building Bee had staked out. While Sacco watched the door, Chloe, Bee, and Paul huddled around the laptop to review c1sman's footage from the hacker space.

"I don't recognize him," Chloe said.

"Think back to that time in Key West, when we were with Isaiah and his whole Crew."

"Oh, I remember the event, but I'm telling you, I don't think this guy was there."

"I was sure I recognized him."

"I'm sorry Paul, but I'm positive I don't."

"Really? Fucking hell."

"Are you sure you recognize him?"

"Not anymore I'm not," Paul said, cursing to himself.

They spent the next day confirming the target's identity and concluding that this freelance web site designer and part-time NYU student was probably not connected to Isaiah in any way, especially given how easily Sacco hacked his wireless network and his e-mail accounts. They'd wasted four days on this wild goose chase, and then there was fucking c1sman.

Bee got an e-mail from him the next day, but by then they knew what had happened. Using his own name and his own credit cards he'd gone straight to JFK, bought an airline ticket and flown back to Atlanta. The e-mail was short and simple, "This isn't for me. I can't do this. Sorry." Paul had thought Bee would be upset, but she was just pissed at him, calling him a coward and a turncoat. Paul didn't think that was quite fair—they really had demanded more of c1sman than he'd ever wanted to give. He did what any sane person would have done in his position.

Not that Paul was going to tell Bee that right now; she was much more productive when angry than when depressed. The big issue was, they were down another man and had got exactly nowhere with trying to find Isaiah.

"We need to think about alternative plans," Sacco said.

"Like what?" asked Chloe. "What else is there?"

"Chasing Isaiah sure as hell isn't working, is it?"

"I should never have taken you to meet him. If I'd known you'd develop this huge man crush on him, I wouldn't have."

"What, I have a man-crush and am behaving like some sort of fucking fanboy just because I don't want to screw a good man over?"

"Hey!" said Paul interrupting them. They'd been bickering like this all week. "Hey, let's just think here OK. Either we find Isaiah and turn him over to Marsh or we warn him that she's after him. Or, I guess, we do both. But all of that depends on talking to him, right?"

"Yeah," said Sacco, Chloe nodding in agreement.

"So let's just reach out to him. Send him a message through the one channel we have left."

"That will take days," said Chloe. "We don't have days. Marsh is going to pull the trigger on us soon."

"Then we need to make it not take days. Either that or make Marsh give us more time."

"And how're we going to do that?" asked Sacco.

"Give me an hour," said Paul. "I think I've got a plan."

Chapter 29

Chloe

Chloe walked down the street in Bethesda, looking for a quiet place to make her phone call. The rest of the Crew was back in the Baltimore squat, but she needed to be in an entirely different metropolitan area before she was going to talk to Marsh. She had to assume that the phone call would be traced. She found an office building with an empty lobby and some chairs that were far enough away from the front desk that she wouldn't be overheard. Plopping down in the surprisingly comfy chair, she slipped the battery into her cell phone and dialed Marsh's number from memory. She got the receptionist, who put her on hold. That would be them tracing me, thought Chloe, although she couldn't know for sure. Five minutes crept by before Marsh picked up the line.

"Ms. Lanier, what can I do for you?" she said, without a hint of irony or menace in her voice.

"Ms. Marsh, I just wanted to check in with you and let you know that while we are making progress, we've run into some unforeseen delays and might need some more time."

"Well, I'm certainly glad you're making progress, but I'm afraid I'm operating on a very strict timetable here. I don't think I'll be able to accommodate any significant delays."

That's pretty much what Chloe thought she would say, but there was a little wiggle room there. "I'm not foreseeing a significant delay, just a matter of a week or so at the most."

"A week. I fear that's just not feasible. Let me tell you what, why don't you send over what you have so far and if I agree with you as to the quality of your information, and I'm sure I will, then I'll do what I can to get you a couple more days. How does that sound?"

"That sounds fine, Ms. Marsh. I appreciate it."

"We're in this together after all. Now, if I need to reach you, is this the best number to use?"

"Not always," said Chloe, who'd never used this phone before now. "I can't always be sure which phone I'll be near."

"Oh, that must be confusing. You know, my son has three different phones and I can't ever understand how he keeps them straight. Sometimes I have to call all three before I get through to him. Listen, since time is such a factor for you and me right now, why don't you do me a favor and hold on to that phone. After I receive your update, I'll call you at this number to confirm the time extension. I don't want to have to have Larry hunt around for you. Does that sound alright to you?"

Crafty bitch. "Yes, yes," said Chloe. "Not a problem at all."

"Good. And when should I be looking for that update from you?"

"I'll e-mail it over this afternoon."

"I look forward to it. Goodbye, Ms. Lanier."

"Bye," said Chloe, hanging up and taking the battery back out of her phone. She ignored the curious look from the security guard at reception as she ducked back out onto the street in search of a bus.

An hour later she was in the library at American University logging in with an account Sacco had scammed from some poor student over IM. Chloe just wanted to use the net access. She inserted a USB thumb drive into the computer and ran a linux distro on top of the computer's own Windows OS that allowed her to read and send encrypted messages without leaving her keys on the public machine. She used these accounts to keep in touch with some of the other Crews out there in the world, including Isaiah's and Marco's cruise-ship based Crew. She sent out a few feelers and pinged Marco to make sure she could still reach him if she needed to. There was also an e-mail forwarded to her by the letter drop service she used down in Miami. Not only was it encrypted, but the contents required another form of decryption as well, one that she couldn't do online. She took a piece of scrap paper and copied down the 100 character long stream of gibberish before logging off and heading upstairs to find a quiet library corner to work in. She took out a well-worn moleskin notebook and flipped through it looking for the right page. There were ten one-time only code keys hidden within the ramblings and doodles that filled most of the book. The mail service down in Miami had the matching ten one-time codes. She found the right one and decrypted the message, revealing a ten digit phone number. It was a time consuming way to send messages, and the mail service charged them $500 each time they used it (they'd paid up front for ten messages), but it was also the most secure way she knew to keep in contact with other people who were as security conscious as she was.

Chloe went back out onto the campus and crossed the street to the art center where a small sculpture garden offered both protection from the wind and some privacy. She dialed the number and let it ring three times before hanging up and dialing again. Two rings, hang up, then one and hang up. On the fourth call the person at the other end picked up before she even heard it ring.

"I thought we weren't talking," said the voice on the other end.

"It's an emergency."

"Go on."

"Isaiah, we need to meet, I'm not comfortable talking about it on the phone."

"We're not going to meet."

"I know you think there's heat all over us, and you're right. But this is important."

"I know."

"If you knew, you'd want to meet."

"I don't think so. In fact, the only reason I agreed to take this call was so I could express to you in unequivocal words that our dealings are now and forever through and that I consider you an enemy."

"What? Why?"

"Your newfound relationship with Emily Marsh is anathema to me."

"..."

"Yes, I know about the Marsh woman and her machinations and have concluded that there can be only one reason for your wish to meet me face to face. You're trying to capture me."

"Isaiah, no, no! I'm trying to warn you. I wanted to tell you what's going on and try and come up with some sort of plan to—"

"Please, don't embarrass yourself. I think we're done here."

"You can't believe I'd ever do that."

"Of course I can, for many reasons, not the least of which is that it happens to be true."

"Isaiah—"

"There is one last thing you can do for me in fact. Since you are on such good terms with Marsh, you can deliver a message to her for me. It's somewhat complicated, so hopefully you're recording this. Marsh must immediately cease all investigations into me. They will avail her nothing in any event—she knows even less than you, and you, really, know nothing about me. It will be impossible for her to find me, while it is beyond simple for me to find her. Indeed, I have already found her. I know about her sick husband, bed-ridden in their Georgetown home. I know about her work patterns, her finances, her political interests. I know when she sleeps and when she rises. And I know about her children. I know of her son in New York and her daughter in California. In retaliation for her interest in me, I will be striking back at the two of them tonight. Go ahead and warn her if you wish, although I don't think it will do them much good. If we miss tonight, there is always tomorrow, or next week, or next year. Unless she's willing to make her own children somehow disappear, we will find them and we will have our revenge."

"Isaiah, this isn't right. Those two had nothing to do with this."

"I simply don't care. However, there is a way to avoid all this. If she transfers 500,000 Euros into a bank account of my choosing within thirty minutes of me giving her the account and routing information, I will simply walk away. Her children, her husband, her life, will all be left alone. Left alone as long as she leaves me alone. I will e-mail her the information first thing in the morning. That gives her the rest of today to assemble the funds and prepare the transfer. One week later, once the money is secure beyond her considerable reach, I will call off my hounds. Did you get all that?"

"Yes," said Chloe. He hung up. "Fuck," she said into the dead line. She didn't have time to take the train. She called a cab. She needed to be back in Baltimore right now.

She threw the door wide as she burst into the Baltimore flat. Bee looked up from her makeshift workbench in alarm. Sacco was sitting on the rotten old couch, a laptop on his knees. Paul was nowhere to be seen.

"Where's Paul?" she asked.

"Using the piss bucket," said Sacco, eyes locked on his screen.

"We need to talk," she said.

"It told you, he's in the—"

"No, you and me. We need to fucking talk."

"Not yet."

Chloe looked at him, her head cocked to one side, her lips caught mid-snarl. She wanted to yell now.

Something changed on the screen Sacco was looking at and he nodded, looking pleased with himself. Then he put the computer aside and looked up at her. "What's up?"

"I just talked with Isaiah."

"And?"

"And he already knew. He knew fucking everything. He knew about Marsh, he knew we were trying to capture him, he knew fucking everything."

"What? How?" said Sacco, looking shocked.

"Oh, I think you know."

"I have no idea."

"What's going on?" asked Paul, coming out from the bathroom, balling up a wet nap.

"What's going on is, someone tipped off Isaiah, and I'm pretty sure I know who it was." She stared right at Sacco.

"You think I did what?"

"Someone told him. It wasn't me or Paul, and I'd bet my life it wasn't Bee. But then there's you. You never wanted to turn on Isaiah and you went with me to use the messenger service, so you could have tipped him off. Go ahead, deny it. I fucking dare you. Deny it."

Sacco stood up, his face indignant, "Fine. Fuck it. Fine. Yeah, I told him. You know why."

"Why?"

"It wasn't a question. You know why. Because it was the wrong fucking thing to do. Because you don't sell out your friends. That's fucked up. When you recruited me into this doomed band of misfits you two promised me you weren't just criminals. You talked about ideals and doing good and fucking with the bastards of the world. Well you know what, selling out Isaiah was a bastard fucking move, and I wasn't going to be part of it."

"Get out!" shouted Chloe.

"Fuck you. I found this place. It belongs to my friends."

"GET OUT!" Chloe shouted again.

"FUCK YOU!" Sacco shouted, chest out as he got up in Chloe's face.

Paul stepped forward before she could hit him, pushing the two of them apart. "Calm down, calm down. Sacco, can you give us an hour? Would you go take a walk or something?"

"I've got a better plan," said Chloa. "I'm going out for a walk. When I'm back he'd better be gone."

"Chloe," said Paul. "Come on, wait."

"Gone. Take your shit and go. But leave that fucking computer. That belongs to the Crew."

"Whatever. Fine by me," he said. "But I'm not sorry."

"You fucking will be," said Chloe as she walked out the door. "You will be."

Chapter 30

Paul

Paul didn't try to convince Sacco to stay. At this point, that would've been counterproductive. He did make him promise to check in in a few days using an e-mail address that Paul had never used before. Sacco left the laptop, just like Chloe had demanded. Paul handed it over to Bee and asked her to try and ring Chloe up on it using an encrypted Skype connection. The phone rang twice before Chloe picked up.

"He's gone," Paul said.

"Good," replied Chloe. She still sounded very angry.

"I know what he did is fucked, but I'm not surprised. But listen, maybe we can—"

"Paul, honey, this is one of those times."

"When I shouldn't press it?"

"Yeah. Besides, there's something else to worry about."

"What?"

"Marsh just sent me a text message. She wants me to call in."

Paul could almost feel his blood pressure go up twenty points. "OK. That's good timing."

"Yeah, I was a little worried about that too. So should I warn her?"

"I think we have to."

"I hate being Isaiah's fucking messenger girl."

"I know, but she needs to know. I mean, Isaiah's after her kids for fuck's sake. She should take some measures to protect them."

"No, no, you're right. Shit, this is all spinning so far out of fucking control." Paul heard a slight hiccup of silence that he knew signaled Chloe's call waiting.

"Christ, I think that's her. Hold on, let me talk to her."

Paul waited as Chloe switched over to the other call. He sat down at the table next to Bee where they'd set up Sacco's laptop. Bee had pulled up an app that combined info from the GPS tracer in Chloe's phone with Google Maps. It showed Chloe was in a park about a mile away from them. He put his phone on speaker and laid it down next to the computer and stared at the map.

"Do you think she's going to be OK?" asked Bee.

"I think so. She's been through worse. Speaking of worse, have you heard from c1sman?"

"Just another e-mail. He went out west to where his kid is. I think he might try and reconcile with his ex."

"That sucks. I'm sorry."

"Sucks for him. There's no way she's taking him back. I wouldn't. He's kinda, well, you know, needy? Latches on real tight."

"That's not always bad."

"Does it matter?" asked Bee. "No going back now."

"I guess not."

They sat in silence for a minute or so, watching the screen and the phone, waiting for Chloe to come back on the line. Then her dot started moving on the screen. Moving fast. "Did she get in a fucking car? What the hell?"

The dot moved fast, and five minutes later, with Paul shouting into the phone for Chloe to pick up, it got on the highway. "Jesus, come on!" Paul said, pulling Bee up out of her seat and grabbing the laptop. "Come on!"

He wished they were parked closer, but security concerns had dictated that they leave the car at least three blocks from their hideout, and both he and Bee were huffing and puffing by the time he fumbled with the keys and unlocked the door. Paul still had the phone connection open and there was still no word from Chloe. It wasn't until they were on the interstate and headed towards DC that he heard her voice again. It was muffled, like she had the phone in her pocket. Paul covered the microphone on the phone with his thumb and motioned for Bee to keep quiet. They both strained to listen over the car noise and Paul tried to concentrate on driving down I-295 as fast as he dared. According to the dot on Bee's laptop, they were about twenty miles behind Chloe.

"It's not my…" he heard Chloe say. "Come… fuckers… explain… the hell?… me."

Paul could make out other voices, male voices, but couldn't understand what they were saying. Chloe wasn't screaming, but she was talking louder than normal, probably so the phone would pick her up and alert Paul and Bee. It continued like that for another ten minutes or so, but then one of the male voices very clearly yelled at her to "Shut the hell up!" and she did. Paul hoped she wasn't riling them up too much that they lost control and did something even worse than whatever it was they were planning to do with her.

They followed the dot down the highway and into Washington DC, getting off at Highway 50/New York Avenue, which offered a straight shot towards Capital Hill. They caught up some as the car holding Chloe ran into city traffic, but then they got snarled into it as well and things got slow. They were still at least fifteen minutes behind when the dot came to a stop. "I think they're done," said Bee.

"Where are they?"

"Somewhere in downtown. Lemme zoom in on the map. It's like midway between the White House and Capital Hill. They're close to four different metro stops. There's a bunch of stuff there. National Archives, the Internal Revenue... oh heck. They're a block away from the J. Edgar Hoover FBI Building."

Paul felt his eyes bulge and rocked his head back. He blinked a few times. "That's... that's not possibly any good at all. Oh fuck, oh fuck, oh fucking fuck. This isn't what was supposed to happen. Is the dot still moving?"

Bee, giving off waves of tension, watched it in silence for thirty seconds. "No. No. It's stopped. It's still in the building."

"It's in the FBI building?"

"No, no. A block away. You want to turn left on 6th Street. That's coming up in a quarter of a mile. The dot's holding steady. It's just some building. I can't tell what. It's near like a Shakespeare Theater and some restaurants. In half a mile you're going to want to make a right on D Street and then a right on 8th."

Paul followed Bee's directions and slowed to a crawl as they came onto the street. The GPS tracking software they were using couldn't get much finer detail than this. He wasn't sure what he was looking for, not even what kind of car Chloe had been taken away in. "What about there?" said Bee, pointing out the window. It was a parking garage.

Paul hoped they were still in the parking garage and not in the office building connected to it or, much, much worse, the FBI building less than a block away. Looking at the toll booth and gate arrangement guarding entrance and exit from the garage, he decided that he didn't want to get trapped in there. But there was no on street parking in sight. "Bee, I'm going in there. You keep circling the block or find a place to park on the street somewhere nearby."

"Are you going to be on a phone? I want to know what's happening."

"No phones," he said, pointing towards the sky. "None except Chloe's."

"If I don't hear something in fifteen minutes I'm coming in."

"Twenty."

"Seventeen point five."

Paul slipped out of the car and jogged across the street to the parking garage entrance. He had no way of knowing which floor Chloe (or at least her phone) might be on, but since going down was easier than going up, he took the elevator to the top parking level, planning to work his way down. If they were waiting for the elevator up there he might be screwed, but he risked it.

On level four he stepped out and listened. There were voices echoing up from somewhere, angry tones bouncing off concrete until the only discernible content was an unmistakable urgency. Glad he was wearing rubber soled sneakers that didn't clack against the hard floor, Paul inched forward. Every parking space near the elevators was filled, but looking out farther he saw plenty of open spots, except in the far corner where they were full near a stairway. People liked to cluster near the exits, which made sense. Paul crept towards the center of the floor, where a gap ran from the ground floor to the ceiling above Paul's head. The voices grew louder. They were definitely coming from below him. Paul trotted on tiptoes across to the stairway and opened the heavy door as quietly as he could, making sure it didn't slam behind him. Down one level, he cracked the third floor door. He couldn't see anyone, but he could still hear something. Again he carefully slipped out, easing the door closed behind him. He crouched behind a nearby Toyota.

The voices were coming from the other side of this level, he was sure of it. He used the sound of a loud car or truck approaching from the lower level to cover his sprint across open concrete to a pillar that offered both cover and a better view of the rest of the garage. Peeking around the corner he saw a black SUV about fifty feet away, two men in dark suits stood beside an open door, talking to whoever or whatever was inside. A second SUV, twin to the parked one, pulled to a stop behind it. It didn't bother to park in a space, even though there were empty ones to every side. The driver got out, another man in a dark suit, although this one seemed familiar to Paul. He circled around to the passenger door on the right side, which was obscured from Paul's position. He heard the door open and then the clack of hard heels on concrete. The driver came back into view, and once he saw the passenger his identity came to Paul. It was Marsh's assistant Larry, and his boss was right behind him.

One of the nameless suits reached into the properly parked SUV and yanked Chloe out by one arm. Paul drew in a sharp hiss. It was weird to see her out in public without a wig on, her short pink hair showing some dirty blond roots. Paul willed her to notice him, but she never even looked his way. Everyone's attention was now focused on Marsh. She wasn't quite facing him and the others were facing her, so Paul risked exposure and dashed across the open space to hide behind a VW Jetta that was about fifteen feet closer to them. He ran hunched over, an awkward, off balance action that ended in him sliding to a painful stop on his knees just behind the car. Now he could hear them, even as he bit his lip to stifle any sounds of pain that might give him away.

"Do you know where we are?" asked Marsh. Her voice was calm and even, just as Chloe had described it.

"Washington D.C.," said Chloe, sounding just like a smart ass.

"Did you notice the building down the block? The FBI headquarters?"

"Yeah, I recognized it from X-Files. Are your friends here agents?"

"They're licensed security professionals on my payroll. They've been keeping tabs on you and your friends for me. No, the FBI doesn't know about you, yet. But I'm going to have them walk you down the street along with a fat file full of evidence against you in about ten minutes if you don't do as I say."

"That would definitely suck. What is it you want me to do?"

"Give me Isaiah."

"He's after your kids," Chloe said, her voice urgent. "I was trying to warn you about that when your goons pulled me into their truck. You need to warn them. He's going to—"

"I've already warned them."

"You've what? How?"

"We've been tapping your phone for a week now. And following you. Do you think I trusted you and your accomplices for even a moment?

Of course not. I know everything. And unless you give me Isaiah, you're going to the FBI."

"If you really know everything like you say, then you know there's no way I can hand you Isaiah. He wants nothing to do with me! He's cut all ties. You want to know what I know? He's in New York. Maybe. He's got a wife named Dualla. Maybe. He's super fucking smart and ruthless and talented. No maybes there. He's after you and your family and there's nothing I can do about it. And unless you're willing to put your kids in witness protection and surround yourself with these hired goons for the foreseeable future, there's nothing you can do about it either. Unless he screws up. Very unlikely. Or you get lucky. Not great odds. Or you pay him off."

"Do you imagine that I'm bluffing? The FBI doesn't customarily have suspects delivered to their headquarters by helpful citizens, but I assure you they'll make an exception for me. They'll make an exception for you."

"Ma'am, I absolutely do not want to go to jail, but I swear, there's nothing I can do about Isaiah. Polygraph me, water board me, whatever. I was trying to warn you! There's nothing I can do. Put me in jail, fine. Sucks for me. But Isaiah's still out there. Just pay him off and leave him alone and you'll be fine. Don't and you won't."

"Both impossible and immoral. I'm not giving in to your threats."

"Not MY threats," insisted Chloe. "Isaiah's. His threats. You know what he managed to pull off in Florida. What makes you think you're any better protected than they were?"

"I know he's coming, and shortly he'll be on the FBI's most wanted list."

"And they'll catch him right after they get Osama, I'm sure. You don't know anything about him. I don't know anything… OK, listen. Is there anything else? What else can I do to appease you? I'll tell you everything I know about him over and over if you want. I'll try and reach him again if you want. Whatever you want, but it has to be something I can actually do. If I could give him to you, I would. But I really, really can't."

"Then I don't see that there's much more you can do for me besides serving as a convenient scapegoat for Ken Clover's problems, and I don't need your cooperation for that."

Paul's knees were killing him. This wasn't what they'd planned at all, but Christ, he needed to do something, and he needed to do it right now. He closed his eyes, rearranged the words he'd planned on saying into something that might save Chloe's ass right now and stood up. "But our cooperation would help," he said in a loud, clear voice that didn't quaver a bit. OK, maybe a bit, but not so he thought they'd notice.

The two goons, Larry, and Chloe all turned to look at him. One of the goons started reaching into his jacket, so Paul raised his hands high above his head. Marsh had started back towards her SUV, but had stopped dead in her tracks when Paul revealed himself. Without looking back at him, she said, "Mr. Reynolds." She turned and looked at him, her expression revealing nothing. Was she surprised? Pleased? Paul had no idea.

"I'm unarmed," he said, walking down the middle of the space between him and them. The goon kept his hand in his suit coat, but at least he wasn't pointing a gun at Paul.

"Are you surrendering yourself to the authorities?" Marsh asked. "That makes things easier for me, then."

"I could do that, yeah, I guess. Don't want to though. I've got a better offer."

"You can deliver me Isaiah?"

"I can't. No more than Chloe can. He's in the tall grass, beyond my reach for sure. I stick my nose in there and I'll get eaten." Paul stopped when he was about five feet away. If someone tried to grab him he could still run for it, although run where remained an unanswered question. "But there are other things."

Marsh's head tilted slightly to one side, her chin raising just enough that Paul knew she wanted him to continue.

"Right, so, here's the deal. You're in this for Ken Clover, right? He's your paying client. And I'm sure you're charging him for all of this—the surveillance, the security, the gas for those SUVs. Right?" Marsh didn't nod but she also didn't deny it. "So this is just one more charge. You pay off Isaiah with Clover's money. Doesn't cost you a dime. Now wait! I know what you're gonna say. You're going to say you don't give in to threats and paying off Isaiah doesn't do any good for Ken Clover. But what if it did?"

Marsh kept staring at him. Paul felt himself flashing back to his days in the video game business when he was giving pitches to venture capitalists and publishers. The same dead, skeptical, bored look that implied they'd heard it all before. Very few of those meetings had gone well. In fact, none of them had.

"Here's the deal I'm proposing. I'll give you a confession. I'll give you solid, unimpeachable evidence that Ken Clover was in every possible way framed. Server logs, original and then edited e-mails, bank records.

I'll give you all the details of what we did to him. That's what you need isn't it? You need him off the hook so he can get back to his old life? Well fine. I take all the blame. I'm a known criminal. Hell, I can even give you stuff linking me back to the shit I pulled in San Jose a few years back. You put me on that wanted list if you want. You bring in that kind of evidence to get Clover off the hook, and he'll gladly pay your normal fee plus the money to pay off Isaiah. Everybody wins."

"Everyone but you," Marsh said.

Paul's stomach did flips, he was so pleased to hear her say those words. "I win because Chloe and I don't get handed over to the FBI tonight and you get them to let Sandee go down in Florida. We run away. We go underground. We turn over a new leaf. At this point, that's all we want. We just want it to be over."

Marsh didn't say anything for a long time. Long enough that Chloe jumped into the negotiations. "It's a fair trade isn't it? You get everything you wanted in the beginning and it ends up costing your client a little more than he might have paid otherwise. But he gets his life back now instead of six months or a year from now or never. I've seen his books. He'll make back that much money in six months, easy."

Marsh looked at Chloe. "Why pink?"

"Excuse me?"

"Your hair is that shockingly ugly shade of pink. Why?"

"I like it," said Chloe. She pointed at Paul. "He likes it."

"It's awfully dangerous. Very recognizable, stands out in a crowd. Which I suppose is why you always wear a wig. I guessed right about the wig, but I never would have guessed pink."

Paul and Chloe exchanged blank faced looks. What was this woman going on about?

"The pair of you," Marsh said. "You're a couple?"

"Yes," said Chloe.

"I see that. Interesting. You've picked a strange way to live. A stupid way, really. I don't think you're quite cut-throat enough to be criminals, not successful ones anyway. It's your sentiment that's gotten you in so much trouble, that led me to you." Paul started to say something and then stopped, deciding it was better for him to wait and see where she was going with this. "I don't much care for your deal, but I'm not sure I much care for any of the alternatives."

"Can I just say what you probably can't?" Chloe said.

Marsh nodded.

"We go to jail, we plead out to the feds, that helps Ken a little bit. But you're right, we're sentimental, and maybe that makes us bad crooks, but it also means we didn't choose Ken at random. We chose him because he's a bad guy who does bad things for even worse people. You know as well as we do, that if the whole truth comes out about what we really did to Ken, well, there's no coming back for him. He's fucked because, quite frankly, he deserves to be fucked, and I think you know that."

Paul thought, maybe just imagined, he saw a flicker of something in Marsh's eye. Maybe anger but, really, maybe delight? "That's if we have to cut a deal with the feds instead of you," Paul said. "But we deal with you and you get a custom tailored confession, one with plenty of details that exonerate your client in ways an official FBI investigation never would. Plus, from a purely selfish point of view, we don't spend the next twenty years in a federal penitentiary."

"I'd need more than just your files. I'd need a confession from you. A confession people can believe in. Not written, not something that could have been faked. Something on video."

That she was even talking about making a deal thrilled Paul. His mind raced, thinking back over everything that they had done to see if there might be something to win her over. The pieces started to come together for him and he let the ideas pour out. "OK, I getcha. A believable confession. Well, cynics and experts, they know that no confession got under any form of duress is really believable. What you want is not a confession but an admission."

"Explain the difference in your eyes."

"I make a video. We make a video. A video demanding more money from Ken, extorting him, threatening him, saying we're going to make it seem like he's done even more horrible things, or whatever. We can back date it, say we're going to make it look like he's done the horrible things that he has in fact actually done, right? And I use something to blur my face and my voice. But here's the deal. I use something that can be reverse engineered. Those programs that swirl or blur faces? There are algorithms out there to undo the swirling. They caught some child molester that way from pics he posted online. So you'll have this video and you can get your experts to unblur me and then you'll have me admitting to trying to blackmail Ken. It will look like you've outsmarted me, which, I think, the media and Ken's clients will find a lot more convincing then a straightforward confession. Plus, hey, it makes you look pretty damn smart too, doesn't it? That's gotta be good for business."

"I'd have to see proof that this works."

"Sure, yeah. Or we could just give you the unblurred video and you could do the rest on your own however you want. Whichever way."

Marsh turned her back on them and walked a few steps away, looking up at the ceiling as she did. She stood at the rear of her SUV for a long while there, just staring at the ceiling. "I remain dissatisfied about Isaiah's threats towards my family," she said to the ceiling. "Paying him off galls me."

"I know this won't mean much coming from me," Chloe said, "But Isaiah is a man of his word. And he knows full well how connected you are. He doesn't want a war with you, he really doesn't. If he says he'll leave you alone when he gets paid, I promise you he will."

"Yet still it galls me."

"I'm sorry," said Paul, "But I don't know what else to say."

Marsh stared up for a few more seconds before turning and calmly walking back towards them. "I'll need some other reassurance. A form of probation."

"What does that mean?"

"For one year, I want to know where the two of you are at all times. I want to be able to snatch you up again and drag you to that building across the street if any of this goes wrong. Should one piece of misfortune befall my family, I shall blame Isaiah and, by proxy, you."

"We'd better hope they live charmed lives then," said Chloe.

"So far, they have," Marsh said with a smile. "My call to them an hour ago might well have been the first time in their adult lives they've been truly frightened. I don't want that to happen again."

"Just me and Paul," said Chloe. "Sandee and anyone else, they go free." Marsh nodded. "And how do you propose to keep tabs on us. We don't want to go to jail."

"Jail would be easiest. Some petty larceny charge? But no, it couldn't work. Mr. Reynolds can't be the total scapegoat if he's already in police custody on some other charge. We'll have to work out some arrangement. I'm sure my security experts can think of something. Assuming the details all work out as you suggest they will, do we have a deal?"

Paul looked at Chloe. She pursed her lips slightly, no doubt wondering if they'd made some mistake, forgotten something. Paul couldn't think of anything. He nodded, she nodded back. "Deal," said Chloe, holding out her hand.

Marsh stepped forward and shook it, then shook Paul's. "All your effort, for naught," she said to Paul. "You're left only with your freedom, something that never would have been at risk at all had you but focused your attention on legal achievements instead of criminal ones."

Paul just shook her hand. She had no idea what had really just happened.

Chapter 31

Chloe

Chloe didn't get to see Sacco again for two weeks, when they were back in Florida to celebrate Sandee's release and help plan Paul's funeral.

Going back to Key West at first seemed like a crazy idea. Too small, too few exits, they were too well known. But that was kind of the point wasn't it? Marsh wanted to know where they were all the time. Going back to the last place they'd called home would put her at ease. Now the old house, that was out of the question. The feds had torn it apart looking for evidence, and had probably found a ton of it too. They'd also gone through the Keys Condos and Estates records with a fine toothed comb, meaning the Crew's primary hook up for free housing was no longer an option. Chloe called one of their few contacts on the island who hadn't been questioned by the feds, and she hooked them up with a houseboat that hadn't left the marina in seven years. They did have to actually pay for it though, which sucked.

Sandee regaled them with tales of life behind bars the whole way down from Miami. There were at least three fellow federal felons with broken wrists and one with a cracked pelvis and a guard who had a crush on him. He played it off in his typical joking style, but Sandee was clearly happy to be free. He looked tired, worn, and, for the first time ever, Chloe thought she saw wrinkles around his eyes. Not that she said anything. Bee filled Sandee in on everything else, from c1sman's chickening out, "he never was cut out for this," she'd said, to the final chase and negotiation with Marsh that resulted in

Sandee's release. The two of them joked and teased in the back seat, sucking in the sea air as Chloe raced south over the water with the windows down.

The houseboat smelled a little too much like the sea, the fishy part of the sea to be precise, but it was home for the moment anyway. Once they were inside, Chloe showed off the GPS ankle bracelet that was locked to her left leg and then checked in with Marsh's security goon over the Web cam, proving she was where she said she was. Bee had figured out within the first few hours that the thing not only had a GPS in it, but a hidden microphone as well. Basically a whole phone set up. Chloe had suspected as much. The really shitty part was that its battery only lasted 72 hours, which meant every three days she had to plug her leg into an outlet for a couple hours while it recharged. Well, not much longer, she thought.

Having checked in as ordered and knowing by now that the Marsh goons never did their random spot checks within the next couple of hours, she motioned to Bee. Her techno-savvy best bud pulled out the cloned unit from under the couch and orchestrated the careful switchover from the live one on her leg to the fake one that would cover for her. The first time they'd tried the trick, they almost got caught and had used every ready-made excuse they'd prepared ahead of time to convince Marsh it wasn't their fault. Sunspots, electrical storms, lead paint in the walls, everything. A week later Bee had perfected the process and they could come and go as they pleased. Chloe removed her slave bracelet and placed it on the table behind the computer next to Paul's, its microphone safely muted.

"Did she really think you wouldn't be able to find a work around for those?" Sandee asked.

"I don't think she did," said Bee. "She can't have thought we were that stupid."

"I just think she didn't realize you were that smart," said Chloe. "It's a subject of running debate."

They opened up a bottle of champagne and drank out of Dixie cups for the next hour. They were halfway through their third when Chloe heard familiar footsteps on the dock outside the door. A moment later Paul came in, with Sacco right behind him.

"You piece of shit," said Chloe.

"I'm sorry," said Sacco.

"You said you'd be here yesterday."

"I got hung up."

"Was it a girl?"

Sacco actually blushed a little. "Maybe. But it was a girl at a bank in Belize, so it's not like I wasn't working."

"Fine, fine," said Chloe. "Tell me good news and all is forgiven."

"Good news. The money made it through all the way. 500,000 Euros into the Frankfurt Account, then moved over to the Overseas Holdings Group Account there and then to Belize and then to our bank in Belize and then to our other bank in Belize. I took out a little traveling cash to bring with us and the rest should be waiting for us wherever we go next."

"Well all mother fucking right," said Chloe.

"But he's got no idea how to kill me," said Paul.

"I told him we could hire a hit man," Sacco said.

"He also said he wanted to give Isaiah a cut."

"I did not!"

Chloe laughed and laughed and poured them both cups of champagne. There had also been a running debate about whether or not to tell Isaiah how egregiously they'd used his name and reputation in vain. Chloe hadn't spoken to him since their last face to face meeting, nor had Sacco. They'd paid one of Chloe's contacts, a member of Marco's Crew in fact, to play the role of Isaiah on the phone call knowing that Marsh had the line tapped. And when Chloe had "stormed" into the Baltimore squat to confront Sacco about it, they'd waited until Sacco detected that Marsh's security had secretly (they thought) activated the phone's microphone and were using it as a bug. Thus, Sacco was moved out of the picture without arousing suspicion and more credence was given to Isaiah's invented threats against Marsh's family.

They hadn't quite imagined that Marsh would actually seize Chloe. She'd left the flat in supposed anger so there was a plausible reason to remove the bugged phone from the house while Sacco packed up and Paul and Bee planned the next move. She'd intended to call Marsh and then make the offer over the phone. Instead she'd been snatched. But Sacco's laptop was tied into Chloe's phone just like Marsh's security team had been. She'd been flooded with relief when skinned-kneed Paul had popped up in that garage. From there things had gone almost as planned, certainly close enough to make it work out in the end. Sacco had been left hanging at his rendezvous point for Bee to contact him and thus had missed the entire FBI adventure, instead spending his time setting up the location they'd hoped to lure Marsh into for negotiations. If they'd been delayed a couple more hours, Sacco would've bugged out himself, cutting all contact. At least that was what his orders had been. Who knows what he would've actually done. Probably try and bust them out of federal prison on his own. Luckily they'd cut a deal with Marsh before Sacco knew anything had gone wrong.

The hiccup with the leg bracelets had thrown them off a little, but Bee had sorted that out. Yes, Ken got some semblance of his life back, but they got his money and Sandee's freedom, which she counted as two points to his one. They still argued over whether or not to warn Isaiah that Marsh thought he was the devil incarnate. Chloe didn't want to, Sacco said they should. Paul and Bee agreed it was better to leave that particular sleeping dog lie. Since Paul was the one who's face was all over the news the following week (again), his vote carried extra weight.

Even with the scruffy beard, the spray on tan, and the waving jet black locks of his wig, Paul was still a very wanted man. Clover, in his self-righteous, self-aggrandizing, self-important press conference had offered a $100,000 reward for information leading to Paul's arrest. They hadn't foreseen that little wrinkle either, but it only confirmed the wisdom of their original plan: it was time to leave the country. Even old Ollie had gotten in on the act, blogging incessantly about Clover, Paul, and spreading the word about his desire to form a hacker posse to bring the rogue black hat to justice. Apparently Clover had subsequently hired Ollie on as his full time computer security guy. With all that heat out there, they only had Marsh's word that they would be safe and there was no way they could trust her anymore than she could trust them. And she couldn't trust them at all.

"So, Paul says the plan is to kill him," Sacco said. "That seems a bit extreme."

"I don't see any other way," Paul said. "Hell, even after they think I'm dead, it'll probably take them years to remove me from the wanted list. Might as well get started as soon as possible."

"It's a tough one, especially since we can't actually kill you."

"We'll think of something," Chloe said. She and Paul had already tossed some ideas around. Yesterday she'd picked up everything they'd need to draw a few pints of blood and remove one of his teeth without causing too much pain or permanent damage. Paul had even offered to give up a couple toes, but Chloe drew the line there. That was the other reason for coming back to Key West. People knew him here, people they could fool. They'd figure it out in a couple days, maybe three at most. In two weeks she was betting they'd be out of here. "The next question is, where do we go from here?"

"Belize," said Sacco. "That's where the rest of the money is."

"And then?" asked Chloe.

"I know where I'm not going, kids," said Sandee. "I'm not going back to jail. I love you. I love all four of you to death, but babies, I ain't up for any more hard time."

"We'll be more careful from now on," Chloe said. "You don't have to do anything you're not cool with."

"I'm done, Chloe. I'm sorry, but I'm done. It was all a game. It was a lark. It was an adventure. Right up until when it wasn't any of those things. Then it was scarier than sin. I'm sorry, but it just won't work."

"No," said Bee, "No, please, San, you can't."

"Oh honey, we'll keep in touch. I'll come visit, if you'll have me. I swear I will. But right now I'm staying right here." He looked around with a critical eye. "Well, not right here on this awful boat, but here in Key West for another few days. Then I think I'll try LA. I took a shine to California when I was there, and you know, there's a city where a girl like me can get comfortably lost. And despite the brown skin, I'm just not cut out for third world countries or life on the run."

"But…" said Chloe, before she could think of anything to follow it up with.

"He's right," said Paul. "If he wants to stay, he should stay. Fuck, if I could stay, I'd stay. It might feel like we won, and I guess we did, but being wanted by the feds, it just plain fucking sucks. I mean, really. This was all too close a call. Listen to me, talking like we're already free and clear when there's probably some private eye or fed or fucking Blackwater mercenary sitting on the dock watching our every move. Sandee should make a new life for himself and so should anyone else who wants to. The rest of us have to go. But what we do when we're gone, I'm not sure anymore."

This was the first Chloe had heard of these new doubts of Paul's. Well, probably not new doubts, but never before said out loud ones. "Now, what are you saying, Paul?" she asked, afraid of the answer.

"I don't know what I'm saying, Chloe, I really don't. But I'm with Sandee, we can't do this again. This was too close. Like I just said, it's still too close."

"What the hell else do we know how to do?" she asked, which was, she realized the wrong question. Paul could write and draw. Sacco could program. Bee could build or repair anything. All Chloe knew how to do was lie, cheat, and steal. What the hell else would she do?

"I don't have any answers," Paul said, staring into her eyes. He understood what she was thinking, no doubt about it. And right then, as scared as she was to face her own limitations, she knew he'd stick by her. They'd figure it out together. "Whatever it is, it'll be something we all want to do, and maybe something that'll do some other people a little bit of good."

"And cool," said Chloe.

"Yes, and cool."

"And exciting."

"Exciting, absolutely."

"OK," she said. "We'll figure it out. We will. Right now though, I need another drink. Anyone else with me?"

They all were. She skipped the half-empty bottle of champagne and pulled out the Glen Morangie. They drank and thought of ways to kill Paul. She liked the shark plan, personally, but some of the others weren't too bad either. When Sandee volunteered to make a run to the store for fresh supplies, he asked if anyone had any requests. Bee needed some AA batteries. Sacco wanted different beer. Paul said he was fine.

"I'm out of pink hair dye." Chloe said.

"Maybe it's time for a change of color?" said Sandee, who'd long lobbied against the pink.

"Oh no," Chloe said. Some things she wouldn't give up. "Get me pink."

THE END

Geek Mafia
PB ISBN: 978-1-60486-006-1
$15.95

Fired from a job he hated at a company he loved, videogame designer Paul Reynolds is drowning his sorrows in late-morning margaritas when he meets an alluring, pink-haired conwoman named Chloe. With her gang of technopirate friends, Chloe helps Paul not only take revenge on his former employers, but also extort a small fortune from them in the process. What more could a recently unemployed, over-worked videogame designer in Silicon Valley ask for?

In return for Chloe's help, Paul agrees to create counterfeit comic books for one of her crew's criminal schemes. In the process he falls in for their fun loving, drug fueled "off the grid" lifestyle almost as fast as he falls head over heels for Chloe. Wary of the Crew's darker side, but eager to impress both the girl and the gang, Paul uses his game design expertise to invent a masterful con of his own. If all goes according to plan, it will be one for the ages. But can he trust any of them, or is he the one who's really being conned?

PM PRESS, PO Box 23912, Oakland, CA, 94623
www.pmpress.org

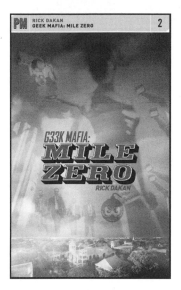

Geek Mafia: Mile Zero
PB ISBN: 978-1-6048-6002-3
$15.95

Key West—southernmost point in
the United States, Mile Zero on
Highway 1; and as far as you can
run away from your past troubles
without swimming to Cuba.

Key West—originally Cayo Huesos
or Isle of Bones, for centuries a
refuge for pirates, wreckers, writers,
scoundrels, drunks, and tourists.
Now home to a Crew of techno geek
con artists who've turned it into
their own private hunting ground.

Paul and Chloe have the run of the sun-drenched island, free to play
and scam far from the enemies they left behind in Silicon Valley. But
that doesn't mean they can't bring a little high tech know-how to
the paradise. They and their new Crew have covered the island with
their own private Big Brother style network——hidden cameras, FID
sensors, and a web of informers that tip them off about every crime
committed and tourist trapped on the island.

But will all the gadgets and games be enough when not one but three
rival crews of con artists come to hold a top-secret gang summit? And
when one of them is murdered, who will solve the crime?

Inspired by author Rick Dakan's own eventful experiences in the
video game and comic book industries, the Geek Mafia series satisfies
the hunger in all of us to buck the system, take revenge on corporate
America, and live a life of excitement and adventure.

PM PRESS, PO Box 23912, Oakland, CA, 94623
www.pmpress.org

ABOUT PM

PM Press was founded at the end of 2007 by a small collection of folks with decades of publishing, media, and organizing experience. PM co-founder Ramsey Kanaan started AK Press as a young teenager in Scotland almost 30 years ago and, together with his fellow PM Press co-conspirators, has published and distributed hundreds of books, pamphlets, CDs, and DVDs. Members of PM have founded enduring book fairs, spearheaded victorious tenant organizing campaigns, and worked closely with bookstores, academic conferences, and even rock bands to deliver political and challenging ideas to all walks of life. We're old enough to know what we're doing and young enough to know what's at stake.

We seek to create radical and stimulating fiction and non-fiction books, pamphlets, t-shirts, visual and audio materials to entertain, educate and inspire you. We aim to distribute these through every available channel with every available technology - whether that means you are seeing anarchist classics at our bookfair stalls; reading our latest vegan cookbook at the café; downloading geeky fiction e-books; or digging new music and timely videos from our website.

PM Press is always on the lookout for talented and skilled volunteers, artists, activists and writers to work with. If you have a great idea for a project or can contribute in some way, please get in touch.

PM Press
PO Box 23912
Oakland CA 94623
510-658-3906
www.pmpress.org